DOWNHILL WITHOUT BRAKES

DOWNHILL
WITHOUT
BRAKES

Val Binney

T

Troubador Publishing Ltd
Unit E2 Airfield Business Park,
Harrison Road, Market Harborough,
Leicestershire. LE16 7UL
Tel: 0116 2792299
Email: books@troubador.co.uk
Web: www.troubador.co.uk

ISBN 978 1836280 200

British Library Cataloguing in Publication Data.
A catalogue record for this book is available from the British Library.

Printed and bound in Great Britain by 4edge Limited
Typeset in 11pt Minion Pro by Troubador Publishing Ltd, Leicester, UK

For Ed

PART ONE

PART ONE

CHAPTER 1

Ezekiel Mabuza had a lot on his mind as he walked out from behind the reception desk in the foyer of the Durban city hall, where he had been a doorman for twenty years. A big man in his mid-forties, he had been a heavy-weight boxer in his day.

As he passed, someone called. '*Haai* Ezekiel.'

Usually, he had a smile and a word for everyone but today he had no time to stop on his way upstairs. He loved this high-ceilinged old building with its black and white floor tiles, but today he failed to dwell lovingly on each feature as he passed. His old friend, the stuffed dodo in the glass case, seemed to have a particular expression on its face and he wondered if it was trying to tell him something. Feeling even more uneasy, Ezekiel made his way up two flights of red-carpeted stairs, with mahogany handrails, towards the museum director's office.

On this autumn morning, Ezekiel found himself sweating as he climbed the stairs. His breath came fast. It had not been easy to find the courage to ask his boss for today's meeting. If Gallagher refused his request, Ezekiel didn't know what he would do. He reached the floor housing the Natural Science Museum and his last bit of courage deserted him.

He stopped. He had known Gallagher, director of museums, for years and liked him well enough. An easy-going man, who often stopped to swap a story with him in passing. But this matter was different. He was not sure a white man would understand. For my children's sake, he murmured to himself. He straightened up, stepped forward and knocked on Gallagher's door.

'Come in.'

As Ezekiel opened the door, Gallagher's lean figure came forward, smiling broadly. The man's mop of wiry, grey hair was much admired by the Zulu staff, as signifying potency.

'Ah, Ezekiel, *sawubona*. Good day.'

'*Sapila*, Mr Gallagher, *gunjani wena*, how are you?'

'Take a seat, my man. What can I do for you?'

'Mr Gallagher.' Ezekiel's large hands twisted in his lap and he tried to still them. Gallagher had been generous during his wife's long illness but still the doorman hesitated. As he searched for words, his eyes roved Gallagher's room with its books piled everywhere, its desk strewn with papers, pens and coffee cups. The scene made him smile and he relaxed a little.

'You see, Mr Gallagher, I need some time off...' Ezekiel mopped his brow. 'I need to go up-country to Nkandla, the place of my birth...to consult my *sangoma*.'

'Of course, you are entitled to time off to see a traditional healer, same as for a doctor,' Gallagher said. 'But Nkandla is a long way to go for such a visit. Can't you consult a local *sangoma*?'

'Mr Gallagher, my problem is a very big problem. This one is a special *sangoma*. Not your two-for-ten-cents ones at Durban market, who sell people love potions and lucky charms.' Ezekiel paused. 'I need someone powerful enough to appease the restless spirits of my ancestors.'

Ezekiel did not know why his ancestors were so angry with him that they were taking his loved ones from him, one by one. One son from AIDS, another in township violence and most recently, his wife from cancer. He needed urgently to find out where he was going wrong in his life and to make the necessary appeasements, before disaster struck again. He thought with fear of his two young daughters, his only remaining children.

'Let's see whether you have enough leave left,' Gallagher said, going to a cabinet and rifling through files.

Ezekiel breathed heavily while he waited.

'Ah!' Gallagher was frowning. 'It seems you'll have to wait until the next leave year. If you travel on public transport, I reckon you would need three to four days to get to Nkandla, see your *sangoma*, pay your respects to your elders and make it back here. Only one of those days can count as sick leave, the travel must come out of your own time. You have already borrowed five days leave from next year, so there is no more leeway.'

'But Mr Gallagher...'

'Of course, you can take time off to visit a *sangoma* in Durban but to be away for so many days...' Gallagher ran his hands through his hair, leaving it sticking up on end.

'But you see sir...' Ezekiel started to breathe heavily again, feeling stiff with apprehension. For months he had saved his wages to pay for this consultation, for the medicines that the *sangoma* would recommend and for the cost of the long journey back to his home area. How to explain all this to Gallagher?

'I'm sorry, Ezekiel. You're a good worker but you've had

a lot of extra time off already, when your wife was sick. I would gladly agree but if I give you more leave, everyone else will want it too.'

'Mr Gallagher...' words failed Ezekiel. His palms sweated. He knew that he could not wait until the following year for this special visit.

Gallagher shut the file and stood up. 'January will be here sooner than you think, you'll see.' He smiled at Ezekiel with his teeth but not with his eyes, crushing his hopes of relief as though they were dung-beetles underfoot.

Ezekiel stumbled out of the room without another word. Although he was distraught, he remembered to turn away and cross himself, as he passed the body of the Egyptian mummy, so disrespectfully removed from its burial place. No Zulu could understand how white people would display the body of another's ancestor in public like this. He worried that passing it so often would bring him harm from the restless spirit of this disturbed prince.

Usually, on his journeys up and down the stairs between the city library, the art gallery and the museum, Ezekiel lingered over his favourite exhibits – the life-sized tyrannosaurus towering over him, the gallery of stuffed animals, each in a glass case made to look like its natural setting. He especially liked the elephants and rhinos, great proud beasts that still seemed alive. Most days, Ezekiel felt his heart almost burst with pride for this wonderful building and his job there, when so many were unemployed. He knew every corner of the place by heart, the smells of the museum exhibits, the paintings in the art gallery and the much-fingered books in the library.

Today he turned away from them all. The very thought of making it to Nkandla to the *sangoma* had kept him going through these weeks and months since his wife, Thandiwe, had died. To think of Gallagher playing high and mighty with him, after all his years of faithful service. Ezekiel felt his usually upright bearing slump and his feet drag heavily down the stairs. He caught himself. This would not do. In his maroon uniform with its gold trim, he was a representative of Durban city hall. He hastened to stand up tall again. But he was reeling. He could not stop his feet from shuffling. He could feel himself going under. Too much had happened in his life these last few years and he desperately needed someone who could cure a heart made too heavy for living.

****

I freewheeled down the steep slopes of the Berea towards the central business district of the city, leaning hungrily into my waiting day. Whistling to myself, I lifted my butt off the saddle instinctively in all the right places. This was my big day.

The cool morning air rushed at my face, the reds of hibiscus, bottlebrush and bougainvillea flashing past. I smiled to myself. I hadn't made so much effort for a long while. I'd resurrected my beige linen suit from the back of the wardrobe, pressed it and folded it carefully into my pannier, ready to woo these European funders. People used to say of me, 'Ben Gallagher has a silver tongue'. Well today that tongue would sing again.

My route flattened out into the bustle of Warwick Junction. Through the city centre I had to dodge the usual press of newspaper sellers weaving between the morning traffic, calling 'Mer'cry, Mer'cry' and the squeegee merchants yelling 'easy klee-een .' Most whites avoided the centre these days, but I enjoyed the way it had livened up since apartheid had ended.

The traffic eased as I approached the gracious old part of the city, with its colonial buildings around the square. The Cenotaph and statues of by-gone royals gazed out from formal gardens, huge palm trees waving in the breeze. I liked the contrast of old colonial Durban with new, urban Africa. Stalls of garrulous stallholders spilled baskets of colourful fabrics and beads, group-taxis touted noisily for business around the square. The sounds and smells of the beer-garden beyond rose up, even this early in the day.

My bike stuttered to a halt outside the city hall. I always felt a tickle of amusement, that this was a replica of the Belfast civic building. The two cities couldn't be more different, except for their bigoted pasts. As I wheeled into the bike-shed, my mouth went dry. Three hundred million rand was hanging in the balance today. Sipho Zikhali, director of art galleries, Bettina Mtwetwe of libraries and I had sweated over our joint funding application. Only three South African cities would be chosen for this Swedish grant and we had to be one of them. It would put an end to my worries of being transferred to some tin-pot place in the sticks, as positive discrimination bit hard in public services. Of course, I was all for the idea in the abstract; the evils of apartheid had to be put right. But I'd die in a place like that. And there was no way Miranda would come with me, let alone our teenage kids. Today was my big chance to secure my job here and I couldn't afford to blow it.

I bounded in through the splendid double doors of the city hall, across the marble vestibule and up the elegant staircase to my office in the museum. I slipped into my suit, patting out the worst creases. It was a bit tight around my middle. As I ran a comb through my mop of hair, there was a knock at the door.

'Hey, bra!' Sipho and Bettina greeted me like co-conspirators. We made a good team – Bettina bristling with go-get-em energy, formidable in the bosom and colourful outfit department, as well as in sheer personality. Youthful Sipho exuded competence and warmth. Today I needed to put over a modern vision of the role of our museum in South Africa, for educating a young black generation's enthusiasm for science.

We made our way to the wood-panelled surrounds of the chamber room, which was used to impress important guests. The Swedish funders were announced and we began our charm offensive. Their lead player was a good-looking woman with trade-mark blond hair piled on top of her head, two younger men deferring to her, their manner cool. We would have to play the Swedes' ice with our African fire.

As our morning presentations ended, I let out a long breath and ran my hands through my hair, my adrenaline still pumping. The Swedes had warmed towards us, I was sure. Even their ice-maiden was shaking hands in a way which must mean something. All we had left to do this afternoon was some PR with local big-wigs and to show the Swedes around some of the city's flagship library, art and museum projects in the townships. Just the sort of thing these funding bodies loved.

I slapped Sipho on the back and grinned. 'Sweet-talk them over lunch and it's ours!'

'Don't count on it bra, until it's in the bag,' Sipho replied.

'Drinks on me tonight, for our star performance.' I wasn't going to let him spoil our moment.

Even in autumn the sub-tropical heat of Durban simmered on the pavements as we led our visitors a few streets away for a slap-up lunch at the Roma Restaurant. After all, they were paying.

One hour later, I steered our guests back up the city hall steps. We were standing in the foyer chatting, when suddenly Ezekiel Mabuza, the doorman, veered out from behind his desk. Red-eyed, his face strangely twisted, he staggered towards us, one hand behind his back, cursing loudly in Zulu. The Swedes leapt back, faces panic-stricken.

Furious, I stepped forward. 'Silence, Mabuza and move back to your desk. Or your job is at risk.' This normally quiet man must be the worse for drink or drugs. Today of all days.

He ignored my instructions and continued towards me. Suddenly, he pulled a knife from behind him. I reeled backwards. Mabuza froze warrior-like, his weapon held up high above his head. There was a moment of hushed silence around us.

Then, face contorted, he let out a war-cry and flourished the knife at me, slashing it this way and that.

I leapt about to avoid his blade. 'What the fuck? Call the police, someone, for God's sake!'

Onlookers screamed and began rushing from the foyer. Mabuza's attack seemed to be totally directed at me. He was blocking the stairs to my office. When he glanced away, I seized my chance and bolted for the outside doors. As a marathon runner, I would easily outpace him.

I clattered down the steps into the bright sunlight. Headed right down the street, hurtled round the corner, then swerved left down Anton Lembede street, instinctively heading for home. I heard Mabuza's heavy frame lumbering after me, yelling insults in Zulu. I pushed my way through the lunchtime crowds, indignant shouts from passers-by trailing after me. The pavement smashed through the thin soles of my smart shoes. My trousers felt too tight after a heavy lunch. The red wine rolled about in my gut, making my head spin. I was sure I would throw up any minute. I could hear my breath rasping, my knees jarred. A sharp pain jabbed me beneath my ribs. I didn't normally run on a full stomach.

I looked back, hoping I'd lost him but there was Mabuza, far too close, his mad eyes, the metal blade in his hand ready to strike through my soft flesh. I shuddered and rushed on, pushing myself to the limit to widen the gap between us. No-one else would tackle a guy brandishing a knife. Oh God, my bowels were threatening to give way. All the time I kept asking, why? Why me? This was not the Ezekiel Mabuza I knew. This must be a nightmare. Any moment now I would wake up back in my civilised meeting with the Swedes. But the horror went on and on… My mind felt stunned by the picture of our kindly doorman coming at me, face contorted with rage. My morning had started on a such a high and now I was running for my life.

I veered off the pavement, onto the street, dodging between hooting cars, trying to lose the homicidal maniac. But he followed me into the road. I slipped onto the crowded pavement on the other side, sure I'd lost him now. But the hot sounds of his grunting were behind me again, this side of the road. I should have run in the other way to the nearest police station, but I never thought Mabuza was fit enough to keep going this long.

Surely someone must have called the police by now. I listened for sirens coming to my rescue but heard nothing. The long vista of Anton Lembede Street stretched out before me. The whole thing seemed to be taking place in slow motion. At last, the marathon runner in me slipped into gear, lungs easing, legs settling into that steady pace that I could keep up for miles, even in thin shoes.

By the time I reached Warwick Junction, Mabuza's cries had faded and died out. But nothing would persuade me to turn round and walk bang into that knife again. Mabuza had nearly stabbed me, could have killed me. My legs were making the decisions and they kept on running, all the way up the tree-lined Berea and home. Finally, I panted into Cadogan Avenue and the bolts of tension around my head began to ease. The squeal of our garden gate welcomed me home. I let out a whoosh of relief, my legs went slack and I had to drag myself the last few steps to the front door. I breathed in the sweet *yesterday-today-and-tomorrow* bush as I scrabbled for my house keys in my trouser pocket. By some miracle they were still there. I opened the door. Mamba, our dopey dog, bounded out, almost knocking me over. Carefully I locked the door behind me again, made for the cool darkness of our living room and collapsed onto the sofa.

'Can you believe it, Mamba? Ezekiel Mabuza of all people!' I rubbed her neck and she threw herself on top of me, licking my face with her slobbery tongue. I was too damn tired to push her off.

I didn't feel safe for long downstairs. I could imagine unseen eyes staring at me through the windows. My legs flip-flopped up the stairs, Mamba pressing close behind. I shut us both in the soft greens of my bedroom and pulled the curtains tight shut. I burrowed under the duvet and couldn't imagine ever coming out again. What was wrong with me? Mabuza didn't know where I lived. I pictured someone seeing me in this pathetic state and felt the tinny taste of self-disgust in my mouth. Weird shudders welled up from deep inside my body and I couldn't control them.

I pictured the steadying image of Miranda and reached for my phone. I struggled to find the number of the law centre where she would be this afternoon, then dialled with fumbling fingers. She wouldn't like me interrupting her clinic, which would be overflowing with a queue of needy people.

'Ben?' Miranda's voice was irritable.

After a few false starts, I managed to spit out: 'Ezekiel Mabuza…tried to stab me with a knife…chased me down Anton Lembede…'

'Oh my God! Are you alright? Where are you?' Miranda's voice went up high. Once she realised that I was back home, I got her mother-to-child voice. 'OK, calm down Ben, it's over now.' I never liked that tone, as if I was making something out of nothing.

'It was terrifying. I can't stop my t-teeth from juddering.'

'You're in shock. Get some sweet tea down you and have a hot bath.'

'Can't you come home?'

'Are you safe in the house? He's not outside there, is he?' Her voice rose again.

I peeked through the curtains. 'No sign of him.'

She sighed. 'I'd come home if I could, Ben. But I can't walk out on a packed clinic. Habib would sack me.'

'Jesus, Mirrie. Someone just tried to kill me, for God's sake!'

'I'll see how soon I can get away. Have you spoken to the police?'

'Not yet.' It hadn't occurred to me.

'I'll find out whether he has been reported yet. And I'll

get Ellen or Tom to come home early. Don't forget the sweet tea.'

I put the phone down, heart pounding. I felt suddenly as though somebody was pressing down hard on my chest. I struggled to breathe. Was I having a heart attack? I couldn't slow things down, sweat was pouring off me and the different bits of my body seemed to have wills of their own. Who was this weird person? Mamba whimpered at my feet.

Eventually I calmed down enough to stumble downstairs to make the tea, Mamba was close behind, nuzzling my legs. I had gone from too hot to icy cold by now. Mug in hand, I went back upstairs, trying not to slop the tea. Focus, focus, I told myself, looking at the weave of the beige carpet. It seemed to help. I went straight into the bathroom, pushed the plug in, turned on the taps and squirted in some bath foam. I watched it fill as I sipped my tea. The comforting sound of water gushing in, of steam rising and finally, the blessed relief of sliding into the hot, foamy bath. As the water embraced me, my muscles began to unwind and slowly, slowly to let go of the strange physical rigors that had me in their grip. I wallowed in the soapy bath, a hippo puffing and snorting, trying to warm myself back to human. The image of hippos carried me back to that trip to the Okavango Swamps long ago, when Pete and I were still young – big water-lily pads with vivid pink flowers, the humid air thick with insect life. Then we had rounded a bend in the river and found that the light, flat-bottomed boat we were using to manoeuvre through the swamps was surrounded by the vast backsides of hippos – sleepy and benign-looking one moment, active and terrifying the next. Two males had taken issue with each other over a female and unleashed bloody warfare into the green-grey river. The frightening creatures rose up out of the water above our boat, screaming unearthly sounds as they gouged great pieces out of each other's bodies, leaving the water running red with blood. I remembered the two of us rowing backwards as fast as we could, to get the hell out of there.

The hippo memory cornered me, setting my heart racing again. Danger could sideswipe you from the most benign quarters. I scrabbled for a safer image, reaching in my mind for pictures of my kids and gradually my breathing slowed down again. I topped up the hot water and I lingered there, only my nose showing, until all the hot water in the tank ran cold. I emerged dripping onto the mat, my fingers and toes wrinkled like prunes.

Back in the green cocoon of our bedroom, I padded around in front of the television. I felt slightly unhinged. Mamba kept watch but had retreated behind her paws. The familiarity of test match cricket was restoring me by the time Ellen came in and dumped her book bag on the bed.

'What's up? Mom said you needed me home.'

'I think I'm starting the flu,' I lied. I couldn't bring myself to frighten her with the truth. 'Just snoozing it off with the cricket.'

'Is that all?' she said and stomped off. It seemed to pass her lie detector test.

CHAPTER 2

E zekiel zigzagged to a halt and doubled over as he choked on the fire in his lungs. He looked up to catch a last sight of Gallagher pulling further and further away. Slowly, his breathing eased. He stood up, blinked and shook his head. What was he doing in this street, trying to catch up with Gallagher? He stared down at this *thing* clutched in his hand. He could tell from the familiar feel of its wooden handle that it was the knife he normally kept in his shed at home. How had it arrived here with him?

The crowds were backing away from him, voices loud and turning back to stare, before they hurried on. He stuffed the knife down his trouser pocket until it slit through the lining inside and was almost hidden. He covered the hilt with his hand, his eyes sliding this way and that for the reactions of others. Fear sent him scuttling down a side street until he doubled back towards the anonymity of the bus station. All the time his mind grappled with what had happened. His head throbbed with what felt like a hangover. He recalled being out last night with Maphulo and the boys.

A survivor's cunning took over. Where to get rid of this fearsome object in his pocket? Had he committed a crime with it? His fingerprints must be all over the thing but he could see no blood on it. He recalled some rough ground on the other side of the station, with a culvert running through it, which was used as a dumping ground. He glanced round to see who was watching him, before he ducked under the barbed wire onto the wasteland. The few individuals in there, rummaging about in piles of rubbish, seemed engrossed in their own business. He climbed down into the culvert and dropped the knife into the water, then picked it out with a dirty cloth lying nearby, trying to wash off any evidence of his hands. He hesitated briefly at the thought of losing his useful tool, then shoved it deep into some mud at the side of the culvert, under an overhanging bush. Who would find it there? He made as if to pull up his trousers after emptying his bladder. Then, with his heart throbbing in his chest, he went back to the station, to join the throngs waiting for buses to the townships.

After what seemed like an age, his Umlazi bus pulled in and Ezekiel squeezed onto the vehicle, along with the rest of the queue. He was exhausted but did not manage to secure a seat, so he swayed with the tightly packed mass of standing passengers as the vehicle swung round corners at speed on its long journey to Umlazi township. He swallowed hard. This might not be the end of his troubles. People who had seen him with the knife might talk. Someone may have called the police. He had no idea what he had been doing with it in his hands, running down the street trying to catch up with Gallagher as if his child's life depended on it. He screwed his eyes up to peer inside his heart but he saw nothing. His head ached. He clutched in vain at yesterday and his safe life as doorman at the city museum.

The swaying and jolting of his regular bus journey gradually soothed him, with its familiar sounds and smells of closely packed humanity. The rhythms of voices around him exchanging the stories of their day rocked him into some sense of normality. Only as he stepped out of the bus at last and into the shrieks of taxi-drivers, the squeal of bus brakes pulling into Umlazi Station, did fear engulf him again. The chill of the autumn afternoon grabbed him in the throat like a secret assailant. He started to shake.

Where should he go? Home would be the first place the police would look for him. He made his way to the dusty station cafe to think what to do next. He fretted about his daughters, left alone at home. Surely they would walk round to their Aunty Nomsa's if he didn't come home? As darkness fell, he longed for somewhere warm and safe to hide. In the throng of the bus-station, he was apart, alone. He would see if he could lie low at his friend Maphulo's place, until this had blown over.

****

At around six pm, I heard Miranda's car roll into our garage. A little later she came clinking up the stairs, with what sounded like a welcome tray of tea.

She set it down and came over to the bed. 'How are you feeling now?'

'Better than I did.' I took her hand and stroked it. 'You were right about the tea and hot bath.'

'Sorry I couldn't get away sooner.' Her voice was thin and tired. 'You know how Habib is about trainees running out early on clinics.'

I tried to smile, but my lips wouldn't perform the required gymnastics. I'd read somewhere that it took twenty-six muscles to smile. Miranda wriggled out of her suit and into a pair of jeans and a jersey. She flopped down on the bed and sipped her tea.

'Ezekiel looked…possessed,' I said. 'He just went mad and in front of our Swedish funders.'

'So unlikely, Ezekiel Mabuza. Have you done anything to upset him?'

'Don't start to blame me.' I could hear my voice rising. 'I've cut him a lot of slack this year with his wife's cancer.'

'That's true, you have looked out for him. The trouble is, it's becoming second nature for people in this country to resort to violence, even decent people. The ANC is making the fight against crime a top priority this year, not before time.'

She had on her 'political' voice that annoyed me so much, especially after the day I'd been through. Miranda had never been that involved in politics in the old days, when the rest of us were in the thick of anti-apartheid stuff. Now she had joined the ANC, just when I had begun to have serious second thoughts about Mbeki's government. They were ignoring the needs of the poor, while handing out too many directorships to a few top comrades. This was not what we had been fighting for, all those years. Mbeki even claimed that there was no such thing as AIDS, that the idea was a white plot. That's when I tore up my membership card.

I looked up. Miranda had disappeared into her own thoughts. Simply having her here in the room was enough to calm me. I had stopped having bouts of shaking but now I began to feel a tide of anger towards Ezekiel. The idiot could have killed me. After all I had done for him too, when his wife was dying.

Miranda jumped up. 'I almost forgot – the police are coming round later for a statement. I'd better ring our senior partner for advice.'

'No, please Mirrie. I can't handle them tonight.'

'How are they supposed to arrest Ezekiel without your information? He could attack other people.'

'Someone will have called the cops straight after it happened and he'll have been restrained by now. He'll have come down from whatever high he was on earlier. Drink, drugs, whatever it was.'

'I suppose we can leave it until tomorrow.' She picked up the tray. 'I better check on Ellie. She's pretty agitated now she knows what happened.' She turned back at the door. 'What happened to your Swedes?'

I jumped up. 'Jesus, the Swedes! That'll be our grant down the pan.' I had completely forgotten our visitors with their coffers full of funds. I grabbed the telephone.

Sipho wasn't answering and I didn't have Bettina's number. I rang the Royal Hotel where our guests were staying. They had checked out earlier today. Oh shit! Suddenly the bedroom felt too hot.

The phone rang. 'Sipho, thank God. What happened with the Swedes?'

'They freaked out bigtime after Mabuza's crazy turn but me and Bettina managed to calm them down. We explained that nothing like this had ever happened here before. They weren't keen on the township visit, scared witless! But we arranged bodyguards and got them there in the end.'

'And?'

'They seemed impressed by the projects but the shine had gone off their visit. You could feel it. I think we'll have our work cut out to re-engage them.'

'Oh hell! And it was going so well.'

'How are you doing, bra? That attack put the fear of God in me and I wasn't in your shoes.'

'It bloody well did me too! And he kept up with me right to the other end of Anton Lembede street.'

'We called the cops straight away but we haven't heard if they found him yet. Personnel were going mad apparently, ringing them for updates. Going on about how they couldn't have someone like that on the loose, threatening their staff.'

'Let me know when he's found. I know it's crazy, but I keep thinking he's at my door.'

'Will do, bra. The cops have your details. They'll get in touch, I guess.'

'Don't count on it! Catch you tomorrow.'

Miranda popped her head back round the door. 'Any luck?'

Before I could reply, the phone rang. 'Mr van Rensburg? Yes, he's quite safe, thank you.'

'Human Resources,' she mouthed to me and, ignoring my headshaking and throat-slitting gestures, she passed the phone over and left the room.

I finally made it off the call and followed Miranda down to the kitchen.

'Mabuza's been arrested in Umlazi,' I announced. 'I'm meeting HR on Monday, to take it from there.'

'We're perfectly safe now, so you can calm down, Ellen,' Miranda said in her mumsy voice. 'Our take-outs are about to arrive.'

'Fantastic!' Ellen shrieked and jumped up. I could see the atmosphere was volatile. I felt ashamed that I'd been entirely caught up in my own reactions. I held my arms out and folded Ellen and Miranda in them. Tom wrapped his lanky eighteen-year-old frame around us all.

'Christ, Dad,' he said in a low voice, his unshaven chin tickling my face. 'Fucking lucky escape. What will happen to Ezekiel now?'

CHAPTER 3

'Ezekiel Mabuza, *woza*,' the constable called.

Ezekiel tried to stand up from the cement floor of the police-cell but his knees refused to unbend. He had been sitting there for many hours without space to move. Pitching forward as he stood, he rescued himself on the shoulders of the next man.

'Mabuza!' the constable shouted.

Ezekiel staggered towards him, between the mass of bodies huddled in the half-dark. It must be late afternoon by now, he guessed. It hadn't taken them long to track him down at Maphulo's last night. He wasn't sure how.

The constable reached for his hand to attach handcuffs. What else could Ezekiel do but go along with it, if he wanted to get out of this place, with its stinking bucket of piss and shit and human misery, its acrid smell of the sweat of men in fear? He had spent a restless night in a cell with twenty strangers, wondering who might steal his shoes or stick a cold blade in his back.

As they tramped the corridors of Umlazi Police Station, his eyes followed the tidemark between dark and lighter grey paint along the wall. He wished his head didn't feel as though someone had been at it with a jackhammer all night.

He assumed he was being led into this little cubicle for a police grilling and he was in no state to give the constable the right answers.

'Nomsa!' he cried out in surprise at the sight of his sister-in-law in the room. 'You got my message from Maphulo.'

Nomsa faced him with her mouth pursed, hands planted on her hips. 'And what would my sister Thandiwe have said about this?'

Ezekiel winced at the mention of his Thandiwe, lying cold under the earth. He hunched away from Nomsa's accusing eyes. 'Are my girls all right?'

'They are getting used to your behaviour! They brought themselves round to my place for the night.'

'Thank you for taking care of them. Tell them I'll be home soon.' This was not a time to pick a fight with his late wife's eldest sister. Where would he have been without her help this last year? Right now, he needed her to help him get out of this police station.

Nomsa heaved her bulk into a plastic chair and shifted her swollen feet off the floor, first one and then the other. He lowered himself onto a chair on the other side of a table, criss-crossed with scars and pocked with cigarette burns. He was grateful for the barrier between them.

'Just as well it's Saturday or I would be at work. I suppose it's a drunk and disorderly charge?' Nomsa sniffed. 'I have brought bail money.'

'I don't know if I will be charged, or with what. They are behaving very strangely towards me.'

Nomsa sucked her teeth to show her disapproval.

Ezekiel buried his head in his hands, trying to clear his thoughts about the last twenty-four hours. 'The cops are hinting that I won't get bail.'

'What did you *do*?' She sat up straight.

Ezekiel didn't want to admit that he couldn't recall very clearly what had happened yesterday. He remembered drinking with Maphulo at the *Jazz Queen* s*hebeen* the night before last; arriving home in the early hours, the struggle to make it to work next morning. He could picture himself coming out from behind the reception desk to argue with Gallagher in the foyer of the city hall and then…nothing… everything went blank…until he recalled jumping on the bus to Umlazi, a pain jagging in his chest, as though he had run from the devil.

'Wake up.' Nomsa elbowed him sharply. 'We need to make a plan. We don't know how much time they will give us.'

He shook himself and tried to concentrate on his predicament. 'Maybe *you* could ask them why I am here? I could wait all day to be told.'

Nomsa shrugged. 'You know how arrogant these policemen are.' But she rang the buzzer on the table next to her.

'Maybe if you tell them you are on Umlazi Women's Committee?' he whispered.

The constable returned and insisted on speaking to Nomsa alone. He put the cuffs back on Ezekiel's wrists and began to lead him away. Ezekiel reeled at this close-up of the man's foul breath.

'If they don't let me speak to you afterwards, see to my girls…' he called over his shoulder, as he left the room.

Nomsa tossed her head, as if to say, 'Would I do otherwise with my own sister's kids?'

Back in the cell, Ezekiel burned with shame at being led away from Nomsa like a criminal. This was his first time this side of a police cell, although he had often had to come in the past to bail out Sipho, his younger son. His mind clouded at the memory of Sipho, of the times he'd had to turn up here, as Sipho was drawn deeper and deeper into the Razor gang that had begun to flex its muscles in Umlazi township. Until he had realised it did no good trying to rescue the boy. In the end, there was no bail for the sort of activities that Sipho was involved in.

Remembering his son here left Ezekiel's heart raw. He tried to think of something else. It was a long time since the bread and tea they had been given this morning and his stomach rumbled. He had forgotten to ask Nomsa to check how much bail money he would need. If he got bail at all.

The door of the cell opened. 'Mabuza,' the constable beckoned him with his head. Ezekiel heard the clink of their cuffs being joined and down the corridor they went again.

'Why didn't you tell me what you had done?' Nomsa asked, tight-lipped. Her voice had a new layer of chill, her hands clasped her cheeks.

'What did he say?' Ezekiel licked his dry lips and tried to catch her eye.

'You could be charged with attempted murder, that's what!' She raised her eyes to heaven as her voice reached a crescendo. 'What in the name of Jesus made you do it?'

'No, no, there must be some mistake…' He looked around but the constable had shut the door and disappeared.

'And why did you bring a knife to work?' Her bosom heaved as she wiped away a few tears. 'If my beloved Thandiwe were still alive, to witness this.'

Ezekiel crouched at this blow. At the mention of the knife, the room had become stifling. He struggled to get air into his lungs, which felt as though they had been pressed flat. Ragged pieces of yesterday afternoon began to float into his mind. A picture of himself doing a crazy dance in the city hall foyer in front of Gallagher and then he lost it. Another glimpse of him and Maphulo talking big in the *shebeen* the night before. And 'pop' – that was gone too.

'I don't think you'll be getting out soon,' Nomsa sounded bitter. 'They say you're dangerous.'

'Dangerous! How can that be?' his voice was thin and hollow, as though coming down a long tunnel. 'Take care of my girls until I sort this out. And find me a lawyer, please.'

'I'll see what I can do.' She rose on ankles that looked painful and straightened her clothes. The air in the small room was stale and beaten.

He caught a glimpse of Nomsa going down the corridor towards the outside world, as he was being led back to his cell. What could they charge him with? Surely there had been no crime. He had been foolish to carry a knife but he had never used it. He had never caught up with Gallagher. His heart sank at the thought of even one more night in the dank cell.

****

Next morning, a policeman called to see me. He wanted me to describe yesterday's events which set my heart racing again. I could have done without it.

'OK, thanks Mr Gallagher,' he said when we finished. 'Let me assure you again that your assailant is now safely under lock and key.'

I saw him to the door, peering out carefully before I opened it fully. I knew it was crazy to fear other assailants now Mabuza was locked up but I couldn't help it. I locked it again as soon as he left.

I could hear Miranda on the phone. 'Shocking, I know, Ezekiel Mabuza! Yes, I'm sure he'd love to see you.' She rang off as I came into the lounge. 'The Listers are calling round. That'll be nice. Come away from the window Ben, there is no-one there.'

I followed her to the kitchen, after a last glance backward. I didn't feel like visitors.

'You lay out the tray, while I make the tea,' Miranda said. 'Let's hope we have some biscuits.' She reached for the cake tin.

A while later, the doorbell made me jump. This was ridiculous. I went to check through the window that it was the Listers, before unlocking the door.

'Ben, I'm so sorry. How dreadful for you,' Penny said, enveloping me in a warm hug.

'You OK, man?' Stocky Neil clapped me on the shoulder. 'You gave us a helluva fright.'

'Thanks for coming round…' I said, trying to steady my shaky voice. I hated Neil seeing the state I was in.

'Welcome, welcome,' Miranda came in and hugged our old friends. 'Come through to the kitchen.' We followed her and sat down around our long wooden table.

'Coffee, everyone?' Miranda asked.

'To think of Ezekiel turning on you, after all these years,' Penny shook her head, pushing back her wispy, blond hair.

I nodded. 'He just went crazy. Like he was a stranger.'

'What makes a decent man do a thing like that?'

'I wish I knew.'

'You're both personalizing it too much,' Neil waved our words away. 'There is a kind of collective psychosis in this country…' he paced up and down pontificating, as though we hadn't heard it all a dozen times before. 'We haven't really made the transition from apartheid yet. The poison is still oozing out.'

'Take no notice.' Penny rolled her eyes. 'Neil tries to reduce everything to this theory.'

'You're so bloody naive, woman.' Neil raised his voice.

'Don't "bloody woman" me because you're in a bad mood.'

The silence was tense.

'Throw me that jersey, Neil,' I said. I'd started to shiver, although it was a warm day.

'You'll sack the guy, of course,' he said.

'It's not that simple,' I said, struggling into the jersey. 'Right now, the police have him locked up. He'll be suspended from work. There'll have to be a tribunal first but he will be sacked in the end. We can't have our doorman running amok with a knife.'

'You'll charge him with assault in the meantime.'

'I'm not sure…'

'Don't be crazy, man. Hit him hard. Teach him a lesson. South Africans have to give up using violence as the solution to everything or this country will go to the dogs.'

'This is Ezekiel Mabuza we're talking about. Decent man, twenty years of good service. Something weird happened to him that day, totally out of character.'

'Christ! I don't care how decent Ezekiel usually is. He came at you with a knife.'

'You tell him, Neil,' Miranda said, handing round the mugs of coffee. 'Ben escaped serious injury only by sheer luck. And now he doesn't want to press charges.'

'He didn't actually touch me,' I said. 'So I probably can't charge him with assault. And the police in Durban have bigger fish to fry, they won't be interested.'

Penny gave Neil a look which silenced him. She turned to me. 'Did it happen out of the blue, Ben?'

'Yes, Ezekiel was standing quietly at the door as I came in from lunch with our Swedish visitors. Suddenly he jumped up yelling. I called him to order and he came at me, pulling out this bloody great knife!'

'Terrifying.'

'He was swiping at me this way and that.' I found myself acting out the scene for them. 'I managed to get out of the main door but I didn't expect him to chase me so far down the street. Or so fast. This heavy, middle-aged guy just kept pounding after me.'

Neil punched me lightly on the arm. 'Just as well you've been doing all that Comrades training.'

We tried to laugh but his joke fell flat.

'Let's take our coffee into the garden,' Miranda said. 'It looks lovely out there.'

'Too cold for my liking,' I said, so everyone stayed put. There was no way I was going to step outside into a world of possible assailants.

I sat hunched and silent as the conversation swirled around me. It was easier to stay in the room than to be alone, where panic threatened to well up. My mind returned to the scene in the foyer yesterday. What had Ezekiel Mabuza yelled as he brandished the knife at me? And why on earth was he angry with me in particular?

I looked up at the others. 'I've been thinking...what may have...why he picked on me.'

'Spit it out,' Miranda said.

'It may not be relevant but...last week I had a small incident with Ezekiel.'

'What sort of incident?' asked Neil.

'He asked for extra leave to go back to his home village…
to consult his *sangoma*. But it's a long way and he's had a lot
of extra leave already this year, when his wife was dying… so
I refused. I told him to visit a *sangoma* in Durban.'

'Surely that wouldn't be enough to provoke this attack?'
Miranda asked.

'Well…it depends what he wanted to see the *sangoma*
about,' Penny said thoughtfully. 'If it was a life and death
issue, he'd want to see one he knew and trusted.' I took note
of Penny's words. She had grown up on a farm and had a
much greater knowledge of Zulu culture than we townies
did.

'I should have given him more time to explain that day
but I was having a bloody awful afternoon.' I could feel
my face flush as I recalled the incident. How Ezekiel had
struggled to get his words out. How impatient I had been
with him.

'This is ridiculous,' Neil exploded. 'You're trying to take
the blame for your own attack!'

'Leave Ben alone,' Penny said. 'This has only just
happened. He's still in shock.'

'You're just as bad. Bleeding hearts brigade.' Neil threw
up his hands in disgust.

'I think we should be going, Neil. Ben needs to rest.'
Penny stood up and came over to hug me. 'Give yourself
time. You've had a very nasty shock.'

I felt tears smart my eyes and blinked them away
furiously.

We walked our visitors to the door. 'Thanks for coming,
guys.'

'*Vasbyt*, man, hang on in there.' Neil said. 'We'll have a
drink soon.'

'Stay well,' Miranda waved them off and turned to me. 'A bit of tension between those two today.'

'Yeah.' I put my arm around her shoulder, 'Thank God we're all right.' I needed to believe that.

She didn't reply. I wanted to kiss her but she was likely to say that I always took things *that* way. This weekend of all times was not the moment to rock the boat between us.

My thoughts veered inevitably back to Ezekiel. Why was I so reluctant to charge him with assault? Or so upset that he might go to prison? He had brought it on himself. And because of his crazy actions, we might lose the Swedish grant. I flinched. In public services, older whites were being demoted all the time to give black colleagues a chance, to make up for some of apartheid's wrongs. My manager had hinted to me that I was next in line if we didn't get the Swedish money. My days as director of museums might be numbered.

CHAPTER 4

'Greetings, Bra.' A cocky young man shambled down the prison visitors' room and sat down opposite Ezekiel, on the other side of the glass. He raised his hand in a salute. 'Mathias Dutu's the name.'

Ezekiel frowned. Who was this man? Why had he come to visit him?

'The guys in the union send you fraternal greetings.'

'Ah, you're from the union…' Ezekiel struggled to clear a voice that he hadn't used all day.

'Union sent me to see how you're doing. You're a hero, man, challenging the director like that.' The stranger grinned.

There was a long pause. Ezekiel glanced down the row of men lined up on his side of the glass, spitting out their private business in loud voices. He didn't want his *indaba* known all over D section of Westville prison and spread around the townships.

'Thanks to you, bra, all the guys are talking about our municipal strike call.' Mathias rocked back on his plastic chair, thumbs hooked low in the waistband of his trousers. Then he swung his chair back upright with a thwack.

Ezekiel shuddered at the thought of everyone knowing what he had done that afternoon. It must have been because of his trip to the *shebeen* the night before. Nomsa was right. He had got in with the wrong crowd since Thandiwe went to join her ancestors. He needed to sort himself out.

'It's all round the municipality. The union meeting will be massive next week,' Mathias crowed, his hands stretching out to indicate how big. 'We'll give the managers a thumping.'

Ezekiel coughed. 'You don't understand. It wasn't about the union. I was not well that day.' He couldn't look the young man in the eye.

'Man, anyone would be having second thoughts at this stage.'

There was a long pause then Ezekiel said. 'Listen, tell the union I'm not your pin-up boy for the strike. This has left me in deep trouble.'

Mathias looked taken aback and remained silent.

Ezekiel could not bring himself to mention out loud the charge of attempted murder but the very thought of it started him rocking – a steady backwards and forwards rhythm of his upper body that calmed him. The men in his cell had begun to laugh at him for it. All day and night, he worried how his girls were doing and what would happen to his job. How he would pay his rent from inside here. Rock, rock, rock. How would Thandiwe have responded to his situation? Only, it would never have happened if Thandiwe had still been alive.

Mathias spoke more quietly. 'It'll work out man. And don't worry, union will pay your costs. For the lawyer etc.'

Ezekiel found he could focus more easily on that. Would the union really pay for a lawyer? But could he trust this stranger who seemed to be taking over his life?

'My sister is already organising a lawyer.'

'Our guy will know union business. You can't rely on a tin-pot township lawyer.'

Nomsa would be very annoyed after the effort she was making to find him a lawyer but Ezekiel had been worried sick about how he would pay for it. He would explain to Nomsa that the union was paying, so they must choose the lawyer.

'Yes, the union knows about these things. Give them my thanks.' Let the union think he'd done it for them. He knew that whatever he'd done, he'd done it for Thandiwe and his girls.

'Good, bra. Union will find a razor-sharp lawyer to get you out of here.'

Ezekiel slumped with relief that he'd allowed the union to take over his case. He felt his bowels loosen and quickly tightened his sphincter. He reached over to grasp the man's hand, but the glass screen was in the way. He mimicked the grasp of hands and Mathias did the same from his side. The boy grinned his toothy grin and Ezekiel managed a watery smile back.

'Is this your first time inside?' Mathias asked and Ezekiel nodded. 'Union will have you out of here in no time. Strike is a good cause, heh?'

'Yes.' Ezekiel didn't mention his dead son's visits to Westville prison.

'You short of anything we can send you, bra?'

'Toothpaste and Lifebuoy soap. I've got nothing.' Ezekiel's voice was urgent. He was too embarrassed to ask for cash. He would have to wait for Nomsa's visit.

The bell rang, making Ezekiel jump. The guards stepped forward and ordered visitors to clear the room.

Mathias stood up, stretching as if he'd been squashed in a box. He threw Ezekiel one last salute and was gone.

The sound of all the visitors scraping their chairs on the bare floor, felt like the rip of cat's claws in Ezekiel's brain. Prisoners stared longingly after their vanishing visitors, then rushed towards the door opening behind them, pushing and shoving to get through. But nothing was waiting for them, not even an evening meal. Ezekiel could not get used to the fact that their last meal was bread and tea at three in the afternoon. Then the long, gnawing evenings locked in their cell together, forty of them packed in tight like the ticks round a cow's backside. With only a few night staff they hardly ever saw. That's when his panic rose to a silent scream inside and he pleaded with his ancestors to save him.

Back in D section, he returned to his task – trying to piece together the missing shards of memory from the fateful afternoon. If only Gallagher had given him time off to go to Nkandla to consult his *sangoma*. That was where the trouble had started. Ezekiel recalled the powerful medicine woman living deep in KwaZulu, who could help someone who had displeased his ancestors so badly. But what exactly had he done that could give rise to a charge of murder?

****

I dawdled at the bike sheds, struggling as I did every day, to step inside the city hall. Gone was the happy carelessness of one who had not been chased with a knife by a wild-eyed madman, replaced by a choking fear of every passing stranger. Now anyone might suddenly turn on me like Ezekiel Mabuza had. But I couldn't stay out here all morning. I braced to enter the building.

I raised my hand to today's doorman. 'Samuel, *gunjani wena* – how are you?'

The young man rose smartly to attention, inclining his head respectfully to an elder. '*Sapila,* Mr Gallagher. *gunjani wena?*'

I hoped that he didn't notice me suppress an instinctive shiver. Every day this encounter with the doorman brought Ezekiel's attack flooding back. My hands balled into fists, my mouth clenched. I had to fight an instinct to turn and run right out of the building. I stretched my mouth in what I hoped looked like a smile and rushed up the staircase, two at a time, hoping no-one would waylay me. Once in my office, I could concentrate on getting my heart rate down and with any luck I'd be OK. I cringed with shame at what I had become.

As I turned the corner, I slowed down and groaned. Van Rensburg from Human Resources was waiting outside my office. A slight man with sharp features and mousy, brown hair, neatly slicked back, van Rensburg was twisting his Biro and seemed to be contorting his face at his own effrontery at calling on me uninvited.

'Sorry, sir,' he cleared his throat. 'But we need to discuss Mabuza's disciplinary hearing.'

I was annoyed by the implication that I needed to be reminded. I snapped back into manager mode. 'Come in, van Rensburg. Let's make it quick.' I had to be careful, with my job no longer secure. I'd run the Museum for years but recently people had recently started to take issue with my management style.

'OK, let's get started.' Why had they assigned the case to this pipsqueak Afrikaner deputy, instead of to the head of Human Resources? 'And for God's sake stop calling me sir. This is an informal organization.'

'Yes, s-sir,' van Rensburg said in his clipped accent. 'We

need to discuss the code of conduct line by line. Make sure you are fully briefed.'

'You do your nuts-and-bolts stuff, I'll just tell it how it was.'

'That isn't an option sir. Unless we want his union to out-manoeuvre us.'

'You do things your way on Wednesday, I'll do things mine. End of story.'

'The man could have killed you.'

'I realise that.'

'I hope you'll be suing him in court, sir.' Van Rensburg flushed at his own impertinence.

'Don't you start. I've already got my wife on my case.'

'I'm sure a charge can be made. We have to show people…'

I leaned back, eyeing the piles of paperwork threatening to topple over on my desk. I could do without hearing van Rensburg's views on crime. Why wouldn't this horrible little man go away? I could hear the tea trolley making its way down the hall and I didn't want to miss out.

Van Rensburg persisted. 'Surely it is our Christian duty to make South Africa a safer place. God's own country!' Fervour shone in his usually meek eyes.

'Look, I know what happened but I'm still here, not a mark on me.'

Van Rensburg looked defeated. He stood up to leave. 'Very unpleasant incident, sir.'

'It certainly was.' I shook his hand and I followed him out to catch the tea trolley.

Back at my desk, I drank down the warm liquid as if it was an intravenous fluid I needed. How come I always felt the weight of South Africa's past pulling me down below the water, while this young Afrikaner acted as though he had walked squeaky clean into the Rainbow Nation, as if his kind had no blood on his hands for what apartheid had done? I would not have van Rensburg telling me what to do about Mabuza. Inside, I was being torn between rage at the man for ruining our presentation to the Swedes and the growing feeling that I had tipped him over the edge. If only I had listened to his plea to visit his *sangoma* back at home. And I didn't want to punish his family. What would happen to his daughters, if he was sent to prison? They had already lost their mother. And hadn't he lost both his sons a few years ago?

There was a knock and I found Bettina and Sipho at my door.

'Have you read it?' she asked. 'The email from the Swedish woman.'

'Haven't had time to get on my computer yet.'

'Here, I printed it out.' Sipho waved a page in my face. My eyes ran down the page.

Dear Durban City Hall applicants,

Many thanks for your excellent presentation and the township visits, where you showed us the type of projects you want to expand upon if you are awarded a grant from us.

Before we move your application forward to the final shortlist, however, I must be reassured that you have built in sufficient protection against the type of violent incident that we witnessed in your city hall foyer. You will understand that we can't fund a project whose staff will be put at risk of such violence. This will be the case more especially in the townships. I noted we needed bodyguards to visit your projects.

I look forward to receiving a detailed outline of your security proposals as soon as possible. The committee's decisions will be made on 18th May.

Yours cordially,

Astrid Bergdahl

'Christ, what do they expect?' I said. 'This is South Africa, things happen. We have the highest levels of violence in the world. Didn't they do their bloody research before coming all this way to assess us?'

'Just what I said to Sipho on our way over,' said Bettina. 'These same problems apply to any South African proposal they fund. Why even bother to come out here?'

'Calm down, both of you,' Sipho said. 'We know that's the case but they saw violence on their visit here, nowhere else. So, we have to find a form of words that satisfies them and moves us on to the final shortlist.'

'You mean, as long as it sounds as though it meets their expectations?' I grinned. 'We will know it is merely a little finger in the dike but we don't have to spell that out to them?'

'Exactly!'

'I'm too angry to make a good job of it,' I said.

'Oh, I can rattle off a first draft,' Sipho said. 'I'm so used to writing this sort of soft sell about township projects. We'd never get any money without it.'

'Go ahead,' said Bettina. 'I find it difficult to bend the truth. I'm always thinking "what would my minister say about it?"'

'It's down to you to save us, Sipho,' I said. 'And don't forget the good news. We have made it onto their final shortlist, apart from this hurdle.'

CHAPTER 5

A man in a smart suit came forward and offered Ezekiel his hand. 'Robert Dlamini, your lawyer. Let's work out how to get you out of this mess.'

Ezekiel was startled. The fellow looked too young for an important job like a lawyer. At least they didn't have to shout through glass, as he had with Mathias. They sat down opposite each other in a small room, with sun streaming in through a small window. Ezekiel looked out on a strip of green grass. All he had seen since he arrived here had been the grey exercise yard or shit-coloured prison walls. This little patch of green conjured up for him the summers long ago in Nkandla, where the goats nibbled the grass flat. If he and the other herd-boys didn't keep moving them to another patch, they would eat it right down to the roots. Then the boys would get a beating from their fathers. Looking beyond the patch of grass, he was startled to see, coming up the hill towards the gates of the prison, many people, large and small, old and young, baskets weighing them down, women balancing bundles on their heads. It was prison visiting time.

'Mr Mabuza.' Dlamini called his attention back. 'I am afraid you have been charged with attempted murder.'

Ezekiel buckled over at hearing the words again and grasped the edges of the table that sat between them.

'Do not despair. This is the first thing we must challenge.'

Bit by bit they went over 'the incident' as Dlamini called it, that Friday that had brought on his troubles. It made the day shrink into something Ezekiel could think about. Until now, the memory of it had been a moth-eaten blanket, full of holes. In the long dark hours in his cell, more pieces kept floating to meet him. He remembered waking in a dark mood the morning after his night at the *Jazz Queen*. And arriving at his doorman's booth in the city hall foyer and hiding a knife in a drawer there. He had no plan to use it, he was sure.

'So why did you bring it to work?' his lawyer asked.

'I don't know. Maybe it was to give myself courage to ask Gallagher again about having time off.'

'And what made you take it out?' Dlamini asked, holding him with his eyes. 'In front of all those people?'

Ezekiel hung his head. 'I'm sorry...my mind goes dark when I try to recall...'

'Take your time; try to put yourself back in that day... where were you just before you pulled out the knife?'

'I...I think I was sitting at my desk at the door to the city hall. I am senior doorman there, twenty years,' he added proudly.

'And what was the trigger? What made you pull the knife out of the drawer?'

'I...I don't know...I remember Mr Gallagher entering the building...'

'Were you angry with Mr Gallagher?'

'Yes. I needed time off to visit a *sangoma* in Zululand, because my ancestors are angry with me. Mr. Gallagher refused me.' Ezekiel could feel again the anger from that day. How Gallagher had no idea how he had been struggling to keep his head above water since Thandiwe had died. 'But I only wanted to talk to him, to ask him again for time off.'

'What happened next?'

Ezekiel frowned hard as he thought, then shook his head. 'I can remember nothing…just running as if the devil was after me and…and then looking down and seeing a knife in my hand. I didn't know what it was doing there…'

'And the union business?'

'The union was also angry with Gallagher for trying to stop the strike. I am a union man.'

Dlamini nodded and then was silent for a while. 'So it could be argued that it wasn't just for yourself that you confronted Mr Gallagher, but for your union. A misguided gesture but well intentioned.'

Ezekiel thought he understood what the man was saying. He nodded.

'So, you chased him on impulse then?'

'Excuse me?'

'You're saying that you didn't plan to chase Gallagher with the knife?'

'No, definitely not.' Ezekiel shook his head vigorously. 'I am not a violent man; ask anyone who knows me all these years.'

'You didn't intend to attack him?'

'No, I did not.' He'd only had a few beers that night at the *Lucky Queen*. How come it had tipped him over the edge like that?

'Are there any witnesses who can confirm your side of the story?' Dlamini was scribbling words down in his notebook.

Ezekiel thought back hard to that day. 'I can remember no-one but Gallagher coming towards me.'

Dlamini stopped writing and looked up. 'It sounds as though it was the union business that swung things. We'll play on that. You were making a gesture for the union. You had no intention of doing any harm.'

Ezekiel was puzzled. 'But…'

'Don't worry, I think I have it in hand,' Dlamini said.

Ezekiel was glad somebody knew what to do. 'When will the case be heard?'

Dlamini rubbed his hands together as though they were cold. 'Ah, difficult to say. It depends how long it takes me to collect the evidence. There is also a bad backlog in the courts, unfortunately.' He eyed Ezekiel with a look the prisoner could not place. 'Of course, there are ways on speeding matters up.' He paused and looked at Ezekiel expectantly. 'If you could see your way to…you know, butter up the clerks of the courts.'

It dawned on Ezekiel that he was being asked for money. 'But how much? I can't manage very much on my wages…'

Dlamini's face fell. 'In that case you could wait a long time for your case to be heard.'

The warder led him back to his section, shoved him into his cell and slammed the door shut behind him. Ezekiel staggered and almost fell, his heart thumping so loudly he expected his cellmates to hear it.

Terror Mangoba, the main man in his cell, was holding court. He looked up. 'So, there is life in this one after all,' he drawled, looking up at Ezekiel. His cronies brayed like mules.

Ezekiel swallowed. 'My lawyer says I may be in here for a long time.'

'China, a case like yours will be dropped "poof" just like that,' Terror clicked his fingers. 'Unless you're big in the Numbers gangs like me. Then you have to pay plenty money to get your case heard.'

Terror should know. They said he'd been in the twenty-sixes gang a long time and that he had been in and out of Westville prison since he was a kid. Ezekiel's world had turned upside down in the few days since he'd arrived here. In his old life he would have crossed the street to avoid someone like Terror but the twenty-sixes gang ruled D section. In their large cell at night, he had to rub shoulders with forty other snoring, farting, moaning bodies, including Terror and his crew and he knew he needed to avoid offending them. He didn't know the name of Terror's thin, sad-faced sidekick – everyone called him Doris or '*wyfie*'. It hadn't taken Ezekiel long to work out what was going on in the beds of the top men like Terror at night. Doris hardly ever spoke but he seemed pathetically grateful for Terror's protection.

The bell rang for the noon-day meal and everyone crowded towards their section gate, waiting for the key to turn, so they could push and shove down the long corridor to the canteen. Ezekiel hated these corridor runways most. Grudges could easily be set up, punches lobbed. On his first evening he had been sent sprawling by a well-aimed kick. Last night he'd seen a knife drawn on someone just ahead of him.

D section shuffled past the food hatches and on to their tables. The food was lousy. The dining room roared with noise. They said Westville was one of the biggest prisons in South Africa. He still had to shake himself to believe he was in this strange new world, while his familiar one went on somewhere out there without him. Ezekiel sighed and forgot about the food on his plate.

'Stop stressing and enjoy your moment of celebrity!' Jazz said, scraping the gravy up off his plate with balls of maize *putu* and smacking his lips. 'You've been in the newspapers, man. I'd give my back teeth for that.' Jazz was part of the group who had adopted him at their table on his first day. 'You look lost, man. Come with us.' They named Ezekiel *Ukuthula* – the Quiet One.

'You can walk tall in your township after this. No one will rob your house,' Phineas said. 'It will be useful in here, too.'

Ezekiel cringed at being reminded of how the papers had run the knife story. 'But will they give me back my job at city hall after all this publicity?'

These things didn't seem to worry the others. Did they even have steady jobs to lose? Jazz was facing an assault charge – a late night punch-up that turned nasty, when his band was playing alongside their rivals at the *Blue Lagoon* Cafe.

Phineas had been charged with grievous bodily harm. He had come home early one night from performing to find his wife in the arms of his neighbour. He couldn't see why he was in here at all. What else should a husband do to restore his honour? He said he was sorry he hadn't finished both of them off. Ezekiel could just imagine what Nomsa would say about him mixing with guys like this. But laughing with them tonight felt like a branch snapping, letting go of some of the tension that had held his body so taut for the last days that he felt sick and giddy. He was grateful that Jazz and the gang had adopted him. It felt much safer than rolling around in here on his own. As he scooped up his gravy and *putu*, he wondered if he might survive this place after all, at least until his lawyer got him out.

****

I woke feeling drained. All night long, I'd tossed in sweaty sheets. Every time I had shut my eyes to sleep, I'd been tormented by images of a knife-wielding Ezekiel Mabuza. Today I would come face to face with my attacker again at his disciplinary hearing. I tried to shrink the frightening figure in my mind back into the friendly doorman I had known for years but I couldn't manage it.

Downstairs, Miranda was in the hallway, kitted out in another of her smart, new suits. Not what I'd expected when she went back to being a student after all these years. She said she had to dress the part for her law placement.

She'd turned to me, briefcase in hand. 'You're cooking tonight, remember? I've got my late Law Clinic and then an ANC meeting.'

'Ja, ja, every Wednesday…' I backed off, raising my hands as if it was a hold up.

'Good luck with the tribunal,' she said. She checked her smooth, dark hair in the hall mirror. 'Ellie, we'll be late!' she called upstairs as she left the house. Ellen ran out, trailing her open school bag. I watched Miranda drive off in our blue Mazda, taking the corner into the street a bit on the sharp side. Whizzing off to sort the sheep from the goats in the outside world. I found myself fretting over how my art-teacher wife had become this intimidating trainee lawyer that I felt I hardly knew anymore. Yet another of the world's mysteries that seemed to be thickening around me. I tried to shake off the feeling that things were slipping from my grip.

By eight am, I was at the city hall. Outside the door of the tribunal, I had another panic attack, sweating, heart racing, the works. Gradually, it wore off. I tried to steady my legs as I made my way to my place with the other witnesses in the municipality chamber, the site of our meeting with our Swedish visitors. If only I could rewind the clock to that day and secure a different outcome! Ezekiel was led in, manacled to a prison guard, his head hung low in shame. The terrifying figure of my nightmares melted away. The poor man looked dazed, crushed, as though he did not understand how he had ended up in this situation. I felt an answering shame flush my cheeks, sure that I was somehow responsible for bringing him down. I tried to catch his eye but he didn't raise his gaze. The panel chair called the meeting to order and the tribunal began.

Two hours later, it was over. I shoved back my chair and ran my fingers through my hair. 'Geez, that was a long morning,' I said to van Rensburg, seated next to me. Stage one of Mabuza's disciplinary tribunal was over, thank God. I felt another rush of shame at seeing Ezekiel led out in chains. I must try to find out if his family was alright. See whether his union was helping them. Van Rensburg and I made our way out of the chamber and down the corridor.

'I jus' don't understand Mr Gallagher,' he said, nervous tic appearing at his jaw. 'We could have had him sacked by this afternoon if you hadn't let it go, sir. Now we have to go through another panel meeting, after his psychiatric assessment. It could take months.'

'I have to admit to having similar thoughts, after the way he scared the hell out of me that day. But there are more important matters to consider…'

'I'm sure you have fears for your family, sir, if you come down hard on him,' van Rensburg said, 'But there is a principle at stake. What safety message are we sending to the staff?'

'It's not that,' I said, irritated by van Rensburg's self-righteous tone. 'You want me to kick the guy out at his age, with a week's wages?'

'He should have thought of that before he pulled the knife on you, sir.' Van Rensburg danced to one side as a crowd of schoolkids swept noisily down the corridor. Outside, the mynah birds in the flamboyant trees joined in.

'How long have you known Ezekiel Mabuza, Matheus?'

'It's seven years since I joined the Department.'

'Well, he has been here twenty years. Did it occur to you that he is probably supporting ten family members on his wage?' I hated my self-righteous tone.

'No sir,' van Rensburg whispered. I guessed that these issues were not included in his Human Resources Training, Disciplinary Section.

'Or that he'll never get another job at his age, after being sacked for something like this, not with unemployment running at forty percent?' My lip was curling more with dislike at myself than van Rensburg. When did I start picking on such easy targets?

He waved his hands vaguely. 'I'll have to discuss it with my *dominee* on Sunday. But we have to have law and order in this country, sir.'

'Well, let's start with the fat cats higher up with their Volvos and BMWs and leave this poor bastard with a hot temper until last, hey?' I said more gently. I patted him on the back and said goodbye. Then filed away the folder marked *Mabuza, E.*

I shuffled through the post left on my desk by my secretary, Mira. An official looking envelope with foreign stamps stood out and I pounced on it. It had to be our reply from the Swedes! I ripped it open.

'Dear Durban applicants,

Thank you for your addendum about additional staff security measures in relation to the concerns we raised. I am sorry to inform you that, despite our admiration for your project, we still had safety concerns. As a result, I regret that your application is not one of the final three which have been funded...'

The letter dropped from my hands. I felt sick in the stomach as I saw our plans crumble around me, all the work we'd put in, how much Durban municipality had been banking on this investment. The grant had seemed such a sure thing. Bloody Europeans with no grasp of our circumstances here. Then the impact of this news for me personally bubbled up. It would be only a matter of time now before I was demoted, relocated somewhere in the sticks like the Battlefields Museum in Ladysmith, and my directorship passed on to my thrusting, young deputy, John Gwala. Or I would be offered early retirement, just as bad. I needed to alert Miranda to my looming disaster. But the picture of her going ballistic at the news made me change my mind. Better to wait until it actually happened. Something might still come up to save me. I'd talk to Bettina and Sipho, perhaps we could challenge the Swedes' decision. I reached for my phone. Soon the three of us were gathered in Sipho's office.

'Durban can't be more dangerous than the places that won,' I said, exasperated. 'Who did win, anyway? I didn't finish the letter.'

'They haven't announced them yet,' Sipho replied. 'You're right. But it was our bad luck to get caught out being dangerous, right under their noses!'

'Damn Ezekiel! If he hadn't...' I went no further. 'Let's

challenge this verdict. Make a strong argument, pointing out all their winners operate in places that are just as dangerous.'

'Or threaten to accuse them of bias?' Sipho said excitedly.

'Calm down, you two,' Bettina said. 'This is futile. You saw the application forms we filled in. "The judges' decision is final". It would be chaos if every team started challenging the outcome.'

We were silent. I knew Bettina was right. My rush of hope began rapidly to dissolve. Everyone at city hall would end up blaming me for losing the grant, even though I'd been the victim of the attack. Muck from the incident had already begun to stick to my name.

I was back in my office, head in my hands, when Mira put her head round my door, cheerful as usual. 'A huge pile of messages for you, Ben.'

'Not now, Mira. Something really big has come up.'

'I don't think these can wait. Lots of people want to talk to you about the union meeting tomorrow.'

'That's all I need after this morning.' Reluctantly I took the messages.

'There's still time for the union to settle, isn't there?' she asked.

'I doubt it.' I said, doing a mock hair-tearing. 'Why can't people get it that there is no more money? The Government isn't going to budge on municipal pay.' Thank God I could let off steam to Mira.

'Surely staff won't want it to turn bad like last time.'

If only Mira were right. But the unions had tasted power during the last municipal strike and they'd want to go one better this time.

'Don't worry, the secretaries won't vote to strike,' she said.

'Thanks.' I managed a weak smile.

I couldn't focus on my messages, my mind constantly returning to the Swedes letter. If only... my brain kept repeating...and what if...? People kept knocking on my door all afternoon about the strike. At one point I hid in the gents to escape them all. My office grew hotter and stuffier. The bloody aircon must be off again.

CHAPTER 6

Inside the municipality chamber, Ezekiel watched the important people leaving his tribunal. His union rep, Kangisa, and his lawyer stayed behind, discussing what had happened as if he was invisible.

Dlamini looked very learned today in his pin-striped suit. 'It's not your average open-and-shut case,' he said, his hands clasped before him as if in prayer. 'We have our work cut out on this one.' Ezekiel didn't like the sound of this remark.

'They didn't produce any hard evidence of Mabuza's alleged misconduct,' Kangisa slapped his thigh in delight. 'Anything Gallagher says, we'll dispute that he has a vested interest in distorting events because of the strike action.'

'Gallagher was very quiet today,' chuckled Dlamini. 'Convenient for us.'

Ezekiel shook his head as he tried to figure out what all the big words at the tribunal had meant. Seeing Gallagher so close up had clogged his brain. If he had really gone after him with a knife as they claimed, would Gallagher do something to him in revenge? Maybe he would try to catch him on his way out and, and… Ezekiel's mind closed shut. This was the city hall, not the township, he tried to reassure himself. This was Gallagher, who had been a fair boss and had been kind to him many times. He tried to concentrate back on what Dlamini and Kangisa were saying.

Kangisa slapped him on the back. 'We'll get you home and dry, bra! We'll help you prepare for this psychiatric assessment, don't worry.'

Ezekiel didn't trust Kangisa and his crocodile smiles. He knew from union meetings that the man had a way of making things look the way he wanted you to see them, rather than how they were. Behind his back, they called him 'the dog that nods both ways'.

'I thought you were going to tell them that I did it for the union?' Ezekiel said to Dlamini.

'Ah, that is when it comes to court on a criminal charge. It wouldn't go down well here in the city hall. Here, we need to emphasise the personal strain you were under.'

'And Gallagher's lack of cultural sensitivity to your need to go home to consult your *sangoma*. We'll accuse him of racism. That works well these days,' Kangisa added.

In the pause, the prison guard raised himself to his full height and patted his watch. 'If you are completing your business, sirs, I must return the suspect to prison.' Ezekiel felt shamed once more at the sight of his hand still cuffed to the guard's.

'This is also part of the business of the tribunal.' Kangisa's chest puffed up. 'Mabuza has a right to review the hearing with his union representative and his lawyer.'

With everyone starting to argue, Ezekiel's heart struck loud, uneven beats, like the thunder that used to frighten him as a child. How had he ended up in the middle of all this?

'I think that's all we need to say for now,' Dlamini cut it

short, nodding to Ezekiel. 'I will visit you in the prison next week.'

Ezekiel nodded back. Kangisa was a bit of a windbag and he put his money on his lawyer to get him out of this mess. His guard bustled him out of the building down the back stairs.

Thankfully there was no sign of Gallagher on the way out. For once Ezekiel would be glad to be locked up, somewhere Gallagher couldn't find him. When he arrived back at the prison, it would be bread and tea, followed by an hour in the exercise yard and then the early lock-up in their cells, tight as worms. The cell's blankets were crawling with bedbugs, or 'bed-warmers' as the guys in his cell called them.

****

I watched Miranda lean back in her easy chair, her stockinged feet draped over the side. She looked pale and tired after her long day's work at Habib's. The kids were upstairs doing homework. I was grateful the two of us still managed some time alone together, at the end of most days.

'How did your tribunal go?' she asked.

'OK. Ezekiel has been referred for a psychiatric assessment as the next step.'

'What went on? How did you find it?'

'Oh, not now please. I can't face talking about it anymore today.'

'Come on, I'm your wife.' She sounded exasperated.

'Well, what do you want to know?'

'What was it like facing Mabuza again? I've been worrying about you all day.'

'If you must know, I went into a bloody panic when I was

about to enter the room. Breathing fast, heart hammering, the whole works.' I turned away from her gaze.

'I wish you'd see a doctor about it,' she said. 'There's nothing to be ashamed of. Panic attacks are quite normal after this type of event. I looked on the internet. It's called post-traumatic stress.'

I ignored what she said. 'But I calmed down as soon as I saw Ezekiel. He looked so crushed and defeated...so harmless. I felt sorry for him.'

Miranda's mouth tightened and she gave me that look, as if she wasn't going to give this sort of talk any airtime.

'His life is completely wrecked, because of this one incident. He'll lose his job of course.'

'He nearly wrecked your life too. He should have thought of that before...' she started, with her lawyer's face on.

I stood up abruptly. 'I've choked on enough platitudes today.'

'You insist on seeing things from his side.' Her voice rose to a high pitch. She sat up straight, her feet hitting the floor.

'Not now Miranda!' My emotions were like loose wires springing out all over the place.

'So, breaking the law doesn't count?'

'Don't give me one of your law lectures, not tonight,' I said in the quiet voice that meant I was only just holding onto my temper. I made for the door and managed not to slam it.

In the kitchen, I snapped the kettle on, clattering the cups around with unnecessary force. Miranda could be impossible. This definitely wasn't the moment to tell her that the Swedes had refused us the grant. I'd had enough aggro for one day.

I'd calmed down by the time I carried the tea back in.

'Sorry,' I said. 'It's been a bloody awful day,'

Miranda seemed glad enough to step away from another

of our recent precipices. 'I'm sorry too. Let's take our tea up and catch the late evening news in bed.'

'Good idea.' I poured a glass of red wine to take up as well. Something to tranquilise me if there was to be any hope of sleep.

I sat bolt upright in bed, bathed in sweat. The image of a knife, inches from my face, took a few moments to fade. The dim, familiar shapes of our bedroom wobbled into view. Four am on the clock. My regular nightmare, waiting for me. I spent hours either side of it, tossing and turning, trying to avoid another encounter with the terrifying Ezekiel leaning over me, ready to plunge in the blade.

Why was this still happening? I thought that seeing the real Ezekiel, looking so frail and crushed, would ease my nightmares. But the attacker in my dreams seemed to be a different person to the bowed man I'd seen at the tribunal. This one had a life of his own.

I headed downstairs in search of a pre-dawn cup of tea. Mamba's big paws skittered along the kitchen tiles, as she scooted to greet me. My fingers reached for her head and massaged behind her ears. Upright, my brain thought saner thoughts. The sound of the kettle and reassuring tone of the World Service describing mayhem around the globe, helped me regain my sense of calm. I snorted out loud. I was turning into my old dad, with my night-time wanderings. My old brown dressing-gown was almost a replica of his.

I sat at the kitchen table, trying to shine a spotlight on the muddle of emotions swirling around in me since the knife incident. At the nasty centre of it all, the acid sense of shame eating away at me; that I had run at the sight of Ezekiel with that knife, like a coward, like any racist whitey from the past, instead of holding my ground and dealing with the situation as a head of department should have. Like the solid anti-apartheid activist I had always believed myself to be. I'd known Ezekiel for years; I should have grasped the situation, talked the man down, calmed him into handing over the blade. I could picture how different the newspaper headlines would have been – '*Chief of Museum restrains knifeman*' instead of '*Knifeman pursues terrified head of Durban Museum*'. That would be written up in lights for the rest of my life, cancelling anything else I'd ever done. I pictured on my tombstone – 'This man was a phoney; he cut and ran'. My soul shrivelled up inside me. How could I face anyone again? How could I face myself?

CHAPTER 7

Nomsa looked up from the stew of chicken's feet and potatoes that she was stirring on the stove, as she heard her husband banging the township dust off his boots on the back step. It made their little four-room house rattle when he announced his return every evening this way. However clean and tidy she kept the place, the dust swept in. Years ago, when they were young and just in from the rural area, she and Thembu had been grateful to get passes to live in Umlazi township, in the big city where there was work, but by now these older township houses were falling apart. She longed for one of those new ones they were building in S section. There were still only four small rooms but solid, with no leaks anywhere.

'Ah, *uMama!*' Thembu called as he shrugged off his jacket and hung it on its hook. 'How did it go today?'

'*Eish*, these lawyers!' She waved her hand, casting them into the outer darkness that Pastor Mabena described on Sundays in his thundering voice. 'They want to smell your money before you can get close enough to see if you can trust them.'

Thembu pulled that face that implied 'that's the way the world is, so why upset yourself'. It never failed to annoy her. Where would they be if nobody expected more?

'Did you settle for one of these lawyers?' Thembu asked, stretching his arms up with a yawn, after his long day at the rope factory. He was a reliable man; she had always said that. She watched him ease himself into their one comfortable chair. She could see that his fingers were itching to flick open today's copy of *Isolezwe*, the most popular Durban newspaper.

'All my efforts were wasted,' she said. 'Ezekiel seems to have found his own lawyer. He should have told me before I wasted my time.' She tossed a letter across the table to him. 'I always said Thandiwe should have married the Tambu boy. Look where this Ezekiel is dragging our family.'

Thembu read the letter. 'So the union is providing him with a lawyer.'

'Never mind that I wore my feet out today for no purpose', she sniffed, raising her chin.

Thembu remained silent, fiddling with the edge of his newspaper.

'Men!' she snorted half to herself. The way they stuck together. 'How do I know how to choose a lawyer, anyway?' Her voice trembled with emotion. 'What need has our family ever had of a lawyer before?'

'I thought, with your experience on the Women's Committee…'

'I don't deal with legal matters for the committee. How many times have I told you this?' Everyone else in Section F knew what she did on the Women's Committee but not her own husband.

He glanced at the letter again. 'I see Ezekiel's tribunal was today. Just as well he had already found a lawyer.'

Nomsa closed her eyes and tried to concentrate on the delicious smell of her stew. She stole a taste of it with her spoon, then lifted the other lid. The *putu* was almost ready, white and fluffy and smelling just right. She turned it off and left the lid on. Cooking calmed her. They would find out Ezekiel's fate soon enough.

'Gugu!' she called to the bedroom where her niece was doing her homework. 'Come and set the table, girl.'

Her children had always had jobs to do in the household and it would help Gugu cope with her father's troubles. It was the uncertainty about what was happening to him that was so difficult for them. She studied Thandiwe's youngest as she edged into the kitchen, her eyes red. She had been crying again.

'I take you to see your *baba* on Saturday, hm? You can see for yourself that he is well. We'll take him oranges.' She put her arm around the girl. 'Call your sister and your cousin in from the yard and come help me serve the dinner.'

Gugu laid the table and slipped out into the yard to join her sister. The child took things hard, Nomsa fretted. How was she going to survive in this world? She was like her mother, the little sister Nomsa had brought up all those years, while their *mama* was out working long hours. Thembu looked up and caught her eye, as if to say, 'I see your soft side, you can't fool me!' She let out a throaty laugh and gave him a 'be off with you' flick with her tea-towel. She sat down heavily opposite her husband.

'At least we won't have to pay for this lawyer; the union is paying. We already have food and bus fares to pay for the girls. And for how long?' She sighed. 'Ezekiel could lose his job.'

'You always worry before things have happened,' Thembu said but his voice didn't match his smile.

They were only just making ends meet as it was, with Jabu, their last-born at the Umlazi Technikon rather than earning. They were so proud. To think that the son of a black cleaning woman could now go on even beyond secondary school. Ezekiel must sort this all out but meanwhile, she would never let Thandiwe down. They had had difficult times before. It was hard to believe that they had once fitted into this small township box with four children and managed to pay their school fees. She would work Saturdays, give up her work on the Women's Committee, find a better job if she had to. She could try to put up her hourly rate with her existing *medems*. She eased herself up off the chair and carried the pots of food to the table. Then she went to the back door.

'Jabu, Mbali, Gugu!' She called above the chatter of the neighbours' yards and the *'bik-bik-bik'* of chickens pecking everywhere.

Gugu was the first to arrive. Jabu emerged from his hut in the yard rubbing his eyes. Whenever he said he had been studying in his hut, he came in looking like this. Maybe he had his eyes too close to his books.

Nomsa threw her hands up to her husband. 'Again, Mbali has not come when I call! She seems to be going wild without mother or father, running around with boys from the street, always disappearing.'

Father and son sat down at the table, as Nomsa served steaming plates of stew and *putu* and Gugu passed them round. Where was Mbali now that night was falling? It was never fully dark here in Umlazi, so close to the flares from the huge refinery and the Isipingo factories, which lit up the night sky with lurid orange. But it wasn't safe for a young girl to be out.

'Jabu, when you have eaten, see if you can find Mbali. Did she not say where she was going?' Nomsa felt she was too old to do this teenage business all over again.

****

At five o'clock in the afternoon, I cycled across the university campus towards the athletics track. It had been one of those warm, sunny autumn days and I felt a touch of the old Ben come to life again. I locked my bike up and stepped into the pungent air of the sports centre change rooms.

I raised a hand to my mates. 'Hey, guys.'

'Howzit Ben!' They grinned and then we concentrated on climbing out of work clothes and into our running kit.

Where would I be, without Tuesday and Thursday evening training with these friends to keep me sane? Neil and Pete went way back, to Varsity days. Neil the scientist, stocky and driven, took the whole business of training more seriously than the rest of us, annoyed that we were simply in it for the camaraderie and because we just couldn't stop doing it. Pete was tall and lean, his freckled face still boyish, when the rest of us looked as dried out as *biltong* by now. Pete ran like a mis-wired robot, as though he had too many hands and feet, but always arrived with the rest of us. His easy-going nature had probably held our group together all these years. Without Pete, Neil and I had enough temperament between us to have blown the group apart. Bram, the only Afrikaner amongst us, was a more recent addition, who worked with Pete in the Politics Department. He wouldn't let us get away with 'all your English colonial bullshit'.

We took our time over warm-ups nowadays, not wanting to risk our ancient hamstrings. As I breathed in deeply and stretched, joints and taut muscles relaxed and I felt the tension of the day easing out of me like tyre pressure being released. It felt good. I'd missed a lot of training and the Comrades double marathon was looming fast. I could rely on the guys not to press me about Ezekiel's tribunal. They knew how I felt about anyone bringing up the whole business. I wondered whether to tell them about losing the Swedish grant, try it out on them before telling Miranda? Maybe in the pub afterwards.

'Ten circuits and then we'll start our time trials, right?' Neil took the lead as usual.

We murmured our assent.

'Slacker buys the beers,' Bram called, as we set off around the track. Marathon running was steady and paced so once we were in our stride, we could natter as we went.

'Vice-chancellor was up to his tricks again today,' Neil said. 'McLaughlin had a run-in with the dean about it.'

'For chrissakes, Neil, not now. I've spent all day in that academic cesspit,' Bram said.

None of it meant more to me than the soothing sound of windscreen-wipers in rain, voices in their usual grooves. It wasn't my workplace; it didn't mean my blood on the carpet. That was the attraction of having friends who orbited around another work planet.

Then Neil snapped me out of my state of grace. 'I applied for that job in Vancouver. I've got an interview in two weeks.'

The shock of his words disrupted the easy rhythm of my stride. For a few seconds I was in danger of crashing into Bram until I steadied myself. Our feet sounded loud on the track in the silence that followed.

Then we all burst out together. 'Where the hell did this come from?' 'Canada of all places! Bloody freezing.' 'But why?'

Neil snapped. 'I've been talking about it for months, you deaf idiots.'

'We didn't think you were serious,' Bram said, as though

Neil had declared membership of some weird sect. We'd always mocked whites who left since apartheid fell, not giving the new government a chance.

'You just don't get it, do you?' Neil raised his voice.

'What does Penny think about it?' Pete tried to lower the temperature.

I missed his cue and blundered in. 'We've all talked about leaving on a bad week...but we've always said we wouldn't abandon ship, wouldn't remove our skills from South Africa.' The minute it was out, I knew I'd gone too far.

'Well, no-one seems to want my skills, so fuck them!' Neil glowered and set off down the track. We couldn't get him to work with us for the rest of the session. Without him to set the pace, our times were hopeless.

In the changing rooms later, we enjoyed the pleasure of hot showers after hard physical effort. When the noise of the showers died down, none of us dared to raise the subject of Canada again, talking instead of the coming marathon.

Neil walked away as the rest of us made towards the staff bar for cold beers.

'Don't take it like that, man,' Pete caught up with him and clasped Neil's shoulder. 'We're just a bit blown away, that's all.'

'Give us the low-down over a pint,' I called. 'This is too important to wait until next week.'

In the rundown surrounds of the university staff bar, we had to drag the details out of Neil. How long had he been thinking about this? What had brought it on? Was he that fed-up with the Mbeki government or what?

'You have to give the new country time, man,' Bram

said. We'd been over these points before, as we felt more and more disappointed in the ANC government.

'You don't get it,' Neil said. 'This is personal. The Chemistry Department is strapped for cash. I can't pursue my research interests anymore. My career is finished here. Would any of you be happy to be shuffled off into early retirement? It's not as if we're big businessmen taking capital out of the country!'

There was a long awkward silence, then mutterings of 'Sorry, man, we didn't know.' Someone brought up Saturday's match with the All Blacks and we left it at that.

I considered dropping my lost grant into the conversation but reckoned we'd had enough drama for today. In any case, one of their wives might mention it to Miranda in passing before I'd told her myself. Then there would be trouble.

As we were leaving, Neil said sotto voce to me, 'Now Penny says she doesn't want to go to Canada after all.'

'Jesus, man, you have to work that one out…otherwise that'll be the end of that idea.' I couldn't disguise the relief in my voice. Neil was one of my oldest friends.

'It doesn't work like that,' he replied in a hoarse voice. 'If they offer me the job. I'm going.'

He jumped into his red Toyota, reversed with an aggressive squeal of brakes and drove off, leaving the rest of us to exchange looks.

'Proud bugger. He'll back down,' said Bram but I didn't pin much on his pronouncement.

CHAPTER 8

'Ah Mabuza. Sit bra.'

In the low light of their cell, Terror Mangoba reclined his bulk on his bunk. It was covered in purple silk, strewn with gold cushions. He waved Ezekiel to the opposite bunk, his smile stretching slowly wider, the scar down his cheek gleaming like an oil slick.

'You and I have matters to discuss, heh?'

Ezekiel stared around him, trying to take in the world this side of their cell. No-one else had a bunk. The other forty of them had to grab mats from a pile each evening, sharing their bedbugs around. Terror and his cronies were well set up here under the cell's high windows, through which the sun streaked red and orange, like a revelation, as night began to fall.

Terror patted the cushions at his side. 'You like my pad heh, Quiet One?'

'V-very nice.' Ezekiel's shaking knees folded under him and he sat abruptly.

He didn't need to ask where all this came from. Inside or outside prison, gangsters ruled. He suppressed a shudder. He must have been stupid to think it would be any other way. But you didn't walk away from someone like Terror when you have been summoned – not without big trouble.

Terror flicked open a cigarette case and offered him a Lucky Strike. 'D section not treating you nice, heh?' His voice was like golden syrup.

'I…it's been a bit rough.'

'Some rude boys in cell, I hear?'

It had started with his trips to the canteen. One guy had sent him sprawling. 'Careful!' he'd called out. Until he realised it happened every time he stepped out of the cell, accompanied by oaths and jeers. Ezekiel had a strong build; he had been a boxer in his younger days. He could have taken on any one of them singly, but he could see they were luring him into a group beating. Inside the cell it could be bad too. Last night, a man called Brutus had accused him of stealing his blanket and he had given it up, rather than provoke more trouble. He had assumed these must be the standard initiation rituals at Westville prison.

'I can do something to end your troubles.' Terror's voice was as soft as the pigeons in the wattle trees above Ezekiel's mother's hut back home. 'Join us.'

Ezekiel felt his muscles go rigid. Was this how his boy Sipho had been lured into the Razor gang in Umlazi?

'Join my twenty-sixes gang,' Terror waved to the men on his own side of the cell, laughing, slapping thighs, playing cards, 'and *shap-shap*, my boys won't touch you again.'

Ezekiel held his breath. So, this was where all the bullying had been leading. He played for time. 'But why do you want me? Do you invite everyone?'

You are in here for attempted murder I hear, so you must be tough. And you look strong, well built.'

Ezekiel was silent. It would almost be a relief to shift over and end his torment. Even the air on this side of the cell didn't smell as bad. But after what had happened to his Sipho?

He squared his shoulders up to Terror, trying to steady his shaking hands. 'What do you want in return? I have no money.' Even if he had, thought Ezekiel, he would not pay protection money with the blood of his son.

'Rela-ax bra! Who's talking money? You're the man of the moment, after what you did for the strike! Your name in the newspapers.' Terror's smile was so affable that he wanted to believe him. More difficult to refuse when there was no payment demanded. He was not sure he could take much more, trapped like a rat in a cage waiting for Terror's men to pounce.

Terror would see an outright refusal as a provocation. Ezekiel stood up, sweating. 'I will give you my answer in two days.'

Terror seemed to be counting the seconds. 'As you will,' he said, in a bored voice and waved him away.

Next morning, as Ezekiel queued for the showers, they went for him. He was hit on the head from behind with something hard and remembered crashing to the floor as they beat him. And then things went blank. When he came to, he was in the laundry area, boots kicking him from all sides, pain throbbing in every part of him. He curled up in a ball to protect his brains and his guts. When he came to again, they were gone.

A warder was calling to him. 'Looks like you got it bad, eh? Who was it?'

Ezekiel hadn't caught a clear view of who they were, but he had heard Brutus's voice, he was sure. But what else would these men do to him if he named any of them?

****

The following Friday evening, I ushered my family into Dino's Trattoria, our favourite eating place. Its huge pizza oven glowed to one side, while from the bar, sounds of Pavarotti spilled out. We had been coming here for years and it never failed us. This evening I couldn't help scanning the guests for danger and looking around for a table with a quick exit route. I was relying on Dino's to see off my recent craziness and to wrest Miranda away from her daytime lawyer's persona. I was acutely aware that I still hadn't told her about the Swedish grant but this clearly wasn't the right moment. I needed a laugh with our kids. I'd always teased Miranda about how she succumbed to Dino's mellifluous voice but I was banking on it tonight.

"Bellisima!' Dino admired Miranda's dress, kissing her hand. Even Ellen seemed to be falling for the Dino treatment, when she usually made frank vomiting sounds by this point.

'Howzit going Dino? Business OK?' I asked.

'Ah, Mr Gallagher! So-so, you know, so-so.' We clapped each other on the back. Dino knew how far he could take his Italian charm with a middle-aged South African male like me.

As we settled at our table, I said. 'How about half a glass of wine for Ellen? It is Friday after all.' Our teenage diva deigned to smile. She'd respond well to being treated like an adult tonight.

'All right. As I'm celebrating,' Miranda said. 'Today we won the first case that I've been involved with from start to finish.' Her face lit up.

'Good one, Mom,' Tom called.

'Terrific, Mirrie!' I hoped she couldn't tell I was putting it on. I cursed her bloody law course, for the bad effects it was having on us all.

We went through our usual ritual of studying the menu but it was a foregone conclusion. Pizzas for the kids – Tom all peppers and meat, attacked with ravenous vigour, Ellen's favourite – *Quattro Stagione*, neatly picked at one quarter at a time, starting with 'I'm starving' but we knew it would end with 'who wants to finish mine?' I'd long ago given up trying to talk them into choosing something more adventurous.

'If it's a celebration, you should go for *Risotto con Frutte di Mare*, Mirrie – price no object tonight.'

She smiled. 'Mmh – calamari, mussels, scallops, baby clams. You too?'

'No, I'll have Veal Masala.'

Ellen glared. 'Baby calves! How can you, Dad?'

I put on a mock drool and she couldn't keep up her severe face. She burst out laughing. I smiled. We seldom caught her even half-tolerating us these days.

The drinks arrived. 'To the most hot-shit lawyer in town,' I called as we clinked glasses. If I couldn't beat this lawyer thing, I'd try joining it.

'It's such a good feeling, getting this far, after the academic slog. ' Miranda paused. 'To all of you, for putting up with my late nights, my *occasional* snappiness. Once my lawyer's salary starts rolling in, it'll be worth it.' Her eyes dared us to disagree.

When she disappeared to the Ladies, Ellen giggled. 'I thought Mom would raise a toast to 'our dear leader', she's so over the top tonight.'

'Don't,' I groaned. 'President Mbeki and her ANC are subjects we keep Mom off.'

We were still laughing when Miranda came back. 'What's so funny?' she asked.

By the time we left Dino's, I was mellow, as if deep under the turbulence of Ezekiel's mad chase and my fear of losing my job, my core was still solid. Under the shifting plates of my world, I was still the old Ben. It could have been the wine speaking but I wasn't going to argue. As Miranda drove home through the night, I decided there was nothing wrong between us except that she was overworked and I was still shaky from Ezekiel's attack.

We approached the house and Miranda parked the car. I found myself glancing around carefully for intruders.

We went into the house and Tom asked, 'Want to hear that *Arctic Monkeys* track, Ellen?'

'Cool,' she replied and raced after him up the stairs.

'It's a bit late for that,' Miranda called after her.

Ellen's gesture was ambiguous, just this side of rude, as she streaked upstairs to her brother's room. I rolled my eyes at Miranda and made as if to shoot our stroppy teenager.

For once, she laughed rather than pursuing the argument with Ellen. 'Where did we get one like this?'

I breathed out – scene avoided. 'You were worse at this age, weren't you? Running off to rock festivals without your parents' permission, hippy-girl.' I waltzed her under my arm.

'Don't blow my cover,' she said in a stage whisper.

I put my arms around her and kissed her. 'Let's make it an early night.'

She gave me that bad girl laugh that I hadn't heard for a while. She was always too tired, too busy or had a big case next day. I had thought I might be about to join that throng of middle-aged men whose wives made out that sex was a childish habit they should have grown out of.

In the bathroom I brushed against her as she cleaned her teeth. Her smile lingered back at me in the mirror. I pressed against her beige, silk dressing-gown, caressing her hips. Saw the reflection of her smile broadening as she closed her eyes, toothbrush forgotten in her hand. I nibbled the back of her neck, hands feeling round to cup her breasts.

'Beautiful,' I murmured.

We made straight for the bedroom, tumbling together onto our bed like young things, her lips soft and full in a way I found achingly arousing. My hands pushed open the folds of her gown. She arched up to meet me, her kisses more forceful.

'Like our good old days.'

Mirrie stiffened and pulled away from me. 'There you go again. The bloody "good old days"! What's wrong with the present?'

'I...I just meant before we were both so busy, when we used to have more time for moments like this...'

She sat upright, switched her bedside lamp on and hugged her knees. 'You're always hankering after the past. We've just had a lovely evening with our kids and...'

'I was thinking that too. You've got it all wrong, Mirrie. I wasn't hankering after our "when we were young" days, honestly.'

'It sounded like it...'

'A misunderstanding. Forget I said it,' I sat up and put my arm around her shoulder. 'The words 'good old days' shall henceforth be expunged from my vocab if m'lady doesn't approve of them!' I grinned.

I felt her stiffen. 'Don't patronise me, Ben.'

'That was meant to be a joke, love.'

'Not a very good one, then.'

'Sorry…' I brushed her hair out of her eyes and kissed her forehead. 'Let's turn the light out…and see…'

'I'm not in the mood now…' She stood up and shrugged into her dressing-gown. 'I think I'll sleep in the spare room.'

'Jesus, Mirrie…you never give us a chance.'

She didn't reply. Just left the room without looking back at me.

I sighed. Mirrie was bloody impossible sometimes. Why did she have to spoil a special evening like that? Why didn't she give us a chance? And why had I grovelled. I threw the sheet off and stood up, yanked my dressing gown from the hook on the door and heard it rip. Damn and hell. I stomped downstairs, flicked the kettle on and paced up and down in front of the window. The wind had come up, whipping the trees against the night sky, more desolate in moonlight. This wasn't how this evening was meant to turn out.

CHAPTER 9

Ezekiel limped along beside the warder, his body aching all over, his head still ringing from the blows it had received. It was taking forever down long passages to the sick bay.

'OK Mabuza, we are almost there,' the warder said.

It was strange suddenly arriving somewhere so clean and white and neat, so ordered and quiet, after D section. A long room with empty beds or figures lying still. Behind the drawn blinds must surely be windows, maybe to the outside world. The sound of a woman's voice soothed his frayed nerves. He looked around through swollen eyes and saw a young nurse coming towards him.

'*Yebo* – what have they done to you? We will take care of you here. I am nurse Mtwetwe.'

At the tenderness in her voice, his eyes spurted tears but he was too exhausted to feel shame. Gently she helped him onto a bed. Then she brought clean clothes and warm water and began to wipe encrusted blood from his face. He held his side, each out breath tearing at him.

He looked around to check if any gang members were here. He could not see anyone bearing their trademark tattoos.

The nurse said, 'Open up,' and slipped two tablets in his mouth, then offered him sips of water, 'These will help the pain.'

With great care, she peeled off his clothes, with the help of the damp cloth. He closed his eyes, letting his battered body relax. The relief was short-lived as she began to clean and bandage cuts and bruises. To take his mind off the sting of the disinfectant, he concentrated on her soft features and tried to recall when he had last felt this safe.

'They are animals,' she muttered, her fingers weaving their deft work.

Did he imagine it, or did she look a little like his Thandiwe when they were young and newly married? He drifted off to sleep, remembering.

Later, he woke and looked up to see a tall, stern woman with a fussy sort of bonnet clickety-clacking down the ward. She stopped at his bedside. 'This one can go back to his cell this afternoon.'

Nurse Mtwetwe was by her side. 'But Sister – we need to dress Mr Mabuza's wounds again tomorrow at least. And I think he may have a broken rib.'

The older woman frowned. 'Until tomorrow then. But those warders must sort out their own discipline problems. I'm running my ward for sick people, not for their war-wounded.'

As she left, his nurse whispered, 'You are in luck. Sister must be in a good mood.'

Ezekiel had no idea how long he had been here but it was a relief to be staying longer in this clean, white world. He was afraid to fall asleep again, in case the kicks and punches started up once more. In his dream beatings, he did not experience the mercy of blacking out as he had in the showers.

'You all right, bra?' The guy next to him turned towards Ezekiel. 'You been making weird noises in your sleep.' He was as thin as a stick.

'Sorry if I disturbed you.'

'No worries, bra. I feel for you. It looks like you took a hell of a beating.' He coughed horribly into a roll of lavatory paper and pointed to Ezekiel's bandages. 'What did you do to deserve those?'

'Just minding my own business.' Half-way through a bitter laugh, Ezekiel clutched his side in pain.

'I can't laugh either. It makes me cough my insides out with this T.B.' The other man put out his hand. 'They call me Kris.' With his other hand he rubbed his head, so his hair stood up in a comical manner. He seemed harmless enough.

Ezekiel reached over gingerly with his less damaged hand and made contact. He didn't want to start up any bad feelings. 'Looks like you have to be quite bad to end up in here?' he indicated the lifeless forms in the other beds.

'Ja, mainly lungs, head, or guts …and casualties, like you.' Kris ducked his head as though he wanted to say more but didn't.

Ezekiel wondered what mysteries of the sick-bay Kris couldn't entrust to him. He shifted in his bed and swallowed more tablets as nurse Mtwetwe offered them. He kept reminding himself that this was real – the white sheets, the hands reaching out to help, the friendly voice next to him. But outside the door the challenge of returning to his cell lay in wait, with Terror expecting his answer.

'Here she comes,' someone called.

This must be Sister. As she made her way down the ward, those who could sat up to attention. She didn't frighten Ezekiel, not after the *tsotsis* in his cell. She stopped at his bedside. Close up, her face looked furrowed with concerns.

'Go with nurse Mtwetwe to have those ribs X-rayed before we send you back, just to make sure.' She signed something and tucked it down the back of a wheelchair that his nurse wheeled up.

'Climb in and I'll wheel you there,' she said.

He struggled to ease himself gingerly off the bed and into the chair.

She never stopped talking – pointing out other wards, the staff room, as they passed but it didn't take his mind off the jarring bumps along the way. Exhausted by the time he was back on his bed, Ezekiel was too tired to sit up for the noon-day meal. He slipped back into sleep.

When he woke, he could hear the low mutter of voices and see sidelights winking. An unfamiliar nurse with a clipped manner sat him up quite roughly, without exchanging a word, placed his tray across his lap and rushed away. He tried to take the *putu* and vegetable mush to his mouth with his useless hands, spilling it everywhere. Kris had disappeared from the bed next to his, leaving the place too quiet.

Eventually, Kris came hobbling down the ward and flopped onto his covers, chest heaving. 'Jeez it takes it out of you.'

'Where've you been?'

'Jus' out on the veranda,' Kris looked excited as though he was going to say more, then stopped and busied himself in the locker by his side.

Funny fellow, he could suit himself. Ezekiel watched

idly as Kris fidgeted as though he was sitting on an ants' nest. Ezekiel suddenly recalled that tomorrow was Saturday and Nomsa had written to say that she would bring his daughters. His heart lifted and then veered off downwards again, fretting that they might not be able to find him in here.

'Where do you see visitors here on the ward?'

Kris looked up. 'Expecting someone? There's a visitors' room.'

Ezekiel nodded.

'Guys I know, Siswe and Chief, they needed to see someone in private today,' Kris said. 'So, the staff gave them the visitors room.' Another snippet slipping out, then an abrupt end, another rustle of excitement. Ezekiel wondered if the guy was missing something in the head.

****

Late Saturday afternoon, I lay sprawled on the lounge sofa after watching the big match with Bram and Pete. The sound of the doorbell hauled me up from a satisfied haze. It was bound to be for Miranda, so I ignored it. I recognised the familiar tones of Penny Lister.

The living-room door opened and I heard Miranda say, 'What a fug! All stale beer and sweat. The guys were watching the rugby here earlier. I'll leave the door open to air.'

I could picture her pulling a face but I couldn't be bothered to stir.

'Shh,' Penny whispered.

'He's out cold, I heard him snoring. Beer in the afternoon always knocks Ben out!'

Their footsteps receded to the kitchen next door. I

raised myself on one elbow, surveyed the debris of beer-cans and half-eaten snacks and rolled back onto the sofa. The Springboks had beaten the Australians in an exciting, skilful game. I was just dozing off again, when Miranda's voice, sharp and angry through the open door, alerted me. I sat up, listening intently. I couldn't hear quite what was being said but it sounded serious. I struggled up and went into the hallway.

'I can't believe it Penny. He's trying to blackmail you.' There was sobbing and then, 'Oh Penny don't.'

'I don't know why I let Neil draw me into this crazy idea of emigrating. I never thought he'd follow it through,' Penny said. 'I'm South African through and through. Our kids would be completely out of place in Canada.'

'Don't you have to go with Neil and take a look?'

'I suppose I'll never hear the end of it if I don't.' Penny said. 'But I'm not leaving South Africa for good.'

'Neil's one who knows what he wants, I'll give him that,' Miranda said, in a voice of grudging respect. 'I wish Ben had half his strength of character.'

I stiffened, hardly able to believe what I was hearing.

'It seems more like selfish and rigid to me!' Penny's laugh turned into a sob. 'Neil needs a wife more like you. Someone who could tough it out with him. He wears me down.'

Miranda laughed: 'He'd not bad looking either, Neil.'

I jolted at this casual infidelity tossed in.

'You've no idea Penny, how difficult Ben has been since the knife attack. That's what is wearing me down.'

I was wide awake now. I moved towards the open door to hear better.

'What do you mean?' Penny asked, in that tone women use when encouraging a confidence too far; territory no self-respecting bloke would enter. I was riveted but queasy about what I might hear next, my body rigid with tension.

'When you think of what he's been through recently, Mirrie, it's not surprising.'

'He won't talk about it, let alone consider seeing a counsellor about what happened. He tosses all night long, muttering and groaning. And then bites my head off when he's awake.'

Shit! I swallowed hard. Miranda sounded as though she had had enough of me. I had promised myself I would tell her about the Swedish grant tomorrow when I'd recovered from the rugby-fest but I scrapped that idea. Not if she was feeling like this about me.

'I've never said this before, but things started to go wrong a while before the knife attack,' Miranda continued. 'I sometimes feel …as though…as though I've been left with the empty shell of the Ben he used to be.'

My God, who was this pathetic creature Miranda was describing?

Penny was silent, as though she too was shocked.

'You know how he used to be; out front, full of optimism and charm, believing in the future. That's the Ben I fell in love with.' There was a silence and then she added so softly that I had to strain to hear. 'That Ben has slipped through my fingers somehow…and I don't know what to do about it.'

'We've all changed since those idealistic, anti-apartheid days,' Penny said.

'Yes, but most of us are coping with the rough and tumble of how things have turned out; we're made of tougher stuff. What did he think would happen when it came to rebuilding this country? It's as though Ben is heart-broken that his dream country hasn't come to pass.'

I only just stopped myself from storming through to yell 'That's not true!' I pretended to myself that I didn't know what Miranda was talking about but damn her, she had put her finger on the hopelessness I had felt, as my belief in the ANC trickled away. I punched the wall and clutched my hand. 'Fuck!' It wasn't meant to hurt that much.

Rubbing my knuckles, I hopped about, scrabbling for my shoes in the darkening room, probably looking just like the idiot she had described. I jammed my feet into them and stamped down the hall, not caring if Miranda had heard me. I slammed out of the house, feeling that I couldn't even make a grand exit these days.

CHAPTER 10

Ezekiel woke next morning and gazed at the sun pouring in through the bars of the high ward window. He eased himself over in bed as though he were a parcel of eggs, grateful that sister had not missed out the X-ray and sent him back to his cell, to the rough boys of D section and a night on his thin rubber mat. Although his body was laid low, his heart bobbed and veered up to the enamel blue sky he saw out there. His Gugu and Mbali would be here this afternoon. Would he be able to touch them, or would there be that glass barrier again?

'You're cheerful considering,' nurse Mtwetwe said. 'Had a good night?'

'My girls are coming today. My Mbali is fifteen, such a *medem* since her mother died. All for the boys and won't do her schoolwork. Gugu, my baby, the shy one – she is twelve.' It was more personal than anything he had said since he had arrived in prison. He felt his mouth curve in the near-forgotten shape of a smile. He wanted to tell everyone about his girls, to conjure them up in this unlikely place.

'A big day, heh?' nurse said. 'Let's see how those bruises look this morning.' She turned his sheets over and peeled back his bandages. '*Haai*, your body is the colours of rotten fruit!' She washed him gently. 'I see on your chart that the X-ray showed a cracked rib.'

'How long does that mean I'll be here?' was all he asked, as she tended his bruises and started to bandage him up again.

'That's up to sister,' nurse Mtwetwe replied. 'But I'll do my best to keep you here as long as I can.'

It was almost worth the beating, Ezekiel thought, to escape that cell, the trips to the shower and the canteen and Terror Mangoba pressing for an answer.

By two o'clock, Ezekiel was tormenting himself with all the possibilities that might steal his visitors from him. They might get lost on the way to Westville prison, which was way off their usual bus routes. Nomsa might come on her own the first time, to make sure how he was, before bringing his girls. Their old bus might even overturn, as they sometimes did when they were overloaded and turned a corner too fast. Worst of all, Nomsa might not be able to come at all. He asked nurse ten times if it was two o'clock yet and marvelled at how the clock stood still.

'A very special visit, I can see,' Nurse Mtwetwe smiled, slipping the thermometer under his arm. 'Time goes slowest for those.' She propped a magazine on his lap as a mercy to him. 'Your visitors will be able to see you in here.'

'Not through a glass window?' Ezekiel beamed.

Two o'clock came and went. Exhausted, he had given up patrolling the door with his eyes and fallen into a half-doze, when Nomsa's voice jerked him wide-awake. His family were making their way down the ward. They stuttered to a halt half-way. They didn't seem to recognise him, wrapped up in bandages. Nurse had to point him out.

'*Baba*!' Gugu broke into tears and ran towards him. Mbali held back.

'My girls,' he called, trying to hide the pain from his face.

Gugu in her Sunday best, red ribbon in her hair. Mbali in a pink dress, too, too short. That must have caused a fight with her auntie.

'Lord save us, what have they done to you?' Nomsa exclaimed when she reached him. Her breath was heaving.

'It looks worse than it is,' he lied.

'I thought our prisons had changed since the old days,' her voice was angry but her eyes were soft.

'Come and hug me girls,' he reached out. 'But be gentle – it hurts on this side.'

As Gugu came close and hugged him, he swallowed the urge to groan. She fixed him with her rabbit eyes. Mbali stood like a cat torn between pouncing and fleeing, all red nails and sullen looks.

'Come closer so I can feast my eyes on my big girl.'

Mbali came closer with a flicker of a smile. His heart sang at the sight.

'What did you do to deserve this?' Nomsa asked, pointing to his bruises.

'Some initiation ritual, I think. Hopefully it is over now.' He lied again and hoped God would forgive him. 'Bring a chair over for your auntie, girls. And go ask that nurse how long you can stay.'

Nomsa heaved herself onto the chair. '*Yebo*, this is terrible. What really happened? I know you are protecting the girls.'

'There are gang members in my cell,' he began. 'They want things from me that I don't want to give. Shhh,' he pointed with his eyes as his girls made their way back. 'How have things been since I have been away?' He looked at Mbali and Gugu. 'Helping your auntie, I hope?'

Gugu was glued to his side, stroking his hand as though she could detach it and take it with her. '*Baba*, when are you coming home?'

'As soon as I can, child.'

'Yes, but how many days?'

Nomsa said, 'We have to wait and see how *baba's* lawyer goes in court.'

Why had he not thought of something as simple as that, Ezekiel thought, something to put some bones on their worry?

'They've had to put up with some cruel gossip at school,' Nomsa said. 'But we don't take any notice of troublemakers, do we girls?'

Mbali scowled and buried herself in picking bits of lint from her skirt.

'And Mkhize, that no-good neighbour of ours,' Nomsa continued. 'He can't keep his mouth shut, once he is in the *shebeen*. He must have heard what had happened to you and now it's all over Umlazi.'

Ezekiel shuddered. He hadn't imagined the news would travel so fast.

Nomsa leaned over. 'How did it go with the tribunal?'

'It is not decided yet. I am to have psychiatric assessment.'

'And this union lawyer?' A shadow of annoyance crossed her face.

'It is too early to tell.' They talked carefully around the edges of his predicament to avoid frightening his girls but he noticed the worry on their faces and forced a cheerful voice. 'So tell me what you are learning at school? And have you kept up with choir practice?'

'Gugu nodded. 'We are singing in the inter-schools next Saturday. Will you be home then to come and hear us?'

'I would love to hear you, Gugu but we will have to see what happens.' He gazed lovingly at the faces of his girls, saving their images to live on until their next visit.

It seemed no time at all before the sharp sound of the siren ended visiting hour. Sister marched down the ward clapping her hands. Ezekiel's girls hugged him carefully and then were harried out with Nomsa. Did that ward sister have no heart?

'Write me a letter,' he called after them. When would he see his girls again?

At five o'clock that afternoon, Nomsa trudged through the front door of her little house in Umlazi township, the girls bickering after her.

'uMama!' Thembu greeted her. 'Sit down and I will make you some tea.' He reached for the kettle. Nomsa watched her husband struggling to do what he called 'women's work'.

'My poor feet! It was a long way from Westville bus station up the hill to the prison.' She eased herself into a chair and massaged one foot and then the other.

'What news?' Thembu heaped spoons of sugar into her tea and handed it to her.

'Baba was bearing up, wasn't he, my girls?' Nomsa tried to sound cheerful.

She saw Thembu relax back in his easy chair and crack open a beer. She would have to set him straight about Ezekiel when the girls were in bed.

'Baba was all wrapped in bandages!' Gugu said solemnly.

'What!' Thembu sat up, raising his brows.

Nomsa shook her head and rolled her eyes to head him

off but, as usual, he missed her signal. 'What happened to him?'

Mbali rushed out of the room, her face scrunched up ready to cry. Nomsa sighed. 'He was injured.'

Gugu buried her face in auntie's lap. 'Will *Baba* get better?'

Nomsa threw her arms around her niece. 'Of course he will, my princess. Next time you see him, he'll be much better.' She stood up and limped over to the vegetable rack, piling potatoes and pumpkin onto a tray.

'Go and tell your cousin Jabu about your visit to B*aba*.' She handed the tray to Gugu. 'And peel these for me while you are there.'

Thembu's eyes followed Gugu as she went outside to find her cousin. 'What is going on?'

'*Haai*! That man was beaten so bad!' Nomsa replied. 'To think the girls had to see their *baba* like that on their first visit. And if it happens again? We don't want Thandiwe's girls to be orphans.'

'Who did this to him?' Thembu didn't look as surprised as she had expected.

'These *tsotsis*, these thugs. He said something about gang members in his cell wanting something from him.' It was a relief to finally share her news.

'Guys at work are always talking about this one's cousin, that one's boy having a very bad time in Westville prison.' Thembu took a pull on his beer.

'Ezekiel could not tell me the full story with the girls there.' She chopped onions with angry stabs, making her eyes stream. 'Next time, I will go alone to get the truth.' She waved her kitchen knife about like an army general. There was a long silence, while she fried the onions, her brain working overtime.

Finally, she looked up and said, 'The thing is, to get him out of that place I need to talk to this union lawyer of his. Why did I not think of this before?'

Thembu saluted her with his beer can. 'My clever wife. Main thing is to get the charges dropped, heh? Ezekiel did a stupid thing that day but he says he never touched Gallagher. Where is their proof?'

Nomsa slapped down her spoon. She felt better now she had a plan. She hated to sit around, while troubles piled up in her lap. How could she get in touch with this lawyer? The union must have his name.

****

I yanked open the garage door and jumped into the car. As I swung our car into the road, I saw Miranda and Penny waving me down but I ignored them and zoomed off up the road. I was behaving like the young idiot drivers I always complained about but it made me feel much better. I headed down to the beachfront, parked and considered setting off down the boardwalk but that seemed too tame for my turbulent feelings. I stepped down onto the sand instead and headed straight down to the water's edge. It was high tide and a wind was up, the waves roaring into the shore and crashing on the beach. I went as close as I could to the water and joined in, roaring up at the moon, letting go of all my bottled-up feelings. Anyone watching would have thought me a madman but I didn't give a monkey's. Eventually, when my voice was too hoarse to shout anymore, I gave up and sat on a nearby rock, emotionally and physically exhausted.

After a while I made my way back to the road and picked up a coffee at one of the cheap cafes there.

'You OK, bra?' asked a man at a nearby table.

'Yeah, I think so,' I said. 'You?'

'So-so.' He gave a weak grin and then we both lapsed into silence.

When I could delay it no longer, I found the car and made my way back home, dreading my encounter with Miranda. I was sure to get it in the neck for disappearing like that and my body tensed in anticipation.

I drove into the garage and went into the house via the kitchen. Miranda took me totally by surprise. She came towards me smiling, her arms open wide.

It was so unexpected that I froze.

'I'm sorry Ben,' she said, folding me in an embrace. 'I should never have said those things.'

I didn't know what to say, so I said nothing.

'I was letting off steam because I've been so worried about you…'

I bristled that she thought she could brush aside the awful things she had said about me so easily, the things about fancying Neil. But I didn't have the energy for an argument that I was sure to end up losing.

'I didn't mean any of it, that nonsense about Neil. All rubbish Ben, honestly.'

'Are you sure…?' I asked gruffly.

'Of course. It's just been so hard for us to talk lately, after everything that has happened…

'I didn't realise I'd been such a disappointment to you…' I swallowed hard, to stop myself from breaking down. 'Even before the Ezekiel thing. That you saw me as such a wimp.'

'I don't Ben, I really don't. But you have changed. You

take things so hard these days, it worries me.' She put her arm around me again, sounding genuine.

'About the ANC,' I felt myself soften. 'Maybe I was daydreaming about how the future would turn out but…'

'The big political things are bound to have quite a bumpy ride for a long time,' she said. I could see she was happier back on more familiar territory. 'If only you had a project of your own to get stuck into.'

'That's what the Swedish funding was supposed to do. To open up a big project in the townships.' I could hear how bitter my voice sounded. 'And now that is gone.'

'I hadn't realised…quite how much it meant to you.'

'I suppose I could try to set up a smaller version of the project in Kwa Mashu perhaps.' I didn't really believe what I was saying. It was mainly to reassure her. I didn't dare to mention how fragile my hold on my job was by now.

'Good idea,' Miranda smiled, looking relieved. 'We better get on with supper. The kids are both going out soon.'

'Can I do anything?'

'Yes, put the rice on. I'll start frying the veg. Stir-fry seems the simplest meal to do.'

'Glass of wine while we're working?' I asked. 'Red?'

'Thanks, I'll have white.'

I poured both glasses, took a swig and tried to relax. Crisis averted, for now at least. I didn't think I could have coped with an argument about our relationship, not tonight. I knew I would keep finding the ANC government to be a lucky dip of bad surprises but I would keep it to myself more.

After dinner, when the kids had gone, Miranda said out of the blue, 'We need to talk about Michael Drummond. Decide what to do about Liz's anniversary.'

'I forgot it was coming round. Fifteenth of August, isn't it?'

We fell silent, ambushed by memories of last year. Liz's diagnosis with lung cancer, her horrible, swift end, out of reach in Sheffield, leaving friends in South Africa feeling helpless.

'What do you mean, "do about it"?' I asked.

'Michael's only just been holding himself together all year. This could tip him over the edge,' she said. She set the kettle to boil again and rooted about for some rusks.

I thought about poor old Michael, suffering thousands of miles away. Why hadn't he come back here to mourn Liz. He should have buried her here, where she belonged, not in Sheffield. It was one thing to leave South Africa in the seventies to escape the apartheid government but why hadn't they come back here after the first democratic elections, like so many others? Michael always talked with nostalgia about 'home' and yet he stayed away.

Miranda returned with a fat, new packet of Ouma rusks. 'Wholemeal?'

I held my hands open and she threw one over.

'You could fly over to be with him for the anniversary.'

'Whoa, hold on. I need to be here to fight for our next grant.' I had never managed to tell Miranda just how fragile my current hold was on my job.

'Michael is one of your oldest friends…'

'He should come back here for Liz's first anniversary,' I said. 'Be with us all.' At the moment I could hardly leave my front door, let alone make it to Sheffield.

'We can't get him over here,' she said. 'Penny has tried. Maybe you can talk him round. Give him a ring.'

'Sure. Remind me in the morning.'

CHAPTER 11

'This morning we get up,' nurse Mtwetwe said, her hands busy everywhere. Before Ezekiel knew it, she was moving his aching body. He groaned as he was hoisted into a sitting position. *Eish*, who would have thought broken ribs could feel so bad?

'*Haai*, Nurse, not so soon.'

'Is very bad for you to lie in bed,' she said. 'Much better to sit out on the veranda in the sun. I'll be back in a while.' She moved on, leaving him with his bowl of porridge on a tray in front of him.

By the time she returned he was stiff with fear about the ordeal to come. First came the bed-bath, with curtains pulled around his bed. He never imagined he would have his private parts washed by a pretty young woman but nurse made it seem the most ordinary thing in the world. He kept his eyes averted, in an agony that his manhood would misbehave. She chatted about what he would be able to do once he was up and about, as though washing him was the most everyday activity. She pulled out some loose clothes in the usual regulation prison orange.

'Easier to get these on.' As she dressed him, he winced and tried not to groan.

'To be a nurse must be what you were born to,' he said shyly.

'I had good training,' she replied. 'Now come and meet some of your fellow patients.'

As she helped him transfer to the wheelchair, Ezekiel felt as weak as a new-born baby. Then she pushed him through some curtains out onto a veranda, the autumn sunshine streaming across a red tiled floor. They were several floors up and out beyond the ugly sprawl of prison buildings, he saw the joy of wide-open green spaces, trees, hills rising. It felt so long since he had last seen the outside world.

'Take me to the edge,' he begged.

'Just for a minute.'

'Hey, man!' Kris's stick-like figure loped up to them with its uneven gait. 'Come and meet some of the guys.'

'No thanks.' Ezekiel shrank at the sight of knots of emaciated patients standing about, a few others in wheelchairs. Getting to know Kris was like finding a lucky coin in a pile of muck. He didn't expect to meet any more here that he could trust.

'They're different in sick bay, you'll see,' said Kris but he didn't push it, staying by Ezekiel's side.

Ezekiel was desperate to talk with Kris about his worries and the answer Terror was waiting for. He hesitated to share his problem but he couldn't think how to solve it himself.

'When I get back to my cell, I have a big problem.' He held his hands out wide.

'Spit it out, China. Most likely we've all had to face something like it.'

Ezekiel stuttered on the brink.

'A problem shared is a problem halved,' Kris said. 'If you pick the right guy.'

Ezekiel's words tumbled out. 'It's Terror, the main man in my cell. He's waiting for an answer from me…when I get back there.'

Kris nodded slowly. 'Have you had the usual call-up papers? That beating of yours was sugar to help their medicine go down?'

Ezekiel groaned. So, this was common. Terror was trying to drive him into his arms. 'How can I survive bra? Keep out of these gangs?'

'Not easy, once they set their sights on you. But it's also a case of how do you survive once they've sucked you in. I've seen.'

Could he trust Kris? The fellow might just be playing the know-all to his new boy. He stared out towards the hills trying to figure it out.

Kris waited, then said softly, 'Everyone knows how they work, after you've been here a while.' He chewed his frayed fingernails. 'You know why they want you so much?'

'*Aikona*, no,' Ezekiel said. 'Because they want to control as many as they can?'

Kris snorted. 'There are only two types they bother to pull in. The big guys like you, to do their dirty work, collecting their drug debts, carrying out beatings, arm-twisting with threats. Don't think you can avoid it once you're in. Especially if you've been charged with a violent crime. Then they know you can do this heavy-duty work. And the other type…to wait on them, to warm their beds, to meet their 'domestic needs' shall we say. You're not that sort, I'd say.'

'But how do I stay clear of them? I don't want another kicking.' Ezekiel's breath came in short gasps now, as though he was being squeezed between two great boulders that threatened to grind him to dust.

'You're not much use to them with your arm out of action and your ribs broken, so you can play for time. Best to be clear from the start that you won't play, if that's what you want. Maybe they'll get bored and move on to some other poor fucker.' Kris didn't sound convincing.

Ezekiel gulped. 'How many beatings will it take?'

Just then, two guys came up to Kris. 'Greetings bra.' One of them gave Kris a high five. 'Who's the new boy?'

'He's Ezekiel Mabuza. Ezekiel, this is the Chief and Sizwe.' The Chief was a thickset older man, Sizwe a tall young fellow, pulling on a cigarette.

'Had the usual welcome, I see?' Sizwe asked pointing to Ezekiel's bruises.

Ezekiel flinched at this attention. '*Yebo.*'

'Who did it?'

'The men working for Terror Mangoba.'

'The twenny-sixes run your cell?' asked the Chief.

'What difference does it make?'

'Bra, the twenny-eight gang, they're the really rough bastards. The big bosses. The twenny-sixes control the drugs and other rackets in here.'

'Who do I need to look out for on the ward?' Ezekiel glanced around the veranda. He wasn't sure he wanted to know the answer.

'You're more or less safe in here,' the Chief told him. 'Unless one of the top guys comes in. Most rank and file are only too happy to give it a rest.'

Ezekiel felt the knot in his gut loosen a little.

The Chief clapped Kris on the shoulder. 'Meeting today at three at the far end of the veranda.'

Kris nodded. 'Sure Chief.' The two men moved on to the next knot of people.

'What meeting?' Ezekiel asked. Were they just another gang, with someone called the Chief and their meetings?

'No can say.' Kris looked mysterious. 'Something important to do with the ARV campaign but I can't say at this stage. You'll find out soon.'

'ARV? Is it another gang?' Ezekiel felt hope drain from him. He slumped in his chair.

Kris burst out laughing in his wheezy way, which set off a coughing fit. Once he had recovered, he said, 'No man! ARVs – anti-retroviral medication for AIDS. President Mbeki has finally accepted that HIV causes AIDS. At last ARV treatment is spreading across the country. But the bastards won't allow it in prisons yet. So, we are building a big campaign. Can I trust you not to speak about it just yet, hey?'

'*Yebo.*' It all fell into place suddenly. Kris's secretive hints and meetings. Something big was going off, in the prison hospital wing of all places.

'When will it happen?' Ezekiel asked in a whisper.

'Soon, soon,' Kris looked around as he spoke. 'Or most of us will be dead.'

It all clicked into place, Kris's skinny frame and the way he was always coughing his lungs out. But still it was a shock to have it spelled out. Most people never mentioned AIDS, let alone admitting to having it. Ezekiel didn't know where to look. What did they call them…anti-something-viral drugs? If only his first-born had been saved by these magic pills. He didn't often allow himself to think of his son – the pain of seeing him fade week by week from a young man sleek as a bullock to a living skeleton was too much to recall. And nothing, nothing at all that they did – special diets, medicines, *sangomas* – could halt it. Until one morning they had found his wasted body lifeless in his bed.

****

'Morning Ben, I need to talk to you.' Van Rensburg sounded positively upbeat.

I hadn't bumped into him for some time, so I suspected that this was an ambush. I felt torn between staying in the corridor to keep it brief and enjoying my mug of tea at my desk while it was still hot. My baser instincts won out.

'OK, Matheus. Join me for a drink if you like.' I opened the door to my office.

'Thanks, I will,' van Rensburg said and chased after Mrs Shabalala's tea-trolley.

'How can I help?' I asked when he returned with his own coffee.

He seemed in no hurry. 'Feeling any better, since, you know…?' he asked, his eyes burrowing into me.

'Oh, that's all in the past now.' You're not getting anything out of me, *meneer*, I thought. 'What can I do for you?'

'I came to tell you about Mabuza's case.' Van Rensburg sipped his coffee in just the manner I would have predicted, daintily and as though it was an important business. 'Unfortunately, there's been a mix-up.'

'How do you mean?'

He avoided my eye. 'Somehow the psychiatrist carried out the assessment on the wrong remand prisoner.'

'What an idiot! How come the guy's answers didn't reveal that he wasn't Mabuza?'

'I gather prisoners are not very co-operative with this sort of questioning. They don't always say much.'

'Prisoners having the last laugh. I like it!' I slapped my knee.

'There'll be some delay.' Van Rensburg fidgeted with his sleeve.

I was in no hurry to speed up the case. Every direction it might take threatened to make things worse, either for Ezekiel or for me. Having my attacker back on the streets was unnerving. But the idea of him being sentenced for the attack swamped me with guilt. Floating in no-man's land between them seemed the best place I could manage right then. At least Ezekiel was on full pay in the interim, so his family would be alright.

'One more thing,' van Rensburg said. 'This psychiatrist thinks hearing your experience of that day would be useful to his assessment of Mabuza. Would you be willing to pay him a visit?'

I hesitated a moment, then snatched at the opportunity. I told myself that I was simply helping the investigation. But in my churning guts, I had to admit that I was desperate to open the matter up beyond the action-replay of my nightmares. They always started with Ezekiel's staring, wild eyes, and the first horrible sight of that knife waving too near my face. This could be my chance to move on from those scenes.

I nodded. 'I'll do it.'

'Good, thank you.'

'How is Ezekiel doing?' I asked. 'Who's looking after his kids?'

'No idea,' Matheus said. 'His union should be looking after that side of things. Check with Kangisa.'

'I'm not popular with him because of the strike action coming up.'

'If you don't get anywhere, let me know and I'll ask him.'

We finished our drinks, mulling over the growing possibility of the strike happening.

Van Rensburg was beginning to grow on me in a funny sort of way but I quickly squashed that thought.

Later, my deputy, John Gwala and I sat working on a report for the city councillors. I wondered whether they ever read the things. Gwala annoyed me, always hinting that my job as museum director would soon be his.

But I couldn't help saying to him, 'Some movement on the Mabuza case. The shrink assessing him wants to see me.'

Gwala looked up. 'What does he want from you?'

'Dunno. I just hope he finds some answers about why Mabuza went crazy. And about why he picked on me.'

'That's pretty obvious,' Gwala laughed loudly. 'You're the boss. Blame everything on the boss.' He doubled over with mirth, his voice filling the room. The man was always making jokes at my expense. He didn't seem to notice that I wasn't laughing too. I got rid of him as soon as possible. Was everybody talking about me this way?

I pressed on with my list of jobs but the idea of speaking to the psychiatrist burned a hole in my brain for the rest of that day.

CHAPTER 12

Clutching the directions to her bosom, Nomsa looked around at the fine buildings in Durban city centre. The beautiful old ones surrounded by modern ones reaching up to the sky. In the centre of the square were statues of soldiers on horses, a short fat lady, with a long wide dress who looked very important, something strange sitting on her head. It was a long time since she had been to this part of the city. She would have liked to linger there under the palm trees but she mustn't be late for her appointment with Ezekiel's lawyer. What had the woman on the phone called this area? The CBD?

'You don't know the Central Business District? When did you move to Durban?' she had asked Nomsa in a scathing tone.

The woman had posted her a map of this CBD, with a red pen marking her route from the bus station. It was another world from Umlazi or the smart-smart houses up the Berea, where she went to clean each morning. Everything here was so bi-ig, so hi-gh. Not like the dusty municipality offices in Umlazi, where she usually did battle on behalf of Section F residents.

When she turned the map around the right way, Nomsa saw she was very close to the side street where Dlamini's office was. It had been easier than she thought to find out from the city hall the name of Ezekiel's union. And from there, to be put through to a man called Kangisa, who knew about her brother's case. He had given her the name and phone number of Ezekiel's lawyer. She was pleased with herself. She took a deep breath and entered the smart building.

Stepping out of the lift on the second floor, she saw a door marked *Bishop and Dlamini* in gold lettering and hesitated to go in. This was the sort of place where black people would not have been tolerated in the old days. She stepped forward holding her head up high. She wondered if the young black woman at reception, flicking through a magazine, was the same one who had sneered at her down the phone.

She took Nomsa's appointment card. 'Mr Dlamini will call for you when he is ready.' She pointed to a seat in the waiting area.

So rude of her not to greet an older woman properly and make a little conversation. Probably one of these young people who had been to a Model C school, mixing with whites, and now she thought she was too good for ordinary people. Nomsa looked around the modern reception area, chose a red sofa and sank into it further than she expected to go. She tidied herself and looked around at the magazines and the English-style paintings on the wall. Dlamini had done well for himself. She squirmed on the slippery surface of the sofa as her appointment time came and went. She started to sweat a little, wondering how this Dlamini would behave towards her. Should she have come? Until now, she had met only a few lawyers dealing with township affairs. She patted her hair and smoothed her skirt for the umpteenth time.

Nomsa was drifting into a half-doze when she woke with a start. She jumped up to see a neat young man approaching her, his arm outstretched. 'Mrs Silongo?' He seemed polite, friendly, with a nice smile. Perhaps he would help after all.

In his office, Mr Dlamini took down some details and searched his files, talking to himself while she fidgeted on the edge of her chair. He seemed to take forever and she wondered if he had forgotten she was here.

Finally, he sat back down. 'So what can I do for you, Mrs Silongo?'

She took a deep breath. 'Mr Dlamini, how long do you expect my brother's case to take?' She paused but he did not answer. 'He has been beaten badly in prison once already. His young daughters are very distressed. Their mother passed on last year and now this.'

Dlamini coughed. 'I am sorry to hear that. You see, there are many factors which determine when the case will be heard. I will visit him this week to try to take things forward.' His voice was suddenly less reassuring.

'But how long may it take? If things go well?'

He coughed again. This man seemed ill, he was coughing so much.

He busied himself straightening his tie. 'It is difficult to say. Each case depends on so many factors. How long it takes each side to consult and take evidence from witnesses. The law is a complicated business, you know.' He looked up, as if to see if she followed. 'And then the case is at the mercy of the court system. Usually there is a backlog.' He spoke slowly, as if trying to sound important, but he just sounded stupid, Nomsa thought.

'Mr Dlamini,' she waited until he looked her in the eye. 'To be simple – what is the shortest time we can expect this case to come to court?' She wasn't going to be fobbed off, if he knew something. 'I need to be kept informed. We may be able to provide character witnesses.' She was getting into her stride.

'I think his union has all that under control.' Dlamini sounded distinctly less friendly now. Clearly, he hadn't expected her to have so much to say. Hah! She wasn't on the Umlazi Women's Committee for nothing.

'But the background to this incident?' she said. 'Did you know he lost his wife and his two sons in the past three years? This behaviour was not usual for him at all. Surely this counts for something?'

Dlamini pulled himself upright, his face set. He looked at his watch.

'Perhaps you could put all this in writing for me, Mrs Silongo.' He stood up and reached out to shake her hand.

She remained planted on her chair. 'But how long will this take? He will lose his job if it is too long.'

'At the very least, it will take a year to get through the courts,' he said, as though he was no longer bothered to protect her from the truth. 'More often it takes two years to have the hearing.' He opened the door of his office. 'Now please, I have another client waiting.'

Nomsa gasped. 'Two years, for the judge to hear the case?' She stood up slowly.

'I'm afraid so.' He put out his limp hand and steered her to the door. 'That is the state of play in our courts. Most regrettable but that is how it is. Goodbye.'

Nomsa walked through reception in a daze. There was no-one waiting for Mr Dlamini. She made her way out of the building and over to the area with palm-trees and the statue of the lady wearing the strange thing on her head. She found a space on a bench and warmed herself in the sun, trying to make sense of what he had said, this not-so-friendly lawyer.

One to two years, for the case to be heard. How could it take this long, even to prove yourself innocent?

****

On Sunday morning, a chill wind hit us as we stepped out of our cars in front of North Beach. Seagulls squawked and wobbled as they tried to take off. I watched them scrabble frantically to gain a smooth flight path as they were buffeted about.

Bram pulled up the collar of his tracksuit. 'What's happened to our May weather?'

'There must be snow on the Drakensberg.' Pete shivered, running on the spot.

'You Durban wimps! Get a good tailwind behind you and you can break your personal best.' Neil was chipper this morning.

I felt relieved to be out of the house in the aftermath of another senseless row with Miranda. Thank God I wasn't panicking so much now when outdoors. My fear of random physical attacks was slowly dying down.

We set off down the beach toward firm, damp sand. There's nothing to beat beach training, for a double marathon like the Comrades. It had been high tide in the night, leaving seaweed piled up around us. Sand stung our faces as we began running.

'You fly to Canada tonight?' Pete asked Neil. 'Feeling ready for your interview?'

'Sure am.' Neil gave a satisfied grunt. We were struggling to hear each other against the wind and the crashing waves, so we ran on in silence. The raw salt air stung the back of our throats like neat vodka.

I felt like a traitor, hoping Neil's new job didn't work out. The sense of another solid plank of my life breaking up like matchwood pulled me down and I tried hard to dismiss the image from my mind. I needed to concentrate on my run, with the marathon this close. Eventually, the steady crunching rhythm of our feet on the sand helped me to focus, my eyes fixed ahead, where lines of white horses were being whipped up on the sea.

Neil set us a cracking pace, radiating bonhomie for the rest of the morning. You could never tell with Neil. Running with my mates was one of the few times I felt good, since that awful day of my attack. I was never going to be a fanatic like Neil. It wasn't why I ran – I did it more to pit myself against the terrain, against advancing age. And because I couldn't stop running the Comrades. It was part of who I was. I tried again to switch off the voice in my head and give myself over to the run.

'No-one stopping for coffee?' I asked later, as we headed back towards our cars.

'Sorry, mate.' Bram pulled a 'can't be helped' face and reached for his car keys.

'No can do. I've got a plane to catch,' Neil said and jumped into his car.

'Good luck,' we called as we waved him off.

I felt let down. Coffee at the run-down beach cafe was our usual ritual after our beach runs.

'You alright?' Pete gave me that quizzical look he had used a lot since the knife attack.

'Ja, fine.' I knew I didn't sound convincing.

'I'll stay for a quick one,' Pete said. 'Barbara will understand.'

Bending into the wind, we walked to the near-deserted

beach café. The only other man in there nodded at us morosely. We ordered then huddled in the cafe's bleak interior, hugging our coffees.

'Something on your mind?' Pete asked.

'Yeah.' I paused. 'I need to do something about Ezekiel's family.'

'What do you mean?'

'I'm worried about his daughters. They lost their mother only months ago.'

'That's tough. But they'll have family.'

'I need to make sure of that…'

'Why you, of all people? Hasn't he got friends, colleagues, his union?'

I banged the table harder than I meant to. 'Because I can't sleep at night thinking about it, that's why.'

Pete held his hands up. 'Take it easy. I'm just trying to follow you.'

'Sorry, man. It's hard to explain. I feel responsible for where he's ended up.'

'Now that is ridiculous.'

'If I'd handled the incident better the week before…it wouldn't have escalated like it did.'

Pete shook his head. 'Shock headline: Man chased with knife is to blame!'

I couldn't help laughing. It did sound crazy. Maybe Pete was right. 'If I could just find out they were OK, I could stop worrying about them.'

'Then check that someone is helping him. His union should know.'

'I'm trying to do that,' I said. 'And Miranda is suggesting I fly to Sheffield to help Michael over Liz's anniversary. I'm not sure I can handle that.'

'He should come out here. Be with good friends who knew her,' Pete said as he stood up. 'Sorry, I have to run.'

We made our way to our cars.

'Cut yourself a bit of slack Ben,' he said as he waved goodbye.

As I drove home, last night's row with Miranda returned to my mind. What were the phrases she had brought home from her ANC meeting – 'The government hasn't got time for the luxury of debate. The ANC was elected with a huge majority, it needs to get on with governing. We have to make huge changes and make them fast.'

I shivered at how fast she and her ANC friends seemed to be taking democracy for granted, just ten years after the end of apartheid. She'd called me 'a bleeding-heart liberal, past your sell-by date'. All her precious ANC colleagues wanted to talk about now was who got their economic empowerment directorships fastest, bugger poverty or justice. It chilled me that these directorships were being shared out amongst top ANC comrades, rather than spread more widely in black society. The few getting filthy rich. How had Miranda – my funny, affectionate Mirrie – morphed slowly into this imposter? This defender of the indefensible?

The mournful 'cark-cark' of mewling seagulls echoed my mood. The wind was whipping up a storm as my car made its way through the near-empty Sunday city centre and up towards the Berea. Thunder rumbled in the distance and then closer. Ugly clouds built up inland.

PART TWO

CHAPTER 13

'Can you believe it?' Nomsa asked the Umlazi Women's Committee. 'My brother could wait two years in prison for his trial and then be found innocent!' She pressed her hands to her cheeks.

Engrossed in her story, the women sat around the battered table in the Apostolic Church hall, the familiar meeting place for their committee. Afternoon sun slanted though the window, making dust motes dance across the room, its windows silted up with grime on the outside. Cars screeched past on the busy through-road outside.

'I am getting nowhere, I don't know what to do next.' Nomsa had to unburden her heart. After all, Ezekiel was an Umlazi resident too.

Maya clucked. 'Some things have not changed since apartheid days, heh? Is this what our brothers and sisters suffered for?' The others shook their heads.

Hlengiwe, their chairwoman, bustled in and took her seat. Her angular frame exuded disapproval. 'Ladies, we have an agenda to get though. Do you want to raise this matter under any other business, Nomsa?'

Nomsa gave her a dark look. 'Yes, under any other business.' Hlengiwe took her business as chairwoman too seriously. Nomsa wondered how any man had come to marry this thin, miserable woman.

Hlengiwe shuffled her papers. 'Last month's minutes… accepted?'

They all nodded.

'Item 1. The Municipality is trying to drive informal traders from parts of the city centre.' Nomsa nodded. Too many Umlazi residents earned a living in this way.

'Item 2. Plan to stop another bar opening up, outside the Umlazi high school…'

Nomsa's foot started to tap. She tried to concentrate, but her mind returned to the sad faces of her nieces. Since visiting their father in prison, they had bent like young mielie-corns in a hailstorm. Her hands fiddled with the buttons on her blouse.

Finally, Hlengiwe's bossy voice called out. 'Any other business?'

Nomsa's hand was ready. 'Yes. My brother Ezekiel has been told he will have to wait up to two years in Westville prison, for his case to be heard. Sisters, I ask you, how many other Umlazi husbands and sons may be locked up in prison like Ezekiel, forgotten for a year or two, before their trial even begins. This is an important problem for us to tackle.' Her voice wobbled. 'How many Umlazi children lose fathers, how many families lose breadwinners, when that man may have done nothing wrong. Maybe these courts and prisons will discover that we women of Umlazi are not so easy to steam-roll over.'

'*Viva!*' called Ingwe, clapping her hands. Her freedom-fighter name from the old days was not 'Leopard' for nothing.

'*Amandla.*' Thonko rose from her seat. 'We are Shaka's daughters.' The others stood too, caught up by the idea.

'This is more important than stopping a new bar,' Maya said, banging her hand on the table.

Hlengiwe held up her hand. 'Ladies, sit please. We are not a rabble here. Let us approach this in an orderly manner.' The excitable atmosphere collapsed as fast as it had begun. Hlengiwe waited for silence as the others sat back down again. 'Surely this project is too big for us?'

There was muttering around the table, followed by vigorous calls. 'This is the one for us!'

To Nomsa's irritation, Hlengiwe hesitated. She liked to play it safe, tackle projects that were sure to come off. 'I suppose we could postpone some other plans.'

'Yes, yes!' they called out.

Their chairwoman sighed. 'If we do go ahead, first we would need to find out how many residents in our section of Umlazi have experienced this problem. We would have to question our families, our neighbours.'

She was right of course. That was why she had been chosen to chair their committee. Annoying, but very methodical. They started to discuss the idea in raised voices.

'My brother was charged last year,' Ingwe wailed. 'He is still waiting. He was visiting our mother at the time, so he could not have robbed that take-away. But still he is locked up.'

'Is he in Westville prison too?'

'*Yebo*, that Westville,' she said.

'My neighbour too. He was beaten and robbed, left in a street late at night. The police arrested him instead of those thugs. Then they charged him for drunk and disorderly!'

'How long was he locked up?'

'Only one weekend.' Maya looked embarrassed.

'What has that got to do with our survey?' Hlengiwe's lips were tight. The others muttered 'shame'.

After more talk about the details, they took a vote. It was decided that they would go ahead with the prison project. Shadows were beginning to fall across the room in the rising chill of the winter afternoon. They would all need to leave soon.

Thonko snapped shut her notebook. 'I will type up a draft list of questions to ask our residents and drop them round to you all. Send me your ideas to improve it.' She was the only one with a computer. Her son was at the university and she seemed to know about such things.

'We can make a change with this survey,' Maya said as they rose. They all cheered. 'Power to the Women's Committee!'

After the usual boisterous hugs and leave-takings, the women hurried home to cook evening meals, to impatient children and grandchildren home from school and famished husbands coming back from a long day at the factories at Isipingo. Without these friends, Nomsa thought, life would be hard.

****

It was a warm afternoon, as I slipped into the union meeting about pay negotiations. By now there was standing room only in the huge room, which seethed with raised voices and chants of '*basebenzi masimanyane* – workers unite'. I squeezed through the crowd to where I had spotted the other heads of department, on one side, near the front. I felt myself squirm, feeling out of place in the midst of

SAMWU, historically the black municipal workers union, so different from the staid union to which most of us managers belonged. Ours was still in negotiations with the municipality while SAMWU was going full steam ahead for industrial action.

When the apartheid government began to slide out of control, black unions had burgeoned and I'd felt proud of my own small role in encouraging that in the municipality. Now I seemed to be on the other side. Higher management had left us, the middle managers, to take the flack today. Sipho and I ran through the questions that might come our way. The atmosphere in the room grew more and more tempestuous. Too many of us stuffed into the hot, airless room.

Kangisa, the ebullient SAMWU secretary, stood up in front to quieten the room. A powerful presence, he was instantly dismissive of the pay talks. 'The government has sold out, betrayed our election victory. President Mbeki and his pay restraints must go!'

'*Yebo!*' Clapping and cheers reverberated around the room. I felt I was rolling inside the belly of the crowd. The meeting was sure to follow Kangisa's lead.

'Do you think we should have kept out of it?' asked Bettina.

'Too late now.' Moodley, dapper in his well-tailored suit, made a throat-cutting gesture.

It was a foregone conclusion from the mood in the room that me and my kind would be hung out to dry today as bosses' stooges. I hated opposing a union like this, longed for the old days when the enemy had been clear-cut – the ugly apartheid state in all its carbuncled might. I'd been on the side of the angels then, fighting to legalise the unions.

Now I was caught between the union and the government pay restraints. I coughed nervously. On the strike issue, I'd picked a side and I had to stick to it.

'The other unions are taking too long,' Kangisa shouted. 'We can't wait forever for these timid types.'

Cheers rose again. The meeting went on and on, getting more restive and physical. The air was hot and stale. I badly needed a pee but I knew I couldn't get out of this crowded room if I tried.

Kangisa threw in the usual sly threat. 'You know the union doesn't condone violence, but we have to warn you, comrades. If you break the strike, there are always bad apples who go too far – who will burn cars, houses; people can get hurt. Comrades, the union can't guarantee your safety if you break the strike.'

The bastard, I thought, he's blatantly threatening them. The crowd burst into an old favourite song from the struggle days, '*Umshini Wami* – Bring Back My Machine Gun.'

Someone threw in a question for me. 'Will the director of museums support a SAMWU strike call? He once had a reputation of backing our union.'

I made my way to the podium. Mouth dry, I swallowed hard. Reminded myself this was simply democracy in action, the thing I had fought for. 'Comrades, remember, our other unions are still in negotiation.' My voice grew stronger. 'I beg you not to break ranks. Our strength is in unity. The talks must be given time to work. In the meantime, we owe it to the citizens of Durban to continue providing municipal services.'

All around me I heard rumbles of disagreement. Saw fists waving at me. 'Department heads like me are also concerned about our members pay, we too are affected by the wage freeze. We have children to educate, families to feed, like the rest of you.'

The crowd jeered, so that I could barely hear myself. I took a deep breath and raised my voice. 'We must also remember the forty percent of South Africans who remain unemployed. There are limited public funds from the government. If the big unions push for twelve per cent, the municipality will have to cut the jobs of others to pay it.'

I was howled down by the furious crowd. 'Tell that to Thabo Mbeki,' shouted a heavy man just below the podium.

'Sell-out!' Others spewed hate at me. Fists waved up at me from all round the chamber. I was jostled roughly off the podium by those at the front, twisting my ankle on the way down. Shocked by the hatred. I staggered back to my colleagues.

They were given just as hard a time when they spoke. It was no use saying that the municipal coffers were empty. The union was on a roll about fat cats in government – central government, local government – it was all the same to them. No-one could see that they were different coffers and that the government had set its mind on not giving in. The vote went overwhelmingly to pursue the twelve percent claim, to fight to the bitter end.

Cheers of '*Viva! Viva!*' reverberated through the meeting chamber. The noise was hell at such close quarters. My head was thumping. I felt old and tired. We managers were jostled out of the chamber by the tight-pressed bodies of the departing crowd. Outside, the workers *toyi-toyied* to the high-pitched ululating of the women and deep chanting of the men. I was parched.

I retreated with my colleagues to a heads of department meeting in the chairman's office, where I spotted a trolley of welcome tea. I prayed that there would be biscuits today.

Our chairman, Sengani, head of waste disposal, was bursting with energy. 'Looks like it's time to make contingency plans to handle this strike, if and when it comes.' He snapped open his diary. His office breathed order and control, in contrast to my own chaotic den.

'We couldn't be less prepared than we were last year,' Moodley said.

'We'll pencil in regular meeting dates,' Sengani said. I could see the strike taking off from here; there'd be no stopping it now.

CHAPTER 14

In the darkening evening, Ezekiel and Kris hunched on their beds in the hospital ward, hugging the hot drinks that came round shortly before lights out. The blinds were drawn, the other patients at their end asleep or comatose on drips or other machines. It was almost homely in the low light, almost possible to believe you were not in prison. Nurse Mtwetwe, their favourite, was on duty, her voice murmuring from bed to bed down the line. Ezekiel could feel his heart beginning to mend as well as his body.

'Agh, times like this, I get homesick for Cape Town,' Kris said. 'You Zulus are OK but I miss my own people. We Cape Coloureds have our own ways.

'What work did you do in your old life?' Ezekiel asked, trying to lift the fellow's spirits.

Kris paused, as though he was weighing up how much to say. Finally, he said, 'You tell first.'

'Not much to tell. I've been a doorman most of my life at Durban city hall.' Ezekiel stared into space, trying to conjure up his old life. 'I stood at the entrance desk to check people coming in. And I carried a lot of books around but I read none of them.' He remembered the smell of the boxes of new books for the library. He had carried so many over the years. The library staff received them with reverence, as though they were the bones of their ancestors. He'd never understood why, but in the end, he had come to treat the books with the same respect.

'So long in one place!' Kris looked amazed. 'Such a steady job?'

'Yes. I had uniform, security. In later years we had the union to look after us. How about you?' Ezekiel sipped his tea.

Kris threw his hands up. 'Jack of all trades, me. Started in carpentry but had to sell my tools to pay debts, you know how it is.'

Ezekiel wasn't sure he did, but he nodded. Talking about their previous lives like this was a strange mixture of pleasure and pain.

Nurse Mtwetwe reached them. 'You boys alright? Any painkillers needed?' She adjusted Ezekiel's bedding in a way that made him want to weep, remembering the last time a woman had taken care of him like this. The touch of his Thandiwe.

She handed paracetamol tablets to them both. 'Lights out soon, drink up.' She smiled before moving on.

Ezekiel leaned forward and said in a low whisper, 'So what did you do, Kris that put you inside?'

Kris wrinkled his nose. 'Before that, I ran a street stall at Cape Town market. Selling sunhats and beach gear in summer, scarves, woolly hats and gloves in winter. Freezing my butt off in those Cape winds. Sometimes you can make it with that sort of stuff.' He paused. 'But then things went bad, I had to get money somehow…'

Ezekiel hesitated to push for more. 'How come you ended up so far from your home city?'

Kris's face livened, his hands reached for the words he was seeking but he fell into a coughing fit. When he resurfaced, he slapped his thigh and laughed. '*Ek se*, it's some story, man. Where to begin?'

Ezekiel looked up expectantly.

'I was in Polsmoor prison for about two years. Grim place, man. This one has nothing on Polsmoor. Those Cape gangs are tough.' He paused and looked around, his voice a rasping whisper. 'There was a riot, when the pigs wouldn't provide us with ARVs and…'

'You were trying for ARVs in Polsmoor too?' Ezekiel asked.

'Ja, guys were dying all over the prison but the bastards wouldn't give us the *blerry* drugs. We whipped up a riot about it and they came down on us hard. They schemed I was one of the main *ous* behind it – me and my big mouth.' He spat phlegm into a tin that he kept at his side for that purpose. 'They transferred us ringleaders to different prisons all around the country. And I ended up here.'

Ezekiel's head was reeling at this story. Was Kris making all this up…this little fellow with his limp? But here he was campaigning for ARVs again, so perhaps it was true. 'You seem well in with guys here.'

'If you're a little *ou* like me, and a Cape Coloured far away from home, you use your mouth to survive, man. This time we're going to be much cleverer with our campaign.' His voice dropped so Ezekiel could hardly hear him. 'Hunger strike, man, when we have enough people signed up.'

'What the…when?'

'That I can't say man. We need to talk some non-HIV guys into joining us, for impact.'

'*Aikona*, you are too thin already to go on hunger strike,' Ezekiel whispered back, in awe of this little man's bravery.

'With AIDS, I got nothing to lose.'

The two of them were silent for a while. Ezekiel pondered Kris's words as they drained their mugs. He wondered if he too could talk clever like Kris, to side-step what was waiting for him from Terror and his gang back in his cell.

Ezekiel hesitated. 'How did you avoid being sucked in by the gangs when you arrived here?'

Kris shook his head. 'You haven't listened to a thing I been saying, man. You think I avoided those bastards?'

'But…the other day you told me not to get caught up with the gangs.'

Kris shrugged. 'Ja, I'm telling you not to make my mistake. A little one like me doesn't stand a chance if they choose you. But you look tough enough to maybe fend them off.' He shook his head again and threw him a look. 'Where do you think I got HIV, man?'

Ezekiel nodded slowly. '*Haai*, Kris, I am sorry. You are one brave man.'

'I was forced into the twenny-eight gang. Technically I'm still in – they never let you leave, except in a body-bag, those *fokkin'* bastards. They call it the 'slow puncture' when they rape you, because most of them have got HIV.'

Kris looked behind his back again, though his voice was a croaky whisper. The quiet whiteness of the ward seemed like a haven away from the horror of all that he was telling Ezekiel about. But it could erupt any moment with a hunger strike. If Kris was that brave, Ezekiel thought he too could be brave and face up to Terror Mangoba.

****

After my rough afternoon at the union meeting, the near-vertical pull up through the Berea on my bike seemed more difficult than usual. My ankle throbbed after the way I had been pushed off the podium earlier.

Home was a welcoming *laager*. I fumbled my way in through the gate, dumped my bike and slumped heavy -limbed into a garden chair. Overhead, *hadeda*s gave their harsh cries as they flew low across the city, making their way home. I stared out over Durban and towards the sea, to where it merged with the sky. It was a view that could suck the day's pain out of you. I heard the sounds of insects in the grass beneath my feet and smelled the evening scent of frangipani. I could have stayed there forever but I had to prepare a meal for the kids.

In the kitchen, I began searching for the ingredients to use. A stir-fry was about all I could think of making with what was in the fridge. I put the rice on to boil and set to peeling and slicing carrots, mushrooms, courgettes, peppers, enjoying the arty look of their colours on the chopping board. But I was all fingers and thumbs after my bad afternoon. 'Ouch!' I cut my index finger, spattering blood on the vegetables, swore to myself and went in search of a plaster.

Back in the kitchen, I carried on chopping, rummaging for the words to express the uneasy feelings about Miranda that were rising inside me. Last night, as we had relaxed after dinner, sipping coffees, she had dropped in casually. 'You won't want to come to my firm's party in a few weeks. Lawyers aren't your cup of tea.'

I slipped into it, like a fish into melted butter. 'Oh, I love a party, especially if it's full of bigwigs I can bring down a peg or two.'

She'd pounced. 'That's just it. You'll be winding people up. Your usual party piece.' Her voice was tight. 'You don't understand that I'll be looking for a job there when I finish articles.'

Then it was difficult to back-track, given my reputation for a sardonic turn of phrase, especially after I'd had a few drinks. Miranda sometimes tore a strip off me when we got home for digging the knife in too deep but just as often, she used to love it. Not long ago, she'd have joined me in mocking them afterwards, reliving the whole thing. And everyone would still be talking to me the following week, inviting me to the next party.

'I know you'll show me up, Ben. You never know when to keep your mouth shut.'

'I can see it's different if you're wanting a job there. I'll hold my tongue.'

'No, I've made up my mind. I'm going alone,' she'd said. 'I can't handle waiting for you to let rip at one of them.'

I smelt the oil in the wok sizzling, turned back to my cooking. I threw in the onions, added crushed garlic and oregano. Pungent aromas rose as I stirred. I clutched at this tangible activity until my mind was off, chasing the rabbit of my annoyance again. I was determined to go to that law party, frightened of what would happen if Miranda started excluding me from chunks of her life. What I would have given at that moment, to get back that easy feeling we'd had between us until when? I couldn't put my finger on it exactly.

I tried to recall that sense I'd once had of being rooted in the ground as solidly as the plants in our garden – my red-hot pokers, graceful agapanthus plants and luxuriant clivias. But in my mind, these lovely plants started drying up from within, as I felt I was. I tried to shut down the image or reverse it but it continued until my whole garden was a wasteland, the roots shrivelling and turning up to the sun.

I stared blankly at the stove, shuddering in distress. Heard the front door open then slam, teenage footsteps clomping down the hall. I snapped back into the present. Shi…t. I smelled burning. I only just rescued the frazzled onions, a bit blackened but they'd do.

CHAPTER 15

It was mid-morning when Ezekiel was wheeled back to the door of Section D by a warder. The man rang the bell, then robbed him of his wheelchair and handed him over. Ezekiel stood on shaky legs and was hustled into his cell. It had been very hard to say goodbye to the ward, especially to Kris and nurse Mtwewe. He hesitated to step into his old cell, which struck him as airless and stinking.

The warder gave him a shove. 'I got no time to waste, Mabuza.'

'I…I was beaten up bad in here. Can't you move me to another section?' he asked in a low voice.

The warder laughed. 'None of them are any better, I tell you. I can get you a transfer request form if you want. Takes about three weeks, no guarantees.' He sauntered away.

Ezekiel braced himself for the knot of guys hanging around the entrance, to see who was coming in. Boredom was a disease of remand prisoners without daily work.

'*Haai* Mabuza, *injani wena?*' someone called. 'How are you?'

'*Sapila.* I'm OK.' He looked around in the half-light, to see who else had noticed his arrival. His insides turned at the thought of encountering Terror and his boys. But the twenty-sixes were in their usual corner, gathered round someone who was having a new tattoo added to his collection.

Ezekiel saw Jazz coming towards him, calling, 'Yo, bra? Where you been?'

Ezekiel held out his good arm, to prevent Jazz's friendly clap on his back. 'Go easy man, I got a damaged rib here. I been on the hospital ward.'

'We heard something like that but I thought it was just a rumour. Thought maybe you'd been moved for good.'

Ezekiel looked around carefully. 'Brutus and some guys beat the hell out of me. Don't spread it around.'

Jazz studied him more closely. 'Jesus, you look rough bra. You OK?'

'A broken rib is painful but I'm improving. The sick bay was heaven, man, after this place – female nurses treating us kind.'

'You get lucky?' Jazz chuckled, shaping a female body with his hands.

'It wasn't like that. I met a really good guy in there, called Kris.' He looked around again. 'What's been going on in here?'

'Same routine, man. One *fokking* day after the next, same lousy food.' Jazz yawned and stretched as they walked further into the cell. Ezekiel's eyes were darting from side to side to spot any trouble.

'Any fall-out from Terror and his gang, about my beating?'

'Nothing man. The latest is a dust up between Terror's lot and a new gang taking hold here in Westville. Some of them are next-door. A lot of threats being swapped but no blood spilt so far.'

'*Eish*, I've hardly been away!' Ezekiel grinned, relieved that the twenty-sixes would be occupied with something bigger. Maybe they would forget about him.

'Jus' keep out of their way. They's in a bad mood these days.' Jazz started doing imitations of different gang members' reactions to the new boys on the block.

Ezekiel couldn't help laughing, then clutched his painful rib. He wished he could keep his spirits up in here like Jazz did. He took his small bundle of belongings to his locker, put them in and relocked it.

In the crowded canteen that lunch time, Ezekiel could hardly stand the noise of the canteen after the quiet of the sick bay. His tablemates insisted on being entertained with stories from his time away. Every detail about the nurses was pored over, their names and appearances repeated back and forth, as though the guys already knew them.

'Nurse Mtwetwe, she sounds like the one for me!' Jazz declared.

Phineas muscled up to him. 'You don't stand a chance with me around. Can you dance?'

'You wouldn't believe how clean it was in there,' Ezekiel said. 'This cell really stinks.'

The guys laughed, sucking dry every bone of his time away.

I have friends, Ezekiel thought as he fell asleep later, back on his hard mat on the floor. That night, he dreamed of his days as a herd boy back at his father's *kraal* in northern KwaZulu, roaming the freedom of the *veld*, with his closest companions. The stick fights they had, playing at being king Shaka's warriors. He smiled at the memory of how he and Thandiwe had made eyes at each other as teenagers, whenever she passed him on her way to the waterhole with her friends, her hips swaying, bucket on her head. She'd stop to talk to him, while her friends stood back and giggled behind their hands.

But he was never sure, until he received her bead message, delivered by a friend. Hurriedly he had explored the bracelet's secret language, in fear that the beads spelled out rejection. Halleluiah! The bracelet was made of red and white beads, with a layer of black round the outside to signify marriage, with some blue-grey beads, requesting a reply.

Their courtship proper started then, with stolen kisses behind her father's huts, for what seemed like forever, while their families negotiated *lobola*. Her father was a hard bargainer and so was his. In the end, hands were shaken and the final stage of the marriage process began. Cattle were slaughtered and the aunties were busy making food from sunrise. Just as his dream approached the marriage ceremony itself, it was interrupted by the prison's early-morning alarm. It dragged him back to the stench of the cell and men's voices cursing around him.

Ezekiel's hopes of being forgotten by Terror Mangoba's men did not last long. No-one took the subject up with him directly but his locker was broken into and robbed of precious items, his soap, toothpaste and the phone money he had hidden there so he could leave a message for Thembu, should he need to. A few times, a voice behind him said, 'Watch out Mabuza, sign up soon.' After that, Ezekiel was rigid, looking over his shoulder all the time, sure another beating was on its way. Should he sign up and get it over with? Or could he hold out?

****

I loaded cold beers and wine bottles into a box and carried them through to the dining-room. A few mixers, fill the ice-bucket and I'd be done. We'd invited the usual crowd over for our supper club, where everyone brought a dish. Tonight's theme was Spanish. I sorted the music and turned the lights down, my feet *do-wapping* to my favourite Eric Clapton track. At home, I'd begun to relax, to forget about Ezekiel's attack, apart from my nightmares. But beyond the front door, I wasn't so good.

I approached the kitchen as though it was a rogue state that had recently acquired a nuclear missile. Since our fall-out over Miranda's law party, things hadn't been easy. Tonight, we had a pact to get on and I at least was trying. I didn't want my mom to realise how difficult things were between us while she was here. Miranda looked stunning in her red dress, the way it flared from her hips, her dangly earrings glinting in her dark hair.

'*Do-wap-a-doo!*' I jiggled to the music and snapped my fingers.

'You're in a good mood,' Miranda said.

Dora, my mom, came in. 'I've made a lovely flower arrangement for the table centre.'

I could tell from Miranda's face what she thought of the idea, so I changed the subject before she could say anything. 'Everyone will want to know how it went for the Listers in Vancouver.'

'I thought you'd have asked Neil already.' Miranda said, with that critical tone she used to me now.

'I think I'll go and change,' Mom said and disappeared.

'*Do-wap-a -doo!*' I sang to regain my party mood as I laid out the nibbles.

The doorbell rang.

'Ben, darling!' Barbara waltzed though the front door as I opened it, in that extravagantly affectionate way of hers, followed by Pete. Two of my favourite people. She put down a steaming dish of something fishy and delicious-smelling and enveloped me in a hug, kissing me on the lips. With her blonde, bouffant hair and stylish clothes, she always lit up the room.

We went through to the kitchen, where our long table was lit with fat candles, ready for a feast. Miranda and I were good at this kind of thing. She came through, flashing a smile at everyone but me. Bram and Elsa arrived. Corks popped, wine and beer were poured.

'Did Neil get the job?' Bram asked.

'We don't know yet.'

'Shhh! They'll feel as though they're facing a pack of newshounds.'

At this point, the Listers arrived. Penny's face was pale, red blotches high on either cheek, like one of those china dolls my sisters had as kids. She looked straight ahead, back rigid, shoulders high, as if ready to take us all on. 'Sorry we're late.' Her voice was false-bright.

Neil slouched in behind her, growling a greeting, chin jutting out so far you could have hung his running medals from it.

'Neil, Penny!' We called out brightly to paper over the awkward moment. No-one dared to ask about the interview.

Neil's voice was treacherous. 'And how was your interview Neil?' He answered himself. 'Excellent thanks; they've offered me the job.' Before any of us could speak, he threw in, 'Congratulations, Neil, well done!' His look said it all – ask Penny's opinion of the trip and you're dead.

We fell over ourselves, offering our congratulations but they fell flat. Then Penny burst into tears and left the room, followed by the other women. I began to feel that I was in a bad Fifties stage play. We guys stood around awkwardly, somehow finding ourselves on the wrong side. None of us wanted the Listers to go to Canada either.

'Anyone for another beer?' I asked.

Against the pleasing pop of beer-bottles, the smell of beer and the smoke from Neil's renegade cigarette, the atmosphere veered roughly back to normal. We quizzed Neil about the interview.

'So will you take it?' Bram asked.

'I've accepted already.' Neil's face was pugnacious. 'They want me to start by September.'

To drown out the shockwaves and to stop another question from spoiling the evening, I jumped in, 'Let's serve the first course. I'll call the women back. And change the subject, for chrissakes.'

The women came back in and we all took our seats, trying to act as though nothing had happened. I saw Miranda seating Penny and Neil at opposite ends and gave her a thumbs up. Our big yellow-wood table was dressed in its party best, lifting the atmosphere. I went round filling wine glasses. Bram and Elsa carried in the first course, a crunchy *gazpacho* that made my eyes water when I took a mouthful. Through the window, I saw a half-moon lying low in the sky.

'Mugabe must be shitting himself,' Neil said. 'The Zimbabwe elections were a close-run thing.'

Usually, I went straight in when politics came up but tonight I was too busy thinking about Neil and Canada. I couldn't imagine making a move overseas myself, even if it solved my problems at the museum. I was with Penny on this one; I belonged here. I tuned back into the conversation around me.

'Mbeki's the real villain, with his "softly-softly" approach to Zimbabwe,' Bram said. 'Mugabe makes a fool of him every time.'

'South Africa could pull the plug on Zimbabwe's electric supply tomorrow, if we wanted to,' Pete said. Zimbabwe was personal with Pete and Barbara. They had lived there for a while after it first got independence.

'Give Mbeki a chance!' Miranda raised her voice. It seemed there were no safe topics tonight.

'Main course coming up.' Barbara carried a bowl of pungent smelling paella, shellfish popping up from a red seabed, like drowning hands. She spooned the bright concoction into bowls and handed them round.

'Smells divine,' Miranda said. I could see her unwinding now the evening was underway. I raised my glass to her silently and she returned the toast. I began to relax.

'Pass the red.' 'White over here.' The bottles began their table shuffle again.

The closing days of the Schabir Shaik trial for corruption, fraud & racketeering was on everyone's lips. I lost track of the conversation around me as I slipped back into thinking of Ezekiel Mabuza. How would he be spending his night in prison? Was he warm and well fed? Would he be found guilty of something as bad as attempted murder? Guilt washed over me for my own good fortune, sitting here amongst friends.

Miranda called from the fridge, 'Ben, give me a hand.'

I went over to find her fretting about her *Crema Catalana* desserts.

'They'll taste delicious, honestly Mirrie.'

As I carried the little glass bowls over on a tray, an idea bubbled up. I passed them round and then clinked a knife on my glass. 'Hey, listen, this is important. We've known each other since ...forever,' I said as my brain failed the arithmetic. I could hear my voice going sentimental. 'It's easy to take each other for granted...but this group is very special.'

'Sit down Ben,' Miranda muttered. 'You're making a fool of yourself!'

'It's not just this business of Neil thinking of leaving...'

'I *am* leaving,' Neil called in a rough voice.

'Something could happen to any of us...' I knew I was smiling my silly, had-too-much-to-drink grin. 'You're irreplaceable, all of you. Look at Liz. Gone before we had time to say goodbye.' Sympathetic murmurs went around the table. 'Difficult to say you miss the old days but I do. I'm not saying they were better. Apartheid was monstrous but...hell, I miss the camaraderie of working for change. Things were...urgent, we were involved. We knew who we were.'

Everyone's eyes were fixed on my face. They'd lost their surprised look.

'It's weird without that. Dunno about the rest of you but ...I feel lost at times. No sense of mission anymore.' (More murmurings.) 'We need each other, hey.' I looked around, feeling silly then burst out. 'I love you all, live life to the full. Hasta la Vista!' and fell back into my chair, a bit drunk.

'To old friends!' Pete raised his glass.

'Move on, Ben,' Miranda said. 'That was over long ago. Time to look forward.' She tapped her fingers on the table in irritation.

'But Ben's put his finger on something,' Bram said. 'It's not that there's anything wrong with the present. Just that we haven't found a place in it yet.'

'Well put Ben.' Barbara clapped.

'You've been the best, all of you, since the early days,' Penny said. 'They were sometimes wonderful, sometimes scary times, don't forget. Like when we were arrested.' She paused and gave a short laugh. 'I've told Neil I'll go to Vancouver only if the rest of you come too.'

Someone burst into '*For She's a Jolly Good Fellow*' and we all joined in. Except for Neil, brooding and solitary over by the French windows.

Pete stood up and started giving his take on the old days. Penny followed me over to help make the coffee.

She smiled. 'Sometimes you really have the touch, Ben.'

'Other times, I open my mouth to change feet, Miranda says.' We fell about, laughing.

She looked me in the eye and asked quietly, 'Tell me truthfully how you're doing now?'

'Better,' I said. 'As long as no-one reminds me of it.'

'Sorry!'

'I can't stop thinking about Ezekiel, how he's coping in prison. And how his family is managing.'

Penny nodded. 'Can't you find out? See if we can help?'

'You're right, I must try a bit harder to do that. Instead of lying awake at night, worrying. But Miranda would go ballistic if she found out.

'Hm. Do you have to tell her?'

'Maybe not. What about you and Canada?'

'A rough few weeks ahead, I think.' She bit her lip. 'You know how Neil is, once he's taken a stand.' Her face had a scared rabbit look.

I hugged her. 'He-ey! We're always here for you. You know that don't you?'

'Don't, or I'll blub…' She pushed past me and out of the kitchen.

I felt a pang of guilt towards Neil but he had always been able to look after himself.

'Just how bad are things with Neil and Penny?' I asked Miranda as she joined me by the kettle to sort out the coffees.

'Pretty bad,' she whispered. 'Penny thought Vancouver was a marvellous place. But she can't imagine leaving South Africa or uprooting the kids.'

'I didn't think we'd get through tonight without a bust-up between them.'

'Yes, we've managed a nifty double-act,' she smiled at me.

Just then there was shouting at the table, Neil's voice thick with drink. 'Keep out of it, you stupid fucker.'

My hands froze, coffee-cups midway to the tray. Miranda's eyes latched onto mine. Emollient voices tried to talk Neil down. Then there was a loud thwack followed by a cry of pain and a chair toppled.

Bram called out, 'You bastard, Neil!'

Bram was nursing his jaw. Penny started running down the hallway towards the front door.

'Penny don't…' Miranda called and ran after her, but the front door slammed.

'Let's cool it eh, Neil,' I said, gingerly steering my friend through to the lounge. I handed him a strong coffee but it was difficult to get him to drink it in his truculent state. I didn't want a punch like the one Bram had taken, so I left Neil to cool down on his own and slipped back to the others.

'Just like the old days too,' Pete said wryly. 'Too much booze and by the end of the evening, there was always a bust-up over politics or a woman!'

The rest of them looked shaken. Bram was sitting down, carefully exploring his jaw.

Miranda came back in. 'Penny was off in her car before I could catch her.'

'Has Penny told Neil that she's not going to Canada?' I asked her quietly.

'She's stalling for time but she thinks he's figured it out.'

'We better keep him here tonight then.' There was muttered agreement all round. Persuading Neil to stay might not be easy. The good vibe of our evening was now in tatters. The others talked for a while in lowered voices about what had happened and then left for home.

CHAPTER 16

That Saturday, Ezekiel sat on the prisoners' side of the scruffy visitors' room and watched Nomsa's solid shape puff towards the visitors' seats, her bags rustling about her. He saw her eyes search the row for him. Her face lit up when she spotted him through the glass barrier.

She sat down heavily opposite him with a satisfied sigh. '*Sawubona,* my brother. You are out of hospital.'

'*Sapila. Gunjani wena, uMama!' He* felt a rare smile cross his face. He no longer cared about having to shout through the glass in the crowded visitors' room. The other prisoners faded from his mind. 'How are my girls?'

'They are well. They have schools' choir competition today or they would have come.'

She opened first one bag and then the other, pulling things out like it was Christmas – toothpaste, soap, everything that Ezekiel had had stolen from him. Biscuits, cigarettes, a little cash and best of all, a photograph of Thandiwe and his girls. She slipped it under the glass. He held the picture to his lips and kissed it, his heart full.

'I have a good idea,' she said. 'You check in with Thembu at work in the middle of the week, on the callbox here. He can give you news of your girls and you tell him if things are OK here. That way we all feel better.'

'Where would I be without you, Nomsa? You're smart woman, solving every problem.'

She looked at the large clock on the wall. 'We have matters to cover, before that drat bell rings again. Tell me truly, now Gugu and Mbali are not here, why did those men beat you?' Her eyes pierced his, as if to say, 'and don't try and hide the truth from me'.

He hesitated, then lowered his voice. 'It's like this – when you first arrive in prison, you are on your own. Everyone wants to peck your eyes out. They think you are soft meat.'

He watched to see if this made any sense to her. It seemed such an age since he was the simpleton who first came to this place. Since then, Kris and the others had given him a crash course in prison life. But how much of it did he want Nomsa to know?

Nomsa's face was shrewd. 'Like when a new bride arrives in her husband's village. Things can be bad. The other women try to figure if they can push her around, her mother-in-law tries to be too strict.' She nodded to herself, as if she remembered it. 'If she is strong or her husband is very sweet on her, or she makes a special friend, the moment passes. Otherwise, things can go from bad to worse.'

'Yes, just the same,' he nodded slowly.

She leaned forward to hear him better. 'So what will you do about it? You have no husband sweet on you here in Westville prison,' she chuckled.

He shifted uneasily and tapped his hands on the ledge before him. Should he tell her about Terror's offer? He knew what Nomsa would say, with her church ways. Don't go near him. But he might end up having to accept the 'twenty-sixes' offer and then he would never hear the end of it from her. He dared not risk losing her new-found approval.

'To survive, you must be as wily as a crocodile,' she said, when he didn't answer. 'So they don't know where you are coming up to breathe. Do you have one man in here you can trust? Two old crocodiles are always better than one. You have the brains of a crocodile; remember you had a good job at city hall.'

The mention of his job cut through him. But she was right. He wished he had Nomsa in here as his second crocodile. She was worth ten men. He told her about Kris and the crowd he had met on the ward. About the hunger strike they were planning.

'Don't tell anyone. But keep an eye out for anything about it in the newspapers,' he said. 'We won't hear about in here.'

'I'll check Thembu's newspaper every day. I'm pleased you have a friend here.'

'I worry about Kris surviving the hunger-strike. He is as skinny as a plucked chicken already,' Ezekiel said. He drank in her familiar presence, her motherly shape in this alien place. He reached his hand towards her through the glass and her hand came towards his.

'Have a strong heart, my brother. Something will turn up.'

Maybe his bad fortune would turn, with Nomsa on his side. Now he had paid the price of prison, maybe the spirits of his ancestors would be appeased, would stop demanding one more sacrifice from him. The thought calmed him. Maybe there was a purpose in all this.

'Did that lawyer Dlamini turn up to see you as he promised?' she asked, her face like a sour lemon at the mention of the man's name.

'Yes. He went over the plan for the next tribunal with me.' He shifted in his seat. The noise of the other visitors around them confused him now about what Dlamini had said.

'What about getting your charges dropped? I called in at his office to make sure he wasn't forgetting that.'

'You did?' he gave the shadow of a laugh. Nomsa continued to surprise him.

'Did you tell him how badly you were beaten?' she asked. 'I don't think he believed me. We must make him realise it is urgent to get you out.'

He could see she was in a fighting mood. 'For a simple man like me, it is difficult to follow the way that man talks. He has studied at university; he must know what he is doing.'

She snorted. 'Don't be so sure. My committee has many dealings with such men. It doesn't always mean they know much about how things work in the real world. Many times, they are too swollen in the head, only looking after themselves.'

He never realised before how much Nomsa knew about the outside world. To stand up to a man like a lawyer. He knew she was on the Section F Women's Committee in Umlazi but he had never taken much notice of what they did. When he and Thembu had a few beers together, they would laugh about Nomsa and her 'women's business'.

'Never mind your tribunal,' she insisted. 'Dlamini must concentrate on having your charges dropped, then the city hall can't sack you. He is driving the cart before the donkey.'

Maybe she was right. Anxiety gnawed his stomach at the thought that he might not be in safe hands after all.

'I will be on the tail of that fellow,' she said. She told him about the survey her committee was carrying out about Westville prison and he marvelled. Now he understood the saying that 'women are the strength of the nation'.

The shrill of the bell announced the end of visiting time. He heard her sigh and thought of her long journey home, her walk down the hill to her bus. Watched her reach down for her shoes and struggle to squeeze her swollen feet back into them. It was not easy for her to come all this way.

'Thandiwe's spirit is thanking you for your care of our family,' he said.

She looked up. 'I know. Stay well, brother.'

****

While Miranda saw off our dinner visitors, I brewed Neil another coffee and took it through with one for myself. He hadn't moved since I had taken him through earlier. I could cheerfully have throttled him for tonight's debacle, for the way he had embarrassed Penny and popped our party mood, but the priority was to get him to bed if we were to have any sleep. I felt shattered and we had another qualifying marathon to run in the morning.

'Coffee Neil?' I hoped he had had time to calm down and wouldn't take a swing at me too. 'No-one is in a fit state to drive you home so we'll put you up here tonight.'

He grunted and hunched over himself, all the fight gone out of him.

I sat down beside him and handed him a mug. 'We'll both feel better when we've drunk this.'

'Thanks.' His voice was hoarse. He took the mug with shaking hands, mumbling, 'None of you unnerstands...' but he couldn't finish his sentence and we drank our coffees in silence.

When his mug was empty, I said, 'Let's find you a bed.'

Neil let me lead him like a child up the stairs and into our guest room. He sat himself down heavily on the bed, looking

142

dreadful. How much booze had the idiot swallowed? I hoped he didn't throw up on the new carpet that Miranda prized.

'Have some Panadol,' I said, opening the strip-pack. 'I'll have some too. It's been quite a night.'

'Trouble is,' Neil slurred. 'Penny doesn't unnerstand. My career's finished here. Canada's my last chance.'

'Positive discrimination is only fair after apartheid…' I started and then stopped myself. Arguments with a drunk could go on all night. 'You've got your reasons, Neil, I get that.' If I rushed him he would resist even more.

'S'not just ambition, you know.' He looked at me urgently. 'What jobs will there be for our kids if we stay?'

'Let's talk tomorrow when we all feel better, hey? My head's thumping and you don't look too good either.'

'Penny doesn't unnerstand. I'll shrivel up if I stay.' His eyes fixed on me. 'Tell her, won't you? She listens to you.'

'I'll talk to her, I promise.' It was strange hearing the story from Neil's point of view. It helped me make more sense of how bitter he was.

He staggered upright. 'I need a pish.'

I turned down the bedding for him, listening to make sure he didn't tumble down the stairs on his way to the bathroom. I'd never seen him this vulnerable before.

He returned and sat on the bed. I removed his shoes. Without taking off his clothes, he curled up under the duvet, pulling it around his chin. His eyes closed.

'Goodnight,' I said turning the light off.

'Wake me at six.'

'You're not going to try and run that marathon tomorrow surely?'

His eyes snapped open. 'Got to, if I want to make it… Comrades.'

'OK,' I said. He'd never make it out of bed but I'd wake him.

I went through and crawled into my own bed. Miranda was already asleep beside me. I lay thinking about Neil's desperation for a fresh chance and for the rest of us to understand why he was doing it. It was a bit like Miranda's new career start as a lawyer. Both of them trying to find another wave on which to ride the changes happening around us. But what about Penny's need to stay here, what about their kids? I tossed about, desperate to get some sleep before the marathon tomorrow but my mind wouldn't shut down.

CHAPTER 17

Ezekiel surfaced from his nightmare to the sound of a harrowing scream close by. He forced his eyes open, struggling to make out what was going on in the dark of the crowded cell. Shouts, bodies stirring, jumping up around him. Voices rising, spreading like a wave through the cell, louder, more excitable. Men stumbling over each other, knocking him aside. He was wide-awake now and seemed to be near the centre of the disturbance. Someone took a match to the stump of an illegal candle and it lit up a lurid scene, panic on the faces, the whites of eyes large around him.

'*Eish,* he is out cold.'

'He is bleeding bad man. Press the alarm!'

A screeching wail sounded above their heads, over and over, penetrating Ezekiel's skull like a hot needle. Bright lights assaulted them from above.

'Is it fire?' a voice called. 'I smell smoke.' More screams and a rush for the cell door.

'Jazz! Jazz Suleman won't wake up,' someone near Ezekiel shouted.

'Jazz, where is he?' Ezekiel yelled. Jazz had been lying quite near him. He tried to reach him but too many others had pushed in between them, shouting in the cramped space,

'*Yebo*, move aside.'

'That's my *fokkin'* leg you are standing on,'

'Jazz, Jazz.' Still no answer.

'He's floppy like a ragdoll. Give him mouth to mouth.'

'I don't want HIV, man. You do it!'

'Let me through, I'll do it,' Ezekiel called but he couldn't get near his friend.

'Pump his chest. I've seen it in the movies.'

Someone began to heave at the inert man, everyone around giving directions.

Within minutes, warders in heavy boots trampled down the corridor toward them, shouting. The cell was in chaos, everyone crowding around the door. Ezekiel was swept away from Jazz, his face pushed up against the bars by the tide behind him.

A posse of warders burst in, in full body-armour, brandishing guns. 'Stand back – hands up! Face the walls.'

Ezekiel clung to the bars, his hands up, shaking. The air filled with the sound of batons thwacking bodies or cracking skulls and loud cries of pain. His head was reeling, trying to figure out why all this was happening. Would they shoot? Bodies slammed into his, crushing him further up into the bars. Shouts rose from adjacent cells.

Then Terror shouted out. 'Calm your warders. There is no riot here, just one man injured.' His voice rose to a sneer at the end.

How did he dare? Surely they would beat him senseless. But a warder gave the call to halt the operation. They too must recognise Terror as the big man in here. The alarm was silenced, the air punctured only by the low moans of injured prisoners around him. Ezekiel was afraid to turn back and face what lay behind him. His brain was spinning. He wished he was still dreaming but this was a nightmare he could not drag himself awake from. Orderlies arrived with oxygen equipment for Jazz and carried him away on a stretcher. When would Ezekiel find out if he had survived?

Over the next few days, their cell was deathly quiet. Voices were lowered, even when the conversation was not about the attack on Jazz or the warders' crazed attack on the rest of them. Their whole section rumbled with discontent, drawing them together against the warders. A number of guys had been taken off to the medical wards after the warders had charged their cell. They dribbled back bandaged up, bearing all sorts of rumours that Jazz was dead, that they would all be charged with riot. But mainly the whispers in the cell were about who Jazz's attacker was. Ezekiel didn't feel safe with anyone. In the canteen, questions were thrown at their table but none of Jazz's friends had the heart to answer them, stunned silent at meals. Eventually, the warders told them the official outcome about Jazz. It had been too late for doctors to save him and now they were all suspects in a murder enquiry.

Ezekiel's heart froze. He had new nightmares now, of the cell lit up bright, the warders in riot gear charging in and beating him senseless. During the daytime, he was numb, his torpor pierced now and then by painful thoughts of Jazz – cool, affable Jazz making music, making them laugh in this bad place. Gone forever just like that. Why would anyone want to kill him? Had he upset the gang leaders? Was this how far they would go, if he displeased them? Had the spirits of his ancestors found yet another way to punish him?

****

I'd made it, I'd qualified for the Comrades. It was late morning by the time I ran up to the finishing line, the sweat running off me. Pete and I made our way over to the food counter for supplies. We each glugged down a bottle of water.

'No sign of Neil,' Pete said, looking around. 'He won't be happy that he's behind us.'

'Last night's drinking has taken its toll,' I said. 'But I'm not waiting for him. My muscles need a hot bath.'

We piled onto one of the waiting buses just before its door slammed shut. As it took off, we ripped open the sandwich packs we'd been given.

'Bram was furious that he had to drop out,' Pete said, when we stopped for breath. 'He said he could hardly open one eye this morning,'

'Neil's got some mending to do there.'

'He can't go behaving like he did last night,' Pete said. 'One of us needs to talk to him straight.'

'You're the tactful one.'

Pete hesitated before his Catholic altar-boy past pulled him in head-first. 'All right, I'll do it.' He looked as though he had made a dental appointment for root canal work.

We lapsed into silence and I sat back watching the yellows of the up-country autumn flash by. I hadn't told Pete about the meeting I'd arranged with the tribunal psychiatrist but I didn't want to bring it up now. I needed to relax, watching the countryside go by. The noon-day sun cast squat shadows around the trees. Memories of previous marathons flooded back – the freshness of starting the up run from Durban or the dog end of the down run. I shuddered recalling the year when I had pulled a tendon in my knee and almost hadn't finished the race, the spectre that haunted every Comrades runner. I'd hobbled those last miles, rather than fail to cross the finishing line.

'How's work?' Pete broke into my reverie. 'You've been very quiet about it lately.'

'Oh well, the strike is about to start. It'll begin with one-day strikes, then it'll build up. In the end we could be shut down for months.'

'No way of heading it off?'

'Not unless the government gives us the money to settle. That's unlikely.'

'Last time it turned quite nasty, didn't it?'

'Ja, this one could go the same way. And now I'm getting the blame for losing us the Swedish money.'

'You sure you're not being paranoid?'

'No. There's a whispering campaign going on. They shut up the minute I come near.'

'You're bound to get some idiots,' Pete said. He pointed to a runner in the seat opposite us who was snoring loudly and smiled. 'He's got the right idea.'

'My stock is pretty low in the municipality right now. That grant was supposed to be our golden goose and I'm seen to have fucked up.'

'It was Ezekiel who messed it up. Why blame you?'

'Mud sticks, you know. If Ezekiel was gonna try and stab me, he could have picked a better day.' I laughed harshly and turned away to watch the dry winter terrain go by. Then it tumbled out. 'I've decided to contact Ezekiel's family.'

'You're not still chasing that one?' Pete sighed. 'I thought we agreed you'd leave his welfare to other people.'

'I can't. Worrying about him keeps me awake at night.'

'Our prisons aren't nice places but he did commit an act of violence.'

'Yeah, but...' I was silent for a while. 'I can't explain... trying to help Ezekiel...it somehow helps me. When I'm planning how to get in touch with him, I find myself sleeping better. And I don't get so anxious.'

'That makes more sense. You can't go on the way you've been doing,' Pete said. 'Taut as a wire ...'

'Don't tell me to see a shrink like Miranda does!'

'No way. But you've been bottling up a lot. Remember we're mates.' He punched my arm lightly and smiled.

'I know.'

'What will you do when you find Ezekiel's sister?'

'I'm not sure...find out how they're managing. And ... take it from there.'

'Do what you have to do, man. Just don't expect most other people to understand.'

'Keep it to yourself. Miranda will go mad if she finds out.' I felt a wave of relief now I had shared my secret.

CHAPTER 18

Ezekiel winced and clapped his hands over his ears. The voices of the men in the canteen, the knives and forks clattering on the plates, were too loud for him. He sat down and took a mouthful of his food, the usual grey stew of vegetables with a few gristly bits of meat and *putu*, then stared. There was something strange about today's food. Leaning closer, he prodded it with his fork and sniffed.

'*Eish*!' He reared back from his plate. What was the bitter smell invading his nostrils? Someone must have tried to poison them. He stared carefully around the men at his table but they were wolfing down their dinners as usual.

'Careful,' he called to Tala and Phineas, his voice hoarse. 'This food is poisoned.'

No-one paid any attention to him. Could none of them smell it? He cleared his voice again, then stopped. Perhaps it was only him they were trying to poison. He twisted away from the horrible lumps on his plate and clamped his teeth shut. His fists clenched and he began sweating. No-one else seemed to notice anything out of the ordinary.

Ezekiel looked around to see who was after him. Was it the twenty-sixes gang or perhaps even Gallagher? It could be the prison warders. He twisted and turned, scanning the canteen. Someone had put a warning in his brain. Someone was on his side. He looked around again, hands clammy, to see where it had come from. He narrowed careful eyes. No-one seemed to be looking at him, waiting for him to drop down dead. The poison smelled so strong in his nostrils. Although he'd eaten only a mouthful, he could sense it rushing into his stomach and feel its chill seeping through his veins. Surely it would kill him in minutes.

'You all right bra?' Phineas raised his big bushy, grey eyebrows at him. Ezekiel studied them carefully. Did they too carry hidden meaning?

'Eish!' He backed away. Phineas' eyebrows seemed to be crawling with tiny worms. He rubbed his arms hard to get rid of any repulsive creatures that may have fallen on them. 'You OK?' Phineas repeated, leaning forward.

Ezekiel backed off, shuddering. He wasn't going to let on, if Phineas didn't notice them for himself. Those worms would surely climb right into the man's brain. Phineas gave up and turned away.

As the others got up to leave, Ezekiel sat glued to the dining table, watching them surge out of the canteen, a sea of voices, a thunder of shoes.

'Mabuza,' a warder called. 'You think I have time to waste?' He banged the table.

Ezekiel jumped up and trailed the other prisoners. He felt as though he was sleepwalking.

'Move it, Mabuza!' The warder yelled. 'You're on washroom duty today.'

Ezekiel had forgotten that. He followed the group blindly. He found himself sitting stock-still on one of the lavatories, scrubbing brush in hand, grappling with urgent matters of the spirit. And waited to die. Waited for the poison to seep right into his heart. He was by no means certain that he was prepared for a good death. He was afraid he had not done enough to appease the spirits of his ancestors. If only he had been able to see his *sangoma*. All this was Gallagher's fault. He made a heroic effort to keep on breathing, to drive the poison back from his lungs. His lavatory brush fell from his hand.

'Get to work, Mabuza,' a warder yelled and grabbed his arm.

Ezekiel stared at him. He heard a voice very close to his, yelling like a hyena. His body was suddenly moving through the air, his fists working like windmills. The warder fell to the floor. The next moment a posse of warders grabbed him from behind, shouting. So this is how it would end? Ezekiel fought for his very life. He yelled and kicked until a truncheon came down on the back of his head.

'He's gone mad,' he heard a voice call as he fell.

Sometime later he resurfaced, his head hurting like hell. He was half-aware of them dragging him like a stuffed doll, his feet following him along endless corridors. Then he was thrown into the darkness of a small, bare cell. He waited for them to come back to kill him. All this time, the bitter smell in his nostrils tormented him still. It might kill him before the warders did.

****

The sun streamed through my car windows, as I drove to my appointment with Dr Patel, the psychiatrist who wanted to discuss Ezekiel's attack. I wasn't looking forward to reopening the wound of that day but I felt oddly buoyed up by the chance of finding out more about why Ezekiel had gone crazy. Had his attack been random or was it to do with the previous time we had met, when I'd refused him leave to go home to see his *sangoma*? The question tormented me.

At King Edward VII Hospital, I followed the signs to the psychiatric unit. It was one of the faceless modern blocks. On my way to reception, I noted uneasily that it was threateningly open plan. Maybe I would encounter patients like Ezekiel.

A middle-aged man in a grey suit emerged. 'Mr Gallagher? Dr Patel.' He shook my hand. Something about his manner set me on edge. In his office he explained again how I might be able to play a role in understanding Ezekiel's case.

'What do you mean exactly?'

Patel pressed his fingertips together, forming an arc with his hands. 'It would help if you can recall, in as much detail as possible, the events of the attack,' he enunciated slowly as if I was a bit stupid. 'If possible, the actual words that Mr Mabuza used.'

'I have trouble remembering much about it, apart from running away as fast as I could up Lembede Street.'

'Cast your mind back to that day, again. Where you were, what was the weather like, who was with you. These prompts all help us to recall.'

I shut my eyes. 'I'm in the foyer of city hall with important Swedish visitors, it's a sunny day...' I shook my head. 'I've tried before. Nothing comes back, except in nightmares. But they're gone by morning.'

'Hypnosis can be helpful in recalling blocked memories if you are willing to try it,' Patel said.

I jolted upright in my seat. 'No way, I'm not trying any funny business like that...'

'There is nothing strange about hypnosis, it's not like stage hypnosis which is a con. I would simply help you gain a state of deep relaxation in which you feel safe enough to recall these blocked memories.'

'But what if… if recalling that stuff damages me?'

'In the very unlikely event of your recall of events causing you any distress, immediate psychiatric help would be made available to you free of change.'

I hesitated. 'OK, I'll try it.' What was I thinking of? But I had an inkling that remembering that day would help me move on from my nightmares. I asked a few more questions, then agreed to give it a go. It probably wouldn't work anyway.

'If you could sign my consent form. And consent to my recording your responses for the court case. You can end the session at any point if you feel uncomfortable.'

I took the pen and signed.

Patel came out from behind his desk and sat opposite me in an identical easy chair. He held up his hand. 'Relax back in your chair and keep your eyes focussed on my hand as I count from ten down to zero.' His voice took on a slow, soporific tone. 'Ten…nine … eight…seven…zero. Your eyes are so heavy that they just want to close. Let them go, relax, sink deeper into your state of relaxation. You feel totally safe here, safe enough to allow your mind to return to that day, to that moment in the foyer of the city hall…just allow the events to run before your eyes as if they are on a newsreel. Imagine you are right there, you can hear the sounds, smell the smells, see exactly what was before you that day but know you are totally safe. Tell me everything you see and hear.'

Patel's mesmeric voice soothed me into following his instructions, I heard the click of his recording machine before he faded from my consciousness. The newsreel in my head began – from the moment Ezekiel's glazed stare caught my eye in the city hall foyer. I could see the worn sheen on his uniform.

'I'm passing the reception desk with my guests…Mabuza jumps out from behind his desk. The Swedes look terrified, they back away…Ezekiel has one hand oddly behind his back. Suddenly he pulls it out…holding a knife.' I heard myself let out a strangled cry.

I sensed Patel leaning in closer. 'Keep saying what's coming up for you…'

'Ezekiel starts doing a crazy sort of dance. He looks off his head. I'm telling him to calm down, to step back…that there will be trouble if he doesn't. He leaps toward me, making horrible sounds, waving the knife at me, he's very close. I can smell his breath. I'm jumping around to avoid the knife. Everyone else has pulled back, it's just the two of us in the centre of the foyer. I can hear people leaving through a side door. I want to race upstairs to my office and lock the door but Mabuza is blocking my way. He is shouting at me…'

'Can you hear what he is saying?'

'Something like… "You pay Gallagher." That's odd, I'm thinking.'

'Anything more,' Patel pressed.

'He seems to be cursing me or all of us, it isn't clear. Something about "on my wife's grave"!'

'And?' Patel's voice is low.

'No…nothing more. Someone yells, "Head for the front door, Ben, we'll get him from behind." Ezekiel's a bit further away from me now, so I make a run for the doors. Oh God, I hear him thundering down the stairs onto the street after me. I'm thinking I'm a marathon runner, I can get away but… I've just eaten a full meal, I feel sick, I'm in the wrong sort of shoes. I can hear him close behind me…I run across the road, cars are screeching to a halt, people swearing at me. Oh no, he's followed me. But I'm getting into my stride, I think I'm leaving him behind. I glance back. Yes! I've pulled ahead and see him almost collapse, he's giving up…but I just keep running…I look back and I can't see him anymore. My legs want to collapse but I run all the way home. '

'Is that the last you saw of him that day?'

'Yes, thank God.'

Patel's voice was suddenly everyday again. 'That's all, Mr Gallagher, thank you. Bring yourself back to the present, look around my office. Take a few minutes to recover yourself.'

I came to and realised that I was sweating profusely, as if I really had been back in the city hall foyer. I felt wrecked, as if I'd vomited it back up all over the beige carpet. I was surprised to find that I was still sitting on my chair. I could hear Patel scribbling his notes. I watched a column of ants making their way up the far wall, then with shaking hands, I took a paper cup of water that Patel handed to me. I glugged it down and held it out for more. I was shocked at the way my memory had opened up, the details pouring out of me so unexpectedly. Miranda had tried to get these details out of me several times but my mind had clanged shut each time. But Patel, with his snake-charmer voice, had opened it again.

'Feeling OK?' Patel broke in. 'Miss Biko will get us some tea.'

When it arrived, I tried to drink it but I felt as though I was swishing tea round someone else's mouth.

'You've been very helpful, Mr Gallagher, thank you. It's all part of the jigsaw that helps me to make my assessment. Recalling events like this generally helps the victim of an attack too, lances the boil, so to speak.'

I wanted to smack him. 'I'll take your word for it. At the moment, I feel as if I've been driven over by a bus.'

'Take your time,' said Patel. 'By the way, Mabuza seems to be making out his attack was because of some *sangoma* woman? Does that make any sense to you?' He went on writing his notes.

His words imploded in my head. So it *was* why I had been attacked. The fear in the back of my mind was true. By refusing to let Ezekiel visit his *sangoma* up north, I had tipped him over the edge.

CHAPTER 19

Slowly Ezekiel came to and opened his dry, scratchy eyes. He glanced around him. He was lying flat on the floor. The walls seemed to be going round and round, shimmering and floating. He could see no furniture in the small room. His hands reached down to the floor under him. It felt soft, as though it were made of cloth. Where was he?

When he tried to sit up, his head swam and strange shapes spun around on the grey walls. He slid back down again. He must be coming round from one hell of a bender. He retched but nothing came up. His stomach felt empty. He couldn't remember when he last ate or drank anything.

He wondered if he had died and that this strange place was the land of his ancestors. He had made it after all. He felt too sick in his stomach to be happy about that. His hands explored the soft sensation of the floor. Slowly a memory trickled back to him of warders tackling him and dragging him down corridors. His mood spiralled downwards. The only thing he could remember before that was that he had been in the lavatories with his work-team. And then…? His head felt too weak to think. He tried again to sit up but when he was on hands and knees, he stumbled flat again. He saw a plastic cup go tumbling, grasped frantically at it and wept when he missed and the water spilled out. He had a gasping thirst.

A door creaked open.

'Water,' he croaked, trying to open his eyes again.

'Coming round, eh?' A man in white came across and eyed him warily. 'Something to eat?' He set down a plate, topped up the water and backed away.

Ezekiel managed to prop himself on one elbow, grabbed the cup and drank greedily, slopping water about.

'More!' he croaked and drank it down again. 'Where am I? What happened?' His voice seemed to come from a long way away.

'Man, you went crazy. We had to zap you with meds.'

Ezekiel's hand went like a memory to the ache of a needle in his buttock. He began to shake.

'It's OK,' the man said. 'No more injections. Doctor will give you tablets to keep you calm.'

Ezekiel tried to ask what he meant but his tongue was too thick in his mouth to shape the words. By the time he stuttered them, the man had gone, shutting the door after him. He didn't come back and darkness overcame Ezekiel once more. He felt he was falling slowly through space and he hoped the spirit world would open up and welcome him in.

He was sorry to surface later and find himself still in the same small soft room. He gave up then, days and nights coming and going, all much the same, just like the warders.

Ezekiel came to, crouched in a corner trying to hide, from what dangers he was not sure. His head seemed too heavy for his neck and shoulders to lift it and he felt a stone in his chest, where his heart had once been. Slowly he managed to lift head, to unravel his body from its tight ball against the world. His eyes had stopped reeling and he sat up and looked around.

'*Sawubona*, Mabuza! You have come back to us, eh? I will call doctor.' A man smiled as though Ezekiel knew him. He deposited water and bread, removed a dirty cup and plate and disappeared.

Ezekiel was still looking around from his newly upright position, trying to make some sense of things, when a man in a white coat bustled in, followed by the first one.

'He is doing well eh, doctor?'

The whitecoat was very strange, telling him to try and stand up, asking him all sorts of odd questions. The men hummed and clucked to each other. There must be something wrong with these people.

Finally, the whitecoat said, 'Mabuza, I think you've stabilised enough on your medication now. We'll move you out of solitary and onto a ward. We'll get you back on your feet.'

Ezekiel cringed at the thought of leaving his safe cocoon, of facing other people again.

****

I hesitated outside van Rensburg's office. I hated to ask him for a favour but where else would I find out how Ezekiel's children were? Since my session with Dr Patel, it felt more pressing than ever to make contact. I knocked on the door.

'Ben, come in,' said van Rensburg, smiling his thin smile. His office was a colourless, uptight version of himself. Shelves of grey ring-binders in neat rows, desk bare, not a family photo or picture in sight.

'I'll get straight to the point, Matheus. I need to contact Ezekiel Mabuza's family.'

Van Rensburg's face registered surprise. 'You know I can't do that, Ben. Staff confidentiality and all that.'

'For Christ's sake, Matheus. I just want to make sure his kids are OK. He lost his wife earlier this year.'

'I appreciate your concern but you're the last person who should be following this up. People could get the wrong idea.'

'What do you mean?'

'It might look like you want to take revenge.'

'What…?'

'His sister-in-law might complain of harassment.'

'Ah! So, the kids are with his sister-in-law.'

Van Rensburg winced at his mistake.

'At least tell me how they're doing? I can't sleep at night from worrying…'

'That's not my department,' van Rensburg said, looking relieved to be back on safe terrain. 'His union welfare department is keeping in touch with them.'

'You mean I have to go and ask that shit Kangisa? He can't stand my guts and the feeling is mutual.'

'I'm not sure he will tell you any more. Staff are entitled to…'

'Yes, yes, professional privacy. You don't have a human bone in your body, do you Matheus? I might get further with Kangisa!' I pushed back my chair and walked out.

Two days later I sat in the cramped waiting area of SAMWU union's offices. I wasn't looking forward to my appointment with Kangisa. Bound to be less than helpful after our recent clash at the union meeting.

Kangisa opened his door. 'If you've come to try and talk me out of the strike…'

'No, nothing like that. This is personal.'

Kangisa was silent until we were seated. His office was reassuringly human, piles of papers scattered everywhere, folders falling off shelves.

'Personal, you say?' He raised his bushy eyebrows. 'You aren't a member of SAMWU, are you?'

I laughed. 'You've not recruited me yet. I've come about Ezekiel Mabuza.'

His face shut down. 'What about him?'

'Is anyone keeping in touch with him?'

'Of course, we are. He is a union member in trouble. We are providing the lawyer for his case. What's it to you?'

I hesitated. How best to put it without sounding as though I was prying? 'I'm concerned about his family.'

'That's rich, coming from you,' he said. 'You could shut this whole tragedy down at a stroke.'

'What do you mean?'

'Because of you, he is being charged with attempted murder!'

'Attempted *murder*!' I felt the blood drain from my face.

'Yes, with a long sentence hanging over him. You must have cooked this up with the police.' His tone was bitter.

'No, not at all. I haven't heard from the police since the day after the attack. They said nothing about attempted murder!'

'So, you didn't set all this up.'

'Hell, no. Mabuza doesn't deserve that. He was unhinged that day but thankfully I wasn't harmed. He's a longstanding employee with a spotless record until that day.'

Kangisa looked taken aback. 'How do I know you are telling the truth?'

'The police have done this off their own bat. I'll contact them, see if I can stop the charges.'

Kangisa nodded. 'I'll mention this to his lawyer. He'll get in touch with you if he thinks it's useful.'

'And his children? I worry about them…'

'Their aunt is caring for them. Nomsa Silongo.'

'How can I get in touch with her?'

'I don't know about that! She'll think you are trying to cause more trouble.'

'I assure you I'm not. I'm just concerned. I know Ezekiel well; I used to be his manager.'

'You know I can't give you Mrs Silongo's address. But if you put something in writing, I'll pass it on to her.' Kangisa's voice was warming towards me.

'Thank you. This means a lot to me.' I stood up and shook his hand. Who would have thought the old bastard had some humanity in him? He was probably thinking the same about me at that moment.

CHAPTER 20

Nomsa waited at her open door for Thembu to come home, anxiously tapping her foot. As he came into the shared compound, she rushed forward.

'Something is wrong, I am sure.' Her breath came in short, sharp bursts. 'Ezekiel has not answered my last few letters. And he hadn't called you at work this week as he promised, has he?'

Thembu sat down on the front step and shook his boots off. 'Maybe he has no news to report. Prison is not a very interesting place.' He sniffed the air as he entered the house. 'What is that cooking for dinner?'

She threw up her hands. 'You think of nothing but your stomach! Ezekiel and I had an arrangement. His lawyer was due to see him. How can I help him if he doesn't keep me informed?'

'Talking of Westville prison,' Thembu sat down at the kitchen table and held up his newspaper. 'Listen to this: *Hunger strike over lack of AIDS treatment at Westville prison*, it says.'

Before Nomsa could react, the door burst open and Jabu stumbled in, blood running down his face and smeared on his shirt. He was holding a cloth over one eye.

'*Eish*, my boy.' She grabbed a towel, wet it, went over and tenderly removed his bloodied cloth. 'Thembu, get me the *zambuk* ointment.' Every day she lived in fear of something like this happening to her young son in the township.

'I'm OK.' Jabu was hoarse. 'Luckily there were four of us or I might have been in trouble.'

'How did it start?' Thembu's voice remained calm as he handed her the *zambuk*. He was her rock when bad things happened. She cleaned the wound and applied the ointment gently.

'It turned out that these guys don't like students from the Technikon in their bar,' Jabu said. He looked shaken, although he was trying to sound cool.

'You're lucky they didn't have a knife. Don't wander off your own patch, eh?' his father said.

Nomsa bustled about, setting the kettle on to make sweet tea for all of them for the shock. She knew Thembu was right. In Umlazi a young man had to watch his back, always. She was still trembling at what might have happened when the girls arrived home and buzzed around Jabu. Now the family was gathered, she could not finish talking to Thembu about her worries for Ezekiel. Or read the article about the hunger strike. Would Ezekiel's friend Kris be involved? He had told her that Kris had AIDS. She was certainly not going to tell Thembu about the letter she had received from that no-good Ben Gallagher who had got Ezekiel into all this trouble. It had gone straight in the bin.

'*Medem*,' Nomsa said to her employer next day, when she had finished the housework. 'I am so worried about my brother. Can I please use your phone to ring the prison?'

'Yes, of course, Nomsa. I'll give you some privacy.' The

woman left the room. Thankfully it was *medem* Mackay today, who had a soft heart and not that *medem* with a stick up her backside, who she cleaned for on Fridays.

She rang the usual callbox in Ezekiel's section but it rang and rang. If she was lucky, a warder would pick up and call Ezekiel but nothing happened. She didn't know where else to ring in the prison. She couldn't imagine that the prison reception desk would help, so she rang Dlamini, his lawyer. She had to battle it out with his receptionist but she wasn't going away until she had what she wanted.

'Mr Dlamini, I am sure something has happened to my brother. You must find out for me, please.'

Dlamini humoured her with his honey-voice. 'I am due to see him next week, Mrs Silongo. I will let you know his news. It is a worrying time for families.'

'No sir, this is urgent. I know something has happened. After that beating, he usually lets us know every week that he's OK. This week I have heard nothing.' She paused. 'And when you find him, tell him I will visit Saturday.'

She could tell from his voice that he agreed to ring, simply to get rid of her. He called the prison on his other line and she sat holding her phone, her ears twitching to catch his conversation. She could hear him being passed from one person to another, like yesterday's porridge. Finally, he reached someone who seemed to know something but she couldn't make out their conversation. Every now and then Dlamini said, 'Hm, hm. When do you expect that to be?' She could barely restrain herself from shouting her own questions but feared that he would cut her off. At last, Dlamini came back on-line.

'Is that man still there?' she asked. 'Tell him I will visit Saturday.'

'No, he's gone. You'll have to ring the hospital wing yourself on 273-41117. It seems that Mr Mabuza is there. That is why he has not been able to ring you.'

'Please God, not another beating?' She buried her face in her hand.

'No, not that.' His voice was softer. 'He is sick, that is all.'

Sick was better than beaten. 'What kind of sick? He must be bad to be in prison hospital?'

He seemed to be weighing up his words before he continued. 'You know, Mrs Silongo…' He paused and her heart seemed to seize up. What was this something that could not be said? 'Some men in prison…well, they can have a mental reaction to prison, especially the first time.'

She breathed again. So, they had realised his nerves were not strong and given him refuge back on the hospital ward with that nice nurse. 'So that is it? His nerves are bad. I understand.'

Dlamini sounded surprised by her answer. He didn't realise what Ezekiel had been through in the last few years, all the family members who had passed away. This lawyer probably believed the nonsense about Ezekiel ending up in prison because of the union and the strike.

'Thank you very much for helping me, Mr Dlamini. Goodbye.'

Nomsa found Mrs Mackay and told her the news.

'I'm sorry, *Medem*. Can I make one more call, to see if I can visit him this Saturday? To find which ward he is on?'

'Go ahead Nomsa; put yourself out of your misery.'

****

I decided it would be better to speak to the police in person about Ezekiel's case. It took a few days to get an appointment. I wore my suit, in the hopes of exerting more influence. Of course, I said not a word to Miranda about my visit.

I drove out on the southern highway and turned off into Umlazi township, following the instructions I'd been given. Luckily the police station was well sign-posted, a squat modern building.

'Mr Gallagher? Sergeant Victor Galu.' The middle-aged man shook my hand. In a small interview room we sat down across a small desk. Was it a room like this Ezekiel had been interviewed in, perhaps this very room? I tried to imagine him here. Had he still been crazy or had he calmed by then? He must have been terrified.

'You want to enquire about the Mabuza case?' Galu scanned the notes in his folder. 'And you are the victim of the alleged attack? How can I help?'

'I understand he has been charged with attempted murder. Is that true?'

'Here is the chargesheet.' He pulled out a page. 'Yes, attempted murder…'

'I'm the alleged victim, I didn't ask to press charges.' I said, aping his police jargon. 'There has been some misunderstanding. I don't want the case to go any further.'

'If the crime is serious enough, the police make the decision.'

'It's all been blown out of proportion. It was just a falling out that got a bit out of hand. He never touched me. See, I'm as right as rain!' I stood up and raised my arms in mock bravado. I was lying of course but poor Ezekiel's nightmares about the episode were probably worse than mine.

'It's really not up to you…it's a police matter now.'

'I refuse to give evidence against him,' I said, raising my voice. 'And I'm your main witness. You won't get far without me.' Damn, I had planned not to lose my cool.

'I see here that your statement didn't add much to the case.' He pulled out another sheet and read, 'Mr Gallagher not in a fit state to add data. Says he can't remember anything.'

'Well, I remember now and it has all been blown out of proportion.'

'We do have detailed statements from other key witnesses to back up the change, Mr Gallagher. But I'll make a note of your views. Please write down anything further that you remember now. I'll inform you in writing of my superior's decision. But don't get your hopes up.'

I walked out feeling totally frustrated. This case was a bloody train hurtling down its track and it was going to be difficult to stop it.

That evening I dressed for Habib's dinner party. Miranda had finally relented to include me and now I wished I weren't going, bored at the thought of an evening with her legal guru and his team. All I had heard since her placement began, was 'Mr Habib this, Mr Habib that.' I'd never met the man but already I loathed him. And now Miranda was calling him 'Tariq' in a breathy tone.

'To what do you owe this state of grace, a place at Habib's dinner table?' Pete had teased me in the bar last night.

'I'm reduced to being a poor man at the gate, accepting what sops come my way,' I'd shrugged. I was making moves in a game with my own wife, in a way that never happened before. I felt I'd had to crawl through muck to get into her new social scene. We no longer shared the other parts of our lives like we had done, magpies bringing home bits of treasure. When had it stopped? And now I had a new secret from Miranda. She would be furious if she knew I was trying to shut down the charges against Ezekiel and chasing up his sister-in-law in Umlazi. I twitched nervously. Miranda had always been good at guessing when I was keeping something from her.

I came downstairs freshly dressed in smart new shirt and trousers that I thought the new Miranda would approve of. She began drilling me about how to behave at the Habib's.

I butted in, 'If you carry on like this, I'll be sorely tempted to play up.'

'Talk like that and you're not coming with me!'

'Have you had a humour bypass?' My laugh sounded false.

'Try anything tonight and it's the last team event that you come to,' she said. 'No wise cracks about our profession and no snide remarks about their ANC clients. Habib is sizing me up for a future job in the firm.'

'Well, that's killed the evening stone dead for me. Any topics I am allowed to raise?'

'Your problems with the strike would interest them,' she said. That was the last subject I wanted to take with me on a night out.

'Terrific! Take a stuffed doll instead,' I snapped and left the room.

I stood on the veranda, cooling my temper. Sharpening my tongue on Miranda was something new too, as though my work persona had escaped home and gone mad. But who was this woman in Miranda's skin, who kept closing in on me, buzzing around my head like a mosquito. We both had to stop this before it was too late.

When she re-appeared, Miranda was dressed like someone else's wife, someone that I probably wouldn't like. I picked up the car keys, resigned to one of those evenings you do on sufferance.

As she opened the door, Miranda said, 'Best not to mention your parents' store out in the sticks. Might give the wrong impression.'

'Fuck that!' I said. 'I'm not going to pretend my parents were anything other than who they were. It'd be like killing them off.'

She didn't reply.

'That's it. Go without me.' I flung down the keys.

She gave me a look to freeze my balls off, picked up the keys and held the door open for me. I didn't take up her offer. She turned and slammed out of the house.

CHAPTER 21

Ezekiel sat in his chair in a corner of the ward, facing the window that stared out on a brick wall. He hunched against weird noises, against strangers wandering up to push their faces into his. This was a new kind of hell they had brought him to. He scrunched his eyes tight shut and in his mind tried desperately to cling to the image of the cool, grey world of soft landings which he had recently left. He willed himself back there. When he had flung himself against its walls, they had embraced him, bounced him gently and slid him back down. And there was no-one else there to bother him.

Here, he might shut down to those around him, to the trays of food deposited beside him from time to time but he could not escape it. Eventually he began to bring the grey room back to mind and felt safer. He allowed himself to think of other times. Until, joy of joys, Thandiwe began to appear to him out of the shadows. Before he could catch her eye, she was gone again. He held his breath so as not to frighten her away. The wonder of it, of waiting for her to slide into view again, kept him enthralled. If he kept his eyes shut and waited, she would be back. Patience, he told himself. She did come back and little by little she began to stay a bit longer. He waited to see if she would speak to him. But nothing came.

In the end he caught her eye and breathed, 'Thandiwe.'

She glided closer, her hair greying, the Thandiwe from her final weeks, lines of pain around her mouth. He reached out his arms but she turned and slipped away.

'Come to me, my wife,' he called softly. She would come next time. The wonder of seeing her gripped him still, left him contented all day, his eyes closed. Except for the harsh voices that passed by or gathered round him now and then. Then he played 'dead cockroaches' as his children once had, not moving a muscle until they went away and left him alone.

Next time Thandiwe's spirit appeared, she came forward more boldly. He waited for her to speak. He would let her lead but he could not help smiling.

She fixed him with a stern eye. 'Husband, what are you doing in here? Why have you abandoned our daughters?'

He reeled at her complaining tone. How to explain what had happened? A lump filled his throat, as though he had swallowed a cobra whole.

'Thandiwe…'

'Just like you once neglected me.'

His whole body tensed in shock. 'Ah, Thandiwe, I tried always to do my best for you when you were sick.'

She shook her head. 'In the hospital…you did not make them fight hard enough… you let me go.'

'*Yebo* my wife, those doctors did their best…I prayed for you, willed you to live.'

She slid away again, leaving him shaking. Had she died with these words in her mouth, an unquiet spirit who could not find rest? Thinking it was his fault? She didn't realise how he had harangued her doctors every day, until the nurses had begged him to leave them be. He buried his face in his hands, trembling. Animal sounds came from his throat. He tried to retreat to the grey place in his mind but he could no longer find it. He wandered arid spaces instead, his eyes clamped shut. His hands were two tin cans rattling against each other in the wind.

'Is this where the weave of my thatching began to un-fray? Is this why my hut is falling down?' Ezekiel moaned. 'My wife roams, an unquiet spirit who cannot join the land of her ancestors.' He plucked at his clothes. 'Thandiwe thinks that I failed her.'

****

After Miranda flounced off to Habib's dinner, my knees turned to putty. I'd never gone this far with her before and she was not the forgiving sort. I dreaded her coming home.

Hunger drove me to the kitchen. All I could find to eat was a battered old pizza in the freezer. I waited for it to heat up. It felt too bloody quiet with Tom and Ellen out. I didn't want to spend all evening worrying about Ezekiel's next tribunal session this coming week. Had I said too much to that psychiatrist? Would I ever find Nomsa Silongo? I skimmed the TV guide, gave up and reached for the novel I was reading, 'Bitter Fruit' by Achmat Dangor. Its characters were being pulled under by the legacy of their apartheid experiences. I threw it down. Too heavy for tonight.

As I was taking my pizza out of the oven, the doorbell rang. Mamba skidded ahead to answer it. I followed, peering through our recently installed peephole.

It was Penny. I opened the door and hugged her. 'Come in, come in! Miranda has abandoned me for her law cronies, the worthy Habibs.'

'I'm so glad you're in, Ben.' Penny shivered in her padded jacket and stifled a sob. 'I went out for milk but I can't face going back home.'

'Hell, are things that bad?' I put my arm around her as we went through to the kitchen. Under its bright lights, her face looked white and pinched.

'It's not been easy. You know Neil.' She sniffed and pulled a tissue from her sleeve.

'Tell Uncle Ben.'

'Where to start…? This week a kid at school asked Harry when he was moving to Canada. The boy's dad works with Neil.'

'Didn't Harry know yet?'

'We were about to tell the kids. We just couldn't agree on what to tell them,' Penny groaned. 'It's a mess. Harry has finally calmed down but Kaz won't speak to us.'

'I can just imagine! Our kids would go ballistic at news like that.'

'Neil is so determined to go.'

'That's Neil, I'm afraid. Can I get you a glass of wine?'

'Why not,' she laughed. 'Or something stronger? I can get a taxi home.'

I hesitated. 'OK. I suppose we both need cheering up!'

'I'm too damn well-behaved most of the time,' she laughed recklessly. 'I'll have a gin and tonic please.'

I took a bottle of tonic from the fridge and led the way through to the living room. 'Want to give Neil a ring and tell him you're staying a while?'

'Damn Neil,' she said.

Taken aback, I poured the drinks, then handed her a G and T and took an appreciative swig of my whisky.

'Why does he want this so much?' she asked, choosing the soft chair.

I sat down on the sofa, reluctant to guess at how to make sense of Neil.

'Isn't a professorship enough?' She snorted. 'A lot of academics settle for that as a crowning achievement. And as for us ordinary mortals…'

'Maybe for some, but Neil? He'll be saying, "Jesus, I'm only fifty-five".' I made a typical Neil gesture.

Penny took another swig and laughed. 'You've got him just right. Your career may very well go pear-shaped but you're not dashing off to Canada, are you?'

'Hell Penny…I wouldn't say I was satisfied at work but maybe I lack Neil's courage…or I care more about other things.' I looked up to see that she was staring blankly into the distance. 'You alright?' I asked but she didn't seem to hear me.

It was interesting how Penny and I had talked about deeper things since Canada had come up than we had in years. This Penny was a bit alarming but much more interesting than her everyday self. She was making me think hard about my own life. Why didn't any of us talk to each other like this much anymore?

Mamba woke suddenly from a twitchy dream and made for the door clearly in need of a wee. I went to let her out and stood at the back door, feeling the cool night air as she barked at something up a tree.

When I came back inside, Penny said, 'I've realised that Neil will go, no matter what I want. The boys and I will probably stay here. Neil's finally suggested we take six months or so to get used to the idea. To make sure it's working out there before we join him. I thought as long as I held onto my point of view, he would step back…but no.'

I couldn't think of anything to say so I sat down and held her hand. I took a slug of Scotch and concentrated on the warmth running down my throat. 'It could work out. He'll be back and forth to see you. Those extra months will give both of you time to think.'

'I suppose. If I can forgive him…I'm so bloody angry Ben, it's almost blowing the top of my head off.'

'He'll either find it's not as wonderful as he's expecting or…'

'Or he loves it and stays. And we're stuck here, a single parent family.' She began to weep quietly, her face buried on my arm. Penny, the great coper.

After a while, I said gently, 'So, you stay here and he keeps coming over and you and the kids visit him. You'll be able to afford it on Canadian pay. After a few years, he decides it isn't worth the hassle and he'll be back. This isn't *permanent* Penny.' I wondered where I found the nerve to make up futures for her. I couldn't even do it for myself.

'I wish I could see it that way,' she said. 'Pour me another G and T thanks Ben.' She handed me her glass and walked over to examine the books on our bookshelves. Eventually, she turned round and reached for her glass, taking a large slug.

'How about you, Ben? Are those panics still happening?'

'Not so bad now. I had hypnosis and it seemed to help.'

'You're more like your old self.' She smiled and sat back down on the sofa.

I almost blurted out that I was chasing up Ezekiel's sister-in-law but I stopped myself. What if Penny let it slip to Miranda?

'And how are things with Mirrie? Why didn't you go to the Habib dinner?'

'You don't want to know,' I said. 'Another stupid row.' I wasn't going to break the first rule of husbands – never come between your wife and her best friend.

'What was it about?' Penny seemed never to have heard of that rule.

'Miranda telling me how to behave at the Habib dinner. Including not to mention my parents' humble origins.'

'I know she's very keen to make a good impression but that's taking it a bit far.'

We were silent for a while and then she asked, 'Do you think doing law has changed Miranda?'

'Ja, certainly.'

'In what way?' She asked. 'I won't say anything to Miranda, if that's worrying you.'

'Oh, you know, she's tougher, less tolerant, had a humour bypass.' I laughed.

'How much of that is from being so loyal to the ANC?'

'Oh God yes, that too. Another drink?'

She offered her glass and recklessly, I poured us both another tot.

'To abandoned spouses everywhere.' I raised my glass. 'Whose loved ones are off chasing baubles of one sort or another.'

She stood up and we clinked glasses. 'Abandoned spouses!' We laughed.

The phone rang. 'Neil. Yes, she's here.' I handed it to Penny.

She pulled a face as she took it. 'Hello Neil. Is it that late, I didn't realise? You'll have to pick me up. I've had a couple of drinks.'

I could hear Neil's angry tone.

She rang off and handed the phone back. 'He doesn't like

a taste of his own medicine. Not being consulted for once. Let's enjoy ourselves before Mr Angry arrives.'

I went to answer the doorbell when it rang finally.

Neil brushed past me, radiating tension. 'Where is she?'

'Take it easy Neil. We're in here.' I led him into the lounge.

He stood glowering down at Penny. 'Is this a responsible way to behave? Disappearing like that.'

'Calm down. How often do I not know where you are?'

'You went out for a bottle of milk over two hours ago. We were worried.' I could see a vein pulsing in his neck. 'You think it's OK to frighten your kids?'

'Oh, for heaven's sake, Neil!' Penny stood up and went to fetch her jacket from the kitchen.

As Neil and I waited in the hall, I heard Miranda's key in the door. She walked in, flushed and smiling secretly to herself. 'Hello Neil,' she said, avoiding eye contact with me. She turned to see Penny arrive from the kitchen. 'Oh Penny, you're here too.'

When Miranda saw Penny's tipsy state, her face mirrored Neil's offended look. I caught Penny's eye and we tried to suppress the giggles, two naughty kids being carpeted.

'Come on, Penelope. Let's get you home.' Neil's voice was stiff.

Penny hugged me. 'You're a good friend, Ben. Bye Miranda!' She followed Neil out of the house.

'How was your evening?' I asked Miranda, hoping we could forget about our earlier spat.

She ignored my question. 'Let Mamba out and lock up.' Her voice was cold. I heard her making her way upstairs. At least there would not be a second row tonight. So I was banished to the spare room, again. What was new?

CHAPTER 22

Nomsa trod the prison corridors, retracing the signs she had followed last time to the hospital wing. It was much better for Ezekiel than being in the cells, she was sure. Safer and more peaceful, with nice staff like nurse Mtwetwe. She remembered how frightened she had been the first time she came to Westville prison and now it was a familiar path. Arriving at the prison hospital desk, she gave Ezekiel's name. The receptionist pointed her in the wrong direction.

'Aren't the wards that way?'

'Psychiatry is to your right,' the woman pointed. 'Press the buzzer and they will let you in.'

Nomsa didn't like the sound of this 'psychiatry' but if that was what he needed, so be it. She hesitated. 'And do you have Kris September in the hospital wards? He was there with pneumonia.'

The receptionist searched her book. A guarded look passed over her face. 'He is no longer on our wards.'

'What has happened to him?'

'That sort of information can be divulged only to next of kin.'

Nomsa tried to stay calm. Could Kris have been discharged back to his section in the middle of the hunger strike? It didn't seem likely; he would be too weak. She looked at her watch. She didn't have time to investigate further. And if Kris had passed away, this was not the time to tell Ezekiel.

She made her way down long corridors to the Psychiatric Wing, pressed the buzzer and waited. The door looked as though it had had a good kicking. When it opened, she was accosted by such a powerful stench of urine that she struggled not to retch.

A tough-looking nurse grunted at her question and led the way to a large room where there were no rows of beds, as Nomsa was expecting, just chairs and tables. Men staggered about a room as though they were mechanical beings. Some came up and shouted in her face. One rocked in a corner and screamed to himself over and over in a high-pitched wail. Another was being dragged along the corridor by two strong male staff. The man was swearing and struggling to get free. It was a scene from hell. These were nothing like the few harmless 'mad men' who lived in their own private worlds, that she remembered from her country childhood. Was this why there were no people like them in the townships? Were they all locked up in horrible places liked this? Ezekiel did not belong here. He was simply suffering from a grief too big to hold.

'Don't worry,' nurse said. 'They won't mess with me. Your Mabuza is on the quiet ward.'

She led Nomsa through another locked door and the unearthly sounds faded. In the second room she could hear only low sounds of moaning here and there. A few shadowy figures moved about in the background at half-pace. Another was curled on the floor in the corner, like a cat. The scary nurse led her up to the far corner of the room and pointed to a chair with its back to them, with a thin figure half-folded into it. She looked around her to find Ezekiel.

'This one,' the nurse gestured, standing in front of the man, who cowered as though she might hit him.

Nomsa followed the woman round to face the figure in the chair. God almighty, was this Ezekiel? She let out a strangled, 'No.'

'Yes, that's Mabuza,' scary nurse said as she left. 'Press the buzzer on the wall when you want to go.'

'Wha…what has happened to him? How can this be?'

'You will have to ask doctor,' the nurse said and was gone.

Nomsa pulled up another chair and sat down alongside Ezekiel. He had his head turned into his chest and his eyes tight shut.

Softly, she called, 'Brother, it is me, Nomsa.'

She took both his hands in hers, stroking them gently. His eyes flickered open eventually, then snapped shut again. This was a man with all the innards pulled out of him. She could just recognise a shadow of the old Ezekiel. As she worked his hands, she began to sing a lullaby she used to sing to her children, calming herself at the same time as she hoped it was calming Ezekiel.

'Tula Thul Tula baba, tula sana tul' umama 'uzobuya ekuseni…

Hush my baby, hush now Mama will be back in the morning.'

Tears spilled down her cheeks as she sang the words over and over.

When he seemed calmer, she spoke in a low voice. 'Ezekiel, it is Nomsa, your sister. I bring greetings from your

Mbali and Gugu, from Thembu and Jabu.' Her voice was shaking.

He began to cast her little glances. She stroked his hands all the while, relieved when at last he made fleeting eye-contact. But it was as though nobody was there behind the empty eyes. What had they done to him, in such a short time? Inside, her anger threatened to erupt like boils on the skin. She would find a doctor and strip his hide for what they had done to Ezekiel. How could his tribunal and his court-case go ahead? Dlamini would not know how to work with a man in this state.

When the bell signalled the end of visiting time, Nomsa embraced Ezekiel with tender goodbyes. As she tried to release her hands from his, he looked into her eyes and cried '*uMama*, mother' in a pitiful voice.

She was hustled out of the ward by scary nurse. She must find a doctor before she left but this would be no easy matter. If they thought they could get rid of her easily, they had reckoned without Ladies Committee member Silongo for Umlazi F.

Nomsa sat in a tiny box room, with a harassed young doctor. It had taken two hours to get this meeting.

'I understand that it can be a terrible shock to see your relative at this stage of a breakdown,' he said. 'The heavy drugs were necessary to bring him down from a florid psychosis. He will come out of it when he is more used to the medication. I'm sorry I couldn't speak to you beforehand, to warn you what to expect.'

He seemed a nice man and her anger began to dribble away. 'But why did he go crazy? Something must have happened?' These people must not think she was stupid.

'No trigger event was noted on the admission sheet,' he said, glancing through the file in his hand.

'It must have been something? He was doing OK beforehand. Don't you need to know what caused it, if you are going to make him better?'

The doctor explained that it didn't work like that. That the drugs worked on the symptoms, but it made no sense to her.

'I will ring Section D to check about a trigger event,' he said, picking up the phone. As she listened to the young doctor's call, all she could make out from his side of the conversation was that he was getting very angry. He put the phone down.

'Someone has been totally remiss. This should have been reported to us on admission.' He scribbled with a fierce pen in the notes. 'Shortly beforehand, Mr Mabuza witnessed the death of his friend. A stabbing in his cell. All the inmates are under investigation in a murder enquiry.'

'*Eish,* another murder charge?' Nomsa rocked herself back and forth in anguish, imagining the horror of what Ezekiel had seen. 'No wonder his spirit has gone missing from his body. The world is too much for him.'

'For a while, at least. But our medicines are powerful. He will get better, you will see.'

'Like those others next door, screaming like the *tokoloshe?*'

The doctor looked embarrassed. 'No, those cases are different.'

'How long do you expect this to take?'

'No more than weeks. Now I know the circumstances, I will investigate further what we can do.'

Nomsa's heart sank. Was this one just like Dlamini or

would he really find out? At least he had Thembu's work number and had promised to keep her in touch if anything else happened. As he began to rise from his chair, she remembered Kris and the hunger strike.

'One last thing,' she said. 'My brother had a friend on the medical ward, Kris September. He was on hunger strike about AIDS. Is he OK?'

The doctor's face shut her out. 'Ah, I'm afraid I can't say…it is not my area. And the information is confidential.' His buzzer went off. He stood up again. 'I am sorry, Mrs Silongo. I am needed on the wards.'

'You must find out what happened to him. It may affect my brother's case,' she said, as he rushed off.

This doctor was her best bet, she thought, folding the piece of paper bearing his name and phone number. She set off with a heavy heart to find her way out of the prison. The long way home on her bad feet stretched ahead, her knees ached. She had to see if she could afford a better pair of shoes if she was going to keep doing this journey. On the bus back to Durban, she couldn't get out of her mind the picture of Ezekiel in that horrible ward. The way he had called her '*uMama*' had almost torn her heart in two.

****

Every morning I haunted my in-tray in Mira's office. It was two weeks now since I had written to Nomsa Silongo. Would she reply?

'Expecting something special?' Mira asked.

'Well…yes,' I spluttered. 'I…a reply to a new funding application form.' I felt my face flush. I was hopeless at lying.

Back at my desk I tried to concentrate on my quarterly report but more urgent thoughts kept bursting through. Why had Nomsa Silongo not replied? What if my letter had been lost in the post? Or, worse, that she wasn't prepared to meet me? My mind snapped shut to that possibility. I tried to work but I kept sliding back to Ezekiel.

Ever since my hypnosis session with Patel, images of Ezekiel had plagued my waking mind, not just my nightmares. Mostly it was the scene of Ezekiel's visit to my office that day he had asked for time off to go to Nkandla. I found myself replaying it with a more helpful response from me. After all, the man had worked here twenty years. It would have been so simple to say, 'Sure Ezekiel, you deserve this. Just don't spread it around, or they'll all want more leave.' Banging on in the back of my head was the refrain 'It's my fault. None of this need have happened, if…' I knew I would have no rest until I did something to put things right. Nomsa Silongo was the key. How could I track down where she lived or worked? I stared out of my office window at the mynah birds in the trees. Suddenly I jumped up, almost knocking over a pile of papers on my desk.

The internet, of course! It's a long shot but… Nomsa might have no visible trace on the web, she might never have had access to a computer, given her likely age and income bracket. There might be dozens of Nomsa Silongos in Durban…which township had Ezekiel lived in? She might live nearby. I went to my filing cabinet and pulled out Ezekiel's folder, flicking through for his address. Section F, Umlazi. I'd try typing that in. Only a couple of Nomsa Silongos came up on the screen. One was listed as staff at Rocco's Bar…too young? The other was a member of Section F Women's Committee…more likely? I scribbled down the details for both and looked up Umlazi Women's Committee. All its 2005 members names were listed and there was Nomsa Silongo.

I scrolled down. Yes, this was what I needed. Dates and times of their meetings, at Umlazi Methodist Church. There was one next week. I could catch her outside their meeting. I would also visit Rocco's Bar while in Umlazi, to check out the other woman. I saved the details and shut down my search. I flung Ezekiel's folder in the air and caught it as it fell. I was making headway at last. Too restless to be trapped at my desk, I stood up to go for a stroll outdoors. As I walked I would think about what to say at Ezekiel's tribunal on Friday.

CHAPTER 23

Nomsa tossed and turned all night, grateful when at last the five-thirty alarm shrilled. She rose to make herself and Thembu a cup of tea. The house was silent, before Umlazi began to roar with buses and taxis carrying workers to the factories in Isipingo and beyond. This early morning time with Thembu was normally peaceful but today she felt a sense of foreboding.

Propped up in bed, Thembu reached for his mug. 'All night long, I heard you gathering *mealies* in your dreams, Nomsa.'

'Eheh. I worry about my brother.' She nursed her warm mug. 'What if his tribunal goes badly today.'

'Isn't this why we took on a lawyer from the union? They know about these things.'

'You haven't met this Dlamini. Just out of college and pretends he knows everything. He showed no respect to a woman of my age.'

'Remember, in this family we wait until we receive bad news before we weep,' Thembu said, as he did whenever she fretted.

'If only I could be there to give Ezekiel strength but I cannot take the day off. And how will I find out how it went?' She raised her hands to heaven.

'You can ring his lawyer afterwards.'

'I clean for that dragon Mrs Beaufort today. She never allows me to use her phone.'

'I am sure you can find a phone-box on your way home.'

'If any of them is in working order.' This morning problems loomed up and knocked her flat, like those steamrollers that smashed up the informal settlement on the edge of Umlazi last week. Maybe this is how Ezekiel had felt for months before he went crazy with that knife. Pressure, pressure everywhere and no way out. 'If Ezekiel loses his job, he'll have no money for rent. And how will he feed his children?'

'Whatever the outcome, we will find a way. We always have.'

'This house is spilling over already, with Jabu and the girls. How can we take Ezekiel in, if he loses his house?'

'At worst, Ezekiel can build a shack in the informal settlements. These things happen all the time,' Thembu said. 'People find a way to survive.'

'I worked hard my whole life, so that things like this would never happen to my family,' she wailed. 'And with Ezekiel in the state he is in? You haven't seen him, Thembu, there is no way he can take care of himself.'

'We will take him in then. We can roll out a mat for him in the living-room at night.'

'I suppose I could find another house to clean on Saturdays or do some evening work.'

'I can do more overtime. Mbali could take a Saturday job.'

'Jobs for girls that age? There are few jobs in Umlazi for grown men,' Nomsa said. But despite herself, her husband had managed to calm her. He always did. She could hear township life beginning to rev up outside. They must get going. The factory sirens waited for no-one and her bus journeys into Durban and up to the Berea took a long time.

'Will you tell the girls what is happening to their *baba* today?' Thembu asked.

'Why worry them all day. Let's rather hope we have good news this evening.'

'That's the Nomsa I know!'

'If it's bad news, I'm not sure I'll tell them yet. They'll find out in good time.'

They went through to the kitchen, to breakfast with the girls on thick wedges of bread, margarine and jam and mugs of strong tea.

The girls were setting the kitchen table, squabbling quietly between themselves. Gugu immediately ran to Nomsa's side for a cuddle, her argument with Mbali forgotten. The girl has taken to me like a mother, Nomsa thought, and will be better off staying on with us, whatever happens to Ezekiel. She still needs a woman's care at her age. Mbali is another matter. Mind you, she had already troubled her father before all this. She was the one who seemed to have taken Thandiwe's death hardest, no matter what a cheeky *medem* she seemed to be. Nomsa's throat was so dry that she struggled to get much of her bread and jam down with her tea. She knew she would regret this later. Mrs Beaufort always expected too much hard work and never threw in the usual slice of bread and tea half-way, like the other *medems* did.

As Nomsa swayed on the bus, hanging onto the strap for eighteen kilometres into Durban, her stomach tightened with dread about the day ahead. Was Ezekiel in a fit state to handle his tribunal? She prayed silently to the good Lord not to forsake her brother now.

****

I fidgeted in my jacket and tie, the first to arrive for Ezekiel's second tribunal hearing. The municipality chamber, with its panelled walls and heavy velvet curtains, was stuffy and oppressive. It had been re-arranged to resemble a court room, turning its familiar, wood-panelled surrounds into somewhere much more threatening.

When I thought of Ezekiel arriving, my chest tightened and my stomach began to churn. I clutched the back of a chair and tried to perform the slow breathing that Barbara had taught me. It helped a little. I reminded myself of how frail he had looked last time I saw him here. The bowed and vulnerable Ezekiel at the previous tribunal, not the man who had attacked me but it didn't quite work. Like some sort of talisman, I rubbed the patch of stubble under my chin that always managed to escape my razor. At least Ezekiel would be searched for weapons on the way in. I cursed that this was happening just a week before the Comrades marathon, when I was already tuned bow tight.

Dr Patel arrived in a dark suit, shook my hand briefly and moved on to the front. The lawyers filed in, then Kangisa for the union. Lastly Ezekiel was led in handcuffed to a prison warder. I gave a sharp intake of breath. He looked so much older, his eyes vacant and wandering, his bent figure unkempt. His clothes were hanging off him as though he had lost half his body weight. What had happened to the man?

The tribunal began but I was only half listening. It was impossible to match the images of the rampaging attacker the witnesses described with the broken man before us. Couldn't they see that? And whose fault was all this? My face was hot with shame. I should have handled the whole incident differently.

I sat up and paid attention when Patel's evidence was about to be considered. Surely when they heard it, they would see it as a case of Ezekiel losing his wits. That he was not a bad man in need of punishment.

The lawyer for the municipality leaned forward. 'So you consider, Mr Patel, that Mr Mabuza committed an act of gross misconduct because of resentment that Mr Gallagher had not allowed him extra leave to consult a *sangoma*? That he took the law into his own hands and tried to take revenge?'

'That is correct.'

'Do you consider this action was carried out in the heat of the moment or was it pre-meditated?

'As far as I can establish, it was carried out in the heat of the moment, while the balance of his mind was temporarily disturbed, disturbed by the fear that he was about to lose both his young daughters, the only children he has left.' Patel gave the lawyers that same look that he had given me once, deeply serious, a slight smile. He held everyone's attention.

'I understand that Mr Mabuza has expressed remorse that he attacked Mr Gallagher. But from Mr Gallagher's own description, it is clear he felt in danger for his life. From eye-witness descriptions too, this seems to be the case.'

Geez, put that way, it sounded bad for Ezekiel. Big-time serious in terms of the law. And my own evidence under hypnosis made it worse. When it was my turn to speak, I would spell this out that it was my fault. Tell how I had missed that Ezekiel was in deep distress. My nervous guts went into overdrive and I had to be excused from the Chamber to rush to the men's room.

When I came back in, the union lawyer was trying to put up a defence but what do you say in the face of a report like that. I waited to be called to the stand.

The municipality's lawyer paused to allow due weight to his words. 'I note in your report, Mr Patel, that the state of Mabuza's mind remains disturbed to this day. That he might well still be a danger to members of staff.'

'Mr Mabuza was doing well in prison until his cellmate was murdered. After a melee between prisoners and guards in his cell, however, he has suffered a severe mental breakdown. He is currently being treated with heavy medication.'

Ezekiel would be done for now. His lawyer squirmed around for any loopholes and extenuating circumstances that he could find but it was a lost cause. They were wrapping up without calling me to speak. My talking to Patel had made no difference to this outcome.

I stood up. 'May I add some evidence please.'

'You have not been called by either side, Mr Gallagher,' the tribunal head said. Ezekiel's lawyer was gesturing to me to sit down.

'But…'

'Please sit down, Mr Gallagher.' The tribunal head sounded impatient. 'It is time to make a decision. Witnesses and counsel for both sides will now leave.'

I was shuffled out of the chamber with the rest of them. I fidgeted in the antechamber, picking at my nails, until we were called back in.

The tribunal head declared, 'Mr Mabuza is dismissed from his post on the grounds of his violence to a member of staff and because his persistent mental illness constitutes a serious physical risk to others.'

'But, but…' I stood up.

Van Rensburg tugged my arm and whispered, 'It's for the best, man.'

'He was a good man…' I muttered and buried my head in my hands. It was over and the lawyers bustled out. I raised my hand to Ezekiel but he didn't seem to recognise me. Had he understood a word that had been said?

I buttonholed Patel as he tried to hurry away from the committee room. 'I didn't want *that* to happen.'

Patel looked at me as if I were an idiot. 'Surely you realised that he could not be allowed back after what happened?'

'What's wrong with Ezekiel?' I asked. 'He looks like a different man.'

'It's the effects of anti-psychotic drugs, I'm afraid, but the other option is more of what you saw the day he attacked you. The man seems to have given up on himself after his cellmate was killed. Such a pity. Good day.' And he made for the stairs.

'Bastard,' I muttered after him. 'You could have warned me.' But Patel was gone.

Outside the chamber, van Rensburg suggested a coffee down the Arcades. I needed a strong one. As we walked over, it was one of those leaden days, with low, dense cloud. I could picture the surf rolling into the beach beneath it, grey and churning. My brain churned too, with unanswered questions.

Huddled in the earthy warmth of my usual café, we sipped americanos.

'How long does a person stay "psychotic" or "deluded" or whatever it is? How long will they keep him on that medication?' I asked, ready to hang on to van Rensburg's every word.

'I'm no expert,' he replied. 'This is the worst case of this sort I've seen.'

'The medicine seems to have made him worse. If I hadn't told Patel what I had seen...'

Van Rensburg took on his *dominee* look. 'They said he assaulted a prison guard since your attack. You have to trust in God to see him right.'

'I'm afraid the God thing won't work for me.'

'Then trust the legal system of our country, which is sound.'

'Hmph!'

After coffee, we headed back to our respective buildings. As I passed the doorman I winced, remembering Ezekiel in this spot. If only I could turn the clock back, wipe out that day. Now I had seen Ezekiel in this terrible state, I would track down Nomsa Silongo as soon as I could.

CHAPTER 24

All that morning Nomsa was jittery. On her way to the outside bin, she dropped a carrier bag of empty wine bottles on Mrs Beaufort's kitchen floor.

'For heaven's sake, Nomsa. Now look what you've done!' Mrs Beaufort shouted. The Beauforts always had a lot of bottles smelling of drink, so the kitchen floor smelled rank and had to be washed again. Later she jumped as if someone had fired a shot, as a dinner plate clattered to the floor and smashed,

'What is wrong with you today?' Mrs Beaufort asked sharply. 'I'll have to dock your pay for the plate.'

By the time she left at two, Nomsa was very hungry and desperate for news of Ezekiel's tribunal. The phone-box at the nearby shopping precinct was dead. The one on a windy corner approaching the bus-station stank of urine and the wires were ripped out. She squeezed into the bus-station kiosk in need of a sandwich and hot tea to buck her up, eating at one of the crowded stands. Normally she would join in the banter being exchanged all around her but today she didn't have the heart. What news might Dlamini have in store for her? The tribunal would surely have taken account of Ezekiel's good record all these years. She had given Dlamini names to get references. But what had Gallagher said about him?

She felt better with food in her belly and pushed through the streams of people, to check a phone-box at the far end of the station. There was a queue so it must be working. When it was her turn, she pulled out the piece of paper with the number and dialled. For once, that no-good woman at Dlamini's reception put her through to him without a struggle. She was sweating with anxiety.

'Mrs Silongo, I'm glad to speak to you,' Dlamini sounded anything but glad, unless he was suffering from severe constipation.

'How...how did it go today?'

'I'm... sorry...it did not go well.' The man sounded human for once.

'What do you mean?'

'It was very difficult. We tried our best but...I am afraid we lost the tribunal. The psychiatrist said your brother suffers from a mental illness...he is not safe...' His voice petered out.

She clutched the phone-booth door, her knuckles bloodless and numb.

'Did you tell them that he was not himself when he chased Gallagher?'

'Yes, but he has attacked a guard in Westville too. They say they can't take the risk of violence in the workplace. He is a danger to others.'

'I see.' But Nomsa did not see anything except that Ezekiel had given the city hall twenty years of loyal service and now they wanted to throw him out like the rubbish.

'So, we have another try when his health is better, yes?'

Another silence followed. Her hopes shrivelled.

'I'm afraid he has been dismissed. There is no appeal.'

'No, it can't be…'

'I am sorry.'

The phone fell from her hand and she stumbled out of the booth. As her bus back to Umlazi swung out of the bus station into the busy traffic, her mind was blank, until she was halfway home. Slowly the bad news filtered through to her, not in words but in the image of Ezekiel abandoned, cast out into the street. She had a pain in her side that she could not dislodge, although she rubbed it and rubbed it. As the bus approached the Umlazi turn-off, her fears began to find words. How would she tell the girls? Would Ezekiel lose his house? How could he live without wages. And how would he take today's outcome in his present state of mind? Surely it would send him spiralling further down.

****

The midday sun beat down on my car as I sped past the airport and oil refineries on my way to Umlazi to check out the two Nomsa Silongos I'd identified there. More likely to be the upright citizen on the Women's Committee but sometimes older women were in charge of township bars. I didn't want to entertain the idea that it might be neither of these women and that my search that day might be fruitless.

I veered off the Southern freeway on to the Mangosuthu highway, the state of it deteriorating by the kilometre on its way to the township. Now I was almost there, I was suddenly nervous about coming face-to-face with Ezekiel's sister-in-law. What would I say? How would she react? As I passed the Technikon and drove deeper into the township, my anxiety barometer went up and up. Since the attack, I had avoided visiting our museum projects in the townships. The familiar smell of outdoor fires, dusty un-tarred roads, and the sound of boys kicking footballs on waste ground that I used to enjoy, made me uneasy. Everything here was named after Buthelezi, from the heyday of the Inkatha Freedom Party. My mind wandered back to the many killings of the ANC-Inkatha turf war in Kwazulu-Natal, before the first democratic elections. Whole families and villages wiped out. I shuddered to recall how close we had come to civil war.

I spotted my first stop, the Rocco Bar and pulled off the road. I went inside, my heart beating fast. It took a while for my eyesight to adjust to the dim interior, a typical township bar, very basic with a concrete floor, plastic chairs and tables and a few faded football posters on the walls. Only a couple of men were standing round the bar at this time in the afternoon, making small talk with the woman behind it.

She broke off and turned to me. 'What can I get for you? Castle lager? Lion Ale? Windhoek?

'No thanks. I am looking for a member of your staff called Nomsa Silongo.'

'Nomsa? She's off-duty today.' She glanced back at the board behind her. 'Not in until tomorrow evening.'

I tried to stem my disappointment. 'Is she the Nomsa Silongo with a brother-in-law Ezekiel Mabuza? In Westville prison?'

The barwoman frowned. 'What's it to you, mister?'

'I have a message for her about her brother.'

She shook his head. 'She has never mentioned anything like that…'

'How old is she?' I asked.

'Why you want to know?' She looked frankly suspicious.

'The Nomsa I am looking for is probably middle-aged.'

The men round the bar laughed out loud. The barwoman slapped her thigh.

'No, our Nomsa is hot, a young woman. We don't have middle-aged barmaids here. Not if we want drinkers!' Her customers guffawed.

'OK thanks.' I had eliminated one Nomsa, unless they were just giving me the brush-off. I made my way back out to the car. Three young boys were crowded round examining it intently.

One put his hand out to me. 'We have been guarding your car for you. Lots of robbers here.' I handed over some notes. No point having my paintwork scratched, which was likely if I refused.

I drove deeper into the township, feeling the press of taxis, buses and people surround me. My eyes flicked from side to side, searching for imagined assailants. *The Daily News* had recently named Umlazi as one of the car high-jacking capitals of South Africa. Section F where I was heading was one of the worst neighbourhoods. A bustling outdoor market slowed my car down to almost walking pace, making me more uneasy. Around me, I saw live chickens in cages, whole carcasses of sheep and pigs hanging overhead, street vendors yelling about their wares and holding out rolls of cloth. Women darted across the road with small children clutched to their hands. *Sangomas* sat selling *muti*. I had probably missed my turn-off but I didn't dare stop to consult my map. In the past, I had felt at ease in the townships. When some of my staff had been nervous about coming here, I had teased them for being cowards. Now I was one of them.

I spotted the road I was looking for and soon arrived at the Apostolic Church, a large, yellow-painted building with a pointed roof bearing a cross. I pulled to a halt. A group of women was gathered outside, talking animatedly. This must be the Women's Committee. They would probably be keen to get inside. If I could just identify Nomsa and exchange a few words to arrange another meeting.

'*Sawubonani,*' I greeted them.

'*Sapila,*' the women replied.

'My name is Ben Gallagher. I am looking for Nomsa Silongo.'

They looked at each other silently, as if wondering whether to trust me.

'I have a message about her brother Ezekiel.'

The women made sympathetic sounds. 'Ah yes, Ezekiel.' So, I had the right Nomsa.

'She may be inside,' said one.

Another shook her head. 'No, Nomsa cannot be with us today.'

My heart slumped. To miss her after waiting weeks, driving all this way. 'How can I get in touch with her?'

'If you leave a message, we will pass it on to her,' the tall woman said.

That wouldn't do. Nomsa could ignore it like my first letter. I struggled to think of a new plan.

'It is urgent,' I said. 'Maybe you can give me her address?'

The women eyed each other as if passing a secret between themselves.

'I'll drop your message in on my way home,' the tall woman said. 'I live nearby.'

It looked like this was the best I could manage. I pulled a notebook out of my shoulder-bag and sat down on the church steps to scribble a message that would hook Nomsa in this time.

'Dear Mrs Silongo,

I intend you and your family no harm. I have an idea that might help Ezekiel's court case. Please phone me on 031 311 1111, extension 54. Or contact me via email at ben.gallagher@ gov.za or write to me at the museum, Durban City hall, Anton Lembede Street, Durban Central, Durban, 4000.

Yours sincerely, Ben Gallagher.'

What I'd written was true, that my speaking out for Ezekiel in court might help his case. I folded my letter, slipped it into an envelope, addressed it and handed it over to the woman.

'I'll make sure she gets it.'

'Thank you. It is very important.' I hesitated. 'Do you meet here every month?'

'Same time each month,' one of them said before another frowned at her. I could see I would get no more from them.

I bowed my head. *'Nyabonga gakulu, hlala kahle.'* Thank you very much, stay well.

'Hamba kahle,' Go well, a few of them replied, before they turned and hurried into the church.

On my long drive back to the centre of Durban, I was fretting so much about whether anything would come of my trip that that I forgot all about my fear of being in the township.

CHAPTER 25

Nomsa sweated as she stirred the pots of *putu* and beans for the evening meal. Their small house with its tin roof was hot and stuffy when she cooked, even with the back door open. She itched to show Thembu Gallagher's letter when he came in from the factory. But she would have to wait until the young ones were settled in their bedroom, before they could discuss it.

As the family sat around the table, Thembu joked to the girls. '*uMama* is in a strange mood tonight, I wonder if she is scheming something?'

'Watch it girls, keep out of her way,' Jabu added. They all laughed.

'Can't I have a bad day without being the butt of your jokes, huh?' Nomsa asked. Her fingers twitched with vexation at the contents of the letter in her pocket.

The girls helped her to clean up the kitchen after the meal. Then she found herself in luck. Jabu had run out of cigarettes and he offered to take the girls with him to the store. Mbali never missed the chance to be out of the house, looking for excitement.

Gugu held back. 'I'll stay here with Auntie.'

'Go, get some fresh air,' Nomsa urged. 'Buy yourself some sweets.' She put twenty cents into her niece's hand.

As soon as the young ones were off down the yard, she waved the letter under Thembu's nose. 'So what do you make of this, heh?'

He looked up reluctantly from reading his daily *Isolezwe* in his easy chair.

'The cheek of that Gallagher! Another letter to tell me that he wants to visit me.'

Thembu whistled and pulled a long face of surprise. 'Have you received one before?'

'Yes, I threw it in the bin, just like I will with this one. After the damage he's done to Ezekiel, now he wants to come and crow over us.' She tossed the letter on her husband's lap and watched him study it.

He looked up. 'We must not be too hasty. Ezekiel might benefit from this.'

'Huh?' Nomsa was lost for words, hands on her hips as if to say, 'You better have something good here.'

Thembu cleared his throat and took a swig of his tea. He didn't often challenge his wife when he saw she was in this mood. 'The man sounds genuine. He writes, "I very much regret what has happened. I am concerned for Ezekiel's welfare and that of his children. I'd like to see if there is any way I can help".' He passed back the letter.

'Hmph!' She threw the offending document to the floor. After all the harm Gallagher had caused Ezekiel to suffer, to come poking his nose in their affairs.

Thembu leaned forward, picked up the letter and folded it. 'We must not be too rash.'

'If he is such a fine fellow, why did he lay a charge against Ezekiel in the first place?' It hurt Nomsa even to think about this man Gallagher. 'I thought you would agree that the best thing is to ignore him.'

'Let's leave it for now. I can see how much it has upset you.' Thembu stood up and took the mugs to the sink. Nomsa felt grateful that he knew when to let a subject lie. She began filling the sink with hot water and squeezed soap in to wash the plates.

The girls returned safely and went to their bedroom to finish their homework. She and Thembu watched their tiny television set for a while but Nomsa took in nothing. She couldn't get that Gallagher out of her mind.

Once they were settled in bed, Thembu put his hand on her shoulder. 'I know your brother's business has been very hard for you. Let us think about the Gallagher matter for a few days before we make up our minds.'

Nomsa nodded, too tired to speak. But she didn't sleep well that night, plagued by uneasy dreams involving that Gallagher. In one dream, she chased him around Umlazi with a *knobkerrie*, threatening to beat him out of town. In another, she was on the run with Ezekiel, with Gallagher running after them, vowing to send her to prison as well. Every time she closed her eyes she feared that the dreams would torment her again.

****

The morning of the Comrades marathon arrived. I woke at four am, taut with a mix of excitement and nerves. I dressed in my running gear and pulled on a windcheater and tracksuit bottoms. Downstairs I ate a breakfast of porridge, slow-burning carbs to keep me going. I was relieved that we were running an 'up race' this year, from Durban to Pietermaritzburg. It was demanding, climbing up and up from the coast to 596 metres altitude in just eighty-seven kilometres but it was easier on old knees than the downhill race.

Miranda drove me to pick up Pete, Bram and Neil and dropped us off as close as she could get to the starting point, the square by the city hall. Its lights were blazing in the dark winter's morning.

'Good luck,' she called as we squeezed out of the car and into the crowds. It always amazed me, the thousands of runners who came from all over the world come to take part in the Comrades. We joined the long queue to sign in and be assigned to one of the groups that would set off in batches. Yes, we were in D Group, so we'd leave early. I knew that we could catch up easily on such a long route but it always gave us a boost to set off in an early group.

'Geez, it's fresh,' I said, shivering in the winter morning. I ran on the spot, buoyed up by the camaraderie around me. We started our warm-up stretches, race-happy, as if we'd been sucked into the curl of the wave and there was no going back. There was a lot of milling about until the stewards began shouting instructions over a loudspeaker. Groups were directed to our starter pens. The starter-hooter sounded at five thirty am and the first lot of runners took off. I loved the adrenaline rush of that moment. My group waited, keyed up with tension, for our signal and then we were off too. Clouds of vapour rose from our mouths as we joined thousands of pairs of running shoes swishing through the dark, silent suburbs.

Lights came on here and there in houses and flats as we passed. Soon, we were out of the city and on the Old Main Road, moving north-west towards Pietermaritzburg. Pete and I ran silently in the middle of the pack, until the endorphins kicked in, then we eased into our stride and cruised, as fresh as racehorses. Trails of car lights flashed occasionally from other routes, across the darkened landscape. After an hour and a half, we could sense the sky imperceptibly lightening, until dawn broke around us in deep apricot colours. A magical moment what gave me fresh impetus.

'The old excitement always kicks in,' Pete said, keeping up with me in his odd, shambling gait.

'It's what you do it for.' I felt like my old self, the me from before the knife attack. We started up a long hill. The terrain grew steeper, the breathing of the running pack sounding like an old steam train. Sweat streamed off my face and neck. The clump of runners we were with spread out in a thin trail. As we reached the top of the hill, we spotted one of the official pit-stops up ahead. Volunteers were manning food and drink supplies for contestants and there were *portaloos* to use. We pulled in at tables and reached bottles of water and bananas. Keeping up our calories was the key to finishing the race. Behind us, the waiting crowd of spectators shouted, 'Go Kiwi,' and '*Vasloop*, Pretoria!' to a group of runners. Someone broke into 'Waltzing Matilda' as an Aussie vest ran up.

As we set off again, I said to Pete, 'I'm making progress… with Nomsa Silongo.'

'Thinking of Ezekiel, even on our big day?'

'It gives me…more juice,' I grinned. 'Knowing I'm getting somewhere at last.'

'Have you spoken to her?'

'Not yet. I met her friends outside their Women's Committee meeting. They said they'd give her a note from me.'

'I don't get it…but anything that helps put this business behind you,' Pete said. 'Now concentrate on the race.'

Several hours later, we were well on our way, only the last hour of the race to go. This was where you could relax too much and lose momentum, so Pete and I were keeping each other alert. We'd just stopped for our last top up on water and bananas.

'Damn that food queue,' I said. 'My legs are stiffening up.'

'Mine too,' Pete said. 'We have to take it easy until we loosen up.'

We started out slowly. But I guess that so close to the end, we were too keen to get there. We must have picked up our pace too quickly. The next minute, I heard a weird popping sound and felt intense pain down the back of my leg.

I clutched it. 'Oh shit.' I sat on the ground, rubbing to ease the pain.

Pete stopped and came back to me. 'Geez, bad luck, man.'

'I'll be OK. I just need to massage it until it eases.'

'I'm not so sure. I think that was a hamstring injury. I heard it pop.'

I blocked out his words. 'I can do it. Let me stand up and see how it feels...if I can get some painkillers from the medics.' I tried to stand up, leaning on Pete's shoulder. 'Oh hell! I can't put any weight on it.'

Pete lowered me back to the ground. 'I'll call for an ambulance.' He pressed his cell phone. We had all been given the emergency number.

My mind was reeling. To have to drop out of the race after a whole year's preparation and so near the end. No chance of running into the stadium on a high, with the crowds cheering. No chance of being awash with pride and camaraderie with all the other runners who limped around

Durban for the next few days. No chance of adding another to my string of completed Comrades. The shame of it. The feared nightmare of not finishing was discussed every year by us in hushed tones but had never happened to any of us before.

The ambulance finally arrived and two men hurried over to me with a stretcher.

I looked up, my voice breaking. 'Is there any chance…?'

CHAPTER 26

Maya and Sonto sat with Nomsa round her kitchen table, survey questionnaires piled high around them. Once they had started doing their prison survey, the questionnaires had spread like a bushfire around Umlazi F. Everyone was talking about it. Their committee had had a hard time keeping up with the completed ones coming in, meeting in twos or threes every week to add the results to their master sheets.

But the idea was so popular that their team of helpers kept growing. It took time, training them to explain to each neighbour the reason for the survey, showing them how to fill it in, and reminding them to call back later to pick each one up. Half of the people had forgotten and you had to go back a third time. How far would they have got without women like Sonto, giving their time to help, Nomsa couldn't imagine. Sonto's son had been on remand in Westville for over a year. She would do anything that might speed up his trial.

Maya held up a questionnaire. 'Here is a woman still waiting for trial for over two years, leaving four grandchildren to fend for themselves. I helped her eldest, ten years old, to fill this in. The mother was taken by HIV a few years ago. So, the *gogo* is doing a little illegal brewing to make ends meet.

Can't they give the poor woman bail? But they would rather leave these children to fend alone, to be preyed on by gangs.'

'This one,' Sonto said. 'Was found not guilty, after nearly two years on remand.'

'I never thought we would collect so many,' Nomsa said. 'It makes me feel less alone with Ezekiel's problems.' She was never happier than when working on something useful with her friends from the Women's Committee. Something for 'the greater good' as pastor called it.

'Time for a cup of tea.' Maya stretched. 'I am making too many mistakes now.' She knocked a pile of counted papers onto the floor. 'Lord help us!' She knelt down, gathered them up and took them to the growing pile at the end of the table. The other two stopped counting, stood up and stretched.

Nomsa put the kettle on. 'Thembu is bringing more cardboard boxes home from the factory tonight. They discard them otherwise. We are falling over boxes everywhere in this house. We will have to ask pastor if we can store some in the church hall.'

'I wonder if the others are collecting so many cases. Maybe our neighbourhood is the one full of criminals!' Maya burst out laughing. 'We'll see at the next meeting, huh?'

'Come,' Nomsa called, picking up the tray. 'Let us leave these piles and drink tea in my other room, like ladies on the Berea. What life do I have at the moment, apart from this survey, my job and my visits to the prison?' She led them next door.

'How is your brother doing?' Maya asked.

'He has lost his job tribunal.' Nomsa let out a long breath.

'Oh Nomsa, that is bad, after all his years at city hall.'

'Shame!' Sonto added. 'How is he taking it?'

'Difficult to tell. He is not himself, since his friend was stabbed in their cell.' She didn't want to reveal much about Ezekiel's mental problems but she needed desperately to share her worries.

'Poor man.' Sonto shook her head. 'Did his friend survive?'

'No, he died, Lord rest his soul.'

'That Westville is a terrible place. Did Ezekiel see the stabbing with his own eyes?'

'I don't know. I can't get much sense out of him since it happened,' Nomsa said. 'The prison won't tell me anything, while the murder is under investigation. To think there is a murderer loose in his cell.'

Maya shuddered. 'You must be worried sick.'

Nomsa hesitated and then it spilled out. 'He is out of the cell for now. That murder was the last straw. My brother is in prison hospital while his mind is disturbed. But how can he recover in that dreadful place?' She gripped her mug. 'The gangs inside terrorize our boys. The warders are paid fat bribes to let them run the place.'

'They should send in our Umlazi boys to sort them out,' Sonto said.

'Do we have enough good boys in Umlazi or would the *tsotsis* get there first?' Maya was still smarting from the evening in June when she was robbed by a gang on the way home from the bus-station.

Nomsa hesitated again. 'And now I have this letter from the man who caused all the trouble in the first place. Ezekiel's boss Gallagher.'

Her friends could not look her in the eye. She saw they were embarrassed for agreeing to carry the letter to her from Gallagher.

'Thembu says I should see what the man has to say. That maybe he can help Ezekiel, but how can that be? Just hearing his name makes me so angry!'

'Maybe Thembu is right,' Sonto said. 'At least meet him and see what he has to offer. Tell him the trouble he has caused.'

'Yes, this *umlungu* may be able to pull strings…'

'Maybe.' Nomsa drained the tea in her mug. 'We had better get back to our counting.'

****

It was five pm and I was resting my knee before setting off home on the bus. Another week before I could cycle to work, my physiotherapist had said. I rifled quickly though the post Mira had left on my desk. It was a long shot but each day I hoped for an answer from Nomsa Silongo. One letter looked promising, handwritten and definitely not official. I ripped it open.

Mr Gallagher,

I am receiving your letter. Yes I will meet with you. Come to the Apostolic Church, Lucas Mangope Rd, Umlazi F at 3 o'clock Wednesday 29th June. I trust that this is convenient for you.

Nomsa Silongo

'Yes!' I punched the air. I reached for my diary and checked the date. '3pm – *Meeting with Fielding*'. That would have to be shifted. Nothing was going to stand in the way of meeting Ezekiel's sister-in-law at last.

When I arrived home, I opened the front door and called, 'Anyone here?'

'In the lounge,' Miranda replied.

I tried to wipe the grin off my face in case she started asking awkward questions and guessed at my secret. I wasn't smiling much these days, what with failing the Comrades and the municipal strike coming to a head, so she'd know something had happened.

She was sitting on the sofa, cell phone in her hand. 'Can you believe that I feel nervous about ringing Penny?'

'I thought you'd sorted out the problems with her.'

Miranda's face slumped. 'No, each time I try to re-connect, she shuts me out.'

'Just keep it light. Don't go telling her how to deal with the Canada affair. That's what caused the problem in the first place.'

She looked doubtful as she began to make the call.

I went through to the kitchen to make coffee. As it brewed, I danced a little jig of delight about Nomsa.

Miranda's problem with Penny seemed minor compared to my worries about the strike or Ezekiel. As usual things were tense between us. It was childish but my secret about trying to contact Nomsa helped to still my anger about the way Miranda was shutting me out of her life. Now every time she lorded it over me in her lawyerly way, I thought of Nomsa and felt myself pulling level again.

Miranda came back in and sat down.

'How did your call go?' I handed her a mug of coffee.

She gave a sigh. 'I never thought Penny would hold something against me like this.'

'Cut her some slack until Canada is sorted out. I wonder where things are between her and Neil.'

'She told me. She's definitely not going to Canada and he is.'

'What! Neil's a fool then. What about the kids?' I couldn't imagine tearing our family apart like that.

'Why does everyone see it from Penny's point of view?' Miranda asked. 'Neil's trying to make a bold leap, bettering his kids' chances and Penny doesn't have the courage to back him up.' I had been thrown on the pile of wimpish spouses again.

'Let them work it out themselves, hey,' I said quietly. 'It's not that straight-forward.' I put my hand on her shoulder as a peace offering and she didn't shake it off.

I knew I should do my knee-exercises. But they only rubbed my nose in my failure to finish the Comrades. The more my friends sympathised and tried to hide how high they were since the race, the more keenly I felt it. I was suddenly not part of the gang celebrating their success as I'd always been, and it felt like hell. The only thing going right for me was that Nomsa Silongo had said yes.

CHAPTER 27

Ezekiel sat hunched in his usual chair, his back to the world. He had learned to go deeper and deeper within himself to avoid Thandiwe's accusing spirit. He dared not open his eyes too often. She would be lurking in wait for him, ready to accuse him. In time, he had developed a sense of her presence and knew when to retreat within, to block out her words. But late one afternoon, he was taken by surprise. From the shadows emerged a new figure, someone he thought he recognised but could not place.

Then he realised who it was and called out, 'This cannot be!' He raised his hands to cover his face from the ghostly presence of the bold young man.

His younger self rounded on him. '*Yebo*, old man, I see you cringe. You are worse than a dog! Because of you, our wife's spirit has been left to wander without rest.'

'I see you don't call me *baba m'khulu,* with the usual respect a younger man should show me,' Ezekiel chided.

There was a silence which implied he no longer deserved this title. Ezekiel shrank deeper into himself. 'You do not understand. I did my best for Thandiwe. I took no rest when she was sick. Cared for our children, visited her hospital.' His words trickled away under the fierce glare of the young man.

'Hah! A man who makes excuses for himself is not a man.'

'You dare to speak to me like this?'

'A man who takes a knife to another without good reason, who brings the shame of prison down on our family,' his cocky young self continued. 'Who leaves his daughters alone to fend for themselves in the township.'

Ezekiel cringed in the face of this new attack. It was closer to the truth. He buried his face in his hands. Maybe his young self was right? Had he done enough? Maybe he was no better than a worm in the earth. He opened his eyes to see if his younger self had gone. Coming towards him, he saw a white coat, followed by a nurse. He quickly closed his eyes again but it was too late.

'I know you are awake Mabuza, it's no use pretending,' the doctor said. 'I hear you are not eating. This will not do.'

Ezekiel peeped out. He didn't know what the doctor was talking about, so he said nothing.

'There are only two choices, Mabuza. You start to eat or we will have to put a tube down into your stomach and you won't like that.'

The man's eyes were holding his and Ezekiel could not break free. He nodded and whispered, 'I will try to eat.'

'You need to do more than try, Mabuza or I'll have to use the tube. And it won't be very nice, I can tell you. I can't have you dying on us.

Ezekiel nodded in fear of the man's harsh tone. '*Yebo*,' he whispered.

On this visit, Nomsa braced herself for the shock of the psychiatric ward, for its rank smell, its men with strange stares, their hobbling gait, their moans and screams. She was expecting the nurses with harsh voices, who looked as though they had done karate training in preparation for the job. Not like nurse Mtwetwe.

'He's in his usual place,' one of them said as she led Nomsa through the wild ward and pointed into the far corner of the quiet ward.

It looked as though Ezekiel had not moved since her last visit. She pulled up a chair and sat down by him, dropping her bags to the floor.

'Look at me, Ezekiel. It's Nomsa,' she coaxed. When at last he opened his eyes, his face was more tortured than last time. His eyes were glassy and passed over her as though she were some sort of ghost. As though something more pressing inside him was calling.

She touched his arm. 'Ezekiel. It's Nomsa, your sister.'

He started and stared at her intently. As he recognised her, he veered back, hands raised in front of his eyes. 'So you too come to accuse me?'

'No, no. I have come to see how you are and to bring you letters from your girls.'

'What have I done in my life, that you must all torment me?'

'You have done nothing, brother.' She reached her hands out to his but he pulled back.

'Look, here is a letter from Gugu.' She held it up and then began reading out loud.

'My dear Baba,
I hope you go well. We go well too. At school my test marks are good. Today we take part in the finals of the School Choirs Competition. I am very nervous, Baba…
My love, Gugu'

It shocked Nomsa to see that even this didn't rouse him from his trance. She saw him peer over his shoulder fearfully. Nomsa looked too but saw nothing unusual. Only a few figures wandering about at the far end of the room and one or two comatose in chairs. The window he faced all day looked out into a gloomy inner stairwell, not likely to cheer him up. What went on in his mind, as he sat here all day?

'She is always waiting,' he said suddenly in a thick voice. 'Thandiwe will wait until you go before she starts her usual complaints.' He plucked anxiously at his clothes.

'What do you mean, brother?'

'Because I did not save her when she was ill, she haunts me like this, always complaining.'

She reeled back, sounding angrier than she intended. '*Haai*, Ezekiel, this is too much! Why do you blacken my sister's name? Thandiwe would never say those things.'

'You don't see her…she comes all the time, gives me no peace…' He broke off and looked over his shoulder again. 'If it's not Thandiwe, then it's one of my boys…or myself when I was young. They all accuse me.'

She took hold of both his hands firmly and leaned in closer to him. 'Listen Ezekiel, you are having bad dreams. My Thandiwe would never say those things. She always said you did too much for her when she was sick.'

He kept shaking his head. His scrawny arms had sudden force as he pulled his hands away from her. For a moment, she thought he might strike her.

'And my Philani, he says when he was sick with the AIDS, I let him die.' Ezekiel's face was twisted in grief. He spoke in a hoarse whisper as though his son was there. 'And Sipho, he forgets I tried to save him from the Razor gang. He was bitten by the bug of those *tsotsis* and their easy money but now he blames me. He says that I was never home when he needed a father.'

'That is all nonsense, Ezekiel. You were a good father to your children.' Her voice was strong. 'The AIDS has nothing to do with you. It runs through our people like a swollen river. And Umlazi gangs, they swallow up our boys like pythons.' Nomsa could see it was no use. In his torment, he did not hear her.

'I see it clearly now,' his pitiful voice went on. 'My punishment is to stay here until I die tormented by the spirits of those I loved.'

'Nonsense. I am getting you out of here. My Women's Committee have a big campaign going, you will see.'

He sank back in his chair as though exhausted by his efforts. He was in the grip of something she did not understand. She must speak to a doctor before she left.

****

I struggled to the surface and switched off the screech of my alarm clock. Five am. The first day of the municipal strike. I showered, shrugged on my clothes, added a windcheater, then went downstairs for a cup of tea and a slice of toast before leaving the house. My bike slid silently through the dark streets. A lurid green sheen across the horizon where sky met sea felt like a warning. As I pedalled down into the city, my mind ran over how we had reached this day. The huddled debates in the canteen, as staff tracked negotiations between the unions and management. The build-up of it all on radio and TV. The opposing parties sliding slowly towards the inevitable. Then SAMWU had dropped out of negotiations and the strike was on.

I approached the city centre and locked my bike to a lamp post a quarter of a mile away from the pickets, to avoid it being damaged and went on by foot. The number of strikers milling about the city hall entrance was still manageable this early. I slipped through them, being booed on my way. I leapt up the steps to join my colleagues. Buthelezi, Moodley and Zikhali greeted me with raised hands. Maria Dennison smiled, her face tense.

I prowled up and down the main entrance. Increasing numbers of strikers were beginning to swirl around the city hall, singing a deep melodic refrain repeated over and over with variations. The crowd was good humoured for now. But I guessed from the previous strikes that it was likely to turn nasty later on if anyone tried to report for work. The harsh sound of a loud hailer began to rally the crowd. 'What do we want?' The strikers shouted back, 'More pay!' 'When do we want it?' 'We want it now!' Drums were banged in time to the chanting.

I scanned the crowd. Assembling in front were disciplined ranks of trade unionists with their badges and placards. Further back, the less organised people had gathered. To the sides I picked out the hard core, some probably outsiders come to stir things up. Some of them were cracking *sjamboks*, waiting for trouble. For later, I registered which corner they'd come from. There were some Inkatha supporters in Zulu warrior dress of leopard skins, drumming on their shields to a restless rhythm, their shell bracelets rattling around their ankles and wrists. The noise from the crowd was growing louder and louder with angry slogans.

There seemed to be no policemen around the perimeter. We'd been over the game-plan with the cops beforehand, so what the hell was going on? Our top managers were nowhere to be seen either. Zikhali and I found ourselves propelled to the front and had to try and manage the situation. I called police headquarters, struggling to be heard over the deafening noise, so I slipped inside the building with my phone. Vic Zikhali and Maria followed me in.

'Put me through to your chief immediately. You should be policing the strike at city hall and your men have not arrived.'

'I can put you through to his deputy sir.'

'Not his fucking deputy. Tell your chief this is top priority.' I pulled a face at Vic. 'It's Gallagher, head of museums at the city hall. Your chief agreed to provide a substantial police presence and there is no sign of it. Don't fuck with me man, get him now or there will be hell to pay!'

Vic and Maria cheered. I covered my phone and said, 'Bastard is messing me around.'

'Deputy chief of police speaking. How can I help? We can't locate the chief sir.'

I yelled down the phone, 'Just get some senior police officers down to the city hall strike if you don't want a bloodbath. Think how bad it will look on your record. The press is here taking photos of everything.' I shut down the call.

'We'll see if that shifts their asses,' I said as we went back outside. By now the noise of the crowd was deafening. Most were singing in Zulu the well-known ANC struggle song 'Bring Me My Machine Gun' and beating drums, sticks, shields, anything that made a din. The tempo had built up massively while we were inside and I noticed that the gang at the back of the crowd were edging forward.

'When's the next news bulletin?' I shouted to the others. 'Find the numbers of the press and radio stations.' I turned back to the crowd. 'Oh, hell no!'

On the periphery, I'd spotted a small group of our staff, trying to slip through the crowd, braving it to work. The pickets hadn't seen them yet. Why on earth had they come? I'd told everyone, 'Don't come to work tomorrow. Life and limb are my first priority. I don't want any of you on my conscience.'

Workers from the townships had been intimidated with all sorts of threats, like having their houses torched. Most would sensibly stay away. But here was this little group from my union advancing. I wished Mary Phelps had kept her old bones at home but she was always a fighter.

A sudden rise of yells and a heave near them told me the strikers had spotted them. They came to life in waves, bodies pushing inwards to block their way, the roar deafening. A final heave from the crowd and my little band disappeared under a melee of bodies. I was running on high-octane as I tried to push my way through to them with Moodley, Buthelezi and the others lurching forward with me. Our little crew bobbed up one by one and clung together, except for Mary Phelps, who had disappeared. As I pushed towards her, I held my breath until she staggered up into view again. The crowd let out what sounded like a collective sigh, before heaving once more and she went down a second time. My team called out in dismay but her friends pulled her up again. She appeared to be hurt, making grimaces of pain. It looked like her leg or hip, from the way they were holding her up.

Spontaneously, my lot formed a chain, Moodley in the lead, wading forward in the crowd, reaching out to catch hold of the stranded ones. More by luck than anything, in the end the crowd extruded them like bits of shipwreck onto sand. We passed them backwards to the building where van

Rensburg and the inside crew were waiting to revive them. I found out later that Mary was not as badly hurt as I'd thought, more shocked and bruised than any broken limbs. She might easily have been trampled underfoot. The crowd were calming down now their targets had disappeared.

Back in the building, I was shouting down the phone at the cops again. They had said they were on their way but no back-up had arrived. Now we really needed them. I grew hoarse from screaming to be heard.

Much of the rest of the day was a blur, except that it grew nastier. Those early workers were the only ones who got through. A few later groups were pushed back. The small contingent outside wielding *knobkerries* and *sjamboks* gained the upper hand. They might not even be our employees. I witnessed several of our staff being beaten to the ground and was powerless to help. From an upstairs window, someone saw Mike, from Accounts, carried off on a stretcher by ambulance.

When the police finally turned up, they weren't keen on making arrests.

'We'll crucify you bastards in the press, in the courts. You won't get away with it!' Zikhali yelled at them. But we knew we had no guarantee that our senior managers would back us up when they chose to show their faces. They wouldn't want to risk offending such a powerful union.

'Those strikers who assaulted our members will be taken to the cleaners,' I snapped to the Daily News and Mercury reporters and the television cameras. I was so wound up that my words flowed and I knew it would make good TV. Small consolation.

By four o'clock I felt as though I had been slaying dragons all day. I felt sick with apprehension, waiting to hear how many had been injured. Why had so many of our staff risked so much, when we'd told them to stay home?

'Dad!' Ellen cried out as I stepped through the front door, her face pinched. 'I saw the ambulance on TV...' She buried her face in my shoulder.

'Hey, sweetheart, I'm OK.' I hugged her, feeling bad. I should have rung the kids; should have realised that they might see it on TV.

Once Ellen had talked it over and gone upstairs to do her homework, I watched the news coverage of the strike, over and over, like scratching an itch. The broad highway of certainty down which I'd been running all my life had eroded this last few months, first to one lane, then to a narrow dirt path. After today's business, I felt myself searching for tracks in the sand.

CHAPTER 28

After the morning service, Nomsa stayed back at the entrance of the church, waiting for Pastor Mabena to see his flock on their way. She felt uplifted by the singing, clapping and swaying of the congregation. Friends embraced her on their way out into the sunshine. She loved this plain room with its peach-coloured walls. Her Sunday mornings here were the wellspring of her life.

Pastor patted the last child on his head and turned to her, his broad face attentive. He could be as fierce as a lion in his sermons, pointing out sin. But afterwards he was as gentle as a lamb. His solid frame always offered her a tent in a storm.

He led her to his tiny office. 'How can I help you, sister?'

'Pastor, it's Ezekiel. As you know, he is on Westville prison mental ward.'

'How is he progressing?'

'Terrible Pastor…God is testing me too much.' Her voice was hot with reproach. 'The more I try to help my brother, the deeper he sinks. Last visit, I refused to go home until I saw the prison doctor. I waited two hours but eventually he came. *Eish*, this one had his brain up his backside.' She blushed. 'Pardon my language, Pastor.'

'God will forgive you. He knows you are being sorely tried.'

'This doctor says, "What more can I do if the man is resistant to the medication." I tell him, "You're the doctor, why do you blame your patient when your medicines are no good?"'

'This doctor has met his match.' He smiled.

'I ask him, "Why not try stronger medicine? Traditional healers don't give up so easily." That made him sit up.'

'And what did he offer?'

'He huffed and puffed and finally admitted there is a different medicine they can try. But he says, "Don't expect miracles. Not every man can be rescued from himself". Pastor, he is telling me that my brother Ezekiel may not recover.' Hot tears slid down Nomsa's cheeks. She felt no shame crying in front of pastor. He had a way of making such things feel alright.

'Sister,' he murmured, then stood up and began to brew her some tea.

By the time he passed a mug to her, she had settled herself and was smoothing down her best Sunday dress.

'Because God sees you are strong sister, it seems he has chosen you as a missionary for his work in a very dark place.' He paused, in that slow way he said important things, so you had time to take them in. 'Satan tries to steal your brother's mind while he is weak but I know you will not abandon him now.'

'No, of course not, Pastor! But I have lost my way. I do not know which way to turn.'

He smiled at her gently. 'You forced the doctor to think again, that was your task. Are you not perhaps suffering from the sin of arrogance? To think you have to solve everything for Him?' He paused. 'This can be a danger in such a capable person as yourself.'

She looked away, ashamed. 'But…how can I help Ezekiel, if I don't know…?'

'Sister, remember to bear witness in the darkest hour, redouble your prayer. That is all God needs from us sometimes. He will see to the rest. God will show you the way when the time comes.'

There was a long pause, then Nomsa shifted in her chair. 'Thank you, Pastor, I will try.' She felt very small for forgetting God's place in solving Ezekiel's troubles.

'We all need reminding of this now and then,' he said. 'You have taken on a very difficult task. I am here whenever you need me. Remember the joys in your life too, to give you strength.'

'Ah, Pastor! My brother's younger girl brings me joy. I thought these children would be nothing but hard work, but she has found a way to my heart.'

'I see she is settling well in our choir. And the older girl?'

'She is more troubled, sadly.' She looked at her watch. 'I am sorry Pastor, Sunday School is finishing. I must walk home with them.' She reached for his outstretched hand. 'Thank you for your wise words.'

Nomsa set off to meet her girls. She could not imagine from where God's solution would come but she would try to trust him. In the meantime, she wished she had never written that letter to that Gallagher, the cause of all their troubles. She had enough to do without wasting time meeting him.

****

I fidgeted at my desk, unable to concentrate on the sheets of data, my office strewn with papers. As I stood up and stretched, my mind turned to worrying again about my planned meeting with Nomsa Silongo. Would I be able to handle what came up? I paced my office, running my fingers through my hair. I needed to talk it through with someone who would understand. But who? Certainly not Miranda. There was only one person I could think of who might understand.

I pulled out my cell phone. 'Penny, where are you?'

'Ben?' She sounded surprised. 'I'm just leaving work.'

'I need to talk through something important. Quite soon.'

'Are you alright?'

'Not really.'

'Where are you? Harry is at a friend's house, so I'm free right now.'

'Penny, you're a star. Where is convenient to meet?'

'The Coco Cabana Cafe on South Beach. It's not far from the hospital.'

'I'll be there in ten minutes. I don't know how to thank you.'

After the call, I felt my heartbeat returning to normal, the craziness in my head slowing down. The winter sun was getting low in the sky, as I unlocked my bike and headed towards the beachfront.

Penny was waiting for me in the beach cafe. She stood up and hugged me. 'What's up? Is it the strike?'

'No, we've got used to handling the one-day strikes.' I said, dumping my briefcase on the floor. 'It's about Nomsa, Ezekiel's sister-in-law.'

'Wait until I get us a drink,' she said. 'Then tell all. What'll you have?'

'Oh, black coffee, thanks.'

She went to the counter. I sat feeling blank, staring at the sea through the grubby windowpane.

Penny returned and placed my coffee and a slice of fruit cake in front of me. 'You look as though you could do with this.' She looked at me quizzically.

'Thanks,' I said and drank some of the warm liquid. 'I've tracked Nomsa down at last.' I spilled out the whole story. My nightmares, feeling to blame for what had happened to Ezekiel. How I'd gone to van Rensburg and Kangisa but received no reply from Nomsa at first. How I'd found her via the internet, driven out to Umlazi, how her friends had promised to give her my note. How Nomsa had replied. I heard my voice go juddery and I huddled up feeling cold. Penny took my hands and warmed them in hers. And all the time she made calm, soothing sounds that seemed to bring my fly-away self back to earth, as though she was holding on to me. Her quiet attention was the anchor I needed.

When I finished, she said softly, 'And you've bottled this up for weeks? Confided in no-one?'

I nodded. 'Miranda would be so angry if she found out. Pete thought I was mad to pursue the idea.'

'No wonder you feel half crazy. It's too much for one person to hold onto for so long. Drink up and let's take a walk along the beach.'

We made our way across the sand to the water's edge. The light was fading but it wasn't dark yet. I could smell the sea very close, hear the waves crashing on the sand, the wind salty in my mouth.

'You don't happen to have a cigarette on you, do you?' I asked.

'No, sorry. When did you start smoking again?'

'I hadn't, until this moment. I'm suddenly aching for the satisfaction of that first sweet drag.'

She pulled a sympathetic face.

'I had it all worked out, how I would contact Nomsa. And now she's replied, I'm terrified of meeting her.'

'What's frightening you?' She leaned in, listening, the wind whipping the hair up around her face.

'I don't know, I…'

'What's the first thing you want to say to Nomsa?' Penny asked.

'…um, that I'm so sorry about what has happened to Ezekiel. That I want to help… that it's not me making the charges against him.'

'Just hang on to that and the rest will follow.'

'Also, I need to say that I want to meet Ezekiel.' My chest tightened at the thought. But I knew from my night-time thrashings that this was what I needed to do. 'Do you think I'm crazy?'

'Daring, not crazy,' she laughed.

'You get it!' I yelled. 'You get it.' I flung my arms round her.

'Yes, I think I do.'

We both burst out laughing. And then there was a comfortable silence between us. We looked up at the stars beginning to emerge.

'We've been very remiss, it's probably not safe here this late,' Penny said, peering at her watch. 'I must get home. And so must you.'

As we walked towards her car, I said, 'I can't tell you how much this has helped, Penny. I'm sorry it's been all about me.'

She gave me a little push towards my bike. 'My turn next time. Talk to Nomsa. And let me know how it goes.'

CHAPTER 29

As Nomsa entered the church hall, Maya called out, 'Welcome, sister. We thought you couldn't make it this evening.'

Hlengiwe, their chairwoman, frowned at Nomsa's late arrival. She passed round the survey summaries of the data collected and began to read. 'One in five families returning our survey has experiences of Westville prison.'

There was a ripple of excitement around the table. Nomsa knew the results already because she had helped to write the report. The men and women of Umlazi had poured out to interviewers their sad and angry stories about Westville prison and about long waits on remand. Hundreds of completed survey forms had rolled in, full of complaints from relatives of prisoners.

Hlengiwe continued to read. 'Four fifths of charged residents were waiting at least two years for trial.' She paused. 'One third waited more than three years.'

There were gasps round the table. 'Mother of God, how do families cope if it is the main breadwinner?' Thonko asked.

Nomsa didn't know whether to be outraged or hopeful, now she knew there were so many others like Ezekiel.

'Now people will expect too much of us,' Hlengiwe said. 'I have already received many letters from residents pressing us to do something about the situation.'

Nomsa wanted to stamp her foot at the timidity of the woman. 'Surely this is exactly the result we hoped for. The survey was just the start.'

There were mutters of agreement around the table. 'We must take up their challenge,' Ingwe said.

'This support from the community can make us as strong as lions,' Ingwe spoke, her vision powerful. 'Together we can force the authorities to do something about this problem!'

'We will need a lawyer to advise us,' Thonko added.

'We must circulate this report to those with authority in Umlazi,' Nomsa said. 'And to all members of the community.'

'We need to develop a set of demands,' Maya said excitedly. It is a while since we have taken on a big project like this.'

'It would make us stronger to have other Umlazi sections involved.'

'How long will it take to collect such wider results?' Nomsa asked, picturing Ezekiel in torment in the prison mental ward. How much longer could he survive?

The meeting ended on high hopes. As others said their goodbyes, Nomsa lingered around the table with a few friends.

'This is good for Ezekiel's case,' Thonko smiled. 'How are things with him?'

'Not so good. Pastor tells me to trust God to show the way but how can I trust those doctors at Westville?'

'Sister, God will direct those doctors,' Maya said.

'Yes, yes. But now my brother has lost his job, how will he live? God may not have his eye on that side of it.'

'What will you do?' Ingwe asked.

'I will ask the municipality for help with his rent but I am not hopeful. And I am trying to find a new lawyer who will not just sit on his hands.'

'When my cousin was too ill to work, the government gave him disability benefits. His wife was on her knees giving thanks to Mandela. None of us had heard of such a thing in the old days.'

Nomsa sat up. 'You think it might be the same if you can't work because your mind is disturbed?'

None of them realised that Hlengiwe had poked her head back round the door. 'Surely they don't give benefits for someone who is in prison. For doing things like your brother did?'

'He has not been found guilty. You know nothing about these things!' Nomsa's voice wavered. She didn't want that know-all to see her cry.

'Let's wait until Nomsa investigates,' Maya said. 'So many new things are possible now we have democracy.'

Hlengiwe turned to leave, her voice honey sweet. 'I hope you are right. Goodbye.'

'One day I won't be responsible for what I do to that woman,' Nomsa said.

****

Driving through Umlazi didn't faze me this time. I was wound up so tight about meeting Nomsa Silongo that I hardly noticed my surrounds. How would she react to me? So much hung on the outcome. I pulled into the dusty car park of the Apostolic Church, locked my car and walked towards the door.

A buxom, middle-aged woman came forward. She was not smiling.

'Mr Gallagher?' I could see from her stiff posture that this wasn't going to be easy.

'Mrs...Silongo, *sawubona. Unjani wena?*' I reached out to shake her hand.

She didn't respond, simply nodded and led me into the church hall. 'We can find a cup of tea over in the corner.'

'Yes please. Black coffee for me if you have it.'

I followed her across the length of the room. Knots of people were coming and going; there was the steady hum of voices from open doors. Ezekiel's sister-in-law was a good-looking woman who seemed to command the respect of the people who greeted her as she passed. When we reached the back of the hall, she poured tea and coffee into paper cups from large urns and handed me one. We sat down at one of the wooden tables nearby. Her silence made me jumpy. My own voice seemed to have dried up.

'You wanted to meet me?' She said finally, a note of challenge in her voice.

'Yes...How is Ezekiel?' My rehearsed opening lines had abandoned me.

'What do you expect? His arrest has broken him.' Her voice was bitter.

I nodded. 'He looked in a very bad state at the tribunal.'

'Are you satisfied now?'

'No. It was terrible to see him like that. Ezekiel is a good man. What he did that day was totally out of character.' I turned away to break her accusing gaze.

When I looked back, her eyes were still boring into me. 'Then why did you not give him another chance with his job?'

I shifted in my seat, my hands clammy. 'I tried to speak at the tribunal; to say that Ezekiel has been a good worker all these years, but it was settled between the lawyers. They said there was no chance, after what he did…that he could be a risk to the public.'

Just then, a man in pastor's garb came up to our table, smiling. 'Ah, Nomsa, I hear your prison survey is producing results. And who is our visitor?'

'*Sawubona* Pastor.' Her voice was honey. 'This is Mr Gallagher, Ezekiel's boss.'

The pastor reached his hand out to me. 'I hope you can do something for our brother in his troubles.'

'I hope so too,' I replied, keeping hold of his hand for too long.

'Good, good.' The pastor patted my back and moved on to the group a the next table.

Nomsa's eyes switched back to hostile. 'Then why did you have Ezekiel arrested? If you knew he is not a bad man.'

'No, no…I didn't ask for him to be charged.'

'But what did you do to stop it? Heh? And what did you do to provoke him? Due to you, he is sitting in the prison mental hospital.'

My skin was sweaty. I should never have come. Nomsa had put her finger on my guilt. Not giving Ezekiel leave to see his *sangoma*. It rose in my gullet and almost choked me.

'It is true, I refused your brother three days leave to go to Nkandla to see his *sangoma,* because…because he had already had so much extra leave…for his wife's illness…' My voice trailed away. It would have been such a small thing to give, I could see that now.

'Thanks to you, Ezekiel is losing his mind. He is a broken

man.' Tears seeped from under Nomsa's eyelids and she brushed them away with an impatient hand.

'I…I was hoping… I might be able to…help Ezekiel in some way.'

'Huh! A fine thing. After having him arrested!' Her voice was razor-sharp.

'Truly, it wasn't me. My wife was angry with me for not calling the police.'

'Then who did call them?'

'Probably staff at city hall. I thought the police would hold him until he calmed down, not send him to prison.'

'It is easy to say that now!'

I felt hot with shame at making excuses for myself. It felt airless in the hall. We both reached for our tea which had gone cold.

'I didn't want anything bad to happen to Ezekiel,' I said.

'Then how come he is charged with attempted murder?' Her voice rose.

'Attempted murder!'

'Yes, attempted murder. Someone must have told the police that. Ezekiel would never do such a thing.' Under her bravado, her face looked worn and tired. 'He has had so many deaths these last few years. It has disturbed him but not enough to do *that*.'

I found myself shaking. The horror of that afternoon began to flood back into my mind. The knife so close to my eyes, the terror of running for my life…

'Ezekiel leapt at me with a knife, waving it in my face, shouting. Everyone there was terrified. I ran out of the door but he chased me up the street…'

Nomsa's face sagged visibly at my words. 'He came at you with a knife? He waved it in your face?'

'Yes, I thought he would kill me...'

'I...I am sorry, Mr Gallagher, I did not know...' She looked down and fiddled with her hands.

'It was not the Ezekiel we knew,' I said. 'He seemed out of his mind and determined to stab me. People were fleeing from him in the street. Luckily I am a marathon runner, so I got away.'

'I didn't know...Ezekiel doesn't remember even now what happened that day. Why he had the knife on his person or what he did with it.'

'It was not Ezekiel,' I said again. 'Something had pushed him over the edge.'

She nodded. We sat in silence for a long while. Then she asked in a softer voice, 'If you wanted to help him, why did it take you so long?'

I shifted uncomfortably in my chair. 'I thought he might still want to harm me. Until I saw him at his tribunal. So frail, I could not believe it was Ezekiel.'

'Yes, it is shocking how thin he is now.'

'Why are they treating him so harshly?'

'It is the way in Westville prison. It is very wrong.' Nomsa slumped forward, her elbows on the table.

'Let me get you more tea.' I stood up and went to the urn.

We sat with our hot drinks. 'Has he got a good lawyer?' I asked.

Her anger towards me completely gone, Nomsa filled me in about Ezekiel's case. She ended with his sorry state of mind since the murder of his friend Jazz.

'So it is Dlamini, his lawyer, that is the biggest problem?'

She nodded. 'And the long wait for his case to come to court.'

'Maybe I can add some pressure on this lawyer? And offer to be a witness for Ezekiel's case,' I said.

'Come with me to see him. Two against one is always better.' She showed a ghost of a smile.

CHAPTER 30

The housing officer stabbed at Nomsa with her long, red fingernail, her voice rising to a crescendo. 'You think the municipality is made of money. That we can afford to give your brother rent free?'

Nomsa found herself speechless for once. What has she done to upset the woman? She should be the one who was angry. She had been kept waiting for over half an hour, while this woman discussed with her colleague who was sleeping with who in their department, within Nomsa's hearing. Until she had stood up and poked her head through their open door to say, 'I am a busy woman. I have no more time to listen to your gossip!' Did they have no manners, these black girls with smart jobs, smart suits and expensively straightened hair, treating their elders like this?

'How are we to provide services when half the population in Umlazi doesn't want to pay their rent, huh?' The woman paused for breath and Nomsa was in there.

'Who said my brother doesn't *want* to pay his rent? He has been a working, rent-paying citizen all his life. If he could pay, he would.' Now she held the floor, she wasn't going to let go. 'He has lost his wife and his life-long job at city hall. It has affected his mind, so now he is on a mental ward.' She didn't mention Westville prison. It would only complicate matters.

'You plan to throw him and his children out on the street?' Nomsa could play the drama queen when she needed to. 'Your job is to give me advice on these matters. Is there no way to tide him over? The hospital told me he can claim disability benefit when he comes out.' Her voice rose, beating the stale air in the office. She saw the fight in her opponent start to collapse like a punctured balloon.

'Everyone in this township wants free housing,' the woman grumbled as she went to a filing cabinet and ran her fingers through a drawer. Grudgingly she passed over a leaflet to Nomsa. 'Here are your options. If you think he is eligible, fill in the application form for assistance via a rent-waiver and return it here. That does not mean he will get it. There are a lot of shameless people trying to wriggle out of their rates and rent. We are wised-up to all the tricks.'

Nomsa bristled at being included in this group of no-goods but she decided to keep quiet for now. She rose with all the dignity she could muster.

The housing officer stood up, hands on hips.

Nomsa's hands flew to her own more intimidating hips. 'You have not heard the last from me.'

She left the office clutching the Assistance with Rates and Rents leaflet like a prize. She would be home late because of that damn fool woman and her gossiping session.

****

That Saturday morning, I walked with Miranda, Penny and Harry through the bush of Stainbank Nature Reserve, its wild fig trees looming huge above us. I was keeping us busy over the weekend to distract Miranda, afraid that somehow my meeting with Nomsa Silongo would leak out. She was a long way off forgiving me yet for missing her dinner with Habib. Or for not agreeing to go over to the UK to be with Michael on Liz's upcoming anniversary. I was hoping Pete might go instead. I shuddered at the thought that Mirrie might find out that Ezekiel's case was the true reason I didn't want to go to Sheffield.

I'd risen early that morning to pack a picnic, earning my passage back into my wife's affections. I'd invited Penny and Harry to cheer them up. They'd been low since Neil's departure for Canada. And their presence would make a row with Miranda less likely.

'How's Neil getting on?' I asked Penny as we walked along one of the trails.

'Who knows? He makes out Canada's perfect. I don't think he'd tell me if it wasn't.'

'I'm missing the old bastard,' I said.

'He talks mainly to Harry when he rings,' Penny said. 'I don't have much to say to him. And I don't want the details of his Canadian adventure. Kaz is still too angry to speak to him at all.'

Then Penny and Miranda drifted ahead, their bodies stiff as they made tentative overtures to each other after their recent falling-out. I'd never seen them like this before. Harry latched onto my side, a substitute dad for the day. I pulled a bird book out my pocket and showed him how to identify first a bulbul and then a black-collared barbet.

'What else will we see?' he asked.

'Keep your eyes peeled for other birds. And if we're lucky... zebra, different sorts of buck, *dassies*, maybe snakes.' I pointed each one out in the Stainbank pamphlet.

'Mambas and pythons?'

'Big ones like that aren't likely but you should always keep your eye out for snakes in the bush.' I found myself enjoying the role of tutor. Neil was not an outdoor type, so some of this might be new to Harry.

In the back of my mind, I gnawed away at Ezekiel's case. Normally I talked my worries over with Miranda but not this time. She would have been the best person to advise me on the legal aspects of the case. I wondered briefly, if I explained properly, whether she might just understand but I dared not risk it. I wasn't sure of anything with Miranda any longer.

Around lunchtime we came to a riverbank which made an ideal picnic spot. Above our heads, a troupe of vervet monkeys chattered in the trees. Harry gulped down his lunch and wandered off to explore the reeds by the river's edge. I sat back, feeling the tension ease from my body. Nothing like being in the bush.

'Have you decided whether to go to Sheffield for Liz's anniversary yet?' Penny asked me. I tried to signal to head her off the subject.

But Miranda pounced. 'Ben should have booked a flight by now.' She gave me a sharp look. 'He's Michael's oldest friend. But work comes first, of course, always work. Before family, before friends or sorting himself out.'

I stayed silent. Miranda was winding herself up and nothing I said would help. Her list of grievances was like a broken record. She jumped up and stomped off towards the river, calling in a tight voice, 'Harry, come and see this swarm of blue butterflies.'

'Sorry…I should have thought,' Penny said.

'Don't worry, it's an ongoing subject.' We watched Miranda and Harry following the butterflies.

'Have things been this bad since that night we were both in the dogbox?' Penny asked. 'I don't know what's happening to us all, Ben.'

'It'll sort itself out,' I said unconvincingly. 'Listen, I met up with Ezekiel's sister Nomsa.'

'How did it go?'

'Much better than expected. I'm going with her to see Ezekiel's lawyer. See if we can push his case on.'

'Things have really moved on since we last talked.' She smiled.

'Nomsa Silongo is an amazing woman, you'd like her.'

'Have you seen Ezekiel yet?'

'No but I'm hoping to.'

'Does Miranda know anything?'

'No, and for chrissakes don't tell her.'

'I understand.' Penny made patterns in the sand with her finger. 'Mirrie can be a bit black and white about things.'

I peered over my shoulder nervously and spotted Miranda making her way back to us.

'You missed a treat,' she said as she sat back down. 'I've never seen so many butterflies all together like that. Spring is on its way.' There was a short silence. 'You haven't scoffed all the ginger cake, have you?' She found it and cut a slice.

'We'd better get going,' I said after we'd all had a slice of cake with the last of the tea in our flasks. We gathered up the remains of our picnic. I found it more difficult to pack away my unfinished conversation with Penny.

PART THREE

CHAPTER 31

After Nomsa's meeting with Gallagher and Dlamini, she sailed out of the building, her head steaming like a fresh pile of cow's dung. That man made her so angry. And Gallagher hadn't been as much use as she'd hoped. But at least he had seen what Dlamini was like, twisting this way and that to avoid answering their questions. Her throat was dry from battling her points with that donkey, so she was happy when Gallagher offered to buy her a coffee.

He led the way down the street and stopped outside a smart-smart cafe. She'd never been inside anywhere like this before.

He held open the door but she hesitated to step inside, although she was fascinated by the place. Inside there were black people as well as whites, all dressed like people in magazines. She felt out of place. I am neat and tidy, she thought, and I have nothing to be ashamed of. So she held her head up high and walked in.

'Try their coffee,' he said. 'You can choose latte, espresso, americano, cappuccino.' His eyes were wide with delight.

She shook her head. 'Tea please.' What was it with this *umlungu?* He was such a child at times. A hot drink was a hot drink and she didn't know what all those fancy names meant.

She squeezed her bulk into a slide-in seat. The air was filled with delicious smells she didn't recognise. She eyed the cakes and biscuits on other tables, the fancy cups and saucers, just like in the posh houses she cleaned on the Berea.

A waitress came to take their order. Gallagher said, 'One English breakfast tea and one cappuccino. And a lemon drizzle cake and a chocolate torte please. We're starving.'

Nomsa looked around. The black women were dressed in tight fashionable clothes. Blacks and whites mixing as if they were friends. Is this what went on in the CBD, as she must learn to call the city centre? At the table next to her, a group of black people were speaking English to each other. Although she could understand each word on its own, it made no sense, full of strange words like NGO, CBD and BEE. She shook her head.

The waitress returned and set down their drinks and some odd shapes on a plate.

'Which would you like?' he asked.

'I have never tasted them before,' she said stiffly.

'Then you must try a piece of each.' He cut them in half and passed her a plate.

As she bit into the lemon drizzle piece, she couldn't help herself letting out an appreciative 'Ooh!'

She dusted sugar off her fingers. 'What did you think of Dlamini?'

'I can see why you are fed-up with him,' Gallagher said. 'A blatherer who avoided our questions.'

'Why didn't you tell him straight to get Ezekiel out of prison? You were too polite. He will think he can push you around.'

'I'm holding fire for our next meeting,' he said. 'Just sussing him out today. Lulling him into a false sense of security.'

'You did ask him a lot of questions, yes. Like a dog gnawing its bone.'

'So, what do we do next?' Gallagher asked.

'You heard him. When I tell him to move ahead with the case, he says he can get no sense out of Ezekiel. But he is the lawyer, he must decide the way ahead,' Nomsa said, turning away. The smell of Gallagher's coffee nauseated her.

'I get the impression Dlamini and the union have lost interest in Ezekiel's case.'

'Because he is no longer of any use to their strike.'

'Then we will have to get rid of him.'

She was shocked. 'But the union is paying for Dlamini. He is their lawyer.'

He tapped his fingers on the tabletop for a while then said, 'We will just have to find a better lawyer.'

'No, no, my family have no money,' she said. Gallagher was getting carried away.

'Just one session. Sometimes there are free clinics. Or we will raise funds somehow.'

'You know so much about lawyers, heh?' she challenged.

He laughed. 'My wife is training to be a lawyer.'

'*Haai!*' This man was full of surprises. 'Tell me more about this free clinic.'

'Some are run by trainees of law firms. And university law lecturers do clinics too, to keep up their skills. I will find us one.'

'The Umlazi Women's Committee is also working on Ezekiel's case. We can each chase our side of the problem.' She described the survey they were carrying out about Westville prison and the long waiting times to get cases heard.

'That's excellent. The new lawyer can maybe use that information. Let's meet up again when either of us has more information,' he said.

'Leave a message with Thembu at work, like last time,' Nomsa said, wiping her sticky fingers on the serviette. She had a satisfied feeling that they had achieved something here. But it was only an idea; they had no new lawyer yet.

'In the meantime,' Gallagher asked. 'Would you like to write Dlamini a letter demanding action? And giving him a deadline to achieve it?'

'Maybe you know better the right language to use? As your wife is a lawyer.'

'OK. I'll send you a draft to check first.'

'Yes.' She hesitated. 'My brother's doctor in Westville says Ezekiel's best chance to improve is to get out of prison. They give better medicines for his condition outside prison. And they offer other treatments too.'

Gallagher nodded. 'We can't leave it to Dlamini.'

'We must teach him how to do his job or get rid of him,' Nomsa chuckled. 'We cannot fight him with sweet medicine only.' She was suddenly buoyed up with hope. It was easier fighting this lawyer with two. She looked at the time.

'*Eish*, I must get home for the children.'

On her way to the bus station, she crossed the square and looked up again at the statue of the fat lady with the crown. 'Maybe this Gallagher is not so bad, hmm, lady?'

****

The smell was what I would remember most from the all-out strike. The bin-men were out solidly and in the city centre the rotten stench of overflowing rubbish hit you full on. Each morning I'd hunch into the building, past figures shouting 'scab' and waving placards in my face. Most of the ugly anger from the early days had evaporated and the pickets sullenly let in those of us who weren't in their union. More noise and ritual than anything, now the police were back keeping watch.

The strike had given rise to a thriving temporary village on the city hall steps; makeshift shelters, hawkers selling ice-cream, hot food and drinks. The ground was slippery underfoot with accumulated orange peel and discarded sandwiches. Empty packets blew around in the August wind. The smell of stale urine rose from the corners. I'd slip indoors, past the empty doorman's post and up the dirty stair-carpet. Then, just when I thought I was almost used to it, something horrible would catch me, like vomit rising. On Monday, a schoolboy trying to gain access to the library had the hell beaten out of him. He was carried in, blood leaking from his pulpy face. The culprits claimed he'd given them some lip about the strike.

The strike affected my fellow managers in different ways. Griffiths would rush into the building waving his hands, saying, 'These streets are apocalyptical; something awful is going to happen!' None of us would have expected him to turn panicky. Moodley was his usual self, as though nothing out of the ordinary was happening, every crease of his tailored suit in place. I felt numb, coming and going like a mechanical thing. I would need to sleep for a month when it was all over. I was on sleeping pills, otherwise I prowled the house all night, worrying about every bloody thing. Miranda said I was driving her to distraction, so I was back in the spare room. When I looked in my shaving mirror, I hardly recognised the face I met – grey skin, bloated around the eyes, a fish-like mouth. I couldn't even rise to giving myself a morning pep-talk.

Every day I expected one side or the other would cave in, but both the union and management negotiators kept holding out. Then one afternoon a young bloke from Libraries ran in yelling, 'The strike's over!' No-one believed him; we thought it was a silly prank. When someone else confirmed it, everyone started whooping with joy and turning radios on to check the details. They shouted down their cell phones, spreading the news. The union had finally settled for a small concession from management. Too many strikers had been drifting back to work, unable to support their families.

I'd been in the secretaries' office when I heard the news and found myself clutching Mira's desk as waves of tiredness threatened to topple me. This is good, it's over, I told myself. But I didn't feel good. Just a sense of what a mess. And sympathy about how much the strikers had been through for so little gain. On my way back to my office, putting one foot in front of the other seemed difficult. Nothing a few good nights' sleep wouldn't sort out, I told myself. In the privacy of my office, I laid my head down on my desk.

By the time I left work, I was strangely unsettled. I slung on my shoulder-bag and headed down to the Mazda dealers to pick up my car. Waiting to exit, I watched people criss-crossing the city square or driving round it, all with a sense of purpose, while I wasn't sure what to do next. I couldn't simply drive home and watch TV now the strike was over. The sense of everything pressing down inside me was urgent.

I found myself driving past the racecourse, heading towards the Umgeni river, past the bird park in the old quarry site, deafened by all the different bird calls at the end of the day. The squawking of parrots, macaws and hornbills reminded me of the agitation around the city hall during the strike. As I approached the river mouth, pelicans flapped low over the reed-beds. I swung north up the freeway, not sure where I was going, whizzing on past each turn-off. I could keep going all the way up the North Coast, surrender to impulse and take off to a game reserve for a couple of days. I laughed out loud, a buzz of adrenalin tingling through me. When had I last done something this spontaneous?

As I approached Umhlanga Rocks, I pulled into a parking bay overlooking the sea and stepped out of the car. I stood watching the waves roll in and spread up the sand as the sun was setting behind me.

My cell phone vibrated in my pocket but I ignored it. I didn't want the world to intervene in my reverie. It stopped and then rang again, on and on.

I gave in. 'Hello.'

'Ben. It's urgent. Please come home…' Miranda's voice broke.

'Mirrie, what's wrong?'

'Michael Drummond phoned from Sheffield…it was awful. He sounded suicidal.'

'Shit! Give me twenty minutes to get home. I'm up at Umhlanga.'

I jumped into my car and raced back down the freeway, my mind running over possible bad scenarios with Michael. It was darkening now and the oncoming headlights half blinded me. I got stuck behind a lorry and couldn't overtake. This was supposed to be a fucking freeway. I managed to pass it and pumped the accelerator, the blazing spread of Durban's lights pulling me towards them.

I reached home and pulled the car into our drive at a crazy angle and leapt out.

Miranda was waiting at the front door. 'Thank God you're back.' She choked up. 'It was so frightening with Michael…' Tears ran down her cheeks.

'Hey, hey, it's all right.' I wrapped my arms around her. I was not used to my fierce warrior girl being this vulnerable.

'He's in a bad way, Ben. He rang for you but it all spilled out. He was pretty drunk.'

My pulse slowed down a bit. 'Yeah, he's been hitting the bottle lately. It could have been just the drink talking. He's probably sobered up and has forgotten what he said.

Miranda shook her head. 'He wasn't threatening to do it this minute. But he sounded deadly serious about killing himself.'

'Oh God. Let's go inside.' We went in and sat at the kitchen table. 'What exactly did Michael say?'

'Stuff about life not being worth living without Liz. How he's on his way down…to day zero.'

'So it's not an immediate threat of suicide? We don't have to alert UK emergency services. At least that gives us time to think.'

'He said he was thinking of finishing it before Liz's anniversary.'

'God! I better speak to him right now.' I picked up my phone and called Michael's number. 'He's not answering. Let's ring Rosa, see if she knows her dad's in a state. She lives in Sheffield, doesn't she?' I scrolled through my mobile numbers. 'Nothing under Drummond. Does she use her married name? But what the hell is it?'

'It began with "B" didn't it? Bennett? Bernard?'

'Pete will know. He was there last year.' I punched his

name on my cell phone. 'Damn. No answer.' I was trying to think straight but my head was still spinning from the end of the strike that afternoon.

I took the coffee Miranda handed me and drank it down. I tried Michael's number again. It rang and rang. Miranda's brow was furrowed as she watched me.

'I bet he's sleeping off a drunken evening, while we are frantic,' I said. 'He's made of tougher stuff than you think, old Michael.' I hoped I was right.

'We don't know that.'

I came over and wrapped my arms around Miranda and I felt her relax a little. I couldn't remember when she last needed me like this.

She pulled away. 'I know! You could go straight to Sheffield now. Stay with Michael until the anniversary is safely over.'

I stepped back, as if stung. 'What? We haven't even spoken to Rosa yet. She may have everything under control. We may be panicking about nothing.'

'She'll need support. She has a small child.'

'I can't go straight to Sheffield. There's a lot to resolve now the strike is over.' I had also started something with Nomsa now and I couldn't back out. It felt as though wires were attached to both sides of my head, pulling in opposite directions.

'You could fly tomorrow if there's a seat on a plane.' She reached for her laptop muttering, 'South African Airways...' She looked up. 'You can keep him safe, make sure he has medical support. And connect with his English friends too.'

'Let's just think this through... It would be much more sensible to ring a friend of Michael's in Sheffield who can check on him in person now. We can't be his only friends.'

'I suppose so,' she said. 'Pete may have phone numbers from his trip there last year.'

I rang Pete again. No answer. 'Where the hell is everybody?'

I reached into the sideboard, poured myself a tumbler of whisky and took a swig. 'Ah. Do you want one?'

'No, we need to keep clear heads. You're not taking this seriously enough.'

'I'm dog tired,' I said. 'I'm trying to relax a bit so I can think.'

'I'm tired too but we need to get the ball rolling tonight. Michael is a definite suicide risk in the lead up to Liz's anniversary.'

I dialled again. 'Pete, Howzit?' I gave Miranda the thumbs up.

She nodded and headed upstairs.

I told Pete about Michael's call. 'He sounded drunk, apparently. And now he's not answering.'

'He's probably in bed, while we're all worrying.'

I felt relief at Pete's steady voice. 'Miranda's trying to get me straight on a flight to Sheffield. Before we've even spoken to Rosa.'

'It might be serious,' Pete said. 'This close to Liz's anniversary. I've got Rosa's number. I'll give her a ring.'

'You didn't make a note of any of his Sheffield friends' details did you?'

'Yes, I've got a couple of phone numbers. I'll find the notebook and call them.'

'Man, that would be great,' I said. 'I've had a helluva day. The strike ended this afternoon.'

'I'll ring back as soon as I get anywhere.'

'Ring no matter how late it is.'

'Will do. Cheers.' Thank God for Pete.

I staggered upstairs and found Miranda stepping out of the bath. I stopped to enjoy the sight of her drying herself with her rose-coloured towel. I wanted to wrap myself round her, kiss her sweet-smelling skin but I hesitated to take such liberties anymore. Especially at a moment like this.

'It's still warm, jump in,' she said, settling on the cane chair in her white dressing gown.

I stepped into the bath. 'A-ah, I need this.' I slid under the hot, soapy water.

As my head surfaced and my ears cleared, I made out Miranda's voice. 'Did you get any numbers off Pete?'

'He's ringing Rosa and a couple of Michael's friends. He'll ring us back later. We don't have to do it all, you know.'

'Thank God. But you should be ready to jump on a flight if one of his friends can't step in. We can't leave this all to Rosa, if Michael is as bad as he sounded.'

'It's crazy to rush over there until we know who can help locally. And I'll have urgent matters to deal with now the strike has ended. There's a meeting first thing Monday.'

'I sometimes wonder if you'd even put your own family before work,' she said and left the bathroom.

Once I was in bed, I tried Michael's number again. Still had no joy.

By the time Miranda turned the light off, I was still holding out on agreeing to a trip to the UK but it looked as though it was a case of when, not if I went.

Pete rang as I was drifting off to sleep. 'I spoke to Rosa. She's frantic about Michael. Says he's very low. But he won't go to his GP for help. Won't talk to her about it.'

'Oh shit! And his friends?'

'No replies so far. I'll try again tomorrow.'

'I'm up at the university in the morning,' I said. 'I can drop into your office about ten-thirty for an update.'

CHAPTER 32

On Monday morning, Nomsa could hardly sit still as her bus made its way in from Umlazi to the city. Gallagher had said he would be waiting outside the bus station. Just as well her *medem* was away for a few weeks, so she had a free morning. She made her way through the crowds to the main exit and caught sight of him, waving frantically.

'Let's hope Dr Khumalo will be our man,' he said as he opened his car door for her.

On the way to the university, Nomsa sank into the soft seat, enjoying the vision of herself riding along in a car. It was good having help to tackle the problems of Ezekiel's case; someone to come up with new ideas. But she still didn't trust this *umlungu*. Why was he getting involved with Ezekiel's problems?

Up and up the hill above Durban they went, through suburbs with enormous houses and lots of trees. There were no trees in Umlazi F. As the car crested the ridge and drove into the university grounds, she exclaimed, 'I have never been so high up! You can see right over *eThekwini* to the sea.' She turned the other way. 'And such a beautiful building!'

'That's Howard College, the oldest part of the university,' he said. He parked and they stepped out of the car.

'The Technikon in Umlazi is nothing like this,' Nomsa said.

'Let's plan what to say to this Dr Khumalo over tea and cake in the refectory.'

Nomsa nodded. She had had no breakfast and Gallagher was very much a man for his cake.

He led the way towards one of the many buildings and down some corridors. It made her proud to see all the black students here, more than the Indians and whites. Not that long ago, this place would have been for whites only. In the refectory they loaded tea and buns on a tray from the counter, then shuffled along to pay. It was scruffy in here and very noisy, students shouting at each other, their voices echoing up to the high ceiling. Much more like Umlazi Technikon. They sat down with their tray. Nomsa sighed with pleasure as she tucked in to her hot tea and tasty bun.

'How much will this man charge?' she asked.

'Don't worry Nomsa. University lawyers run free clinics, to keep up to date with their subject.'

'That is good.' But she worried still. Whoever heard of anyone giving something for free?

When only crumbs and empty cups remained, Gallagher pulled out his notebook. She wondered why he always needed his notebook, why he didn't keep facts in his head.

'So, what do we need to ask Dr Khumalo?' he asked.

'How to get Ezekiel's case heard sooner. None of this waiting two years. And why are they charging him with trying to murder you, when you yourself say that is not true.'

'Yup, I guess that's it, in a nutshell.'

They set off to find Dr Khumalo's office, struggling through crowds of students moving in the opposite direction. The law department was quiet and ordered. They had hardly sat down, when a tall, distinguished-looking man with grey hair emerged and introduced himself as Dr Khumalo. Old enough to be wise about the law, Nomsa decided, not like that idiot Dlamini. He had a ready smile and greeted her, '*Sawubona uMama*', taking both her hands, before turning to Gallagher. She felt an immediate bond with this man.

Once they were seated, Dr Khumalo looked at them. 'I've read the background summary you provided. Tell me how I can help Mr Mabuza.'

Nomsa felt shy in this new setting. She nodded to Gallagher to begin.

'We are trying to have Ezekiel Mabuza's case brought forward,' he said. 'He has been waiting on remand many months and his health is failing fast. He also has children to look after.'

'The charge seems excessive for what happened,' Dr Khumalo said. 'Certainly, for what could be proven in court.'

'Yes, excessive.' Nomsa nodded vigorously.

'During the chase I was terrified by Mr Mabuza,' Gallagher said. 'But in retrospect I don't think he intended to use the knife he was carrying.'

'He is not that sort of man at all,' Nomsa said. She tried to imagine Ezekiel looking terrifying with a knife but she couldn't. Most annoying at times but never terrifying.

'I didn't bring the case myself,' Gallagher added. 'It was the police who charged him.'

'In my view,' Dr Khumalo said, 'this might be a suitable case for plea-bargaining. It is a much quicker process than fighting the case as it stands. Your union lawyer has not suggested this?'

'No, he has not. All he keeps saying is that we cannot move on while my brother is sick in his mind.'

'Ahah...' he nodded. Nomsa definitely liked this thoughtful man.

Gallagher added, 'This union lawyer has the issue mixed up with the strike that was going on, but I can't see how it serves Ezekiel's case. And now the strike is over, he seems to have lost interest in it altogether.'

'I can't swear that this case will be accepted on a plea-bargain but it is well worth a try.'

'What is this plea bargain, please?' Nomsa asked.

'You plead guilty to a lesser charge and it moves things forward more quickly than a not-guilty plea. But it all depends on which prosecutor looks over the plea, what sort of mood he is in, on the day in question.'

'As bad as that?' Nomsa exclaimed. Her new hopes wilted. Her feet ached in her too-tight shoes.

'I could swear to it that there was no physical contact between me and Mabuza on that day,' Gallagher said.

'That's worth a try. But I don't want to raise your hopes too high.'

'We must take the chance,' Nomsa said. 'It is better than waiting two years. You understand that I have no money? The union is paying the useless Mr Dlamini.'

'Don't concern yourself, my university clinic is free,' he replied.

'That is a great weight off my mind.'

'There are two approaches we can take with the plea-bargain,' Dr Khumalo said. 'I can write a report advising your lawyer on the path to take. He should argue that Mr Mabuza caused a minor public affray at worst.'

Nomsa listened, quivering with dismay at the thought of Ezekiel pleading guilty to anything.

'My report to your lawyer-fellow would spell out in

detail how to proceed,' the professor added. 'If he still won't bite, I can give him a coaching session.'

Nomsa and Gallagher nodded approvingly.

'Or,' his eyes twinkled. 'For the really stubborn mule lawyer who won't shift, I occasionally take the case over myself.'

'Halleluiah!' Nomsa called. The Good Lord was spreading manna from heaven before her. Was this what pastor meant when he told her that He would find a way? A way she had tried to throw off when it first sought her out in the form of Gallagher.

'My plan meets with your approval, I gather?' Dr Khumalo smiled.

'And mine,' said Gallagher. 'But I fear we may be dealing with just such a mule.'

They all laughed.

The professor ran through the steps that a plea-bargain would involve, what could go wrong and how she could back out of it at any time if she wanted to. The court would require Ezekiel to sign over to Nomsa his power of attorney first, witnessed by a member of his psychiatric staff. How much swifter this method could be over than waiting for a full court hearing. How much less stressful for Ezekiel. It sounded heaven-sent. But she must remember that it might not work.

'What would be the longest sentence my brother could get for this business of affray?' Nomsa was afraid to hear the answer.

'It could be as much as a year, I'm afraid. But it is more like to be six months or so. And any time he has been waiting for trial will count as part of that sentence.'

Nomsa shivered at the thought of a whole year. Would Ezekiel last that long in prison?

'So, if he pleads guilty to the lesser charge, he might walk free almost at once,' Gallagher said. 'He has been in prison six months already.'

'Jesus wills it.' Nomsa's excitement bubbled over. 'But his psychiatrist in Westville prison says he will need hospital care for a while.'

'The law would have no further interest in him, so that would be up to the health services to provide,' Dr Khumalo said. 'I think it is the obvious route to try.'

They stood up and shook hands. Nomsa's voice brimmed with feeling. 'I don't know how to thank you, Dr Khumalo!'

'It is my pleasure. We just need Ezekiel's signature on this, giving you power to act for him.' He handed her the document and waved her and Gallagher down the hall. 'Remember, it all depends on the judge who hears the plea bargain. We are in their hands.'

****

I waved Nomsa off at the bus stop and made my way across the university to Pete's department. All last night I had fretted, trying to decide whether to go to Michael or stay and work on Ezekiel's case. When I woke this morning, my mind was made up. Ezekiel came first. What would Pete think of this? And would he step into my place?

'Come in, come in,' Pete said, as he opened his office door, his shirt rumpled although it was only eleven am. 'Coffee?'

'Please. I have to face the mess left by the strike when I get back to city hall.'

'I got through to Michael late last night,' I said. 'He

swears he's fine, that he was just drunk when he spoke to Miranda. But he didn't sound at all good to me.'

Pete brought over our mugs and sat down. 'I got through to two of his Sheffield friends. Bad news, I'm afraid. They hardly hear from Michael anymore. Not for want of trying. He's shut them out since Liz died.'

'That's not a good sign. Can't one of them call in now we've raised the alarm?'

'They both promised to go round,' Pete said. 'Geoff will visit tonight and report back to me.'

'Miranda's set on me getting there for Liz's anniversary. I know it's a risky time for him but I really can't leave right now.'

'The strike?' Pete looked sympathetic.

What the hell, I might as well tell him. 'Not only that. The truth is…I'm in the middle of helping Ezekiel's sister-in-law to sort out his legal case. I can't jump ship now.'

'You're choosing Ezekiel over Michael?' Pete raised his voice. 'You must be fucking crazy.'

'He's in a very bad way…physically and mentally.'

'Everyone in prison is in a bad way, Ben. Michael is in a bad way too. Does he have to chase you with a knife to count as much as Ezekiel?'

I felt a rip of guilt through my chest. 'Of course not. It's just that…we're moving Ezekiel to a decent lawyer at the university clinic. I'm the link. Ezekiel's not eating, hardly drinking since his friend was murdered next to him.'

'I'm sorry for the guy,' Pete said, his tone still sharp. 'But Michael's one of your oldest friends. Why can't someone else help with his case? His family, his union?'

'They haven't made any headway with the union lawyer. Ezekiel is being left to rot in prison. He won't make it.'

Pete snorted and walked away, fists clenched. I'd never seen him this angry before. Pete the peacemaker. I was sweating now. This conversation was proving more difficult than I had imagined. I walked over to the window, wishing I hadn't told Pete the truth.

'I thought you were frightened of Ezekiel,' Pete said finally.

'Not since I saw him at his tribunal, looking like a frightened child. Doing this for Ezekiel…it's made me feel sane for the first time since…my nightmares have gone, the panic attacks.' My voice was pleading. 'I'm doing it for myself Pete, not just for Ezekiel.'

'I see…' Pete's tone changed. 'I don't understand but if that is what you need to recover…'

'The guy's been charged with attempted murder.'

'Attempted murder?' Pete said. 'That's harsh.'

'I have to help him. But Miranda will go crazy when I say I'm not going to Sheffield.' I took my last swig of coffee. 'I know it's a cheek, Pete…'

'Spit it out, man.'

'Is there any chance, you know…that you could go to Sheffield instead?'

Pete held both hands up. 'Whoa! That's difficult in term-time.'

'The thing is, Neil's left for Canada. Bram isn't a friend of Michael's.'

'I went to Liz's funeral last year. I did my turn.'

'I know you did. I wouldn't ask but…'

'Let me think,' he said, rubbing his jaw. 'I'm busiest in the second half of term. If I could get Nelson to cover my lectures for two weeks…and take some marking with me.'

'Jesus Pete, if there's any chance…I could take your

place if Michael needs it, as soon as this lawyer sorts things out.'

'It's only an idea… I'll have to check with Nelson and with my head of department,' Pete said. 'I'll ring you as soon as I get answers.'

'We'll all chip in for your flight, Pete.'

'I could get into the idea of two weeks in the UK. If I can pull it off.'

I looked at my watch. 'I better get to the museum. I can't thank you enough, man.'

'Michael is one of our oldest,' Pete said, his arm round my shoulder. 'He'd do the same for one of us. But don't count on it yet.'

Driving back from the university, I imagined confessing to Miranda that I wouldn't be going to the UK. I shivered.

When I reached the city centre, garbage vans were out in force now the strike was over, loading into their maws the black bags which had piled up in the streets, leaking noxious fumes. The clean-up was stirring the rotten smells afresh. At the city hall, municipal cleaners were sluicing dirt from the area outside the main doors that had housed the village of protesting strikers. Inside, cleaners hoovered up ten days of dust. None of them greeted me as I progressed up the stairs. It wasn't going to be easy improving relations between black SAMWU members and those of us in the other unions.

The museum was grinding back into action, the atmosphere volatile. I witnessed a few skirmishes between staff, with Gwala intervening to break it up. Everything was topsy-turvy, exhibits in the wrong place, rosters out of date.

I sat over my phone all the long afternoon, catching up on calls. Pete's answer was sure to be no or I'd hear nothing until tomorrow. It was three o'clock when he finally came on the line.

'Pete?'

'Nelson took some persuading but he's agreed to cover for me.'

'Alleluiah! I've been sweating it all afternoon.'

'It's not sorted yet. I've put it to Robertson. He's considering it. He always likes to play the power game.'

'Jeez! Call me as soon as you know.'

I was just about to leave for home that afternoon when Pete rang again.

'Robertson has agreed to me taking leave, given Michael's circumstances.'

'Thank God.'

'I spoke to Barbara too. She thinks it'll do me good to get away. You've definitely drawn the short straw.'

'I'll ring Michael and explain,' I said. 'I'll blame the strike.'

'I just hope I can get a flight soon.'

'I can't thank you enough, man. Now I have to face telling Miranda…'

'Say I needed a break,' Pete said. We rang off like conspirators.

As I drove home, there was new metal in my belly, something of my old self. Sorting things with Ezekiel's family was more important than keeping Miranda happy. I wouldn't be straying too far from the truth if I told her that the city hall was in chaos after the strike. And that Pete was desperate for a break.

CHAPTER 33

On the long bus journey from the university back to Umlazi, Nomsa smiled to herself, recalling the meeting with Dr Khumalo. She didn't like to admit it, but her husband had been right. Gallagher had turned out to be very helpful and not at all the man she had hated in her head. She reminded herself the plea-bargaining was only a possibility. But it was the first grain of hope for a long while, on the bleak landscape of Ezekiel's problems. By the time she got off her bus at Umlazi station, she was bursting to tell her news. On her walk home, she rapped on the door of the Apostolic Church.

'Nomsa Silongo. Come in.' Pastor Mabena looked happy to be interrupted. She knew he hated doing what he called his 'wretched paperwork'.

'Pastor, God has put a solution for my brother in my hands, just as you said he would.'

'Tell me your good news, sister.' Pastor smiled and pulled up another chair for her in his crowded little office. She settled into it.

'The Lord moves in strange ways indeed, Pastor. That Gallagher who was the source of Ezekiel's troubles has led me to a new lawyer. This one knows a way to get my brother out of prison quite soon.'

'Ahah.' Pastor beamed.

She could see that he liked being proved right. 'This Dr Khumalo is very wise. He is at the university, *eheh*. He suggested something called…called a plea-bargain to avoid the charge of attempted murder. If it works, he could be out quite soon.'

'Sister, let us give thanks for this blessing.' Pastor raised his hands in prayer and she raised hers.

"*O give thanks unto the Lord, for he is good; for his mercy endureth forever. Who can utter the mighty acts of the Lord? Who can show forth all his praise?*"

'Amen,' she joined in and opened her eyes. 'Thank you, Pastor, for counselling me to trust in Jesus. But…'

'What is troubling you, sister?'

'Pastor, this plea-bargaining…' She twisted her hands in her lap. She did not want to seem ungrateful to the Lord.

'You are worried that it might not work out?'

She nodded. Pastor understood her so well.

'Ah, you must leave some jobs for the Lord Jesus to do. He loves you dearly, sister. He will surely provide, if you pray.'

'I will, Pastor, I will,' she said, feeling ashamed.

'Remember the sin of pride, sister. Of thinking you have to do it all.'

Nomsa nodded uneasily. It was hard to trust the Lord to get it right.

She left the church feeling calmer, walking the rest of her way home on feet that hardly felt their usual aches and pains. She glanced at the clock as she came in through her kitchen door. It was a long time until Thembu came home and she could break her news. And her girls were still at school too.

She treated herself to a cup of tea before getting on with

the ironing and preparing the evening meal. It was only *samp* and beans because household funds were short. She sang as she worked, then chided herself for becoming too excited. This plea bargain could fail, Dr Khumalo had said. She was lost in thought, so that the girls took her by surprise when they arrived home. Eventually Thembu banged his boots clean on the step and came in.

'You were singing, *uMama*,' Thembu said. 'You haven't done that for a long while.'

****

I recognised the angry click of Miranda's heels in the hall before she burst into the kitchen, interrupting the peace of my morning coffee.

'I found this under our bed!'

'What is it?' All I could see was a crumpled scrap of paper in her hand.

She tossed it onto the kitchen table, as though she couldn't bear to come near me.

I unwrapped it and saw in my own handwriting, the words "Dear Mrs Silongo". Oh hell! My draft letter to Nomsa. I had been trying to be so careful.

'Mirrie…'

'Don't you "Mirrie" me!'

I stood up. 'Look Miranda, I wanted to tell you…'

'Well, what stopped you?'

'Frankly I didn't think you'd listen to me,' I said.

'You didn't tell me because you knew I'd put a stop to it. You've been trying to help Mabuza, haven't you?' She turned her back on me and walked over to the window, hugging herself as though she hurt.

'He is not just any old person, Miranda. This is Ezekiel Mabuza who I've known for twenty years.'

'I've had enough of this poor Ezekiel nonsense,' she shouted. 'What about all the harm that his crime has done to you? And the effect that's had on our family?'

I felt suddenly exhausted. I longed to sit down but didn't want to lose my position in the fight. 'Ezekiel's paying his dues for what he did. Why don't you ask me *why* I'm doing it?' I asked.

'I'm tired of listening to you going on about Ezekiel. The country is drowning in crime and you end up supporting a criminal…'

'Oh, for chrissakes Miranda! Not your ANC anti-crime lecture again.'

'It used to be your ANC too,' she said. 'You idealistic types are always whining when the government has to take decisive action.'

Now we were onto one of our favourite battlegrounds. 'Decisive action to line their own bloody pockets, more like. You forget that half the government is prosecuting the other half for corruption. You weren't all that interested in the ANC when it mattered, now you spout the party line at every chance.'

Miranda pulled herself upright, quivering. 'How dare you!'

I'd gone too far. My accusation was untrue. But I couldn't bring myself to apologise. This was not about the ANC but about what was falling apart between the two of us but neither of us could admit it.

'Drop Ezekiel's case or find somewhere else to live for a while.' Miranda's eyes narrowed. 'Just leave me and the kids out of it.'

I felt as though I had been punched in the gut. Neither of us spoke for a while. 'I have to do it,' I said. 'For my own sanity.'

'Then do it elsewhere.' Her tone stayed icily determined. She turned and walked out.

Gradually my breathing slowed down but my thoughts churned. Surely she didn't mean it. She'd calm down. But if she didn't, where would I go? I dreaded the emotional warfare that would result if I refused to move out. I didn't have the stamina for it. I wondered for the umpteenth time why Miranda always won the upper hand in our rows. I could always hold my own at work. But I hated tension at home; always gave way for a quiet life. Not admirable, I thought as I sloped out to do some gardening to calm my nerves.

For the rest of the day I hunkered down at the far end of the garden by the fruit trees, turning the compost heap and spreading it in preparation for vegetable planting. The warm sun soothed my back. When I heard Miranda drive off I snuck into the house for a cup of tea and a sandwich, dreading the evening ahead.

I picked up the phone. 'Hey Bram, are you free for a drink tonight?'

'Sorry mate, Elsa and I don't go out on our own Saturday nights. We could all meet up if you like?'

'Miranda's pretty angry with me – we could both do with a cooling off period.'

'Sorry to hear that. Come and eat with us. About six-thirty,' Bram said.

'Thanks man, I really appreciate that.'

I went for a run but with my hamstring still mending, it wasn't long enough to restore me. I loped back sweaty into the house and straight upstairs to shower. I saw that Miranda had carried out a furious sorting job. Boxes and bags were piled up, labelled to send to charities.

Afterwards I went downstairs. She was emerging from the kitchen. 'I am spending the evening with Penny,' she said. 'Do what you like.'

CHAPTER 34

Ezekiel gagged as a nurse pushed a spoonful of tasteless mush into his mouth. He coughed the food up all over the floor and she 'tsked' in annoyance. Before he had recovered, she was spooning in another mouthful.

'Come on Mabuza, I have other things to do. I cannot sit with you all day. Tomorrow is your weigh-in day. You don't want doctor to see that your weight has dropped again. You don't want to have the nasty tube put down into your stomach, do you?'

All the while, she was spooning in his food and he struggled to keep up, to swallow at the right moment to avoid choking again.

'What is it with you and this not eating?' she asked. 'You could easily feed yourself, instead of wasting my time. You act like you're on hunger strike.'

Hunger strike. Where had he heard those words before? The phrase took his mind back to another time and place. He struggled through his drug-filled haze to remember where it was. Slowly, a picture of the prison sickbay came to mind, of his friend Kris, skinny as a snake, coughing in the bed next to his. He felt again the ache of his own bruises and broken rib after that beating he'd had from the twenty-sixes gang. He smiled at the memory of the two of them swapping stories of their lives, of nurse Mtwetwe coming round at night with hot chocolate before lights out.

Then it came to him, the picture of Kris explaining to him in a hoarse whisper, about the hunger strike that he and his friends planned. Ezekiel struggled through the clouds in his mind to remember more. Why were they going to starve themselves? What was it all about? But the matter escaped him. Still, the picture of Kris with his funny ways, of them both in bed on the safe, white ward with nurse Mtwetwe, comforted him. He longed to be back there now.

'That's better,' nurse said as she showed him his empty bowl. Without realising it, he had finished his food. 'Doctor will be pleased with you.'

'Hunger strike, hunger strike?' Ezekiel whispered to himself. Gradually it came back to him. 'Anti-retrovirals.' He looked round quickly to make sure he had not been heard. His conversations with Kris were re-forming in his mind piece by piece, like a puzzle. The meeting on the veranda with Kris and the Chief, the hints and the air of excitement before Kris had finally shared the secret with him. That the AIDS patients were planning to go on hunger strike to try and get ARV treatment.

Fear gripped Ezekiel. Had the hunger strike happened? And what had happened to his friend? He looked down at his own unrecognisably scrawny body and whispered to himself, 'This is what not eating has done to me and I was a sturdy man. How long could skinny Kris survive not eating, with his TB and AIDS? Kris, my friend…'

Another one gone. Without even saying goodbye. Was Kris another restless spirit, wandering the earth, unable to find peace? Ezekiel started to cry in big, noisy gulps, tears flowing down his cheeks.

*****

I leaned back on Bram and Elsa's sofa, sipping the glass of red in my hand. They were in the kitchen preparing the meal. Through the open windows, I heard the garden pulsing with the sounds of nightjars calling and insects buzzing. I inhaled the heavy evening scent of flowers.

It had been difficult explaining my situation to them; why Miranda was threatening to throw me out. We'd had to go through their inevitable questions of 'why are you helping Mabuza? You're the victim. Why can't someone else sort it?'

Once they understood a little, I felt better for sharing it. I'd been keeping so much from my friends.

'Regardless of Ezekiel,' Bram had said. 'The trip to the UK might be too much for you after the knife attack. Michael won't be easy to deal with right now. Much better for Pete to handle that.'

'True. One minute Miranda thinks I'm mentally unstable and the next she's trying to send me to Sheffield to deal with Michael threatening suicide.'

'Let's try to relax for the rest of the evening,' Elsa added. 'Miranda may have cooled down by the time you get home.'

'She's gone to Penny's,' I'd said. 'If anyone can change her mind, it's Penny.'

I tried to put it out of my mind as I watched bats swoop low across the moonlit sky. I took another swig from my glass. My shoulder muscles were slowly beginning to ease as the wine reached my brain.

A slow sense of sadness came over me. I felt that I was about to lose everything I'd ever had, the old Miranda I'd loved, as well as the uptight one I was angry with now. Our very first meeting, all those years ago at a student party, came vividly back to mind. There was something about her smile and her long dark hair. I'd broken off in the middle of a political discussion and had followed her to the kitchen.

'Why haven't I seen you around before?' I'd asked. Such a cliché but it had worked. She knew who I was. Everyone knew me, president of the students union, confident, sardonic. I must have been an arrogant pain in the ass. That moment we met was still so clear in my mind. I'd been wearing purple bell-bottoms, holding a joint in my hand as I approached her, already smitten. Before long, we were inseparable, doing political stuff together between lectures, our nights in each other's arms on her squeaky, old bed. I'm not sure how we passed our finals but we did. A few years later, our hippie-style wedding in the woods had almost broken her mother's deeply conventional white South African heart. As had the number of black guests. 'Where do you know these people from?' she had hissed in my ear.

The years after Tom was born had changed things. Miranda was buried in nappies and baby sick, just as everything hotted up politically in South Africa. I was always home late with tales of union-building, rent strikes, conscription boycotts. Things seemed to be on the move at last and Mirrie had felt horribly left out. How could I accuse her of not being political back then? Of being a Johnny-come-lately to the ANC? I hadn't done my share as a parent, that's for sure. A rising tide of township violence, massive boycotts from the outside world, history in the making, had seemed much more important.

Then suddenly the struggle was over. Mandela was released and the unbanned ANC won the election. We joined of course, helping to build the Rainbow Nation. At the beginning, we'd been drunk on Mandela worship, like the rest of the country. To see the man himself after so long. Not a single picture of him had emerged since his conviction in 1964.

After a while I wasn't that happy at the way many ANC leaders had slid out of their anti-poverty values almost as quickly as they slipped on evening dress. The banks and big companies had sucked up their brightest and best, transforming some of them into a new elite. That was when my political arguments with Miranda had started.

At first they had been good-natured. She called me an idealist, herself a pragmatist. 'Look how they have steered the country through the rocky transition from apartheid,' she'd say, 'away from the brink of civil war. You take that for granted now.' But in the past year or two our differences had become more personal, more bitter.

I recalled how it was after Mbeki became president that I had really lost faith in the ANC. I'd said to Miranda, 'Black Economic Empowerment has become nothing but Mbeki enriching his ANC cronies. Let the poor go to hell.'

'You expect too much,' she'd thrown back. 'Creating a black middle class is an important step towards racial equality. You're a dreamer, Ben.'

We'd both agreed that Mbeki's beliefs about HIV/AIDS were crazy. We'd shrieked in despair when his health minister advocated a diet of garlic, olive oil and beetroot to cure it. And I couldn't forgive Mbeki for not bringing down Mugabe's Zimbabwe. 'All he has to do is pull the plug on their electricity,' I'd say.

She'd shake her head. 'It's difficult to break loyalties to old comrades, you ought to understand that.' Surely political arguments alone hadn't eaten away the love between us. There must have been more to it to explain the toughness she'd developed towards me.

'Elsa put her head around the door. 'Supper's ready.'

'Coming.' I left my thoughts behind and went through to the kitchen, with an aching a sense of loss. The old Miranda had been there with me again for a while.

'Vegetables with rice.' Bram presented us a dish of roast peppers, aubergine, courgettes.

I inhaled the tempting aroma and realised how hungry I was. 'You're right,' I said. 'I mustn't panic. The Ezekiel thing will blow over.' I scooped some food onto my plate. 'I was dreaming of happier times.'

CHAPTER 35

Nomsa pressed the bell on the battered door to the psychiatric wing of the prison. She had Gugu and Mbali with her this time. They were pining for their *baba* and she had not been able to hold them off one more day. She hoped Ezekiel would not be the tormented soul she had seen on her last visit. The affidavit he needed to sign burned a hole in her bag.

'Psy…' Mbali stumbled over the word on the door. 'What's that?'

'Psychiatric. It's for…people who…who don't feel well in their mind,' Nomsa said. 'Prison is not an easy place and people can sometimes feel bad. As I explained, your *baba* is not his usual self.'

She was saved from having to say more by the door opening from the other side. Gugu clutched auntie's hand, her eyes large. Mbali pulled her short skirt down, as if to make it more decent for her *baba's* eyes. Nurse Nsele, the nice one, greeted them and led them through the difficult ward to Ezekiel's one. The smell of urine hit Nomsa's senses again like a slap.

'Pooh!' Gugu giggled, holding her nose. Mbali laughed loudly.

'Shush.' Nomsa put her finger to her lips. 'The people in this room are ... a little strange,' she said. 'But don't worry, nurse is with us.'

Luckily it was quiet in the severe ward that day, no-one loomed out at them as they passed though. The walls were painted the colour of the custard her *medems* had taught her to make. More cheerful than the grey walls of prison section D.

They entered Ezekiel's ward and Nomsa held her breath. What would they find? Had she made a mistake bringing the girls? She scanned the residents in the dayroom, some staring into space, some pacing up and down, others busy at tables. It struck her how none of the patients spoke to each other, each one locked in his own world. Ezekiel was no longer in his usual chair, facing the wall. That must be a good sign.

'There is your *baba*,' the nurse pointed.

Ezekiel sat at a table, engrossed in a task. This was an improvement. Please God he would recognise his daughters.

'*Baba*.' Gugu ran towards him. She stopped, her face puzzled when he did not respond. '*Baba*?'

Ezekiel turned from his task. He looked them over solemnly for what felt like minutes.

'*Baba* is on some medicine that make him sleepy,' Nomsa whispered.

'Why?' Mbali whispered back.

'Remember, he had a shock, when something bad happened in his cell. The tablets are to calm him down. Soon he will be OK again.'

'What shock?' Gugu pestered, rolling and unrolling the pictures she had drawn for her *baba*.

At last Ezekiel gave a vague smile. 'My girls!' His voice was slight and scratchy, his eyes watery.

'*Baba*!' Gugu approached and threw her arms around him. He allowed himself to be embraced. Mbali came forward and hugged him more stiffly. Nomsa was grateful that the girls had their faces buried in his chest and could not see his blank face.

Gugu checked what was on his table. '*Baba* is doing a jigsaw of lions and elephants! Let's help him.' She bent over the picture on the box and began to pick out pieces.

Nomsa's heart hurt when she saw it was a child's jigsaw that absorbed her brother so.

Mbali started to unpack their parcels. 'Look what we have brought you, *Baba.*' She spread each item out on the table. 'Ginger biscuits, tobacco, soap.' But Ezekiel was too involved in his jigsaw, his hands shaking as he lifted each piece.

'Come Mbali, let's see if we can find some tea,' Nomsa said. 'After that journey, my throat is a dry riverbed.'

Mbali followed her auntie, shoulders hunched, her voice sullen. '*Baba* always plays with Gugu rather than talking to me.' Was she pretending not to notice her *baba's* drastic changes?

They found nurse Nsele, who said the tea trolley was coming round any minute. On the way back to Ezekiel, Nomsa thought of the brown envelope in her bag. Was her brother in any fit state to sign the affidavit, giving her the right to deal with his case in his absence. Dr Khumalo would not take on his case without it.

They saw Gugu threw up her hands in delight. 'We've finished the picture, Auntie, look! Do they have any more jigsaws, *Baba*?'

Ezekiel seemed to have come to life, smiling a lop-sided smile. They drew up plastic seats around him.

'Mbali, tell *Baba* about your choir,' Nomsa said.

'We are in the Durban Inter-school Choir finals, *Baba*. It's very hard to get to this stage.'

'Isn't that good?' Nomsa asked.

'Yes,' Ezekiel said, his voice flat.

The trolley arrived at their table and he fixed gimlet eyes on the assistant until his mug of tea and biscuit were in his hands. The girls were offered squash. So much nicer in here than the main prison, Nomsa thought as she took a mug of tea. There was silence apart from Ezekiel slurping his tea noisily. The girls exchanged looks.

When he had emptied his mug, Nomsa said, 'I have some business to go over with *Baba*. You girls go find another jigsaw and get it started for him.' Gugu ran over to a pile of games in one corner. Mbali threw her auntie a look but followed her sister.

Nomsa looked round. The only nurse available was the bad-tempered Sizulu. She would have to do. She called her over to act as a witness.

Nomsa pulled her chair close to Ezekiel's. 'Listen well, brother. I have something important to show you.' She waited for his full attention. 'I have found you a new lawyer – a professor at the university! If you sign this paper, he will sort out how to get you out of prison.' She looked into his eyes.

Ezekiel nodded. He seemed to be following.

'If you sign here, I can advise this new lawyer for you. I can tell him to do everything to get you out. You understand?'

Ezekiel gave a slow nod. *'Yebo.'*

Nomsa gave him a pen and pointed to the bottom of the document. 'If you agree with that, just sign here.'

For a long moment Ezekiel examined the pen in his fingers.

He was bringing it to the page when the nurse interrupted. 'Ezekiel, do you understand what your sister is asking?'

He stopped and looked up at her with watery eyes.

'Tell me what you are signing,' nurse said.

He stared into the distance. There was a gut-wrenching moment when it looked as though he had forgotten. He looked up at his girls approaching and the moment seemed lost.

Nomsa wanted to weep. 'Brother, tell nurse Sizulu what you are signing.'

Ezekiel cleared his throat and looked at the nurse. 'I am signing for my sister to tell the lawyer how to get me out of prison.'

Nomsa pointed to the page. 'That's right. Sign here.'

He bent over the table and very slowly added a shaky signature.

Nomsa pushed the paper over to nurse, who added hers.

'Thank you, brother, thank you.' She threw her arms around his bony shoulders. 'I will do my best to get you out of here.'

Ezekiel seemed exhausted. He leaned over the table, rested his head on his arms. He turned the side of his face to Nomsa and said, 'Kris, my friend Kris.'

'Have you seen Kris?'

He buried his face on his arms again. Was he crying or just exhausted, she wondered.

'*Baba*, what about this jigsaw,' Gugu said, thrusting it on his table.

'I think *Baba* has had enough for today,' Nomsa said gently. 'Say goodbye and we will come again next weekend. Then you can tell him how your choir has done in the competition Mbali.'

On their way back out, Nomsa dropped in on the medical ward where Ezekiel had once been.

'Just sit and wait for me there,' she pointed to a bench at the side. The girls groaned.

Nomsa went up to the reception desk of the medical wards.

'*Sawubona*, Mrs Silongo,' the receptionist said. 'How is my friend Ezekiel?'

'Not so good. We have just visited him on the psychiatric ward.'

'I am sorry.' The woman spread her hands expressively. 'It is usually the gentle ones who can't take it in the cells.'

'He's asking about his friend Kris September,' Nomsa said. 'Is there any news I can take him?'

'Ah, sadly the hunger strike carried him off. And some others too.'

Nomsa felt dismayed. How could she tell Ezekiel? Could the poor man take more bad news?

****

I was first home that evening and I slumped at the kitchen table, poring over the Daily News. *Rape allegations against Zuma. Is presidency beyond his reach now?* This on top of corruption allegations against him. The whole country was gripped, me included. Everyone kept saying Zuma would never make it to president but I was not so sure. The wheels of power within the ANC ground silently.

My phone buzzed. 'Pete! Howzit going?'

'England's wonderful of course. Not that I get time to see much.'

'How's Michael?'

'Calmer than I expected,' Pete said. 'But he's so thin, as though he might fall over in a stiff breeze. And he's weird, man.'

'How do you mean weird?'

'He's not the old Michael – more sarcastic, more closed down. Won't say much about his suicide talk. Just apologised for scaring us. Says it was after a helluva bender. He tried to convince me it was a one-off but I doubt it.'

'What else do you have to go on?' I desperately wanted to believe Michael's story.

'Wait for this,' Pete said. 'He's painted the whole living room *black*. Walls, ceiling, floor.'

'You're kidding?'

'He says it's after the Rolling Stones song '*Paint it Black*'. He's playing in a band again.'

'I suppose making music has gotta help, if he's depressed.' How would I know? I wasn't handling life too well myself.

'He doesn't seem to see any of his old friends, the ones I met last time.'

'You haven't been there long.'

'Michael says he doesn't see them anymore; that he can't stand their cosy uxorial bliss, as he calls it.'

'I could do with a bit of that here.' I laughed bitterly.

Pete paused. 'The thing is…he's drinking way too much.'

'Understandable… around Liz's anniversary.'

'No, it's bad. He gets to the pub around five every evening and doesn't leave until they close. I'm so tired that I need to bail out on him some nights. I can't stop him drinking even if I stay. I don't know how he's holding onto his job.'

'It does sound bad. Sorry I landed you with this.'

'I just need to talk it over with you now and then. Make sure I'm doing the right thing. I'm repainting those black walls when Michael's at work. At least he says he's at work. Who knows? You wouldn't believe how many coats it takes to cover black. And I'm keeping house, making sure he eats. There wasn't a crust in the place when I arrived.'

I could just picture sensible Pete with his steadying hand on things. 'Sounds like a good start. How was Liz's anniversary yesterday?'

'Awful,' Pete said. 'Just the amputated little family – Michael, Rosa, her partner, little Angela and me. He wouldn't invite any of his or Liz's old friends. He seems so alone. I keep thinking of my pal Adam's anniversary in Durban last May. Friends and family from far and wide, stories about his life shared, friendships renewed. This one was so bleak, no memories recalled. Just the four of us standing in the cemetery, Rosa crying, Michael grim-faced.'

'We've got to get him out here, to touch base with us, with his old life. Try and find out what's stopping him.'

'I'm working on it,' Pete said. 'Something happened last time he came out, that's all I can gather.'

'Like what?' I tried to recall Michael and Liz's last visit to South Africa. 'It was a few years after the first elections, was it?'

'I'm trying to dig out more. He loosens up after enough drink, but soon after that, he's past the point of a sensible conversation.'

'God, difficult.'

'Even if I can persuade him, he says he won't be able to come over until their summer holidays next August.' Pete said. 'He gets just a fortnight at Christmas. He should be on sick leave but I can't get him to his GP.'

'Two weeks at Christmas would be better than nothing.' So much could happen to him before next August. But if anyone could persuade him, it was Pete. He knew how to handle people, whereas I would have made a balls-up of it. I would probably have got drunk with Michael, in my present state.

'How about you?' Pete asked. 'Has Miranda forgiven you for ducking out on Sheffield.'

'Worse. She found out I'm trying to help Ezekiel.'

'Oh shit!'

'She went ballistic. Nearly threw me out. Penny talked her out of it, thank God. We're walking on eggshells in the house at the moment.'

'Seriously Ben, you should drop the Ezekiel business.'

'I can't. Miranda's not dictating to me on this one. We're just getting somewhere with his new lawyer.'

'I hope you know what you're doing.' We were both silent, then Pete asked, 'Has Neil been in touch?'

'He rang the other day. Says things are going well in Vancouver. Says his new colleagues are a friendly bunch.'

'I was hoping that he would say it had been a mistake.'

'We all were. Penny says he would say it's all fine, wouldn't he? It would be hard for Neil to admit he'd made a mistake.'

'I don't know, we're all splitting apart. Just you, me, Miranda, Barbara and Penny left of the old gang, hey? Is this how it goes as we get older?'

CHAPTER 36

The Women's Committee members who had arrived early were catching up as they brewed tea and laid out the cups.

Nomsa took a deep breath. 'Sisters, I have important news!'

The others looked up.

'I have a new lawyer helping with my brother's case. He thinks we can get him out soon.'

'*Haai,* Nomsa!'

'*Siyabonga Nkosi.* Thank the Lord,' Maya said. The others echoed her. 'Thank the Lord. Your luck has turned.'

'How did it happen?' Ingwe asked.

Nomsa felt reluctant to spit out this particular nugget of information. They had heard her strong opinions on Gallagher, so how would it sound now that he was helping her? She had kept quiet about it even to Maya and Sonto when they counted the prison survey results each week.

'Tell us quickly, before Hlengiwe arrives,' Maya urged.

'Well, this Gallagher felt bad about what has happened to Ezekiel,' Nomsa said. 'So, he offered to help.' A silence followed as though a dung-beetle had crawled onto the table. They had heard her views on this Gallagher.

'He took me to see a new lawyer at the university, Dr Khumalo.' Nomsa felt on safer ground with the Khumalo story. 'This lawyer thinks that no-good Dlamini has been hunting leopards up the wrong tree. That there is a much simpler way to try and get Ezekiel out.'

'*Haai!*'

'I always knew that Dlamini was not trying hard enough,' Nomsa said. She explained the plea-bargaining that Dr Khumalo would use.

'Can you trust them? Especially this Gallagher?' Ingwe asked. 'He could be trying to make more trouble for Ezekiel.'

'I thought so at first. But he is taking me to see Dr Khumalo in his car, so why should I complain. And he found the new lawyer for me. He is *free of charge*.' Her chest puffed up. 'And he is a professor at the university.'

'This is good,' Sonto said but she sounded disappointed. 'Does this mean we don't need to complete our prison campaign survey?'

'*Eish*, no sisters,' Nomsa said. 'Don't we owe it to the people who answered our questionnaire, to carry on?'

'Of course, yes.' Everyone nodded. The mood in the room bounced back up. The campaign was still on.

'I thought you would be too busy Nomsa, if your brother is coming out,' Maya said.

'We are all busy, sisters, but when did that stop this committee?' Nomsa laughed and they joined in.

Hlengiwe walked into the room. 'I am sorry I am late, ladies. Pastor wanted to see me about something.' She looked around. 'What is the excitement about?'

They tried to smother their laughter behind their hands.

'Share the joke with me,' Hlengiwe urged.

'Nomsa's brother has a new lawyer. He has a new plan to get him out of prison soon.'

'I am pleased for you, Nomsa,' she said stiffly. She motioned them to sit down. There was a scraping of chairs and they put on serious faces. The room quietened. Hlengiwe handed out copies of the agenda.

'Ladies, let us begin. Any corrections with the minutes of the last meeting?'

As the meeting broke up, Maya said, 'What about arranging a celebration for your brother's new lawyer? If you each bring some food, we can hold a party at my house.'

'That is a good idea,' Nomsa said. But we shouldn't plan anything until Ezekiel's case has been solved. It would give me a bad feeling…'

'You are right, we won't talk more until he is released. Then we hold a bi-ig party.' Ingwe waved her hands in a large circle.

****

As I was about to leave work, an email arrived from Miranda. 'Working late. Can we do the film another night?' I read it in business mode, as information I needed to know.

Heavy rain and gusts of wind buffeted me as I stepped out of the building. I turned back into the vestibule to tog up in waterproofs. I hated riding a bike in this weather, especially on a dark winter evening. As I fought my way to the bike-shed, bits of the usual end of day city litter were being whipped up into the air and cold-slapping against my legs.

I took off cautiously into rush-hour traffic, face into the wind, car lights fractured into thousands all around me, beautiful but lethal in the lashing rain. I took it slow and steady in low gear on the long, hard pull up to the Berea, a nagging sensation at the back of my mind about Miranda's message. Why did I feel so annoyed that she hadn't rung me instead?

When I arrived, our house was cold and empty. I was grateful when Mamba came hurtling over and jumped up to greet me. I hugged her and scratched behind her ears. 'Hey girl, you're still here, aren't you?'

I scrabbled around on the back porch for logs to light a fire. I should be getting supper together but I felt freezing and somehow adrift. The basics of coming together for a family meal at the end of the day seemed to be falling apart lately. Was this what happened as your kids grew up? Or was Miranda leaving me out of the family loop?

'Hell Mamba, I'm getting paranoid,' I said. 'She was just too busy to call.' Other families probably did this all the time. But the uncomfortable throb of something wrong followed me around. I laid logs in the fireplace, my fingers knowing the routines, as they cross-hatched sticks and brushwood on top. The moment of striking the match, the satisfying 'psssh' as flames caught on dry wood, kick-started me. I stood up, ready to prepare dinner.

I poured myself a glass of cabernet sauvignon. Put Eric Clapton on, the sounds of *Layla* drifting through to the kitchen. I started cooking for whoever decided to turn up, whenever. I searched the fridge. What to make with what was there – pasta with mushroom and stilton sauce?

The fire was beginning to warm the house when I heard the front door open, then voices in the hall. When Ellen and Tom burst in I sagged with relief. What was wrong with me?

The kids weren't fazed by their mother being out late. Bags scattering, they competed for airtime.

'I've been asked to stand for leader of students' union,' Tom grinned.

'Fantastic, son. Tell us more.'

Ellen butted in. 'I *said* I wouldn't be able to get that essay in on time and then the stupid woman gave me detention. It's so unfair.'

'Ignore them Ellie, you'll be out of there soon,' Tom said. 'You'll be running your own show at varsity in a year or so. Give her a glass of red, Dad.' He had already helped himself and started pouring one for his sister.

'Whoa, just a drop.' My hand shot out over the glass. 'She's not at varsity yet.'

'Smells like Dad's lit a fire,' Ellen said. 'Can we eat in front of it?'

'Sure.' I raised my glass. 'To Ellen escaping school soon. To Tom's new post!'

'I haven't been elected yet.'

We clinked glasses and I wanted to bottle that moment. I felt I'd waited for it half my life. The grown-up intimacy with my kids, my son getting interested in politics. Of course, it was nothing like in my anti-apartheid days.

'About my nightmare teacher, everyone…'

'Tom's right, you'll be out of school soon. Focus on the future…'

'You never take me seriously,' Ellen said and flounced out. Usual teenage terms restored. Tom eyed me ruefully.

'Try Mom's cell phone, Tom. See if you can find out what time she'll be in. Then tell me more about this election.' I got on with chopping mushrooms and broccoli.

Tom fiddled with his phone. 'Mom's is switched off.'

'Why?' I sounded desperate.

Tom shrugged. 'She's probably run out of juice or is in a meeting.'

Ellie seemed to have forgiven us by the time I called her down for dinner. The three of us sat around in a mood of pleasant togetherness, eating pasta and stilton sauce in front of the fire. Tom made us laugh describing his rivals for the student union role. Still no sign of Miranda. After the meal, Tom and Ellie didn't shoot off upstairs as they usually did. They sat round the fire with me, drinking coffee, egging me on to tell stories from my student union days.

I tensed as we heard Miranda's car pull into the garage. Her key clicked in the door. There was a guilty silence as we surveyed the mess of plates and glasses around us. Miranda came into the living room.

'Nice of you to let us know when you'd be back.' I don't know why I said it.

'Don't start, Ben. I've had the mother of all days.'

I knew I should leave it, at least until she had her feet up and a glass of wine in her hand. But my anger that had been building up against Miranda was pressing dangerously against the dam wall. Why should she join in what we had going here, I thought, forgetting that we'd all pay if my dam wall broke tonight.

'Such a burden isn't it, to make a phone call in this modern age?'

Tom hissed, 'Dad, shut the fuck up.'

I snapped my mouth shut, stunned that he had intervened in that moment between his parents. He was right of course. Miranda would always insist on having the last word and before we reached that point, the air would be thick with ill-will.

With that easy victory, Miranda poured herself a glass of wine, kicked off her high-heeled shoes and carried them upstairs.

During this, Ellie and Tom had been flashing each other telepathic signals. Not long ago, they would both have sloped off to their bedrooms at the first sign of parent trouble. Instead, they remained seated around me, as though setting themselves up as a firebreak between Miranda and me.

I didn't seem able to speak. I'm a bit drunk, I thought, watching Tom and Ellen taking turns to keep the fire going, talking quietly to each other. I must have dozed off and when I next looked up, they were gone. Everything felt strange, the room smaller, different. I felt uneasy. Where was I?

Then I recognised the room. It was where Miranda and I had stayed on our first holiday together. We'd been up in the Drakensberg mountains and had argued fiercely about something as we walked the lower slopes of Cathedral Peak. We had watched two roped climbers high above us attempting the Bell. I remembered holding my breath, feeling that unless I sorted things out with Miranda, the Bell was going to claim two victims that day. Instinctively I had turned to her and found her arms reaching for me. Recalling it now made me shiver in front of the fading fire.

It was never supposed to turn out like this between me and Mirrie. Now neither of us was able to reach out and breach the gulf. Back then, as we arrived at the base hut, we had seen the figures of the climbers coming down onto lower reaches. I remember feeling as though, by resolving our quarrel, *we* had saved those two lives. We were rock solid, from then on. For a long time, we always thought we were better suited than any couple we knew. Until these last few years. Now suddenly, it felt like we were on that precipice in the Drakensberg again.

Someone shook me. 'Come to bed, Dad. It's late.'

'Wha…? Oh, yeah, Tom.' I stumbled out of the armchair and shook my head. 'That fire knocked me out for a while there.'

'More likely the booze!' Tom's hand guided me up.

The image of the two small climbers stayed with me as I made my way upstairs. Miranda was in bed reading. She glanced up.

'I was just dreaming about those climbers we watched on the way up the Bell, when we went to Cathedral Peak in '78. Remember?' I looked at her intently.

'What?' she muttered.

'That time we went up to Cathedral in'78. Remember?'

'Oh, yeah.' There wasn't a glimmer of recognition of the significance of that incident and she turned back to her book. Something fell away inside me.

CHAPTER 37

Nomsa walked home from her bus-stop in Umlazi, weighed down with bags of shopping. It was a long way to her own street. She struggled through the gate, dropped the bags and felt inside the post-box. Nothing there. Still no news from Dr Khumalo. Why was he taking so long?

She flapped at the hens clustering round her, always wanting food. She unlocked her front door and placed her shopping on the kitchen table, then flopped wearily into a chair. She eased off her shoes and rubbed her painful feet.

She brewed herself a mug of tea, before preparing the family meal. Her mind raced with possibilities about what might have gone wrong with Dr Khumalo's plan, each one worse than the last. That lawyer Dlamini had maybe refused to take advice from Dr Khumalo. He was an arrogant young man. She poured the hot water onto her teabag, added milk and sugar and sipped the hot liquid gratefully. Dr Khumalo had said if Dlamini didn't take his advice, he would take over the case himself. But what if Khumalo was all talk, too busy to put in more effort? What was in it for him? What if Gallagher lost interest, leaving her alone with Ezekiel's case again?

By the time the girls came in, bubbling with news about their school day, she was frantic with worry.

'Yes, yes,' she replied now and then as she put a pot of water on to boil and started to chop vegetables.

'Auntie, you're not listening!' Gugu said.

'Can't I have a few moments peace when I'm cooking?' Nomsa burst out. Gugu scuttled out of the kitchen, fighting back tears. 'Lord forgive me,' Nomsa muttered. Why am I taking it out on these girls? She felt the prick of tears at the back of her own eyes. It was all too much, this burden that the Lord had placed on her, no matter what Pastor said. She would talk to him again. How much more was she supposed to take? She wanted to have words with the Lord too but she did not dare. Did He have any idea of a woman's load in life, in this township?

The water in the pot started to bubble and she threw in the vegetables, followed by a can of tinned tomatoes and the beans she had soaked overnight. No meat. Cash was scarce before payday.

Thembu came in from work, slamming the door shut in that careless way of his. Why didn't the Lord make men more thoughtful, she added, while she was complaining to Him.

'Greetings, *uMama*,' Thembu said in a loud, cheerful voice. He sounded as though he had stopped at a bar on the way home. Nomsa came closer to him and sniffed the air. She smelled beer.

'*Eish*, how could you go spending your hard-earned money on drink in the middle of the week when we are short?' She used the tone of voice that normally made her husband quail. But tonight he was quite brazen.

'Short of money? What is this in my hands?' Thembu said, proudly pulling a pile of fifty rand notes out of his pocket and letting them flutter onto the kitchen table.

'And where have those come from? Not gambling I hope? You've done no overtime lately.'

'Rejoice! The manager at the factory puts the names of each team in a hat and pulls one out once a month. That team gets a bonus. For the very first time, my team's name was pulled out.'

'Are you sure that is not some form of gambling?' Nomsa asked, eyeing the notes longingly.

'Definitely not,' Thembu said. He knew how Pastor inveighed against the evils of gambling from his Sunday pulpit.

Nomsa smiled. 'Then I can buy a little meat from the butcher tomorrow. It will keep you all strong. And some new shoes for me and the girls. Mine are falling to bits.'

'How was your day?' Thembu asked.

'Still no word from Dr Khumalo. I think he has forgotten Ezekiel's case.'

'Don't worry so. These lawyers always take their time,' he said, as if he dealt with lawyers every day. He sniffed at the pot she was stirring.

'This waiting will drive me crazy,' she said. 'Tomorrow I will find a callbox and ring Dr Khumalo's secretary. I can't wait for the Good Lord to arrange everything.'

****

Next morning, I took Miranda her Saturday cup of tea in bed. I'd try once again to explain the significance of my dream about our trip at Cathedral Peak. Maybe she would get that it held the key to our future. But she didn't stir though I called her name several times. I left her tea there and went downstairs. Outside, birds were going mad with nest-building and twittering. I had a tussle with Mamba on the living room carpet, then went out to my garden. I had a bad feeling that the magic of recalling the Cathedral Peak story would fail.

Miranda was sitting at the kitchen table when I came back in. 'We need to talk, Ben.'

'Let's forget about last night,' I said. 'We were both tired.'

'It's more than just last night.' She looked deadly serious. 'I can't take it any longer. Your helping with Ezekiel's case. That's why I came home so late.'

'Look, it's almost over, we've found him a new lawyer. This Dr Khumalo thinks that…'

She put her hands over her ears as if in pain. 'I don't want to hear another thing about any of it.'

'Really, it's…'

'How do you think it makes me feel, seeing you obsess about his case? The man who tried to kill you.'

'But…'

'I feel betrayed, Ben. By the way you put him before regaining your own health or the impact on your family. Either drop Mabuza now or move out of the house until you're done with him.'

'I'm not going anywhere,' I said. 'If that's how you feel, we can keep out of each other's way for the next week or two until it's over.'

'That's not good enough. I've tried to ignore it but it's too much. I can't sleep, I'm not eating…'

'If you feel like that, you move out.' I stared angrily at her.

'I'm not the one putting some stranger before our family. And Ellen needs me more than you, especially around exam time.'

'What about the effect on the kids? Me moving out just before their exams?'

'They'll understand. They can sense what's going on. As soon as you stop helping this man, you can move back in.'

'Why should I be kicked out of my own home. Where am I supposed to go?'

'You seem quite resourceful when it comes to helping Mabuza.'

Anger coiled up from my belly. 'Jesus Miranda, you're a hard woman…The children will be far more upset than you think.'

'They're not children anymore. They know that things aren't right between us.'

'They'll be devastated. You've become such a cold, selfish person.'

'I feel the same about you.' She stood up and walked out of the room.

My limbs felt suddenly heavy. I wanted to go after her and say, 'Mirrie, for chrissakes, this is me and you. We can't let this happen.' But I didn't. I just stood there. Mirrie and Ben – the ones our friends had always put their money on lasting for life. That was before her law obsession, before she became an ANC groupie. Before…Ezekiel's attack on me. I had to admit it; I had changed too. I made coffee and sat hugging the warm mug as though my life depended on it.

I dug furiously in the garden, trying to think what to do next. Mamba followed me round whining, as if to say, 'what is going on?' I hauled things about that didn't need to be moved until both I and my anger were exhausted. Miranda didn't mean it. She was just calling my bluff. She would calm down like she had last time.

When I went back into the house, I found a note saying, 'Suitcases out for you in our room. Ellen and I have gone to stay with a friend. I expect you to be gone by the time we get back late Sunday afternoon'.

It hit me in the solar plexus. I wasn't going anywhere but it sounded like things were about to get very ugly. And Miranda had a way of winning in the end. I didn't have her stamina for a fight, not in my own home.

I felt desperate for human contact. I knocked on Tom's door but as usual he was out. University life had taken over and he often dossed on friends' floors at weekends.

If Khumalo could just get Ezekiel out of prison quickly, this would all be over. Maybe it would be simpler to move out briefly until then. Better than fighting Miranda and building up more bitterness between us. Once the court case was over, family life could start to settle back to normal. I could explain this to the kids once I managed to track them down.

I picked up the phone. There was only Bram left to ask, with Neil in Canada and Pete weighed down within Michael's problems in Sheffield. Penny had enough on her plate and was Miranda's friend.

'Bram, its Ben…things have got worse with Miranda. Can we have a drink tonight?'

'Ja, of course. Elsa will understand. I'll pick you up at eight.'

I put the phone down feeling more real. I slumped into a hot bath to wash away the sweat of gardening and wished I could wash away the rest of today too.

CHAPTER 38

Dr Khumalo looked ruffled as Nomsa and Gallagher sat down at his desk. 'You were right. Your Mr Dlamini has proved to be a mule. I will proceed with Mabuza's case myself.'

Nomsa smiled at Gallagher. Things would work out far better with Khumalo in charge. 'Thank you Doctor,' she said. 'Are you sure there is no additional cost?'

'None at all. This is a free clinic.'

'Perhaps Dlamini wants to take the case to trial, to get publicity for the union,' Gallagher said.

'The dirty dog!' Nomsa replied.

'Don't get your hopes up too high,' Dr Khumalo said. 'It is unusual for the courts to agree a plea-bargain in a case of attempted murder. But I will argue that the charge was inappropriate in the circumstances.'

So many ifs and buts and maybes. Nomsa could see her own tension reflected in Gallagher's face.

'This is the next step.' Dr Khumalo reached for his glasses and adjusted them. He opened a folder and passed them each a typed sheet of paper. 'If you are happy with the wording, Mrs Silongo, please sign it and I will send it on to the prosecutor without delay.'

She and Gallagher studied the document intently.

'The language used by lawyers is old-fashioned.' Dr Khumalo's voice was apologetic. 'It simply means that your brother is pleading guilty to making a public nuisance of himself on that day. If the prosecutor won't settle for that, we may have to up the stakes and have him plead guilty to causing a public affray.'

Nomsa frowned. 'This word "affray". It sounds serious.'

'I'm hoping it won't come to that,' Dr Khumalo said. 'In any case, affray is a lot less serious than a charge of attempted murder.'

Nomsa nodded. She looked out over the view from Dr Khumalo's window, thinking it through. She did not want to agree that Ezekiel had done anything wrong. Any conviction brought shame on their family. But it seemed she would have to.

'If we take this approach, Mr Gallagher could send an accompanying letter of support,' Khumalo added. 'If I am successful, I don't think the sentence is likely to be much more than some months, maybe less than Mr Mabuza has served already.'

'I am only too happy to do that,' Gallagher said.

'I drafted something along those lines but please alter it as you wish.' The doctor passed him a document and a pen and Gallagher started reading it. He gave Nomsa a copy too.

'Let us give him some peace,' Dr Khumalo said, leading Nomsa over to the window. They looked out over the city from the university's height on the ridge, a view she could not see enough of, almost like being up in the sky.

'To see all this from your window every day!' she said. Then she read the draft letter intended for Gallagher. She felt sure it would help Ezekiel's case.

Gallagher joined them at the window. 'How does this look?' He passed the letter to Dr Khumalo with a few scribbles on it.

Dr Khumalo leaned across and showed them to Nomsa. 'I'll have those changes made right now. Then you can sign it and I'll post it today.' He collected his papers together. 'It should be only a few weeks until we have a reply, if we are lucky.'

'That will be wonderful,' Nomsa said. Dr Khumalo was definitely part of God's plan for Ezekiel.

'I'll call you as soon as we have a reply.'

Nomsa could hardly breathe. To have arrived so close to a solution at last, made her tremble. But if it did not work out?

In Gallagher's car, on the way down to the bus-station, she said, 'I will tell the prison doctor that we may need to find a place in hospital for Ezekiel soon.'

'Somewhere they can make him properly well,' he said.

'But what if...if our plan doesn't...?' She could not bring herself to voice the thought.

****

All the following week, I kept ringing home, in the hope that Miranda would relent and let me back. Surely she'd have cooled down. I'd sent emails to Tom and Ellen saying that I hoped my move out was for just for a few days.

At last, on the Thursday evening, Tom picked up the phone.

'What's going on?' I asked. 'No-one answers when I ring.'

'Sorry Dad, I'm usually out.'

'And the others?'

'Um…Mom… won't speak to you at the moment.' Tom sounded embarrassed.

'Where's Ellen?'

'She won't answer the phone either.'

'What! She and I haven't fallen out.'

Tom hesitated.

'Spit it out, son.'

'Um…she thinks you put that Mabuza guy before our family.'

'Your mother's obviously been bending her ear.'

'Before you start Dad, it's not my view. I'm keeping out of this row.'

'Fair enough.' I cleared my throat. 'I'll sort it out as soon as your mother's prepared to talk to me.'

'I hope so, Dad. This is weird.' I could tell that he did not want to hear the details.

'I'm sorry Tom, I'll do my best.'

I put the phone down, the reality of Miranda's hardening attitude sinking in. I went through to the lounge where Bram and Elsa were sitting.

'Looks like Miranda is determined to keep me out of our house for now.'

'I'm sorry, Ben,' Elsa said.

'You're welcome here until you sort something out,' Bram added.

I caught Elsa signalling Bram a warning look.

'Penny may be looking for a lodger now Neil is in Canada,' I said. 'I'll ring her now.' I went through to the kitchen to make the call.

'Penny, it's Ben. Can I come round?'

'Of course.' From the tone of my voice, she had the sense not to ask any details.

I set off straight away, driving a little recklessly, reeling at the thought of making my move from home more permanent. My life was splitting at the seams. I needed to get a grip, instead of being buffeted about by Miranda's whims.

Penny hugged me. 'Miranda still holding out?'

I nodded. Of course, she'd have heard all about it from Miranda.

'That's rough.'

'She and I seem to be on different planets these days,' I said.

'I'm afraid it's the kitchen for us. The boys are watching their favourite soap in the lounge.'

'It's cosy in here.' I sat down at the table. 'I don't know how long Miranda is going to keep this going.'

Penny filled the kettle. 'I guess you and I have both been abandoned, one way or another.'

'That's true. Any chance I can rent your spare room until I sort it out?'

'You can be my first lodger,' she said, holding up an advert saying LODGER WANTED. 'I was about to put this up in the local shop windows.'

'That would be wonderful.' I squeezed her hand. 'I can be here for the boys when you're on nightshifts, as your advert requests.'

'I'd much rather have you than a stranger.'

'You've saved my bacon, Penny. It's getting a bit awkward at Bram's. But I may suddenly want to belt back home when Miranda whistles.'

'That's OK. It gives me time to find a long-term lodger I like.'

'I'd still come round for your boys for your night shifts, until you find someone.'

'Move in as soon as you like,' she said. 'I've just had the cottage repainted and it's all ready. Assuming it's good enough.'

'So, you'll put me in the *khayia*!' I laughed. Many whites had done up their previous servant's quarters in the garden to let out as self-contained rooms.

I paused. 'I ought to fill you in…'

'Not unless you want to…'

'Miranda seemed to accept that I was helping Ezekiel Mabuza. But now she says she can't take it another minute.' I groaned. 'She sees it as a betrayal.'

'Yes, I've heard her views on that subject.' Penny got up. 'Come and see if you like the cottage first and then we can talk.'

We went out of the kitchen door, across the garden to a small building attached to the side of the garage.

'It's amazing the difference a lick of white paint can make,' I said as we went in. 'We could have done them up long ago, instead of housing people in ugly red brick.'

'You're right,' she said, as she pointed things out. 'Cupboard space in here. Try the bed.'

I lay down and stretched out. 'It's fine. The room's small but it's perfect for a while.'

'Neat little shower and loo in here. You can fix food in this nook or you'd be welcome to eat with us and use the lounge. As long as you take your turn cooking.'

'I'm well-trained.' I grinned. We stepped back outside. She locked the cottage and we walked back to where the kitchen lights glowed.

Penny switched the kettle on. 'Or would you like something stronger?' She laughed. 'It seemed to work last time we were in trouble.'

'I better not. I'm driving.'

'That'll be one good thing if you take the room, we can occasionally get plastered. Do you need time to think about it?'

'No, I'll snap the room up, Penny. Name your price.'

She passed a sheet of figures to me. 'This is the costs sheet I've done for potential lodgers. Do you think it's too much?' She looked embarrassed.

'It's fine. Too little if you ask me,' I said. 'This is all so… bizarre.'

'It is weird. Every day I feel as though I'm acting like a clown with a smiling face for the kids, when inside I'm raging at Neil.'

'At least we won't have to pretend to each other. We can both howl at the moon once the boys are in bed.'

'I wouldn't give Neil the satisfaction,' she snorted. 'That's what he wants. For me to come crawling over to Canada because I can't do without him.'

'Who would have thought a year ago, that this would be happening to both of us?'

'Why have relationships become so difficult?' Penny asked. 'Neil and I have agreed to give it time before I decide on Canada but deep down, I feel it's the end.'

I was startled. 'How do you mean?'

'I think it's over between us. I'm not bailing out on my life here.'

'Give it time…' I said but I knew that feeling myself.

'Just before Neil left for Canada, we went for a meal at *Hemingway's*,' Penny added. 'He begged me to give his idea a chance. For me and the kids to have time here to get used to the idea of Canada and for him to make sure the job was right. It was the closest we've felt for a long time.'

'That must have been sad,' I said. 'Just when he was leaving.'

'I said yes to his idea but I don't believe in it. It just seemed the easiest way to part without fuss.' Penny was crying now.

CHAPTER 39

Nomsa and Gallagher sped up to the university in his car, desperate to hear how Dr Khumalo's plea-bargaining had worked out. He'd contacted them both a week ago to say that the courts had given him permission to present his plea-bargaining case but had it worked? She didn't dare think what would happen to Ezekiel if it had failed. She sat silently, clenching her hands. Gallagher was quiet too. When they reached the university car park, their feet travelled at double-quick time down corridors towards the law department.

'Ah, Mrs Silongo, Mr Gallagher, take a seat,' his secretary said. 'Dr Khumalo has been held up a little.'

They glanced anxiously at each other.

'It doesn't mean anything,' Gallagher said. 'They may have started late.'

She tried to believe him. He didn't look as though he believed himself. Nomsa could feel herself sweating with anxiety.

'How was Ezekiel this Saturday?' Gallagher asked.

'I took his daughters to see him again. They miss him so much.'

'Those poor girls.' Gallagher shuffled in his chair.

'Something must be up with Khumalo.' He walked to the door and looked up the corridor.

'I also managed to see Dr Methu again,' she said. 'The nice psychiatrist.'

'Has he found a hospital place for Ezekiel?'

'He says if Addington or other Durban hospitals can't take him, they will be able to take him in Pietermaritzburg. But that is so far away. How will we get to see him there?'

'So, nothing definite.'

'No. I hope they don't change his medication again. He was terrible on the new stuff last time, before it settled down. He kept saying that Thandiwe's spirit was angry with him, that she was tormenting him. His sons too. It was like torture for him.'

She shivered at the thought of the girls seeing their *baba* like that. And if he came home too early, who would watch out for him while she was out at work?

The secretary put her head round the door, smiling. 'Dr Khumalo has just rung. He is on his way through the building now.'

Nomsa locked eyes with Gallagher. Emotion welled up in her. This was the moment where all her plans for Ezekiel could fall apart.

Dr Khumalo strode in, looking strangely fierce. 'Mrs Silongo, Mr Gallagher, I am so sorry. It was a tough call.' He turned to his secretary. 'Tea and cake for all of us, please, Xolani.'

He led the way to his office and set down his briefcase, wiping his forehead with a grey handkerchief. They leaned forward, desperate for his news.

'We ended up with prosecutor Landsman, the tough fellow I told you about.'

'But what happened?' Nomsa asked desperately. 'Did it work?'

'Forgive me, yes, we won.' He laughed. 'I am always in this strange mood when I've managed to win by a blade of grass.'

'Viva!' Gallagher punched the air. Nomsa flung her arms around him, tears flowing. Then she sat down, her legs suddenly weak.

'And…what did Ezekiel have to plead to?' she asked, hardly breathing.

'We had to settle for the affray charge, I am afraid.' Khumalo looked serious. 'But because Mr Gallagher swore to it that there was no physical contact, Landsman gave Mabuza only six months.'

'Six months?' she gasped.

'Don't worry, they include how long he has been in already,' Ben said, counting the months on his fingers.

'Thirtieth of October he will be out,' Dr Khumalo beamed. 'Just over two weeks from now.'

Nomsa's mood swooped down. She knew it was silly to be so disappointed. She had hoped for Ezekiel to be released immediately.

Gallagher caught her eye. 'We've won, Nomsa. His psychiatrist will need time to make arrangements to transfer him to a hospital.'

'That is true,' she nodded. 'And thank you, thank you, Dr Khumalo. I am forgetting my manners.'

'My pleasure,' Dr Khumalo said, bowing slightly.

Xolani came in with a tray of tea and cakes. She poured and Dr Khumalo passed round the cups like such a gentleman.

He raised his own. 'To Ezekiel.'

They clinked cups. 'To Ezekiel!'

'To Dr Khumalo, who has solved his case,' Nomsa said. They clinked again.

'And to Nomsa, who has fought so hard to rescue him,' Gallagher added. They raised teacups and cheered once more. Nomsa smiled.

'Doowap-da-doowap,' Ben Gallagher sang on their way to his car, clicking his fingers to the rhythm.

Nomsa laughed and wiggled her hips with joy. She gave vent to a series of trilling ululations.

Students passing by looked up and clapped. Some of the women joined in the ululations.

'I wish I could do that,' Gallagher said, cheering.

'Maybe I will teach you,' Nomsa said. 'Now that we have won.'

****

I shuffled nervously in my seat. Miranda had finally agreed to meet me at a city restaurant; faceless, formal and air-conditioned, all beige and pink. Probably where she hung out with her lawyer friends. I looked up to check each new arrival. Would she do a no-show? I crumbled a bread-roll as I rehearsed my lines. Now that I was here, I felt distinctly less sure about meeting her. I had a bad feeling about it. What if I said the wrong thing? Why had she not just agreed on the phone to me moving back home, now that Ezekiel's case was over?

Then she was standing beside me.

'I thought you'd stood me up.' I laughed awkwardly.

'Would I do that?'

'I don't know anything anymore,' I said and passed her a menu. 'You… look lovely.'

She ignored my compliment. 'I'll have catch of the day, with a salad.' She was as definite at choosing from the menu as she was about most things these days.

I tried to choose but my stomach seized up at the thought of eating anything. I settled for a butternut mousse, whatever that was.

A long silence followed. I hadn't expected it to be so difficult, to feel so separate from Miranda after only a few weeks.

'How is Ellen?' I asked.

'How do you think? Pretty angry with you.'

We paused as the wine arrived. I tasted it and nodded to the waiter, who filled our glasses. The usually delicious *Backsberg* chardonnay tasted sour in my mouth.

'She feels betrayed, Ben.'

'I didn't want to leave!'

'And of all the places to stay, you had to choose Penny's.'

'I had to find somewhere in a hurry, remember. It was getting awkward at Bram's.'

'I would have expected Penny to check how I felt first, but she didn't.' I could hear the hurt in Miranda's voice.

'She was desperate to have someone there for the boys when she worked late. But it's all over, my involvement with Ezekiel's case. I can move back home.'

'I'm not sure I'm ready for that,' Miranda sounded uncomfortable.

'What do you mean…?'

Our waiter arrived with the food.

'*Kabeljou* is your catch of the day, mam,' he said in a chatty voice. 'And yours sir, a delicious Butternut Mousse, our vegetarian special.' He left in a hurry when we didn't respond to his charm.

I watched Miranda working her way steadily through her fish. My mousse lay virtually untouched on my plate.

'Look Mirrie, I'm really sorry all this happened. That Ezekiel's case upset you so much. I felt I had to do it to stop feeling crazy myself.'

'I can't…' Miranda's voice trailed away. She turned away.

'We can put this behind us,' I said, 'I know you find this difficult to believe but helping Ezekiel has stopped my nightmares and my anxiety attacks…'

She stayed silent. I couldn't fathom her expression.

'I want to mend things with Ellen. And with you. I've really missed you Mirrie.'

'It's not that simple, Ben.'

'No, I know it will take time but…'

'You don't understand.' Her voice was strange. 'Things were going wrong between us before Mabuza attacked you.'

I stiffened. 'What are you saying?'

'It's too late, Ben. I don't think it would work. You must have had some inkling this past year…?'

'I know it's not been easy, but…'

'The last six months have been hell. We don't get on anymore.' Her hands were scrunching her napkin into a ball.

I reached my hand over for hers but she pulled away. 'I'm much more my old self again. We can start…'

'It wasn't just that. You must have realised…'

'We can get back to how it was. I've been thinking about some of our recent happier times. The two of us laughing together, you in your red dress.'

'Ben, you're not listening. I want to make a fresh start with my life.'

Her words jerked me back to the present. 'Yes, yes... we can make a totally fresh start.'

She didn't answer. I wasn't getting the right feeling from Miranda. Her hands were folded tightly across her chest.

I had a sudden sick feeling. Of course. I'd been a fool not to realise it. 'You're having an affair with that Habib, aren't you?' Jealousy grabbed me around my throat. 'I can just imagine that prick moving in on you while I've been away...'

'Don't be absurd. He's happily married and fifteen years younger than me. We're finished Ben. It's nothing to do with Habib. We've just moved in different directions.' She looked as though she were going to cry. Her voice softened. 'I'm sorry, I've really tried.'

Miranda stood up and grabbed her bag from her chair, tears running down her cheeks.

'Please Mirrie...don't go,' I called after her but she kept moving towards the door. I stood up but my feet were stuck to the floor. How could she throw away all our years together just like that?

I realised that people were staring at me. I picked up my jacket and went to pay the bill, my butternut mousse untouched.

'You no like your lunch, sir?' the waiter asked.

CHAPTER 40

Ezekiel looked up from his workbench and gazed around the woodwork room. Sunlight poured in the window, catching the sawdust that hung in the air. He had grown to love this place, with all its sawing and banging and sanding. He was putting the last coat of varnish on the pine table he had been working on for weeks. He bent over his table that would be a gift to Nomsa. His time at Addington Hospital was slowly returning him to himself.

'Ezekiel,' Philani called. With a reluctant backward glance at his table, Ezekiel walked over to the woodwork tutor who stood in overalls covered in sawdust. Philani's broad face was smiling. 'That table is looking good, my friend. But it's time for your session with Bongani.'

Ezekiel frowned.

'I know, bra, I prefer the hands-on stuff too, but he has something important to tell you.' Philani gave him a gentle shove. 'Can you find your own way?'

Ezekiel nodded. He liked Bongani but did not like this talking business. And he needed to finish his table to take back home. Like Philani, Bongani didn't treat him like a child to be humoured, like some of the staff did. But these talking sessions hurt his brain. He dragged his feet along the corridor to the office. What important matter could he have to tell him? He tensed. Maybe his discharge date? Was he ready for that?

'Ah Ezekiel, welcome.' The rotund figure of Bongani stood grinning above his double chin. 'Good news, bra.'

They both sat down in the easy chairs and Ezekiel waited.

'We have been talking these last weeks about your fear that the spirits of your ancestors are still angry with you.'

Ezekiel nodded.

'That they will continue to punish you until you get up to Nkandla to see your *sangoma*?'

'Uhuh.' They had been over this all before. Why was Bongani bringing it up again? Ezekiel picked at the cuts and abrasions on his hands from his woodwork. These sessions brought him down, thinking about the curse of his ancestors and everything in his life that had gone wrong.

'Well, I have tracked down your *sangoma* Busi back in Nkandla,' Bongani said. 'I have spoken to her about you on her cell phone.'

Ezekiel looked up, surprised. Bongani had offered to try and bring a Durban *sangoma* onto the psychiatric ward but Ezekiel believed even more strongly now that only *sangoma* Busi from his home village could help him. He was terrified that as soon as he was out of this place, the spirits of his ancestors would begin to wreak vengeance on him again, this time taking his daughters. Much as he wanted to go home, stepping out of hospital was a frightening thought.

'Ezekiel,' Bongani called. 'Your *sangoma* is willing to see you as soon as you can travel to Nkandla.'

'*Sangoma* Busi?' Ezekiel sat up, excited. So it could be arranged just like that. 'But how can I manage the long bus journey?' He had not been out of the hospital gates yet.

'You won't catch a bus,' Bongani laughed. 'We will arrange a taxi to take you there. Nomsa can travel with you. The hospital will cover the cost of your journey.'

Still Ezekiel hesitated. 'Outside is another world...'

'Your *sangoma* had another idea. She said if it is too far for you, she will conduct the session with you by phone.' Bongani clapped his hands with delight. 'What do you say?'

'By phone from Nkandla?' Ezekiel asked. Who had ever consulted a *sangoma* on a phone before? 'Will her power come through the phone?'

Bongani beamed. 'She swears so. She says all the *sangomas* have cell phones now.'

'But how will I pay her?'

Bongani leaned forward. 'The hospital will pay. It's all part of your treatment. It's a little more expensive by phone. She says cell phone prices are high and she will still have to post your medicines to you but we save on your taxi costs.'

Ezekiel shook his head. 'I cannot believe this phone business will be powerful enough to solve my problems. I will travel to Nkandla by taxi with Nomsa.'

'So be it, Ezekiel! I would feel the same.' Bongani patted his shoulder. 'You talk to Nomsa and I will fix the visit with *sangoma* Busi.'

Ezekiel went back to the woodwork room with a light step. This could mean the end of his troubles. He would have to be very brave to undertake the journey but he didn't trust this phone business. He needed to be there when *sangoma* Busi connected with the spirits of his ancestors. To see it happening.

****

I sat outside my manager David Fielding's office. Through the door, I heard him on the phone. I was glad he was running late, so I could get my head into 'meet my manager' mode. I was still trying to steady myself after Miranda's devastating announcement a few days before. It was unusual for David to ask to see me outside our routine monthly meetings. Unless something was wrong. I cast my mind over my department's various projects. They were all progressing well.

I started to sweat. Was this the summons I had been dreading ever since we lost the Swedish grant? So much time had passed that I had imagined that mishap had been forgiven and forgotten. I had assured David that we stood a good chance of getting several local grants I had applied for. None as prestigious as the Swedish one but not to be sneezed at. He must know Durban Natural Science Museum was streets ahead when it came to our township projects. Surely he would cut me some slack after how I had handled things during the strike.

I was worrying about nothing.

David's door opened. He was a tall man, who had an air of one who thought better things should have come his way.

'Ben, come in. Take a seat.' His office was pristine – polished desk bare except for a few well-placed pens, notebook and the obligatory family photograph. He retreated behind it.

'I won't beat about the bush, Ben. I'm afraid it's bad news.'

I held my breath.

'It's your turn to make way for the positive discrimination bandwagon.' His tone was sardonic. 'I have to feed the name of one white manager to the City Council every few months, a sacrificial offering. Replace them with an up-and-coming young black manager. That's the way public services are going.'

'But…I thought…' I laid out my press cuttings about the Umlazi exhibition. 'I have several more funding applications in. We stand a very good chance of getting them.'

David looked almost apologetic for once. 'It's nothing personal Ben. You know how I've always appreciated your approach to putting the museum out there.'

What could I say in the face of such a sweeping explanation.

'I might have been able to push some other poor bugger under the bus if you'd pulled off the Swedish grant. But losing that in such a public manner zoomed your name up the list. The councillors don't appreciate bad publicity.'

I clenched my fists. 'You can't just throw me on the scrapheap David. After all I've done to build up the museum over the years.'

David examined his manicured fingernails. 'I'm afraid that finer heads than yours have rolled, in the interests of the new South Africa.'

'Obviously I agree with positive discrimination, but…'

'John Gwala is the obvious candidate to promote. He's talented, ambitious, you've trained him up well as your deputy.'

My head was fizzing. I had just lost my wife, my kids and my home. There was no way I could cope with losing my job. How would I afford the rent at Penny's?

'I need this job, David. I have a family.'

'Get personnel to work out your pension. You may find you'll not be as badly off as you think. You'll get a lump sum when you leave and others have set up their own businesses.'

'That's not for me,' I said. 'And I'd go mad retiring at my age.'

'There is always the battlefields museum up in Ladysmith.' David shuddered fastidiously. 'The province is always looking for someone who'd make more of it. You'd be ideal.'

'That's out. My daughter's in her final year at school here.'

'Sleep on it.' David stood up. 'I'm sorry it has come to this Ben. But it's the way the wind's blowing. No doubt my own turn will come soon enough.'

We stood up and shook hands and I left his office on unsteady legs.

I pedalled up the Berea, dreading telling Miranda my bad news. I was almost glad that I no longer lived at home and could delay the moment. I could imagine her sardonic tone, her implication that I was a loser. The way she'd say, 'just as well I'll be qualified soon or where would our children be?'

Penny's house was dark. No-one back yet. I unlocked the door to my cottage and poured myself a glass of red. I slumped on the only soft chair and slugged back large mouthfuls. I didn't care if I was drinking too much. My life seemed to be collapsing in on me from all sides. What a pathetic figure I was. A shadow of my former self. I wallowed in self-pity for while.

Then I sat upright. Of course. Why hadn't I thought of it in David's office? I grabbed my cell phone and tapped.

'Put me through to David Fielding.' Please let him still be there. This couldn't wait.

'David? Ben Gallagher speaking. I've thought of another way to resolve the issue of promoting John Gwala.' I could hear that I sounded a bit crazy.

'Calm down Ben. You'll get used to the idea. Just have a stiff whisky and talk things over with Miranda.'

I took a deep breath. 'Hear me out first. I think this will work. I could swap jobs with Gwala.'

'What do you mean?'

'Promote him to director and I'll take his job as deputy.'

'You're prepared to be demoted?' David sounded amazed. 'To work under Gwala?'

'Yes, if that's what it takes to keep a job at the museum.'

'Well, I never! No-one in your position has ever suggested this outcome before. They all want to walk out with their pride intact.' He paused. 'How many years have you got left until retirement?'

'Roughly ten...'

'Hm. That might be acceptable to the powers that be.'

My breathing slowed down and I felt a bubble of hope. Take it steady, I told myself.

'You sure about this, Ben?' David asked. 'It's not easy taking orders from someone you used to manage.'

'Better than shipping out to Ladysmith, in my book.'

'I suppose so,' he said dryly. 'I'll see what can be arranged. Technically it fits the requirements, although someone's sure to bellyache about it blocking another black promotion below Gwala.'

'You'll let me know asap if it's a runner?'

'Yes, of course. But I can't promise anything.'

I put down the phone and found I was shaking. Maybe the whirlwind had been avoided, for now. I thought about colleagues who had had early retirement thrust upon them. Peter had ranted and raged a few months ago, damning the chief executive as he disappeared out of the door, threatening legal action. George had taken it personally, his confidence folding up as he packed up and left quietly. Belinda had been delighted to get out of the rat-race and do something else with her life. She'd held a big leaving party and got a pile of farewell gifts. None of those felt right for a demotion. I didn't care what other people thought about it. John Gwala could drown in all the paperwork I was so sick of. I'd get back to the sort of museum work I loved. I'd earn less but Miranda would soon be earning much more at Habibs. She could pay the kids university fees. As long as David didn't hit a brick wall above him.

I poured myself another glass of red, hoping Penny would be home soon. I needed to tell her my bad news. I knew her reaction would be comforting, so different from anything Miranda might say.

CHAPTER 41

Nomsa sat with Gallagher in the cafe on Anton Lembede Street, he with coffee, she with tea. She saw he had brought a different selection of cakes this time and smiled. Why had she once been afraid to enter this place?

'What's your big news?' Gallagher asked. 'You sounded excited on the phone.'

'Ezekiel's counsellor thinks he won't get better until he consults his *sangoma* in Nkandla,' Nomsa said.

'Of course! That makes sense. It is something he has wanted for so long.'

'You will hardly believe this.' Nomsa laughed. '*Sangoma* Busi offered to do her consultation with Ezekiel by cell phone. But how can that work?' She frowned.

'Very up to date,' Gallagher said. 'It would solve the problem of getting him to Nkandla.'

'Yes…but… what do the spirits of our ancestors know about these new-fangled things? He has turned it down. He wants to go to Nkandla himself.'

'Is he well enough for the journey?'

'I think so, if I go with him,' Nomsa said cautiously. 'But not squashed into a bus, filled to bursting with old men, mamas and children, loud voices, luggage tumbling from the racks. He becomes so anxious, even in a roomful of people in the hospital visitors room.'

'We could take him up in my car,' Gallagher said.

'Thank you but the hospital has offered to pay for a taxi. But I'm not sure he is well enough yet,' Nomsa replied. 'Nkandla is a long way, even in a nice car.'

'But will he get better without his *sangoma's* help?' Gallagher asked. 'He could try this phone consultation first. If it works, he won't need the trip.'

'That's true. Two brains are always better than one,' she said.

'I could drive you both up there. I may have plenty of time on my hands.'

'Are you not busy-busy at city hall?'

'Well…I may not have my job for much longer,' Gallagher said, looking away.

'Why is that? Cutbacks at the municipality?'

'Time to make way for the younger generation, my manager says.'

'I am sorry.' Nomsa's heart went out to this *umlungu* whose very name she had hated not long ago.

Gallagher shifted about in his seat. 'I have asked for a lower job. Better than nothing,' he said. 'I'm waiting to hear.'

'May the Good Lord take care of you.' She patted his hand. 'The hospital will pay for a taxi. But I will arrange for you to meet Ezekiel soon, after his visit to *sangoma* Busi. He will be okay with you, you can be sure. I have told him how you helped me to get him out of prison.'

'Thank you, Nomsa. I understand.'

She thought what a nice smile he had.

****

In the early morning light, I breathed in the salt air. Beyond the sand, my eye following the long curve of rocks that formed the bay, then I gazed out to the sea. I watched as wave on wave crashed, rushed up the beach and was sucked backwards. A few people in wetsuits were diving off the far rocks. Closer in, a father and two boys fished in rockpools with nets. Otherwise, the beach was wide and empty. By midday, it would be full to bursting, another place entirely.

This was what I needed to drive away my demons. It wasn't easy waiting for David Fielding's reply to my job swap idea. And Penny and I had begun to be scratchy with each other lately, our old easiness gone. Kaz had mainly ignored me since I moved in. I was hoping today's beach outing would work it's magic on all of us.

I put down the cooler-bag and shook off my rucksack. Looking back, I saw Penny and her boys laden with more paraphernalia, clumping across the sand towards me. Last night, my suggestion of a breakfast *braai* up the coast had excited the boys. But at seven this morning they'd been grumpy and not keen to get up.

The boys dumped their clobber, went loping down to the sea and flung themselves into the waves.

'It's glorious,' Penny said, clapping her hands. I was pleased to see her mood lifting. She looked so sad these days. We walked to the water's edge.

I pointed. 'Look at the gulls poking their beaks into the wet sand, searching for food.'

'I never noticed details like that before,' Penny said. 'You bring places alive, Ben.'

'I figured we all needed rescuing today.'

She nodded. 'Weekends are so bruising for the newly separated. I never guessed it would be *this* bad when Neil left.'

Newly separated. So that's how she saw herself.

'Fancy some coffee?' she asked.

'Good idea.'

She went over to our gear and pulled out the thermos flask and poured coffee into two camping cups. We stood together companionably, sipping the warm brew. It was quite nippy on the beach this early on a winter morning.

The boys came splashing out of the water and made their way back to us.

'Guys, help me find some stones to build a base for our *braai*,' I said, picking up a smooth stone. 'About this size.'

They nodded and we set off in different directions, searching the shoreline.

When we returned, I checked our collection and showed them how to build the flat base for our fire. I could feel Penny watching me working with her boys.

'OK, good,' I said, patting the surface of the base. 'Now we need to collect driftwood to make the fire on top of it.'

Harry rushed off excitedly but Kaz said, 'Nah,' and walked down to the water's edge.

'Don't take it personally,' Penny said. 'You know how he's been since Neil left.'

'I won't. But I'm sure this will win him over. Any lad loves a *braai* on the beach.'

'I'm seeing a whole new side of you.' She smiled.

'My dad used to do this with us when we came down to the coast for holidays. You just pass it on.'

'Well, it's all new to my boys.'

I walked down to where Kaz stood with his back to us. 'Come, we need that firewood if we're going to cook those sausages. They're so tasty done over a *braai*.'

I expected him to give me the sullen brush-off but as I turned up the beach, I heard him follow me. Yes! We went up towards the high-water mark, collecting bleached dry branches.

'That's keeping them busy,' I said, when I returned to Penny with an armful of driftwood. I began breaking them up and started laying a fire.

'You have them eating out of your hand,' Penny said.

I chuckled, enjoying the pleasure of building a fire outdoors. 'OK boys,' I yelled, waving my arms. Harry returned, dragging a huge branch in his wake, Kaz with an armful.

'Not bad,' I said, examining their spoils. Penny sat back, watching us break up branches and add them to the fire, me explaining to the boys as I went. We stashed the rest of the wood to one side.

'Who wants to light the fire?' I asked.

Both boys yelled, 'Me!'

'Eldest first, I think. You next time, Harry.'

Kaz took the matches and struck one, sheltering it from the breeze. Following my instructions, he held it to the smallest twigs around the base. I could see the pride in his face as a flame flared up. Both boys watched, mesmerised.

'It'll take a while to be ready for cooking,' I said. 'Time for another swim if you want.'

They wrenched their gaze away from the fire and ran down to the sea.

'Geez, its good being out here,' I said as I stretched out on the sand.

'We must do this again,' Penny said. 'To stop us both from going under.'

'Who said anything about going under?'

'Come on! You've been dealt a body blow by Miranda. Now you may lose your job. And I stalk about being Mrs Angry.'

'Just teasing.'

'Truthfully, how do you feel about Miranda? Any chance of sorting it out?'

I poked the fire with a stick, finding it difficult to get the words out. 'I guess I just feel numb. I'm glad to have Ezekiel's problems to take my mind off it.'

'Work's my salvation,' Penny said, sifting her hands through the sand.

'I was going to step aside, once Ezekiel's case was settled. But I might as well stay involved now. There's the worry of how he'll cope, back in the outside world. And Nomsa's campaign group interests me. I've given up on the ANC but pressure from civic groups may shift things in this country.' I felt alive as I spoke.

'Sounds good,' Penny said.

'I never thought anything like this would happen to Mirrie and me,' I said, as I opened my rucksack and got out the plastic plates.

'Me neither,' she said, brushing smoke away. 'Why are our relationships all going bottom up?'

'Dunno. And now I've messed up your friendship with Miranda.'

'Miranda and I fell out when I didn't pack my bags and follow Neil.'

'The lawyer in her has taken over,' I said. 'And swallowed up the Mirrie we knew. It's the old Mirrie I'm missing, but she's been gone for a while. And I miss the kids like hell… the sense of family.'

'Yes, I miss that too.' We watched the boys making their way back up from the beach.

I stood up. 'Fire's almost ready guys. Let's get cooking.'

'I'm starving.' Kaz grinned.

'Me too.' Harry's hair was sticking up all over after his swim.

I placed the metal grill on top of the now smouldering wood, then pulled the long piece of *boerewors* from the pack and placed it onto the grill, enjoying the sizzle. I wiped my hands, played with the fire a bit and sniffed deeply as the smell of the meat cooking began to rise.

That evening, when the boys had eaten and gone upstairs, I helped Penny tidy up the kitchen.

She hung the tea towel up. 'Time for a last cuppa.'

'Thanks for coming to the beach,' I said. 'I'd have been a lonely old bastard on my own.'

'It was wonderful. You saw how cheerful the boys were this evening.'

'I have an inkling you're more relaxed too.'

'You know I loved it.' She smiled and threw her arms round me then buried her face in my shoulder. I hugged her and wondered what to make of it. She lifted her face and paused, nose to nose. I found my lips brushing hers. Penny's mouth sought mine and my arms wrapped around her.

I pulled back. 'I'm sorry. What am I doing.'

'It wasn't just you, silly,' she said, stroking my cheek.

'What about Neil?'

'But he has gone off to the other side of the world, hasn't he? And I am not sure I want him back when he returns.' She held my face in her hands. We kissed again, more passionately, relaxing into each other's arms. Whatever happened next, we both deserved this moment.

CHAPTER 42

Ezekiel could hardly believe that he was on his way to Nkandla at last, after wanting it for so long. It had taken Nomsa and his nurse some effort to persuade him that he could manage the long journey. But the promise that he would finally meet the *sangoma* back in his birthplace, had given him the courage to agree. He knew that only her power could rescue him from further disasters.

For miles and miles, their taxi sped up the North Coast road, past sugarcane growing from red soil. Then they turned inland over hills scattered with villages and grazing goats, past the dusty towns of Gingindlovu and Eshowe. This was his first outing from the hospital and he leaned back exhausted in the front seat of the car. It was a very long way back to Nkandla, even in a nice car like this, with padded seats and air-conditioning. The sense of Nomsa's presence behind him made feel him safe.

Finally, he could see they were approaching Nkandla. It was a long time since he had been back but he smiled to see that Kali's hardware store and the *'Always Welcome' shabeen* were still where they had always been. And there was the Bungane family compound.

'You OK, Ezekiel?' Nomsa asked, patting his shoulder from the back seat.

'*Yebo.*' How could he describe the mixture of fear and elation that threatened to overwhelm him at the thought of meeting *sangoma* Busi face to face? The medicine woman who could put an end to all his troubles, whose help he had needed for so long. If only that Gallagher had given him leave to visit her when he had asked, none of his recent troubles would have occurred. He shut his mind quickly to such thoughts. He knew they led back to madness.

'Let us ask the way,' the driver said. He slowed down and called to a group of passing youths. 'Where is the house of *sangoma* Busi?'

The boldest of them came forward and pointed to a road winding off to the left. Down a long, rutted dirt road, the taxi slipped and slid until they turned into a clearing, half hidden amongst flat-topped thorn trees. Ezekiel could hardly believe he was in Nkandla at last. He felt in the very air around him that his salvation was at hand.

A young woman came out from a beehive-shaped reed hut and moved towards them.

Nomsa stepped out of the car, calling '*Sawubona.*' She explained who they were.

'*Sapila, unjani wena,*' the young woman smiled. She turned back and called into the hut. A wrinkled old woman emerged, her long grey hair twisted in coils around her shoulders. There was no mistaking that she was a *sangoma*, from her beaded head-dress, her bone necklaces and her elaborately beaded skirt. Ezekiel had seen *sangoma* Busi around his neighbourhood since childhood but he had never been up so close. He was awed by her presence.

All the while, he remained glued to his seat, unable to move until Nomsa came back to help him out. The driver said he would stay in the car.

Holding Nomsa's arm, Ezekiel walked forward. In a wavering voice he said, *'Sawubona, sangoma* Busi.'

'Sapila Ezekiel. Unjani wena?' she replied. After further greetings were exchanged, she invited them to sit on low wooden stools around the fire outside her hut. She asked the young woman to bring refreshments and enquired about life in *eThekwini.*

Then the young woman led Nomsa away to the shade of a distant tree and Ezekiel found himself alone with his *sangoma.*

She sat down beside him and looked into his eyes, touching his hand. 'Tell me your troubles, my son.'

Ezekiel's tongue loosened. He told her how the spirits of his ancestors were angry with him and had taken from him first his two sons and then his wife. How he feared for the safety of his daughters so much that he had done a terrible thing and ended up in prison. He told her about some of his prison experiences. How he had finally been freed with the help of his sister Nomsa and a very special lawyer called Dr Khumalo. How he was getting well again in hospital.

All the while, s*angoma* Busi's voice, deep with wisdom and understanding, interjected now and then with *'yebo,* my son' *or* 'Mhm'.

By the end, Ezekiel wept with relief at telling his story to the right person at last. 'Ask the spirits of my ancestors how I displeased them so much?'

'My son, you have suffered grievous hurts. I will speak to the spirits of your ancestors. I will find out what will appease them.'

'Ngiyabonga! Thank you,' Ezekiel whispered, his lips dry with foreboding, in case his ancestors should refuse him.

'Watch and listen as I invoke your ancestors but do not speak until I speak to you again,' she said. 'Do not interrupt my communion with the spirits.'

'*Yebo, sangoma.*'

She drew a handful of small bones from a bag at her side. She leaned over a cleared circle of earth by the fire and cast the bones in a practised manner, muttering to herself. For a long time, she studied intently the way the bones had fallen. Then she reached again into her bag and drew out handfuls of strong-smelling herbs. She threw them on the fire, muttering all the while. A bitter scent rose from the burning herbs, filling Ezekiel's nostrils.

She stood up and began to stamp a rhythm in the dust with her feet. On a small hide drum, she beat long, rhythmic rolls, calling out invocations to raise the spirits, her voice deeper and louder now. Ezekiel watched, transfixed, as she raised her arms to the sky, her beaded hair waving from side to side, her eyes fixed on another world. Her voice wheedled, then rose more powerfully before falling to soft and husky again.

Ezekiel felt an electric current pass through him the moment she connected with his ancestors. '*Sawubonani,* oh great ones! Your son Ezekiel Mabuza understands that he has offended you in some way. He begs your forgiveness. Tell me how he can make reparation to you?'

There was an eerie silence as his *sangoma* appeared to be listening intently to the replies of his ancestors. Ezekiel could hear nothing. Let them be generous, he prayed, his hands clasped together. Her wheedling voice started again, her words so rapid that he struggled to catch them.

At last, the *sangoma* collapsed exhausted on the ground, breathing in deep, jagged breaths. Ezekiel was alarmed but he dared not intrude. Slowly she opened her eyes. Then she rose from her trance and settled herself carefully back on her stool.

'My son,' she said at last, her voice thin and hoarse. 'Your ancestors say that whatever you did to displease them...'

'*Yebo*?' Ezekiel whispered.

. '...that all your suffering – losing your sons, your wife, your job, your time in prison,' she paused dramatically. 'You have paid enough. They say that now you can go in peace.'

Ezekiel collapsed forward over his knees. He could hardly believe it. To be forgiven by his ancestors at last.

'You understand, my son?' his *sangoma* asked.

'*Yebo*, I am forgiven. Thank you, *sangoma* Busi, thank you from the bottom of my heart.' He bowed his head.

'Now I will give you *muti*, special herbs I will brew to cleanse you of the last of the bad spirits. And to make you brave enough to face your future. You must take some every day until the bottle is finished.'

'*Yebo*,' Ezekiel stammered. He was washed clean.

****

It was hot and humid that late December evening, the windows wide open, as Penny and I prepared for the New Year's meal she was hosting for our friends. I piled beers and wine into the fridge, carried bottles of red through to the dining-room.

Penny was singing to herself as she laid the party table. Suddenly, the air was alive with flying ants, homing in towards the lights that she had switched on as dusk arrived. I leapt across to shut the windows but it was too late.

'Why tonight?' Penny groaned, trying to gather up the

creatures in her hands and toss them outside. 'Now I'll have to sweep them off and start again.'

I never understood why flying ants swarmed on some summer evenings and not others. Something to do with the threat of rain. Within minutes, their papery wings dropped off and scattered everywhere, leaving the once-delicate creatures to scuttle away into dark corners. Penny flitted about, sweeping up discarded wings, while I cleared the dinner-table and re-laid things. The house gecko slipped down the wall to gobble up the ants, his long tongue swooping out and back in, quick as lightening.

'Normality restored,' Penny laughed and turned on the party-lights strung across the terrace now the swarm of ants had gone.

I rifled through my CDs for something catchy. The opening bars of *My Girl* by the Temptations filled the room. It was nerve-wracking having our first guests since things had developed between Penny and me. I hadn't meant it to go past that first, unexpected kiss, the day of the beach braai. It had come out of nowhere. Safe Penny, who I'd known for years. But after the last few years of Miranda's growing coldness, that kiss had lit a fuse. We'd been very careful to hide it from Kaz and Harry, no hugging in front of them, always ending up in our own beds for the night. But I was anxious they'd pick up something. And now it was Penny's turn to host the supper club. I'd wanted her to make some excuse to postpone.

'Be careful tonight. We don't want the others to guess,' I fretted when we'd changed into our party clothes.

She shrugged. 'It's going to leak out sometime. This is as good a time as any.'

'It'd be a bombshell. Remember they're Neil's friends too

and you haven't told him yet.'

'You're right. What am I thinking? I have such an urge to burst out with it.'

'It's too soon. Your boys aren't ready for this.'

'I know,' she said. The doorbell sounded.

'Michael, how's it going? Better than your English winter?' I flung my arm around his shoulder. We'd persuaded him out to South Africa for Christmas in the end.

'Cheers,' Michael's face looked weathered by life and probably by drink. But he already looked much better than he had when he had arrived from the UK a few days before Christmas.

'Pete, Barbara, come in.'

Barbara hugged me, while Pete put down a heavy pot smelling of curry. Indian food was our theme for tonight. Bram and Elsa arrived with their dish.

While the others were taking food through to the kitchen, I took Pete aside. In September he'd signed Michael up to Alcoholics Anonymous and was acting as one of his AA buddies.

'How's Michael doing with the booze? Christmas must be a tempting time.'

'I think he's been keeping off it,' Pete said quietly. 'Certainly, since he arrived to stay with us.'

'Good.' I glanced through to the dining table. 'I shouldn't have put so much alcohol out.' I grabbed some bottles and stuffed them inside the sideboard. 'I'll find some soft drinks.'

Once we were all gathered round the dining-room table I raised my glass. 'To all of us, for surviving the last year, some by the skin of our teeth.'

'All of us,' they replied.

'To absent friends,' Bram added. 'To Neil.'

'To Liz.'

I wondered how many of them were thinking of Miranda, so I called out, 'To Miranda!'

The others relaxed. 'To Miranda.'

'That was gracious of you, Ben,' Barbara whispered, beside me.

'I'm in a good mood tonight,' I said. 'Other days I hate her guts.' I wondered who Miranda was with tonight. Would she ever meet with this group again?

I looked around at how it had shrunk. What would I have done without Penny and Pete this past horrible year? Without Bram and Elsa taking me in. Barbara's warmth had been part of the net keeping me afloat. And here was Michael, back from the edge, back in our lives again and in South Africa. I could not face losing any more of them.

Penny came in carrying a platter of pungent curried prawns. 'Let the meal begin.'

Our guests were piling into the food. For the first time, none of our children were here for New Year's Eve. Harry had gone off to Canada to see Neil, the others were out on the town with their friends. I thought with relief about how Ellen was beginning to thaw towards me. She had even visited me at Penny's, although it had left her in tears.

The ghost of the last party that Miranda and I had hosted at Cadogan Avenue played over in my mind. The great atmosphere. The sentimental speech I'd made about our group, not realising what was coming down the line. Then Neil had sprung that drunken punch at Bram. A forewarning of what was to come perhaps.

'Neil seems to be settling in, in Vancouver,' Bram said. 'When'll he be back for a visit?'

Penny shrugged. 'Easter, I guess. This Christmas, he and Harry are learning to ski.'

She didn't sound nearly as miserable as she used to when the subject of Neil came up.

Surrounded by our friends, Neil's friends too, I realised it was madness to carry on with Penny. There was too much at stake. How would we behave when Neil came back at Easter? And if things went wrong between the two of us, there'd be another ripping apart in the group. I was still startled by Penny's boldness about the whole affair.

'Neil abandoned our family,' she'd said several times. 'I can't forgive him for that. I feel it leaves me free to make my own life now.'

I found this new forthright Penny both thrilling and terrifying. But her view didn't take into account the pile-up of consequences that could follow. I dreaded Harry or Kaz realising what had changed between me and their mom. Nice uncle Ben who'd won them over with beach braais and hikes, would suddenly be seen as the viper in their family nest.

Everyone had finished their first course, so I jumped up to clear away the plates. Pete followed me to the kitchen to help.

He clasped my shoulder. 'I'm glad to see you're looking less like a wet weekend.'

'Yeah…I guess I… this break-up with Miranda…it's been coming a long time. Ever since she signed up with that legal firm of ANC fat-cats.'

'Sometimes there is nothing worse than staying together miserable, always at each other's throats.'

I tried to sound casual. 'Do you still see her?'

'Barbara's seen her once or twice. Miranda's always too

busy to meet. We're not taking sides, but you and I have the bond.'

'Thanks, man.'

'Penny seems much happier.' Pete seemed keen to steer off the subject of Miranda. 'She was so low when Neil first left.'

I felt a flush rising up my neck. 'She's been quite up and down.' I turned away and pulled plates down from the cupboard for the next course.

Back in the dining-room, the talk was about the coming year, drawing me into its optimistic mood. Penny smiled across the table at me and I grinned back. I was a lucky man. I might have been a lonely guy in a stranger's rented room. How could I let go of what I was building with Penny?

'Lamb curry,' Barbara announced, as she set down the heavy dish. Pete followed with a tray of yellow rice, naans, *sambals* and Mrs Ball's chutney. As he filled everyone's plates, Bram sniffed the air like a hungry dog.

'Food like this could almost persuade me back here,' Michael said.

'Your visit is one good thing that has come out of this year,' I said. 'Stay as long as you like.'

The main course was over and everyone leaned back, replete. I piled up dishes and carried them through to the kitchen. Penny followed with the rest. We loaded the dishwasher in a smooth two-person routine we had established between us.

She kicked the kitchen door shut. 'Come here.' She drew her arms around me.

I stiffened. 'Someone might come in.'

'They're engrossed, talking to Michael about his life in Sheffield. One little kiss won't hurt.'

'You promised while they were here…'

She kissed me on the mouth and I succumbed, my lips on hers, my arms around her waist. Penny, my wonderful new discovery.

'Oops…sorry.' Pete stood there, open-mouthed. We had not heard the door open. I sprang apart from Penny.

'I never realised you two…' Pete said.

'No, you've got it wrong. We were… just hugging,' I said. 'The evening is going so well.'

Pete grinned. 'That was more than camaraderie I saw there, *boet*. Not my business, anyway. Good luck to you both.'

'It just…happened,' Penny said, her bravado gone.

'Don't say anything,' I said. 'If Neil or the boys…'

Pete put his finger to his lips. 'Your secret's safe with me.'

Penny looked shamefaced. 'You see Pete, for me it's been over with Neil, since he left for Canada.'

'Don't look so guilty,' Pete said. 'I'm glad to see some joining together after all the breaking apart we've had this past year.' He hugged her. 'Neil was a bloody fool to go off to Canada when you didn't want to go.'

I reckoned that if anyone could keep quiet about this, it was Pete. It was a relief to share our secret with someone.

'It's not going to be easy,' I said.

'I'll talk to Neil when he comes home at Easter,' Penny added, twisting her hair around her finger.

'I'm here if either of you need me,' Pete said.

'Thanks mate.'

'What's happened to that bottle of wine?' Bram called from the dining-room.

'Coming,' Pete said and grabbed a bottle from the fridge.

CHAPTER 43

E zekiel stood at the reception desk of the hospital, a couple of black plastic bags beside him. Inside were the meagre belongings he's gathered during his time inside: his wash bag, the clothes Nomsa had brought for him when he left prison, his cigarettes and a pack of cards. Under one arm he clutched the table he had made so lovingly during his woodwork sessions. His present to Nomsa, for all she had done for him. He shifted from one foot to the other, waiting for Nomsa to finish reading the paperwork that would set him free. The receptionist had handed the papers to him first but he had struggled to take it all in. He'd pushed them over to Nomsa. All this writing, writing, why could they not simply walk out the door?

Ezekiel's mind wandered back across his time here in hospital. After everything that had gone before, this place had saved him, put him back together. He shuddered and steered his mind quickly away from the horrors of Westville prison. He moved on to his return to grace, after his encounter with his *sangoma* back in Nkandla. He felt the power of that meeting still strong in his heart.

He looked out of the window at the sun shining on grass, at the builders over to his left, mixing concrete as usual. He had taken a day-by-day interest in their goings on, as the new hospital block went up. There was much he would miss here.

A bevy of nurses came down to Reception, to wish him '*Hamba kahle*, Ezekiel'. Go well. They each clutched his hand in turn. He knew he had been a favourite amongst them.

He smiled. '*Ala kahle! Ngiyabonga*. Stay well. Thank you.'

Nomsa passed the papers to Ezekiel. 'It is all done correctly, you can sign here.'

He produced a rough approximation of his old signature while she began a boisterous round of farewells with his nurses.

'Let us go brother,' she said finally, picking up one of his bags and heading for the front door. He picked up the other and his table. He put a foot forward to follow her, then hesitated, shaking at the thought of facing the world outside. He told himself, to be back with his daughters, he would do anything. And he had *sangoma* Busi's *muti* to keep him brave. He took a few more steps.

'You can do it, Ezekiel,' nurse Mtolo said. She took his arm and walked him through the door.

'There is a taxi waiting for us.' Nomsa pointed proudly. 'We are travelling home in style.'

Ezekiel followed her towards it with his awkward gait. His legs had never been right since he started the medicine the hospital had given him. But it had put him right in other ways. And it was much better than that poison they had given him in prison.

For a moment his mind hung on to those images of his time in prison but he stopped himself. He did what his nurses had taught him to do with such bad thoughts. To shut them out and hold on to a picture of Nomsa and his girls.

'Come Ezekiel, we don't have all day! Your girls are waiting for you,' Nomsa said as she handed the taxi-driver her black bag for the boot. Ezekiel reached her and handed over his bag and table. They settled into the back seat, like *umlungu* with money to spend.

'F Section, Umlazi please!'

As the taxi set off into the city traffic, Ezekiel looked around him. Everything was going too fast. His heart beat unevenly. He clutched Nomsa's hand as cars roared past too loudly. The January sun beat through the taxi windows. Here he was, out in the world again.

Nomsa stroked his hand. 'It's OK, brother, you will get used to it. You are coming home at last.'

'*Yebo*,' was all he could say, clutching her hand. Nomsa, who had been there for him through all his troubles, who had got him out of prison. How could he ever repay her?

'You don't mind staying with me and Thembu for a while? I think it will be best. Until you get used to Umlazi again.'

'My house?'

'Yes, you still have the house,' she said.

'But I have no money…' his lips were dry.

'I have fixed all that up. The municipality needs no rent from you for now.'

'But how…?'

'It is sorted, brother. I explain to you later. For now, let Thembu and me do the worrying. One foot forward at a time, hm?'

He nodded. He tried to picture life outside hospital but it had grown vague in his mind over his months inside.

Everything filled him with fear. He tried to remember his time as doorman at the city hall but nothing came into his mind. He pulled his tobacco and papers out from his pocket and began to roll himself a cigarette. That made him feel safe.

'Thembu and I will be out at work from early morning. I come home about three in the afternoon, but your girls are home for summer holidays, so they will keep you company, run errands for you.'

He pictured his Gugu and Mbali and smiled. They had come often to see him at the hospital with Nomsa, to make him laugh and play cards with him as he got better. It would be good to live with them again. Mr Gallagher had visited him at the hospital too, brought him cigarettes and a few books. With the help of his occupational therapist, he had finally learned to read books, rather than just carry them around in the library. His heart almost burst with pride at the thought.

'At bedtime,' Nomsa said. 'You can sleep in Jabu's hut. He is living in a flat in Umlazi now with his friends.'

'Has he moved out because of me?' Ezekiel asked.

'No, no. He is a working man now; he wants to go his own way.'

'There is so much to worry about,' Ezekiel fretted. 'First I need a job…'

'Easy, brother.' Nomsa stroked his arm. 'You still have some severance pay from city hall. You will get a pension from them too. You worked there twenty years.'

Ezekiel tried to make sense of what she was saying. Someone giving him money without him having to work? All the time, the taxi driver's *kwaito* music buzzed on the car radio, irritating Ezekiel's brain. It had been so quiet at the hospital. By now the taxi was skimming along the southern freeway and he gave up thinking to concentrate on recognising places. All the different factories his bus used to pass every day on his way to work. Clairwood racecourse and then the approach to the airport and the oil refineries. He felt more and more at home as they neared Umlazi. He struggled to shape the words of a question to Nomsa. He rolled another cigarette. Smoking helped him to think. He took a long pull on it.

'When we went to Nkandla…can you remember? Did *sangoma* Busi really say that my troubles with my ancestors are over?'

She nodded. 'Yes, they told her that they have forgiven you.'

'Yes. That with my time in Westville…I had paid the price.'

'That is true, brother.' She patted his hand, brushing away his cigarette smoke from her face. She smiled. 'Your smoking is worse than ever!'

'I think now…my ancestors will leave me in peace.' He let out a deep sigh. No more torment inside his head. 'If that is what my suffering has been for, I can accept it.'

'You have suffered enough,' she said.

'Nurse Bongani told me it was time to move on, to leave the past behind.'

'He sounds like a wise man,' Nomsa said.

By now the taxi was pushing through the Umlazi traffic. Ezekiel felt a rush of old sensations. The smell of dust in the air, of fires burning around them, voices calling out in the melody of Zulu. He was coming home. His eyes peeled the landscape. Familiar places – the Technikon, the bars he knew. He turned away from the Umlazi police station, feeling a sudden rush of blood to his head. So many things frightened him now but slowly he would grow stronger. He had Nomsa, Thembu and his girls to help him. And he would help them however he could.

'Look, Ezekiel, we are turning into my street. Toot the horn!' Nomsa cried to the driver.

The driver gave a series of exuberant toots and the door of their house burst open. Mbali and Gugu were running out to meet them, arms out, calling, *'Baba, Baba'*.

The car pulled up, the driver opened the back door and Ezekiel struggled to move his stiff legs and get out.

As he straightened up, Gugu flung her arms around him, singing, *'Baba, Baba,* Uncle says we can buy ice-cream to celebrate.'

Mbali was waiting her turn to hug him. She smiled in a way he hadn't seen for a long time. Behind them, Thembu stood with a wide grin. He was home. There would be no more going away for him.

GLOSSARY

South African English is peppered with words from the other languages used there. All words below are Zulu unless otherwise stated.

ANC – African National Congress, ruling party, previous political movement

Aikona! – no (said in English for emphasis)

amandla – power (a call used during the anti-apartheid struggle)

baba – father (used as mark of respect towards older men)

baba mkulu – grandfather, old man, elder (term of respect)

blerry – bloody (Afrikaans)

Berg – common name for the Drakensberg mountains, Kwazulu- Natal

boerewors – a tasty South African spiced sausage used on barbecues

boet – brother, matey term of affection to male friends (Afrikaans)

braaivleis – barbecue (Afrikaans) literally to grill/roast meat

chips – South African for crisps

dassie - rock hyrax

Dominee – Pastor of the Dutch Reformed Church (Afrikaans)

eThekweni – the Zulu name for Durban

eikona! – no way!

eish! – An expressive word used to show surprise, disbelief, or frustration

fokking – fucking (Afrikaans)

gogo – grandmother

hadedahs – African ibis birds

haai! – hey!

howzit – common SA greeting – short for 'how is it'

hamba kahle – go well

indaba – business – refers literally to special meeting of the elders

Isolezwe – name of a Durban newspaper ('It is a Country')

khaya – house

kwaito – music genre popular in South Africa

ja – yes, pronounced yah (Afrikaans, but used by many S Africans)

knobkerrie – African carved stick with knob at one end (Afrikaans)

kraal – a gathering of family huts

laager – defensive encampment encircled by wagons (Afrikaans)

mamba – one of Africa's most dangerous snakes; name given to dogs

medem – Zulu pronunciation of madam

meneer – mister – polite (Afrikaans)

melktert – An Afrikaans version of milk tart

mielie - corn

muti – medicine

Nkandla – a country town in northern Kwazulu-Natal

ngiyabonga – thank you

ouma – grandmother (Afrikaans)

putu – a dry maize porridge, staple of Zulu meals

rusks – dried biscuit, an SA favourite, originally used on the Great Trek

SAMWU – South African Municipal Workers Union

Samp – dried maize kernels

sangoma – diviner and practitioner of herbal medicine, usually female (Zulu)

sapila – your health (reply to sawubona)

sawubona – good day

sawubonani – good day to more than one person

Shaka – famed king of the Zulu people

springbok – gazelle found in S. and SW Africa

shebeen– unlicenced bar (used in Zulu but originally from the Irish word)

sjambok – heavy leather whip, originally for driving cattle

tokoloshe – evil spirit

tsotsis – bastards (term used for township bad boys)

toyi-toyi – protest dance with chanting from the apartheid era

ululation – high keening sound of voices made by African women

Ukuthula – the quiet one

uMama – mother (Zulu greeting to women with children)

umlungu – white person

Umshini Wami – Bring Back My Machine Gun – song popular during apartheid years

unjani wena? – how are you?

vasbyt – 'hold fast'; goodbye to someone in a tough situation (Afrikaans)

vasloop – literally 'walk fast' (Afrikaans), said as encouragement veld – open, uncultivated country or grassland in South Africa

Viva! – Live Long! A cry adopted by activists during the apartheid years

wyfie – name for substitute wives in prison – literally 'little wife' (Afrikaans)

woza – come here

yebo – yes

ACKNOWLEDGEMENTS

Many thanks to Neil Reid and the Broomspring Writers Workshop and the Shipyard Writers Group, without whose feedback and support this novel would never have been completed. Also to my fellow-students on Sheffield Hallam MA Writing for their helpful comments. Thanks too to my late friend John Morrison who provided me with a wealth of information about the Durban municipal strike in 2005 and about running the Comrades Marathon. Any errors about these events are entirely my own. My appreciation to Pat Azzopardi, Peter Hannon and Kevin Laue, my novel's first proper readers.

Thanks too, to the staff at Troubador Publishers for helping me through the process of publication. And to Ruth Owen for her brilliant cover design.